"Guarded is an intriguing, emotionally-charged romance coupled with spine-tingling suspense, and filled with well-crafted, loveable characters. Her exceptional story-telling and stellar writing make Sara Davison an author to watch."
—Elizabeth Goddard, bestselling author of the Uncommon Justice Series

"Guarded kept me reading late into the night. The hero was noble, the heroine strong in the face of tragedy, but the little boy, Jordan, stole the show."
—Robin Patchen, award-winning author of fourteen novels

"In Vigilant, Sara Davison has created deep characters and a story that will grab your heart and keep you on the edge of your seat. Days after reading the story, the characters are still on my mind."
—Patricia Bradley, Memphis Cold Case Series, Winner of Inspirational Readers' Choice Award

"Vigilant is a unique boundary-breaking suspense full of emotional depth. Davison's thought-provoking style will leave you breathless as you grapple with tough moral issues long after the story is over."
—Rachel Dylan, Bestselling Author of the Atlanta Justice series

Guarded

The Night Guardians Series

Book One: Vigilant
Book Two: Guarded

Guarded

The Night Guardians Series

By

Sara Davison

Guarded
Published by Mountain Brook Ink
White Salmon, WA U.S.A.

The website addresses shown in this book are not intended in any way to be or imply an endorsement on the part of Mountain Brook Ink, nor do we vouch for their content.

This story is a work of fiction. All characters and events are the product of the author's imagination. Any resemblance to any person, living or dead, is coincidental.

Scripture taken from the Holy Bible, NEW INTERNATIONAL VERSION®, NIV® Copyright © 1973, 1978, 1984, 2011 by Biblica, Inc.® Used by permission. All rights reserved worldwide.

The Author is represented by and this book is published in association with the literary agency of WordServe Literary Group, Ltd, www.wordserveliterary.com.

The Team: Miralee Ferrell, Nikki Wright, Cindy Jackson
Cover Design: Indie Cover Design, Lynnette Bonner Designer

Mountain Brook Ink is an inspirational publisher offering fiction you can believe in.
Printed in the United States of America

Dedication

In memory of my father-in-law, Allen Davison.

Even with so much taken from you the last few years of your life, you never lost your sense of humor.

Which is why, whenever I think of you, it will always be with a smile.

And always and above all, to the One who gives the stories, and who is a shield and refuge in times of trouble. It is all from You and for You.

Acknowledgments

As always, deepest love and gratitude to Michael, Luke, Julia, and Seth. Your love and support keep me going, even on those days. You know which ones those are. You are God's greatest gifts to me.

Thank you to others whose support and encouragement ground me and motivate me to carry on—colleagues, friends, members of my book clubs and writing groups. Your love for God and words (including my words) inspires me to persevere and to do everything in my power to make each book better than the last. Thank you!

To my agent Sarah Joy Freese, and to Greg Johnson and the amazing team at WordServe Literary—thank you for always being behind me and my work. I appreciate you and all your support.

And to Miralee Ferrell, Nikki Wright, and the rest of the team at Mountain Brook Ink, I am always amazed at how much time and effort you are willing to put into my work. Thank you for making me part of the family!

For he will command his angels concerning you,
to guard you in all your ways;
they will lift you up in their hands,
so that you will not strike your foot against a stone.
(Psalm 91:11-12)

Chapter One

God, help me. I can't lose him too.

Nicole Kelly choked back an overwhelming panic and forced herself to stop running, to turn in a slow circle and scan the park. Jordan had to be here. She had seen him ten minutes earlier and it wasn't like him to wander off. A thought slashed through her like the sharp prick of a knife. *Had* he wandered off? Or had someone …?

"Jordan!" Heads swiveled toward her. Nicole forced a tight smile, suddenly aware that the fear in her voice was causing concern on the faces of the other parents at the park. One young mother yanked on the hand of her toddler who had been playing beside her in the sandbox, pulling him onto her lap. He responded to the interruption of his digging with an indignant holler and struggled to free himself from the arms that had tightened around his waist.

Nicole drew in a long, slow breath. Terrorizing young families wasn't going to help Jordan. Her imagination was running wild. From the moment her son was born, Nicole had struggled with the fear that someone would take him, likely because of what her husband had been involved in before his death. But that was in the past. What Gage had done couldn't touch them now. Could it?

She forced herself to start walking in the direction she had last seen him, over by the swings. Beyond the playground area, a small hill rose up that she couldn't see over from her vantage point. Her son was likely there, in the grassy section that widened into an open field. Her six year old had always been fascinated by the people playing football and throwing Frisbees to each other. He'd probably become so distracted that he had forgotten to check in with her.

Nicole climbed the small slope on trembling legs and cleared the top. Holding the side of her hand to her forehead to block out the bright October sunshine, she let her eyes adjust. When they did, she could make out her son's orange jacket and Toronto Blue Jays baseball cap and her chest clenched. He wasn't alone. A man was crouched in front of him on the walkway that wound around the edge of the field, his back to her. The two of them appeared to be deep in discussion.

Anger rose in Nicole's chest, competing with the fear as she started down the hill toward them, almost at a run. When she was close enough that she wouldn't have to scream, she called out, "Jordan!"

The man in front of him rose and turned. Nicole stopped abruptly, the breath that had become ragged over the last few minutes suddenly catching in her throat. "Daniel."

A slow smile crossed his face as he lightly touched the back of her son and the two of them walked toward her. "Nicole."

For a few seconds she couldn't speak. His dark hair was a little longer than she remembered, and ruffled from the wind, but his eyes were as blue and piercing as she always pictured them whenever she thought of him. Judging from the jeans and long-sleeved navy T-shirt, he was off-duty. Or maybe he wasn't even a cop anymore. It had been a long time since she'd seen him. A lot could have changed.

Daniel contemplated her for a moment, then let out a small laugh and stepped around her son to reach out to her. Nicole hesitated before sliding her hand into his and letting the strength of the fingers that closed around hers draw out the last of the fear.

He searched her face. "You're shaking. Are you okay?"

Nicole pulled her hand away. She had no idea whether the trembling was a remnant of her fear over not knowing where her son was, or from being in Daniel's presence again after so much time. "I thought something might have happened to Jordan." She wrapped an arm around her son and pulled him to her side. "He doesn't usually go off without me, so when I couldn't find him, I kind of panicked."

Jordan kicked at a pile of leaves on the pathway. "Sorry, Mom."

"It's okay. Now."

"I found him over by the skate park. He was pretty interested in what those kids were doing. I think you might have to invest in a board one of these days." Daniel grinned.

"A skateboard? I'm still trying to get up the nerve to let him ride his bike on the sidewalk. I'm not quite ready for anything with wheels that actually leave the ground." She tilted her head. "Did you know he was my son?"

"Yeah." A sheepish look crossed Daniel's face. "I've seen the two of you in the park a few times since I've been back."

"Back?" The word clanged around a sudden emptiness in her chest. She hadn't seen him since the night she caught a glimpse of him standing outside the diner watching her. Still, for seven years the thought that he was close by had comforted her as she'd mourned the loss of her husband, given birth to Gage's son, and raised him on her own. The idea that Daniel hadn't been there after all left her feeling irrationally bereft.

"Yeah, I left town for a while."

"Where did you go?"

"London."

Her eyes widened. "England?"

Daniel chuckled. "Not quite. London, Ontario. Couldn't be that far from … my family."

So only a couple of hours away. Somehow that didn't feel much better. And what had he been about to say? "What were you doing there?"

"Two buddies of mine and I decided to try our hand at the private eye game."

"And?"

"It went well, actually. The business took off. They're still at it, but a while ago Toronto Police Services offered me my old detective job, and Sharleen talked me into accepting. We're partners again."

"So you've been back for …?"

"Six months."

And you haven't called. Nicole shook her head. Of course he hadn't called. Why would he? The last time they'd spoken, she'd broken his heart by choosing Gage over him. She was lucky he was even speaking to her now, when they'd accidentally bumped into each other in the park. Or maybe not accidentally? "So you've been watching us since you've been back?"

His cheeks colored slightly. "I prefer looking out for you, but yeah, I guess I have, off and on."

"How did you stay out of sight?"

He offered her an indignant look that was so clearly feigned she had to press her lips together to keep from laughing. "Might I remind you that I am a professional detective? I can blend into any surroundings so well that, unless I chose to reveal myself, you would never know I was there."

"Clearly. So why haven't you talked to us before now?"

He sobered. "I wanted to give you time."

Her smile faded. "Daniel, it's been almost seven years."

"Six years and ten months. Believe me, I know." The sadness in his voice tugged at Nicole's heart. Neither of them spoke for several seconds, until she glanced at her watch. "I should get Jordan home. He has a friend coming over in a few minutes."

"Okay if I walk with you?"

Nicole nodded. "Sure."

They headed in the direction of Nicole's condo, at the far end of the park and across the street. Jordan pulled away from her grasp and ran ahead of them.

"Stop at the corner, Jord," Nicole called out after him.

"I will."

She shook her head as her son veered off the path, chasing a squirrel until it disappeared up a tree before making a wide running arc in the direction of the sidewalk, his arms out to the sides like an airplane.

"He's a great kid."

"Thanks. I think so." Nicole tore her eyes from Jordan and looked up at him. "You really are a great detective. Except for the night I re-opened the diner, I haven't seen you once."

"Well, I've seen you. And you're a great mother."

Warmth flooded her chest. "Thank you. That means a lot. So what made you finally show yourself?"

"I saw Jordan alone and figured you'd be worried, so I thought I'd bring him to you."

"What made you think I'd be worried?"

Daniel looked down at her and smiled.

Nicole stopped walking.

He stopped too and turned to face her.

"I guess I don't usually let him get too far away, do I?"

"Not from what I've seen. Not that that's necessarily a bad thing. It's wise to be careful."

"But you think I'm too careful."

"I didn't say that." Daniel lifted both hands in the air. "I'm not a parent. I'm not about to give advice. I can imagine there are lots of things for a mother to worry about, especially when she's raising her child …"

"Alone?"

He sighed. "Yeah."

Nicole started walking again and Daniel fell into step beside her.

"I know I can be over-protective. It's just that Jordan's all I have left of …"

"Gage. I know. I really do understand that, Nicole. And it's okay for you to talk about him with me."

The muscles across her shoulders relaxed. "Are you happy to be back with police services?"

"Sure. It's where I always wanted to be, working the super-hero thing, on a perpetual mission to rid the world of evil."

"Oh yeah, I always think of you when I see the bat signal in the sky at night."

Daniel laughed. "I wish. I'd love to have some of the toys he gets to play with. And the black cape is pretty cool."

Nicole bit her lip. She hadn't realized until she saw him

again how much she'd missed him. They came to the edge of the park. Jordan stood waiting for them on the corner. "Well, I'm glad you finally came out of hiding. It's good to see you."

"Again, I prefer 'surreptitiously observing' to hiding, but thank you. It's good to see you again too. Up close, I mean, not from behind a bush or while peering around a corner wearing a disguise."

Nicole giggled. "What kinds of disguises did you wear?"

"Oh you know, I like to keep it simple. Sometimes it was a moustache and thick glasses combination. Other days I'd wear my blond wig and brown contacts. The best was the nun's habit, though. That was even better than my old police uniform to make everyone straighten up and behave themselves."

Nicole burst out laughing.

"What's so funny, Mom?" Jordan trotted over and stood at her side, looking back and forth between them.

"Detective Grey was telling me about some of his undercover work."

Jordan swung around to look at Daniel. "Undercover work? That's cool. Do you have a gun?"

"Jordan!"

Daniel smiled. "That's okay." He crouched down in front of Jordan again. "I do carry a gun when I'm working, but not when I'm off-duty, like I am now."

"Can I see it sometime?"

"If it's okay with your mom. Maybe the two of you could come over for dinner one night and I can show you."

"Can we, Mom?"

With both of them looking at her expectantly, Nicole didn't have the heart to say no. "Sure, Jord."

Daniel pushed to his feet. "How about Thursday?"

"That would work. Tuesday and Thursday are my nights off from the diner." She looked at him and wrinkled her nose. "Which I guess you already know."

He shrugged. "You do keep a pretty regular schedule."

"I have to. Between running the diner and being a single mom, it makes things easier if I know what's coming."

"I can see that. Of course, sometimes surprises are good. They keep life interesting."

"They do that." Nicole lost herself in the blue eyes that probed hers. An insistent tugging on her sleeve finally got her attention and she looked down.

"Alex is coming. We have to go."

"Right, okay." Nicole took a deep breath as she held out a hand toward her son.

"Mom, I'm six. I don't have to hold your hand anymore. I can cross with the lights."

Nicole could feel Daniel's eyes on her. She exhaled loudly and dropped her arm. "Okay, fine. But don't run." She watched him until he reached the other side of the street and jogged to Alex and his mother before she shifted her attention to Daniel.

"I guess I better go too."

He nodded. "See you Thursday? Six o'clock? I kept my apartment here, so I'm at the same place."

Her stomach twisted. The place she'd last seen him, where she'd kissed him goodbye. How would it feel to walk into his home again? "Sounds good." She started for the crosswalk then paused. "Daniel?"

"Yeah?"

"Thanks for watching out for us."

"You're welcome. It's been fun. I'm kind of going to miss the skulking, actually."

Nicole grinned. But as she crossed the street after her son, the grin faded, and she pressed a hand to her abdomen. What had she done? Agreed to open up the Pandora's Box she'd shut the lid firmly on a long time ago? Not very smart. Surprises were all well and good, but there was a fine line between life getting interesting and life spiraling out of control.

The knife pricked her chest again. Her life had spiraled out of control seven years earlier, and someone she loved had died. Nicole's gaze sought out her son as he stood with his friend, waiting for her. Chills passed over her skin like a raw autumn wind, and bumps rose on her arms.

No matter what, she could never let that happen again.

Chapter Two

Daniel hung up his jacket and sank into his desk chair.

"Grey?" Sharleen Roberts, his partner for three years before he'd gotten suspended from the force for the last five, stuck her head in the opening of his cubicle as he swung around to face her. "I'm going for coffee, do you want …?" She stepped inside the office and studied him. "What's wrong?"

He forced a smile. "Nothing. And sure, I'll take a coffee, thanks." He started to turn away, but she stopped him with a firm hand on the back of his chair.

"Really? Still think you can fool me after all this time? When are you going to learn?"

Daniel dropped the smile. "Never, I guess."

"So what is it?"

He hesitated, but knowing his partner wouldn't drop it until he gave her a satisfactory answer, he surrendered to the inevitable. "I talked to her."

"Who?"

He gave her a few seconds. It took less than that for her dark eyes to widen. "Nicole Kelly?"

"Yes."

"Finally. How did it go?"

Daniel ran his fingers through his hair and leaned against the back of the chair. "Good. Great, I think. She and her son are coming for dinner Thursday night."

Sharleen let go of his chair and leaned back against his desk. "Wow. So why do you look as though you've made an appointment for a root canal, instead of a date to see the woman you've been pining over for years?"

"Shhh." Daniel jumped to his feet and strode to the door of

the cubicle, shooting a furtive glance up and down the empty hallway before dropping back into his seat. He lowered his voice, hoping she would do the same. "I have not been *pining*. I've been giving her time and space to get over the death of her husband."

"Whatever you say. That still doesn't explain the worried look on your face. I always thought you'd be dancing around here like you'd won the lottery the day you finally worked up the nerve to connect with her again. Aren't you excited?"

"Sure."

Sharleen let out a short laugh. "Looks like it. Come on Grey, spill it. I don't have all day."

"To poke your nose in my business? You've never put a time limit on that before."

She shot him a dark look.

Daniel held up both hands. "Fine. It *was* good to see her again. Incredibly good. And I was happy she agreed to come over. At first."

Sharleen sighed and pulled the black plastic chair in the corner closer to him. "This is going to take a while, isn't it?" She sat down and crossed her legs, settling in. "So what changed your mind?"

"I got to thinking about it."

"That's your problem right there, Grey. You do way too much thinking and way too little doing when it comes to this woman."

Daniel toyed with the plastic tab on the lid of the empty takeout coffee cup he'd brought with him that morning. "I don't know if you remember what I went through last time, Shar, when she married Gage and I thought I'd lost her forever."

She winced. "I have a vague recollection. It wasn't pretty."

"It wasn't fun, either. It was the most painful thing I've ever experienced. I never thought I'd have another chance to be with her, and now that that's at least a slight possibility, I have to admit I'm a little gun-shy. What if I put everything on the line and lose her again? I seriously don't think I could handle that. Plus, she has a son now. She's a single mom. That's a whole different ball-game."

"That's true. A single mom isn't someone you trifle with."

"I have no intention of trifling with her, but I don't really know how I should proceed. Maybe it would be better for us to stay friends."

"*Can* you be friends with her?"

He studied his partner. It was a fair question, and one he'd asked himself countless times over the last few years. The only way that would ever happen, that they actually could be friends, would be if he stepped out of the shadows he'd lingered in for far too long and let her know, like most rational people would, that he was there for her if and when she needed him. The problem was, when it came to Nicole, rational was not the word he'd use to describe the way he had—

"Grey?" Sharleen snapped her fingers in front of his face then leaned back in the chair and crossed her arms. "I guess that answers my question."

He tossed the cup into the garbage can beside his desk. "Mine too. You're right; this was a really bad idea. I'm going to call her and cancel." He reached into his shirt pocket and pulled out his cell phone.

Sharleen covered his hand with hers. "What do you mean, I'm right? I didn't tell you not to see her. In fact, if you want my advice—"

"Do I have a choice?"

"Why would you suddenly have a choice? You know getting my advice isn't optional. Taking it is, although do I need to remind you that whenever you don't, you regret it?"

"You don't need to, but I'm sure you will."

"So listen to me this time. My advice is to see her."

"Why?"

"Because if you don't, you'll always wonder what might have happened. You'll drive yourself crazy thinking about how great your life could have been if only you'd been able to man up and take a chance on being with the woman you've been in love with for years. And you'll end up moping around here feeling sorry for yourself, and I'll be the one who has to deal with that all day every day."

"And if it all falls apart and I get my heart trampled again, you'll still be the one who has to deal with the fallout."

Her expression softened. "That's what I'm here for, Grey. I did it before and I can do it again. But there is a third option. You could take a chance with Nicole and it could all work out beautifully. She'll realize she's in love with you too, and the three of you will live happily ever after. Isn't the remote possibility of that enough for you to be willing to put yourself out there?"

Daniel mulled that over. "Maybe you're right."

"Maybe? Have you ever known me to be wrong before?"

"This would be a really bad time for your first."

"Then don't blow this. For either of us."

"I'll do my best. I'd really hate for my broken heart to do any damage to your ego."

Sharleen squeezed his hand and stood up. "Are you still coming over Friday night for a barbeque? Tom's always happy to have another guy around the place."

"Well, if it makes Tom happy if I come over and help myself to a couple of free steaks then sure, I guess I can do that for him."

"Always the giver."

"I need some time with my girls, anyway. I could definitely use a distraction at the moment."

Sharleen's home had been his go-to place after Nicole had married Gage, and Daniel had gone through the darkest period of his life. In the years since, he'd fallen into the habit of eating with his partner and her family whenever he came back to Toronto to visit his dad and sister. He was more than happy to play uncle to their two daughters, their squealing laughter and innocent trust in him gradually healing and soothing the cracked and broken pieces of his heart. Even now, struggling with anxious thoughts and scared to admit to himself how much he was looking forward to seeing Nicole again, the thought of going over there and spending time with all of them had him smiling as he went back to his work.

"I'll go get you that coffee." Sharleen pushed the chair into the corner.

He twisted to look at her over his shoulder. "Thanks, Shar. For everything."

"I'm doing my job, Grey. You're the cross I have to bear in life."

"Someone has to do it."

"Might as well be me."

He chuckled as they repeated their well-worn mantra, then he swung around and turned on his computer. As hard as she was on him, and as crazy as she could make him by not letting him get away with keeping anything from her, ever, Daniel considered himself blessed every day to have Sharleen as a partner.

Still, he hoped and prayed, for both their sakes, that she had steered him right today.

Chapter Three

"We really have to stop coming here for dinner every week." Nicole pushed back the chair in her brother-in-law Holden and his wife Christina's kitchen and tossed her napkin on the table. "I eat way too much every time. You're a great cook, Christina."

Holden snorted and his wife whirled on him. "Holden."

Nicole's gaze shifted back and forth between them. "What?"

Christina sighed. "I guess you had to find out sometime. It was a good run though." She shoved a strand of her long, reddish hair behind one ear. "I don't cook. I'm a terrible cook, in fact."

Holden nodded solemnly. "It's true."

Christina smacked him on the arm. "You're not exactly Martha Stewart in the kitchen either, you know."

He grabbed her hand, pulled it to his mouth, and kissed the back of it. "I am better in other rooms of the house, I freely admit."

She flushed. "That is true."

The two of them gazed at each other. Nicole watched them, a twinge of sadness working its way through her. She was happy for Holden. When Gage, his only brother, had been killed, two days after he and Nicole had gotten married, Holden had gone through a terrible time. He sank deep into a darkness that only his strong faith, the help of his psychiatrist, and the unwavering love of Christina had pulled him out of, but even that had taken months. He and Christina had married a year later, and they'd invited her and Jordan over for dinner every Tuesday night since. Nicole loved being with them, seeing them together and so much in love, but the sight was always a painful reminder of what she and Gage had shared for only a few days.

She pushed back her shoulders. "So where has all this food

come from then?"

Christina tore her gaze from Holden and turned to her, the crimson on her cheeks deepening. "Antonio's, usually."

"Chris! You didn't have to do that."

"Trust me. She did." Holden pushed back his chair, grinning in response to the look his wife sent him. "Let's have our coffee—which incidentally, we did make ourselves—in the living room."

Nicole followed her brother-in-law into the next room and settled onto the brown leather armchair by the fire. He handed her a steaming cup and she smiled up at him. "Thanks."

Holden and Christina sat on the couch facing her. Holden set his coffee down a second before Jordan barreled through the room and threw himself into his arms.

"Thanks for the cool soldiers, Uncle Holden."

Nicole sent a look of mild reproof in Holden's direction.

"A small set. They were on sale."

She shook her head, suppressing a smile. "You spoil him rotten."

"Hey, it's an uncle's prerogative."

Jordan pulled away from Holden. "Look, Mom. There's a whole bunch of soldiers and they have horses and tanks and guns and everything."

A chill shivered over her skin, raising bumps on her arms, and she swallowed hard. "That's great, Jord." Her voice came out slightly raspy and she cleared her throat. "But remember we don't like weapons in real life, right?"

"But Detective Grey has a gun." He spun toward his uncle. "And I get to see it on Thursday."

Holden met her eyes over the dark curly hair of her son. "That's awesome, Jord."

"I know. I can't wait."

Christina spoke up. "Jordan, your dessert is on the table if you want it."

"Thanks, Aunt Christina." Jordan ran from the room.

Nicole bit her lip, marveling at her son's ability to tear

through a room like a tornado, there and gone in seconds but leaving a wake of destruction in his path. She scraped at an imaginary spot on the arm of the chair with her fingernail, not wanting to get into it, but knowing there was no way to avoid it.

When she looked up, both Holden and Christina were studying her. Warmth flooded Nicole's cheeks as she lifted her shoulders. "We ran into him at the park the other day. Jordan asked him if he had a gun, and Daniel offered to have us over for dinner so he could show him. It's not a big deal."

Holden glanced at Christina. "Really?"

She lifted a hand. "What?"

"You're both blushing like mad. What is it about this guy that has all of you swooning?"

"I am *not* swooning. I limit my swooning to one guy, and only when he's not acting like a jealous fool."

Nicole set her coffee on the table beside her chair. "I'm not swooning either. Or blushing. I haven't seen Daniel in years. He's likely with someone else or even married by now, which is fine with me."

"He isn't."

Holden eyed Christina again.

"What? He's a cop and I'm a Children's Aid worker. He comes to see me sometimes."

"I'm a Children's Aid worker too. Except for that one time when he was investigating Ted Stiller for kidnapping those kids, he never comes to see me."

"We have a long-term relationship."

Holden raised his eyebrows.

"A *working* relationship. When he was with the private eye firm in London, he did some investigating on his own, trying to track down the kids that had gone missing. Since he didn't want to bother you, and he and I had met in your office that one time, he asked for me. We became friends, so I do know he isn't seeing anyone, and hasn't since ..." Except for the crackling of flames in the fireplace, the room went silent. "Well, not for years," Christina finished lamely. She laid a hand on her husband's arm and he managed a smile for her.

"Holden." Nicole leaned forward. "This is nothing, honest."

He sighed. "Even if it is something, that's perfectly fine. It's been almost seven years, Nic. I'd be really happy if you found a good man to be with. Gage …" His voice broke and Christina squeezed his arm. "Gage would want that for you too."

"Well, it's not like that with us. We're friends. I think he partly blames himself for what happened that night, for not stopping Gage earlier or for not getting to the scene on time, and he's been trying to make up for that the last few weeks by looking out for us."

Holden's eyes narrowed as he searched his wife's face. "What is it?"

"Nothing. Except …" She lifted one shoulder. "I don't think he considers you a friend, Nicole. Whenever you came up in conversation, he had this look on his face, a mix of longing and sadness. And he always asked how you were doing and how Jordan was, with a lot more than passing interest in his voice. I don't believe he has ever gotten over you."

Nicole picked up her mug and wrapped her fingers around it. "That was a long time ago."

"And he hasn't gotten involved with anyone since. And believe me, he's had plenty of chances."

"For Pete's sake." Holden dropped his head onto the back of the couch in exasperation.

"With other women," Christina clarified. "I hear them talking at work. He always causes a bit of a stir when he comes into the office, I have to admit. Luckily I'm immune to his charms."

"I certainly hope so."

Christina flashed him a quick smile that faltered when she turned back to Nicole. "Anyway, he's been through a really hard time, especially after they suspended him from the force."

Nicole's head jerked. "Daniel was suspended? Why?"

The pink faded from Christina's face as she pressed her knuckles to her lips and glanced at Holden.

He gestured at her feet. "If you take your shoes off, they'll fit in your mouth better."

She wrinkled her nose at him before dropping her hand. "I probably shouldn't have told you that, Nicole. Daniel likely doesn't want you to know."

"Chris. Why did they suspend him? Did it have anything to do with Gage?"

Christina looked at Holden again, who shrugged. "Might as well tell her now."

Her sister-in-law took a deep breath. "The night that Gage was … that he took the last child, Daniel was the one to call it in. He told dispatch the car with Matthew Gibson in it had gone west when it was actually heading east. After … everything was over, he went to his detective sergeant and told him what he had done. Internal Affairs investigated and found him guilty, and he was suspended for five years. Daniel said it was a testament to the sympathy the force felt for Gage's cause, that Daniel wasn't sent to prison or banned from the police force for good."

Holden nodded. "Especially since they never did track down the car or find Matthew."

Nicole sagged against the back of her chair. Daniel had risked his badge to help save that child? Even after she had hurt him by marrying Gage? What was she supposed to do with that? All three of them were silent for several seconds, lost in their own thoughts. Then Nicole lifted her mug and drained the last of her coffee. "I better go. It's a school night and Jordan will have a hard enough time going to sleep when he's so excited about his new soldiers. He'll likely be up half the night playing with them under the blankets." She pressed a palm to the arm of the chair and pushed to her feet.

"That's the great thing about being the uncle." Holden rubbed his hands together. "You can get the kid all revved up and then send him home for his mother to deal with."

"Well, enjoy that while you can." Christina ran her fingers through his dark hair. "You won't have that luxury much longer."

Nicole sank down again. "What does that mean?"

Christina looked at him and he nodded slightly. She shifted on the couch to face Nicole and pressed a hand to her stomach. "It means Jordan's going to have a cousin in a few months."

Nicole clapped her hands. The two of them had wanted kids for years, and it hadn't happened for them. Until now. "Christina! That's fantastic news. Congratulations."

"Hey," Holden protested. "I had something to do with it too, you know."

"Yes, I vaguely remember how it works." A wry grin crossed Nicole's face. "It's wonderful, both of you. Jordan will be so excited."

The three of them stood up. Nicole slid an arm around Christina's shoulders and hugged her. "Thanks for telling me about Daniel. I appreciate it."

Her sister-in-law nodded and took the mug from her hand. "I'll go see how Jordan's doing and tell him it's time to go."

"Thanks, Chris." Nicole waited until she had gone, then stood on her tiptoes to kiss Holden on the cheek. "You'll be a wonderful dad, Holden. You've been an amazing uncle to Jordan. I don't know what the two of us would have done if we hadn't had you in our lives."

His smile held a hint of sadness. "You always will. Even if you do get married again someday."

"I know. And I appreciate it." She threaded her arm through his as they walked toward the door. "But I don't see that happening any time soon."

Holden stopped and grasped her shoulders. "Don't close your mind to the possibility, Nic. Or your heart. Like I said, Gage would want you to be happy." He pulled her close for a hug. "I do still miss him, though." He whispered the words close to her ear.

"I know. I do too."

Holden stepped back and studied her face. "He loved you so much."

She nodded, her throat too tight to speak. Holden kissed her on the forehead and let her go.

Christina came out of the kitchen, holding Jordan's hand. "I'm not sure how much of it actually got into his mouth, but he's finished his dessert."

Nicole groaned at the sight of her son, chocolate icing smeared around his mouth like a five o'clock shadow. "Let's go, Jord. Looks like someone will need a bath before bed."

"Aww, Mom." He scuffed at the marble tile on the floor with the toe of his running shoe, then lifted his head, his face brightening. "Can I take my soldiers into the tub with me?"

"Sure." She looked at Holden. "Wow. I take back what I said. This might be the greatest gift ever if it gets my son excited about taking a bath." She pulled a soldier out of the bag Jordan had been clutching tightly and held it up. "They are pretty cool-looking."

"Well, there *is* something appealing about a man with a gun." Holden let out his breath in a rush when Christina elbowed him. "Or so I've heard," he added, straightening up and pressing a hand to his ribs.

Christina laughed. In spite of the twinge of pain that shot across her chest at the thought of the deadly weapon that had taken her husband from her, Nicole couldn't help joining her. Jordan screwed up his face. "What's so funny?"

Nicole rested a hand on his dark curls. "Nothing, Jord. Adult humor." She dropped the soldier into the bag and shook her head. "Time to go. Uncle Holden is being very silly."

Holden scooped Jordan up and gave him a hug before setting him down. "See you, J-man."

"'Bye, Uncle Holden. 'Bye, Aunt Christina. Thanks for dinner, it was really good." Jordan yanked open the door and disappeared out onto the porch.

Nicole hugged her sister-in-law and leaned in close to whisper in her ear. "I'll never tell that you didn't make it yourself."

"Thanks. Tell Daniel I said hi." Christina shot a sideways glance at Holden who had raised an eyebrow again. "Or don't. Whatever."

Nicole followed her son to the car and slid behind the wheel, still thinking about Holden's last comment about a man with a gun. A cold autumn breeze, carrying with it the hint of frost, swept down the street. Nicole slammed the door before a cloud of dead, decaying leaves, trapped in a funnel of wind, blew into the car. She shivered.

The last time she had seen a man with a gun, he'd just shot and killed her husband.

Nicole started the car and cranked up the heat. Even as warm air puffed weakly through the vent, she continued to feel the sharp bite of frost on her neck, crawling down her back. She glanced into the rear-view mirror to make sure Jordan had buckled up. A sense of foreboding tightened her throat until she could barely breathe, and she lifted her gaze over his tiny shoulder to stare out the back window. No one was there.

Of course not. Gage's death had occurred years ago. Other than still missing him, what had happened that night had nothing to do with her or her son. Nicole hit the door lock button as they reversed down the driveway.

The past no longer had any hold on them. It had taken a long time, but they had finally moved beyond the reach of its long, grasping fingers.

Hadn't they?

Chapter Four

Troy paced the small cell he'd been caged up in for the last six years. Seven steps from the door, past the metal bed tray bolted to the wall, the navy plastic chair, the stainless-steel sink and toilet, to a set of bunk beds along the back wall. When his shins bumped metal, he stopped and planted both palms on the top frame, ducking a little to peer under the bunk so he could see outside. A tall narrow window with a bar running down the middle of it was set in the wall, offering the same view of the same tree and patch of grass he'd stared at for the past two thousand, one hundred and fifty-six days.

He could practically number the blades of grass in the sparse area that ran along the edge of the bare dirt yard where inmates could walk or play a little basketball during activity period, if they were so inclined. Which he never was. His time behind bars wasn't a game, and he wasn't about to treat it like one. If he did, he might lose sight of his end goal. The one that had nothing to do with sports.

"Count!"

Troy lowered his hands at the sound of the commanding voice of a guard in the hallway.

With a sigh, he moved away from the beds and shuffled the seven steps back to the door. When a guard slid it open with a clang, Troy walked through the opening and stopped in front of his cell. He gritted his teeth as another guard strode down the walkway, counting the inmates off. Identifying them by number. Like robots. Or animals.

Chill out, Troy. Only a few more weeks and he would be out of here, a free man. One wrong in his life righted. And he could finally carry out his plan. He'd need a weapon, which would take some wrangling, now that he had this bogus conviction and prison sentence on his record. Any obstacle could be overcome, though. All he had to do was wave around enough of the cash he'd saved up while he was in here scrubbing toilets and doing endless loads of laundry in the commercial machines in the basement like some kind of nineteenth-century peasant.

His jaw tightened again, but he forced himself to relax. *All will be well. All manner of things will be well.* The guard waved his hand, and Troy meandered back into his cell. His gaze fell on the stack of books on the metal table. He'd done a lot of reading while cooped up here in this tin can. Not just Julian of Norwich, who had also lived a life of isolation in a cell, but a pile of ancient classics. *The Iliad, Hamlet, The Count of Monte Cristo.* He didn't understand a lot of what he read—seriously, if you had something to say, say it in plain English, was his philosophy— but the underlying theme of each of them resonated with something deep inside him.

Something that ached to be free as strongly as he longed to rip out the bars that kept him penned in like some kind of wild beast and force his way out of this place. A desire that he hadn't been able to name until he'd stumbled his way through several of those books, identifying with the protagonist without fully understanding why.

It struck him at last, late one night when he was lying on his bunk, suffocated by the enforced darkness, contemplating the novel he'd been reading that day. Not an old classic this time, but a slightly more modern one, *True Grit.* And suddenly he was able to name what it was he was seeking.

Revenge.

Troy understood exactly how that girl felt. Mattie Ross had been wronged. Terribly wronged. And she'd refused to take it lying down. She'd grabbed her shotgun and meted out well-deserved retribution to her enemy. Mattie had done what she needed to do to obtain justice, to get back at the one who had caused her such pain.

And as soon as he was free of this place, so would he.

Chapter Five

Daniel held the door open for them and watched as Nicole, her blond hair drifting around her shoulders and her eyes bright from the cool fall wind, followed Jordan into his apartment. Her spine was rigid as she scanned the living room, her gaze stopping at the spot where, the last time she'd been here, he had held her, kissed her, and begged her not to marry another man.

His own muscles tensed. Maybe they shouldn't have met here, not the first time. Somewhere a little more neutral, the diner maybe, might have been better. Of course, they'd had their moments there too …

She met his gaze. The apprehension knotting his shoulders eased when a small smile played across her lips. "It's been a while."

"Yes, it has." Daniel pushed the door shut and held out his hand. "Can I take your coat?"

Nicole undid the buttons and slipped off the powder-blue wool jacket. Daniel hung it in the closet and closed the door. "Make yourselves at home. I've got burgers on the barbeque."

Jordan spun around to look at him, eyes wide. "You have a barbeque here?"

"Yes, out on the balcony. Could you give me a hand? I think the burgers are probably ready to flip right about now."

His green eyes, so much like his mother's, widened even farther, and Nicole laughed. "You're fulfilling a lifelong dream for him. He watches the staff flip burgers at the diner all the time and keeps asking if he can try it, but so far I haven't let him."

Daniel winced. "Sorry, I should have checked with you first."

"No, it's all right. As long as you're right there and he

promises to be careful."

"I will. Thanks, Mom." Jordan sprinted for the sliding glass balcony doors. Daniel followed him. The kid had a lot of energy, that was for sure. He was going to have to spend a little more time in the gym if he wanted to keep up with …

Don't get ahead of yourself, Grey. It's dinner, not a lifetime commitment.

Reaching over the boy's shoulder, he slid open the glass door. Jordan started to charge through the opening, but Daniel stopped him with a hand on his shoulder. "Take it easy, buddy. Don't ever rush at anything hot. If you trip and fall, you'll end up with your face on the grill, and I'd much rather have a beef burger than a Jordan burger, if it's all right with you."

The boy giggled, the sound clutching at Daniel's chest. "Here." His hand still on Jordan's shoulder, he guided him over to the barbeque and reached for the long-handled metal flipper. He placed the wooden end in the little hand that grasped it eagerly. "Slide it under the patty, nice and slow."

Jordan shoved the flipper under a burger and looked up at him, face serious. Aware of the magnitude of the moment, Daniel didn't laugh as he nodded toward the grill. "Now flip it in one quick movement. Not too high or it will fall off the barbeque or splash hot grease on you."

He let Jordan do the work, but kept his fingers hovering slightly above the boy's as his hand neared the flames. The patty flipped mid-air and landed neatly on the grill with a loud sizzle. Jordan whirled around so quickly, Daniel had to grab him by the shoulders to keep him from brushing against the barbeque.

"Did you see that, Mom? I did it perfectly!"

She stood in the doorway, leaning against the frame. Daniel caught his breath at the intensity of the look on her face—the heart-wrenching combination of pride and sorrow. *Does it bother her that I'm the one teaching him how to do this, instead of Gage?* When her gaze flicked to his before settling on Jordan, though, a smile of genuine appreciation crossed her face.

"I saw. You did great, Jord." Her eyes glowed as she held up her hand. Still gripping the flipper tightly, Jordan skipped over to slap his free hand against hers.

When he returned to the barbeque, he turned over the rest of the patties, only one half-slipping into the flames before Daniel rescued it with the tongs hanging on the side of the barbeque. A few minutes later, Jordan held the plate for him as he lifted the finished burgers from the grill. The boy carried them into the kitchen and set the plate on the table. As energetic as he was, when he had a job to do, he took his responsibility very seriously. *What a kid.* Daniel slid the balcony door shut and followed the boy to the kitchen.

When they had settled around the table, Jordan looked over at his mom. "Can I say grace?"

Nicole folded her hands. "Sure."

They bowed their heads. The simple prayer of thanks Jordan offered up, his voice solemn and his hands tightly clasped together, slid like a blade through the shell Daniel had built around his heart since the night Nicole left him. He felt the cracking like a physical pain and had to work to even out his features when they opened their eyes.

Her gaze lingered on his face. "Everything all right?"

"Sure." He forced cheerfulness into the word, but judging by the small v in her forehead, he wasn't fooling her. "Your son is a natural at the grill. The food looks good."

Jordan lifted a burger to his mouth with both hands and bit into it. Ketchup and mustard dribbled onto his chin as he chewed. The knots in Daniel's shoulders eased slightly when Nicole grabbed a napkin and wiped off her son's face, her attention for the moment off of Daniel.

Conversation was not a problem, not with Jordan around. The boy talked non-stop about school, sports, and friends. Daniel soaked it all up, loving the fact that the normally silent apartment rang with laughter and childish excitement. He could definitely get used to … Suppressing an impatient sigh, he pushed back his chair. "Who wants ice cream?"

Jordan's hand shot into the air. "I do."

"Dish or cone?"

"Cone, please."

Daniel looked at Nicole, the first time he'd met her eyes since she had asked him if everything was all right. "How about you? It's Pralines and Cream."

"Ooh yeah, I'll have some. That's my fav ..." She leaned back and crossed her arms. "It's disconcerting how much you know about me. If we didn't live on the sixth floor, I'd be worried about what you'd seen the last few weeks."

Daniel nodded, his face serious. "Ah yes, the sixth floor. That did pose a challenge, until I remembered I was a cop and had access to wires, taps, and all sorts of surveillance equipment. After that, it was a simple matter of checking your schedule to make sure you'd be out, gaining access to the building with a very authentic-looking search warrant, and jimmying open your apartment door. Ten minutes later it was done."

Nicole stared at him until he laughed. "I'm kidding. I limited my observations to public sightings only, honest. I don't know anything about you that anyone else couldn't have found out."

She uncrossed her arms. "Only anyone willing to sacrifice weeks of his life to keep an eye on us."

"It wasn't a sacrifice, I promise." Daniel pushed to his feet and grabbed the container of ice cream from the freezer.

When he turned around, Nicole stood in front of him. "Can I help?"

He handed her the container, hiding the slight tremor in his fingers her sudden nearness caused by fumbling through the silverware drawer for the ice cream scoop. "Here." He held it out. Her fingers brushed his as she took it, the brief touch sending shivers of shock shooting up his arm. *Cool it, Grey.* Grabbing the box of cones from the cupboard, he carried it to the table and pulled one out. He held it for Nicole as she scooped ice cream and shoved it onto the cone then he handed it to Jordan, who took it and immediately dove in.

While Nicole reached into the container for another scoop, Jordan looked up, a splotch of ice cream on the tip of his nose.

"What's jimmying mean?"

Nicole's eyes met Daniel's over the cone he held out. "It's a way of opening a locked door without a key, Jord. For emergencies only."

He mouthed the word *sorry*.

Nicole lifted one shoulder. "Actually, this is good. By the time you show him your gun, he'll have gotten a real education tonight. And if he does choose a life of crime, we'll be able to trace the roots of that right here, to this moment in time, which will absolve me of any responsibility whatsoever."

Daniel grinned, relieved that, other than a slight wince when she said the word *gun*, she could joke about her son heading down the wrong path in life, in spite of the way her husband's life had ended. He held out another cone for her and she grasped it, her hand covering his. This time she didn't pull away, and his stomach tightened as her eyes searched his. Swallowing hard, he let go of the cone and stepped back. "I think I'll have mine in a dish."

They ate their dessert in silence. Even Jordan seemed to sense that some kind of veil had descended over their party, dampening the mood. Nicole appeared to have developed a fascination with watching her son take every lick.

As soon as Jordan shoved the last, soggy bit of cone into his mouth, he shifted his attention to Daniel. "Can I see your gun now, Detective Grey?"

"If it's all right with your mom." Daniel licked the ice cream from his spoon and stood.

Nicole covered her son's sticky fingers with hers, stopping him before he could leap out of his chair. "What do you say, Jord?"

"May I please be excused?"

"Carry your dishes to the sink and wash the ice cream off your hands before you go."

Daniel washed his own hands as the boy gave his a half-hearted swipe on the hand towel hanging from the stove handle. He followed Jordan into the living room and told him to sit on the couch and he'd bring the weapon to him. It wasn't loaded, but still he handled it carefully as he brought it over to the boy, wanting him to see that the Glock 27 wasn't a toy, that it had to be treated with the utmost respect.

Nicole settled herself on the arm of the black leather couch. As Daniel perched on the glass coffee table in front of Jordan, her gaze lasered in on the gun in his hand. Although her face remained impassive, he could only imagine the painful memories the sight of it invoked. When she looked at him, he winked, trying to ease not only the disquiet he was sure she felt, but also the tension still quivering between them. It seemed to work—her muscles relaxed as she sank into the couch.

"Can I touch it?" Jordan's voice was hushed, almost reverent.

"Sure. It's not loaded, although you always, always handle a gun carefully. Do you understand?"

The boy nodded and stretched out both hands, sides pressed together and palms up. Daniel set the weapon down gently. Pointing to each part, he explained what it was and how it worked. When he finished, he showed Jordan how they would load it if they had ammunition, and how to release the safety, aim it, and fire it.

"Can I try shooting it sometime?"

Daniel's gaze shifted to Nicole's. "Maybe sometime, when you're a bit older, we could go to the shooting range, and I'll show you how to practice firing at a target."

Nicole bit her lip. What did that mean? Was she uneasy about her son shooting a gun, or uncertain about Daniel inferring that he would still be in their lives in the future? Both, maybe. Since she didn't offer a verbal response, he could only guess. He held out his hand. "Here. I better put it away now."

Jordan nodded and handed him the weapon the way he had shown him, handle first.

"Thanks. And Jordan," he waited until the boy looked at him, his eyes serious. "You know that guns aren't toys, right? They can hurt or even kill a person. Police officers have them so they can protect people and keep the peace. Understand?"

"Yes." Jordan nodded again, solemnly. "Thanks for showing it to me."

"You're welcome." Daniel stood and carried the Glock to his bedroom. When he returned, he waved a hand at the shelf of DVDs above his big screen TV. "Want to watch a movie?" As awkward as the evening had been at times, he still desperately wanted to prolong the visit, not sure whether or not there would be another one after tonight.

Jordan whirled toward Nicole. "Can I, Mom? Please?"

She arched a brow at Daniel. "You have kid movies?"

Daniel slid open the glass door. "Not Disney or anything, but I have a few old classics, Laurel and Hardy, stuff like that."

"Laurel and Hardy should be fine. I used to love them when I was a kid."

"Me too." He pulled out a DVD and pushed the glass shut.

When the movie started, Jordan stretched out on the couch, lying on his side with one arm bent beneath his head. Daniel and Nicole watched for a few minutes, all three of them laughing at the opening scene, before he touched her elbow. "Want a cup of tea?"

"Sure." She stood when he did. "I'll help."

He held out an arm toward the kitchen, and she walked into the small room ahead of him. Grabbing the kettle off the stove, she filled it at the sink while he opened the cupboard and took down the box. "I'm not a huge tea drinker. I only have regular."

"That's fine." Nicole set the kettle on the burner and turned it on, then leaned against the counter. "Jordan stayed at Connie's last night while I was working, and she usually lets him stay up late. There's a good chance he'll fall asleep on the couch before long."

Which would give us a bit of time alone. Daniel shook his head to clear it of the thought as he pulled a tea bag out of the box. When he dropped it into the pot and faced her, an amused look had crossed her face, as though she knew what he'd been thinking. The shrill whistle of the kettle saved him from having to defend himself. Nicole swung around and grabbed it, then poured the hot water into the black ceramic pot he'd nudged closer to her.

While she carried the pot to the table, Daniel pulled two red china mugs and the honey out of the cupboard. "Do you take milk?"

"Yes, thanks."

He grabbed the jug from the fridge. Nicole walked to the doorway. "Like I thought—he's out already."

Nicole filled their cups before taking the seat across from him and contemplating him in silence.

Daniel shifted in his seat. "What?"

"It really is great to see you again."

He wrapped both hands around the warm mug. "You too. And Jordan. He's amazing, Nic." Although he hadn't used it before, the nickname slid easily off his tongue. "You've done an incredible job with him."

"Thank you. I'm not sure what I would have done after Gage died, if I hadn't had Jordan. He was the reason I got out of bed every morning. And he helped me remember that God hadn't abandoned me, that He was watching over us, and that He was still good, no matter what my emotions might have told me."

Daniel's grip on the mug tightened. How many times during those awful days following Gage's death had he wanted to go to her, longed to pull her into his arms and offer some comfort, however small and pitiable a defence it might be against the darkness that threatened to consume her? When the opportunity to leave town came, he'd grabbed it, knowing that if he didn't, he never would have been able to stay away from her.

Lost in thought, he started when she reached across the table and touched the back of her hand to the fingers that gripped his mug. "What are you thinking about?"

A small smile crossed his face. "You."

Nicole pulled her hand away. "What about me?"

"There's something I've been wanting to say to you for years now."

"What?" Nicole caught her lower lip in her teeth.

"That I'm sorry."

"Sorry? Why?"

"For not getting there in time that night. For not figuring out earlier that it was Gage taking the kids so I could stop him before he got himself killed." He stopped and cleared his throat. "If I had done my job better, maybe you wouldn't have had to go through what you've been through, and Jordan wouldn't have had to grow up without a father."

"Daniel." Nicole leaned closer and rested her hands, warm from the mug of tea, on his forearms. "Listen to me. What happened was not your fault, and I never for one second blamed you. Gage knew the risks he was taking by helping those kids, and he did it anyway. There was no way you could have figured out it was him in time to stop him." Her hands slid up and down his arms slowly. If she hoped that would help him focus on her words, she'd seriously miscalculated. "You certainly don't need to apologize to me. If anything, I should thank you."

He lifted the gaze that had settled on her mouth. "For what?"

"For keeping an eye on us. For teaching Jordan how to flip burgers and treat a weapon with respect. And for …"

"What?"

"Christina told me you sent the police the wrong way that night, after the car that had taken the child away. She said you were suspended for five years and could have lost your badge."

Daniel let go of his mug and pulled away from her. Shoving his chair away from the table, he strode over to the counter and, facing the cupboards, braced himself with both hands on the cool, tiled surface. "She shouldn't have told you that."

"Why not?"

"Because I didn't want you to know."

Chair legs scraped across the linoleum. Daniel shifted to face her. The last breath he'd taken jammed in his throat. Nicole stood in front of him, so close they were almost touching.

She rested her hand lightly on his chest. "Why wouldn't you want me to know that? Do you have any idea what it means to me that you would help Gage?"

His heart pounded beneath her fingers. At the moment, with her standing that close, her hand pressed against him, he only had one idea in his head, and it was clearly not one that should be there.

Daniel shook his head. "I did come to understand why Gage did what he did, even to respect him for his convictions. But I didn't do it for him."

"Then why?"

"When I saw Gage go down, I knew that if they found the kid he was trying to save and returned him to his father, you'd always believe that he died for nothing." His chest squeezed at the memory. "So I did it for Matthew Gibson, because he deserved a new life. And for you, hoping that someday you could have that too."

Her eyes locked with his. For several seconds, neither of them moved. Then she slid both her hands behind his neck and drew him down to her.

She's thanking you, that's all this is. Don't do it. When her soft mouth pressed against his, though, Daniel gave in with a groan. His fingers drove into her soft blond hair and he pulled her closer, his lips parting as he deepened their kiss. He wanted to feel her, to taste her, to remember how incredible it had felt the last time he'd held her.

That memory ripped through him like the sharp, blinding ray of a lighthouse penetrating fog, a warning of imminent danger. Every time he and Nicole had kissed—or almost kissed—it had been for the wrong reasons. And every time it had turned out badly, caused far more harm than good. If she was kissing him now out of some sense of misplaced gratitude, the end result would be the same. As much as his brain might short circuit in her presence, he wasn't an idiot. He knew that doing the same thing over and over and expecting a different result made no sense at all.

So maybe it was time the two of them tried something different.

Summoning strength from a reservoir he'd thought had long been depleted from years of not allowing himself to go to her, Daniel broke away and grasped her wrists, pulling her arms gently from around his neck.

Confusion flickered across her face.

He held her hands to his chest. "You don't owe me anything, Nicole."

She jolted as though the words zapped through her like an electric current. "That's not what that was about."

"Are you sure?"

"Yes. I'm positive." She yanked her hands from his grasp and spun on her heel.

He followed her as she stalked into the living room. "Then what was it about?"

Nicole whirled to face him. Daniel tried to analyze what it was that was making the gold flecks in her eyes flash like sparks. Anger? Hurt? Humiliation? All of the above, probably. His stomach churned.

"When I found out what you had done, it reminded me of what had attracted me to you from the first time we met—your heart, your dedication to doing the right thing, even—or maybe especially—that little three-year-old's desire to get rid of all the evil in the world. The fact that you were willing to help Gage, even though he was breaking the law, and even though I had …"

"What? Chosen him over me?"

"Yes. Thinking about all that made me feel close to you, brought back all the feelings I'd experienced the last time I was here. Suddenly I remembered what had drawn me to you so strongly that I almost threw away everything, including the man I had promised to marry, to be with you."

She started to turn away, but he grabbed her elbow to stop her. "You did?"

Deep lines creased her forehead. "Yes. Didn't you know? Walking away from you that night was the hardest thing I have ever done."

He let go of her with a heavy sigh. "Couldn't have been any

harder than watching you go."

"Maybe not. But that's what that kiss was about. No hidden agenda or ulterior motive." She bent down to take hold of her son's shoulder and shake him gently. "Come on, Jord. Time to go home."

"Nicole."

She straightened but kept her back to him.

"Look, I'm sorry. That wasn't fair."

"No, it wasn't." Nicole turned around but didn't meet his eyes. "Although maybe it was for the best. Maybe all this," she waved a hand through the air between them, "is too tangled up with everything that happened seven years ago. Maybe it was a mistake to even attempt to sort it all out, to try and build something new on such a shaky foundation." She bent over her son again. "Jordan!"

He sat up slowly, rubbing both eyes with his fists. "Are we going home?"

"Yes."

Daniel stepped back as she took Jordan's hand and helped him from the couch. His stomach clenched as she crossed the room, her son almost running to keep up. *For ten seconds I had everything I ever wanted in my arms, and I threw it away.* "Nicole, wait. Please."

She picked up Jordan's orange jacket that she'd tossed over the chair by the door and helped him into it before grabbing her blue coat from the hanger in the closet and shoving her arms into the sleeves. One hand on the doorknob, she finally looked at him.

Daniel lifted both hands. "I'm sorry. I don't know what else to say."

Her green eyes showed no sign of relenting. "There is nothing else to say." She twisted the knob and opened the door. "Thank Detective Grey for having us, Jord."

The little boy looked up, his dark curls tousled and his eyelids heavy. The sight tore through Daniel's chest. An overwhelming desire to crouch down and hug the young boy gripped him, but he forced himself not to move, to do nothing more than meet the sleepy eyes that gazed up at him.

"Thank you for the hamburgers, Detective Grey. And for showing me your gun. It was really cool."

Daniel swallowed the lump in his throat. "You're welcome, Jordan."

"Can we come again sometime?"

Nicole's jaw tightened, but she didn't speak. Daniel reached out and ruffled her son's hair. "That's up to your mom, buddy. You're always welcome here."

"Can we, Mom? Can we come next week?"

"We'll talk about it at home."

"Please. Detective Grey said he would take me to his work and show me the jail cells where they keep real prisoners."

"Jord."

"I really want to see that and—"

"Jordan!"

Her son's mouth clamped shut.

"I said we'll talk about it at home. Now let's go." She tugged on his hand and directed him into the hall before facing Daniel. "I'm sorry about that. When he gets an idea in his head, he forgets his manners completely."

Daniel nodded. "I suffer from the same affliction, apparently."

Her expression softened for the first time since she had stormed out of the kitchen.

"For the record, Nic, I didn't think anything about tonight was a mistake. At least, not until I opened my big mouth and ruined everything."

The corners of her lips quirked. "Actually, you opening your mouth was pretty great. It was when you started talking that everything fell apart."

Daniel snorted a laugh, the tightness in his stomach easing when she joined him. Pink tinged both her cheeks, as though she couldn't believe what she had said. He couldn't quite believe it either, but he was extremely glad she had, since it defused the friction rasping between them.

Jordan looked back and forth between the two of them, his forehead wrinkling. "What's so funny, Mom?"

Still grinning, she squeezed his shoulder. "Nothing, Jord. Grown-up humor."

He sighed. "Like when you and Aunt Christina laughed because Uncle Holden said a man with a gun was—"

Nicole wrapped her arm around her son's head and pressed her hand over his mouth. Daniel raised both eyebrows. The flush on her cheeks deepened as he leaned a hip against the doorframe and crossed his arms.

"I don't know when, and I don't know how, but I *will* find out what your son was about to say. I haven't been honing my detective skills for the past ten years for no reason, you know."

"It was nothing, I swear. He talks in his sleep sometimes, but gibberish, nothing that makes any sense."

"He sounds coherent to me. And his eyes are wide open. I'm pretty sure he's fully awake."

"Don't let him fool you. He walks in his sleep too, with his eyes open. It freaks me out all the time. The only thing to do when it happens is get him straight home to bed before he does irreparable damage."

"To himself or to you?"

"Either."

He grinned. The sheepish smile she offered him in return gave him the courage to uncross his arms and lift a hand in the air. "What do you say, Nic. Can we try again? I'd really like to take your son to jail."

She shuddered. "Perish the thought." For a few seconds her eyes met and held his, then she lifted her shoulders. "I guess we can give it one more shot before we abandon the idea altogether."

"Oh good, so long as there's no pressure."

The corners of her mouth lifted. "Next Thursday?"

"Sure. Why don't I pick you up at six? We can grab dinner somewhere and then go to the station for a tour."

"Yes!" Jordan clapped his hands.

Nicole smiled at Daniel. Her eyes had gone soft, and he

clenched his fists to keep from reaching for her and finishing what she'd started in the kitchen. If her son hadn't been standing there, his fingers clutching hers like he'd forgotten he was six and didn't need to hold her hand anymore, he definitely might have.

He watched them walk down the hallway, away from him. This time, though, the sight didn't fill him with pain and helplessness. One thing—the thing that had been missing the last time she'd left him standing there, kept those feelings at bay and brought a slow smile spreading across his face.

Hope.

Chapter Six

Nicole tucked the blankets securely around her son. "Did you have fun tonight?"

"Yeah, I really like Detective Grey." Jordan's eyelids were half-closed by the time his head settled into the tiny indent in his Spiderman pillowcase. She smiled, watching him. Daniel had been so good with him tonight. It had bothered her—a lot—seeing him hand her son the same type of instrument that had killed Gage, but she'd pushed back her trepidation. Better Jordan learn about handling a weapon safely from a professional, even though, if she had her way, he would never need to use that information.

Nicole tapped a finger on his nose. "Hey, Jord, when you saw him at the park the other day, you didn't know he was Mommy's friend, did you? So why were you talking to a stranger?"

Jordan's forehead crinkled as he opened his eyes and fixed them on hers. "Detective Grey's not a stranger. I've seen him before."

Shock tingled through her. "You have?"

"Sure."

"Where?"

"At the park, outside the diner, at school."

"Wait, Detective Grey has been at your school?"

"Yeah. He walks by sometimes when we're playing on the playground. And a little while ago he came to my class with another policeman to talk to us about bullying. When they finished, he met with Lucas and Riley, and after that they didn't bother me at recess anymore."

Nicole gripped his blanket. She remembered Jordan

mentioning that a couple of boys were giving him a hard time at school, but he hadn't said anything about it for weeks and she'd almost forgotten.

"Did he ever talk to you?"

"The day he came to school was the first time. Before that he waved sometimes."

"And what did you do?"

He turned his head to one side on the pillow and stared at her as though the answer was obvious. "I waved back."

Nicole struggled to wrap her mind around everything he was saying. "Didn't it scare you to see a strange man following you and waving at you?"

Jordan closed his eyes, clearly unaware of the impact his words were having on her. "No, I wasn't scared. I knew." His voice was so thick with fatigue she could barely make out the words. She should let him go to sleep, but she had to ask.

"You knew what?"

He yawned and pulled the blue knitted blanket up to his chin, snuggling deeper under its cozy warmth. "That he was good."

Nicole stretched out on the bed beside him and propped herself up on one elbow, watching him until dreams flickered behind his eyelids. Then she eased over onto her back and stared up at the ceiling, her mind racing.

She knew Daniel had been watching out for them the last few weeks, but she hadn't had any idea how involved he had been in their lives. How could she have missed seeing him? How had she not known he was nearby? Tonight, in his apartment, she'd felt his presence as strongly as if he had wrapped his arms around her and pulled her close, even when he was on the other side of the room.

Nicole closed her eyes. *Father, what should I do? I don't want to hurt him again. And I really can't take another loss, either.* Pressing her fingers to her head, she rubbed her temple, trying to absorb everything that had happened that evening.

She couldn't do it. It was too much, and she was too tired. Nicole sat up and touched two fingers to her lips as a slow smile crossed her face. Maybe she and Daniel both needed to do a little less thinking and simply give themselves permission to enjoy each other's company. For the first time since Gage's death, she knew she was ready to at least try to see where things went.

Not sure Daniel is as ready as I am. The look in his eyes—something alarmingly close to panic—when he pulled her arms from around his neck, filled her with misgivings when she remembered it now. At least he hadn't been so scared that he'd let her leave without settling things between them. If he had, she wasn't sure they would have seen each other again.

The pain that shot through her at the thought—so strong she pressed the heel of her hand over her chest in an attempt to ease it—told her what she had already begun to suspect.

Daniel might have recently come back into her life, but even with everything that had happened with Gage, he had never fully left her thoughts.

Or her heart.

Chapter Seven

Mikayla Grant bent forward until her forehead nearly touched the canvas. With her smallest brush, she added a tiny groove to the wooden surface of the table in the center of the painting.

"Mik?"

"Hmm?" Mikayla couldn't tear her eyes away from the canvas long enough to turn at the sound of her best friend and agent's voice.

Leigh came and stood behind her, leaning over her shoulder to examine the new painting. "Mik, it's beautiful. Seriously, I can almost feel the warmth of the sunlight pouring through that window. And I love the big orange cat lying on the kitchen table. Reminds me of a pumpkin."

"Okay," Mikayla murmured, adding a black dot to one of the flowers in the vase on the windowsill with a tiny brush.

"Okay what?"

"Hmm?"

"Mik."

With a small sigh, Mikayla dropped the brush into the holder and spun around to face her agent. "What is it?"

"Did you hear anything I said?"

"Umm …"

Leigh shook her head, her short red hair staying perfectly in place. "I don't know what planet you were on, but I think I'll let you get back to it, since you're doing good work, and we have a deadline hanging over our heads."

"We?" Mikayla's lips turned up in a wry grin.

"Darling, we're in this together, you know that. If you have a deadline, I have a deadline."

"So you're going to stay here and hang out with me until I

get this one finished?"

"Uh …"

"That's what I thought."

Leigh lifted ring-festooned fingers. "There's nothing I'd like more than to stay here and hand you brushes all night, but look how much I'm distracting you already. It doesn't make sense, creatively, for me to be here pulling your attention away from your work."

"Creatively."

"That's right."

"As creative as the way you're managing to justify getting out of here and going home to a hot bath and a glass of wine while I continue to slave away on your behalf?"

"Our behalf, darling. When you slave away, I—"

"Slave away, I get it. What I am a little hazy on is how we're both slaving away, but I'm the only one who's actually working."

"No, you wouldn't get it," Leigh said, waving a hand through the air dismissively. "It's an agent thing." She rested her palms on the arms of Mikayla's chair, her face serious. "Mik."

"Yes?"

"Dinner is in the oven. I don't want to come back in the morning and find the oven still on and something in it that looks like a science experiment gone horribly wrong."

"Of course not."

"Don't *of course not* me—it wouldn't be the first time a travesty like you letting one of my beautiful home-cooked meals go to waste has occurred."

"And by home-cooked you mean you pulled the plastic wrap off the instant dinner and shoved it into the oven?"

Leigh straightened and pressed a hand to her chest. "Are we in a home?"

Mikayla worked to keep a straight face. "I suppose so."

"And is your dinner cooking?"

"Technically, yes."

"There you go."

Mikayla laughed. "All right, all right. Thank you for all your hard work, Martha Stewart. I won't let a single, over-processed, chemical-laden bite go to waste."

Her agent wrinkled her nose at her. "Then I'm off. I'll see you tomorrow morning, first thing."

"What's your hurry, anyway? You have a hot date tonight or something?"

"Always."

Mikayla raised an eyebrow.

Leigh lifted her shoulders. "I've been married for twelve years, honey. When you've been married that long, your definition of hot gets revised somewhat. Nowadays, for me, hot is when Terry takes out the garbage without me having to ask him to. It's all about having realistic expectations."

Mikayla snorted. "I've never known you to have a realistic expectation in your life."

"For my *husband*, darling. Artists are a completely different breed. They need to be handled with kid gloves, led to believe their work is the most important of the century and if they don't produce, they will be robbing the world of a masterpiece that could change the course of art history forever."

"You know I'm right here in front of you, don't you?"

"If I thought you ever heard a word I said, I might worry about that." Leigh grabbed her white faux fur jacket off the back of a chair and slipped it on, her big gold hoop earrings jangling. She zipped it up and waggled her fingers through the air as she pulled open the door. "Tata, darling." The door closed behind her.

Mikayla sat staring at the back of it, her head spinning. *Can you believe that girl, Coe?* She grinned as the words passed through her mind. Coe was the friend she'd conjured up to take the place of all those brothers and sisters she'd never had. On paper, she was a decent substitute. She did whatever Mikayla asked her to, never talked back or said a mean word to her, and not once, in all the years she'd been hanging around in Mikayla's imagination, had she taken anything that belonged to her like a real sibling might have done. The smile faded from Mikayla's face.

All those things her friends had complained about while she was growing up had actually sounded pretty great to her. Having someone argue with you was still better than sitting quietly, listening to the grown-ups ramble on about the latest world events or who they were going to vote for in the next election. Not that her parents hadn't been wonderful, but it would have been nice to have had a sister or brother to grow up with, and to share in the grief and loneliness no one else could begin to comprehend after they had been killed.

Shake it off, Mikayla. She pushed back her shoulders and reached for her brush to get back to work.

When the smoke detector went off two hours later, Mikayla dropped her brush and blinked several times, as if waking from a deep, dream-filled sleep. Leaving the splotches of paint that had splattered across the floor, she jumped up, pulled her dinner from the oven, dumped the charred remains in the garbage, and carried the bag out to the garage so she wouldn't have to listen to another lecture from Leigh when she arrived in the morning.

Chapter Eight

Daniel leaned against the railing of Tom and Sharleen's deck and sipped from his can of cola.

"Here you go, guys." Sharleen came out of the house and handed a platter of raw steaks to Tom. "Do your man thing and cook these over the fire."

Tom took the plate from her and set it down beside the barbeque. "Technically, the man thing would involve going out and hunting this meat with our handmade weapons, then building our own fire by rubbing two sticks together to cook it, but I guess ready-made steaks from the store and twisting the cap on the propane tank will have to do."

Sharleen looked indignant. "Ready-made? I'll have you know I spent hours in the kitchen marinating and preparing those steaks."

Tom cocked his head to one side.

Sharleen's shoulders slumped. "Well, I took them out of the package and threw on some barbeque sauce after I got home from work. That's practically the same thing. Besides, I'm pretty sure they frown on men using homemade weapons to bring down other people's cows these days."

Tom let out a heavy sigh. "Not everything is progress, is it?" He leaned in and kissed Sharleen on the forehead. She smiled, but Daniel didn't miss the look she gave her husband, or the way her head inclined slightly in Daniel's direction, before she went into the house, sliding the glass door shut behind her.

"What was that?"

"What was what?" Tom slid the lifter under a steak. It landed on the grill with a satisfying sizzle.

"That look Sharleen gave you."

"Oh, that." He transferred another steak onto the grill and set the platter down. "She wants me to talk to you about Nicole."

Daniel groaned and pushed away from the railing. "I think it's time for me to go see what my girls are doing." He took a step toward the stairs, but Tom stopped him with a hand on his arm.

"Look, I don't want to have this conversation either, believe me. But you and I know better than anyone that when my wife gets an idea in that beautiful head of hers, the best thing is to go along with it. Or let her believe you are anyway."

Daniel arched an eyebrow.

Tom shot a glance toward the house and leaned a little closer. "It may not be entirely ethical, but I have a plan. If we at least look like we're having this intense conversation, Sharleen will be happy. She'll never know she's been had, and we can all relax and enjoy our dinner."

The corners of Daniel's lips twitched. "Pretend to have a conversation? How does that work, exactly?"

"Follow my lead." Tom pressed a hand to his chest. "Make out as though I said something deeply profound, like there is nothing more miraculous than holding a woman in your arms and knowing she's the one God intended you to spend the rest of your life with, something along those lines. Then nod in agreement."

Daniel forced a serious look onto his face and nodded.

"That's good. It's not *what* we're saying; it's *how* we're saying it. Kind of like reading to a baby. Keep a serious look on your face, use as many expressive gestures as you can"—Tom emphasized that point with a wild wave of his arm, and Daniel bit back a laugh—"and we could be talking about the Leafs' game for all Sharleen will know. And speaking of which, did you watch last night? That overtime goal was spectacular."

Daniel set his can of cola on top of the railing and leaned against the rail again. "Yeah, I saw it. I thought they were going to blow it there when the Rangers tied it in the third."

"Me too." Tom shot another sideways glance at the kitchen window and lowered his voice to slightly above a whisper.

"Sharleen's looking. Let's give her something." He swept an arm across the backyard where his young daughters, bundled up in jackets and wool hats, were swinging on a tire swing.

Childish laughter drifted toward them and Daniel smiled, lost in the sound until Tom's voice brought him back.

"Follow where I'm pointing and try assuming the most thoughtful look you can, as though it has suddenly occurred to you how great it would be to have a couple of kids of your own, calling you Dad and looking up at you with complete love and trust, blah, blah, blah." He started to circle his fingers in a dismissive gesture, then apparently remembered their mission and smacked his open hand hard on the top of the deck railing as though emphasizing a point.

Daniel pressed a fist to his lips to suppress a grin, doing his best to give the action a contemplative air, like the statue of The Thinker. "So what do you think their chances are next year?"

"The Leafs?" Tom winced. "It's tough to be a Toronto fan, isn't it? Even before the season's half over we're talking about how they'll do next year."

"I know. It's been a long time since the '67 Leafs."

"And the '93 Jays, I hear you. At least both teams have interesting prospects coming up. One of these days our time will come again."

The glass door slid open and both men turned toward it. Sharleen stuck her head through the opening and held out a clean platter. "As soon as the steaks are done we can eat. So, you have a couple of minutes to finish up whatever you were talking about and then the hordes will descend upon you."

Daniel took the platter and lifted his can in her direction. "Thanks for the warning."

His partner nodded before disappearing into the house, and Daniel gave Tom a wry grin. "Any last words of wisdom?"

"Hmm, I don't know. How about, it's scary to put yourself out there after you've been hurt, but sometimes you need to be a man and take the leap anyway, or something like that." He shot another look toward the house. "Give her three or four of those slow head bobs, as if you're seriously thinking over everything I've said, will ya? Then I believe our job here will be done." Tom flipped the last steak. The rich smell wafted to Daniel and his stomach growled in response.

"That's it for me. I don't do relationship advice, so you, Nicole, and God are going to have to work this out amongst yourselves." Tom clapped a hand on Daniel's shoulder. "However, I am here any time you want to talk, day or night."

"I know. Thanks. And great pretend conversation, by the way." Daniel nodded his head a few times as Tom had suggested, drawing his eyebrows together as though deep in thought.

"Best kind, if you ask me." Tom glanced over his shoulder. "Better brace yourself."

The girls stampeded up the deck stairs and flung themselves at Daniel. He got so caught up in listening to them talk about their day and what they had seen and done, that everything else in his life faded into the background. At least until he had slid behind the wheel of his car later that evening and was heading home.

Then Nicole's face flashed through his mind. His thoughts drifted to the evening they'd spent together and the trip to the police station the three of them were planning. Daniel tapped a finger against his lips, remembering how it had felt to hold her in his arms again. And to spend time with Jordan. He could definitely get used to hanging out with him, teaching him things and seeing his eyes light up when he tried something out for the first time, like barbecuing hamburgers. He'd never really thought about being a father before, but he could actually see himself stepping in for Gage and doing some dad stuff. Maybe it *was* time for him to be a man and …

Daniel's head jerked up. "Son of a gun!" He smacked the palm of his hand against the steering wheel as he realized, about three hours late, that Sharleen wasn't the one who'd just been had.

Chapter Nine

"Here you go, Troy." The hulking guard pulled a black plastic bag out from under the counter and set it in front of him. Tattoos rose from the collar of his blue work shirt and twined around his neck like living vines. "Everything you had with you when you arrived."

"Thanks, Chuck."

The guard tipped his head to one side and studied him. "You gonna be all right, man?"

Troy pulled the bag off the counter and shoved it under his arm. "Once I'm a free man, I'll be perfectly fine." He grasped the beefy hand of the one guard who had treated him decently. "Thanks for everything."

"You're welcome. Best of luck out there. And take it easy—I'd hate to see you walking back in through these gates again."

Troy started for the door. "You don't have to worry about that. You won't see me in here again. I've done my time and I'm ready to get back to my life."

"What are you going to do?"

He stopped with one hand on the metal bar of the door. "I've got plans. Big plans. That's the one good thing about being in here, lots of time to map out the future. There's someone I need to track down, someone who owes me something. After I collect, I think I can finally find a little peace in my life."

The big man behind the counter nodded. "I hope so. You take care now, you hear?"

Troy raised a hand in salute. "Oh, you can count on it." *I'll take a great deal of care.* The plan he'd had years to concoct and hone while caged up like an animal would have to be carried out with absolute precision. If revenge was a dish best served cold, the serving he planned to mete out had to be about frozen solid by now, but he couldn't rush it. Everything had to go perfectly as he would only have one chance. With a curt nod, he shoved a hip against the bar, pushing open the door. Stepping out onto the cement walkway, he flung his arms open wide, the bag swinging from one hand, and, for the first time in years, filled his lungs with free air.

Chapter Ten

Nicole leaned over the sink, running a finger smeared with cover-up over the shadows two nights spent tossing and turning in bed had left below her eyes. She studied her weary reflection in the mirror and sighed. Even make-up couldn't help her this morning. Nicole adjusted the strap on her cream-colored lace camisole then froze, her eyes narrowing as she stared at the mirror.

Daniel was kidding about putting cameras in here. The thought didn't ease her apprehension, and she grabbed her peach-colored blouse off the washroom door and pulled it on, hastily buttoning it. With another quick glance at the glass, she shook her head, laughing nervously as she turned to leave the room.

"Come on, Jord. Time to go. Grandma Connie's waiting for you."

Her son came out of the kitchen, shoving the last bite of toast into his mouth. Crumbs clung to his cheeks. Nicole pulled a tissue from the pocket of her tan dress pants and reached for him. "How on earth did you manage to get jam on your forehead? You know your mouth is all the way down here, don't you?" She pressed a finger to his lips, and he laughed as she scrubbed him clean before following him to the door of their condo.

Her chest squeezed when Connie pulled open the door of her little apartment above the diner. Deep wrinkles that hadn't been there a few months ago creased her forehead and the skin around her mouth. They crinkled now as a smile crossed her face and she pulled Jordan into her arms. He gave her a quick hug then stepped away and tipped back his head. "Mmm. Chocolate chip muffins, right?"

Connie laughed. "They were supposed to be a surprise, but I

can't fool that nose of yours, can I? Go ahead, you may have one."

She slid the pack off his shoulders, and he sprinted for the kitchen, calling out, "'Bye, Mom," as he disappeared through the doorway.

Nicole shook her head. "I guess the piece of toast I gave him for breakfast didn't cut it." She grinned at Connie. "I never have been able to compete with your cooking or baking."

"We all have different talents, darlin'." Connie wrapped her arms around Nicole. "Yours is raising that boy, and you are doing a splendid job. Although I happen to know your cooking and baking skills aren't exactly lacking, either. Or your management abilities." She pulled away, her soft blue eyes twinkling as they met Nicole's. "The diner is flourishing. Joe would have been very impressed with how well you are running the place."

Nicole's eyes pricked, the way they always did at the mention of Connie's husband, the man she had loved like a father and who had left her the diner as his legacy when he died. "I learned from the best."

Her friend pressed a kiss to her cheek and let her go. "Go on and make him proud then. And say hi to the boys for me." Connie had always had a soft spot for the group of derelicts that came into the diner at eight o'clock almost every evening looking for a hot cup of coffee. And as much as Nicole had fought against taking over the job of serving them when they came in, once she had, she found her own soft spot for the good-hearted, if down-on-their-luck, gentlemen.

Nicole nodded. "I will. And I'll pick you both up in time for church in the morning. Thanks for having Jordan."

"You know it's my pleasure. I thank the good Lord every day for seeing fit to make me a mama and a grandma, even though I never did have any children of my own. What a joy that is."

"See if you still feel that way in a few hours." Nicole laughed and reached for the door handle.

A steady stream of customers kept Nicole running most of the day. By mid-afternoon, the stream had slowed to a trickle, and at three o'clock, when the diner was empty, she stuck her head through the swinging doors to the kitchen. "I'm going out for a couple of hours, but I'll be back for the dinner rush."

Johnny, the tall, thin redhead Nicole had hired as head cook after Joe died, glanced at her from the grill where he'd been using the lifter to scrape grease into the trough on the side. "Sure, Nic."

Molly, a server who'd been at the diner for four or five years and had become a good friend, dropped a handful of silverware into the dishwasher and pushed the door shut, then followed Nicole into the diner. "Don't rush back. We can handle things here. Got a hot date?"

Warmth rushed into Nicole's cheeks. "Of course not. I'm popping over to my sister-in-law's for coffee. No men involved."

"Not even as a topic of conversation?"

Nicole pulled off her apron and stuffed it under the chrome-edged counter. She grabbed her purse before meeting Molly's penetrating gaze.

A smile played around the corners of the waitress's mouth. "That's what I thought. I knew something was up with you. So who's the lucky guy?" She propped an elbow on the counter and rested her chin on her hand, settling in.

Nicole shook her head. "Such an imagination. I'll see you in a couple of hours." She rounded the counter and started for the door but stopped short when Molly called after her.

"It's that gorgeous cop who's been coming by, isn't it?"

Nicole spun around and stared at her. "What are you talking about?"

Molly held a hand over her head. "Tall, dark hair, ridiculous blue eyes? He's been in a couple of times asking about you, so I thought maybe he'd finally worked up the nerve to talk to you directly."

"He's been in here? Why didn't you say anything?"

Molly shrugged. "He asked me not to. He said he was an old friend and wanted to surprise you, but he was waiting for the right time. He seemed genuine when he asked how you were, not creepy or anything. I'm sorry, should I have told you?"

Nicole crossed the black and white tiled floor and set her purse on top of the bar, sinking on to a stool before her weak knees could give out on her. "No, it's fine. He is an old friend, someone I knew before ..." She stopped and drew in a deep breath. "Before my husband died. Jordan and I ran into him at the park last week."

Molly planted both hands on the counter. "And?"

"And it was good to see him."

"How good?"

"Very good. We had dinner at his place Thursday night."

"Are you going to see him again?"

"He promised Jordan he'd take us on a tour of the station this week. After that, I don't know. We're still figuring things out."

"Look, Nic, it's none of my business, but seriously, what is there to figure out? You're both single, and he obviously cares about you. Why not go for it?"

Nicole sighed. This would be a lot easier if she were in her twenties again, when everything was black and white and the path to take always seemed so clear. "It's not that simple, Mol. I still miss Gage, a lot, and I have Jordan to consider. It's complicated."

Molly pushed herself away from the counter. "Like I said, it's not my business. But if I were you, I wouldn't think about it for too long. A guy like that isn't going to stay on the market forever. Although ..." She caught her bottom lip between her perfect white teeth.

"Although what?" Nicole's grip on her purse handle tightened.

Molly looked sheepish. "The first time he came in, I didn't realize he knew you, and I kind of put it out there that I might be interested. He didn't even seem to notice me which—sorry if this sounds like bragging, but I'm telling you to make a point—

doesn't happen to me all that often."

Nicole believed it. Molly attracted men like sugar attracted bees. She was tall and slender, and her shiny, copper-colored hair hung halfway down her back. Besides the fact that she could easily get work modeling if she were so inclined, she had an outgoing, high-energy personality and killer smile that netted her far more in tips than Nicole handed her every week. The fact that Daniel hadn't seemed to notice what every other red-blooded male who came into the diner clearly did, said a lot. The heat in her cheeks intensified.

Molly rested a hand on her arm. "Don't freak out on me, Nic. I'm only saying that even if he isn't wearing a ring—and I know he isn't because, believe me, I checked—maybe he isn't exactly on the market. Not for anyone except you, anyway."

"I'm not freaking out. Not completely. But all of this is happening too fast. I need to try and process what it means." She slid off the stool. "I'll be back soon."

"Take all the time you need."

"If I did that, I might not be back for a week or two."

"Whatever it takes. There are more important things than serving burgers and fries to people, you know."

"I hope we do more than that here. Joe always said we should be serving love and coffee. He said that combination would take you a long way on a cold night."

Two dimples appeared in Molly's cheeks. "I can think of one or two other things that will take you a long way on a cold night." She lifted both hands when Nicole raised her eyebrows. "Just sayin'."

"You're just sayin' a little more than you should, Mol, although …" Nicole lifted her chin as she headed for the door, "… I'll admit your point is well taken."

The sound of Molly's contagious laughter mingled with the jangling of bells as Nicole pulled open the diner door and stepped outside.

"Nicole."

She stopped and looked around. The crowd of people

surging along the busy Toronto sidewalk separated to stream by her like water around a rock. Her forehead wrinkled. Had someone said her name? No one glanced in her direction, and Nicole shook her head. Must have been the hum of traffic or the blare of music from the record store down the street. Still, the sound echoed inside her head.

Nicole strode toward her car, barely resisting the urge to break into a run. *Calm down.* Maybe it had been a friend, trying to get her attention. She glanced back over her shoulder. Nobody appeared to be following her. If a friend had called out her name, why wouldn't that person show themselves?

She tugged the keys from her pocket. They caught on the lining and clattered to the sidewalk. Nicole bent to pick them up, stabbing the button to unlock the doors as she straightened. The sound she thought she'd heard reverberated through her mind again, and she shivered as she yanked open her car door.

If someone *had* said her name back there at the diner, she was fairly certain it hadn't been a friend.

Chapter Eleven

Nicole blew on her hands and stared out at the street as she waited for Christina to come to the door. It was late October and fall had definitely settled in. The cold wind sweeping down from the north, scooping up the leaves lining the curb and sending them swirling through the air, carried the promise of frost. Unfortunately, the heater in her car was misbehaving more than it had last winter, refusing to come on today even after she'd slammed her fist on the dashboard a few times. When the door behind her swung open, she whirled around and lifted half-frozen fingers in a wave.

"Nic! Come on in." Christina pushed open the screen and held it as Nicole brushed by her and into the warm house. "I thought you'd be at the diner today."

"I was." Nicole pulled off her blue coat and tossed it onto a chair. "I needed a break and thought I'd pop by."

Chris shut the door and grabbed both her hands. "Your fingers are like ice. Come into the kitchen and I'll make us tea."

Nicole followed her through the living room.

"Holden had to go into the office to take care of some paperwork," Chris called over her shoulder, "but he should be home soon."

"All right." Nic crossed the pale green linoleum floor and rubbed her hands together as she leaned a hip against the counter, watching her sister-in-law plug in the kettle and pull a basket of assorted tea bags out of the cupboard.

"Take your pick." She set the basket in front of Nicole, who rifled through them and pulled out raspberry, her favorite.

Nicole opened the cupboard and took down the bright yellow mug she always used when she was there. "I was hoping to have a few minutes to talk to you alone anyway."

"About Daniel?"

Nicole almost dropped the mug. Clutching it in both hands, she set it carefully on the counter before facing Christina. "Why would you say that?"

Christina grabbed a mug for herself. "Wishful thinking. I'm hoping that's what you're here for, because I've been dying to know how your dinner with him went the other night. I wanted to call you, but Holden told me not to bug you about it, that you'd let me know if you wanted to talk. And then you showed up here, which is even better."

The dishwasher door was open. Nicole reached for a clean plate and set it in the cupboard. "Are you sure you don't mind talking about this? Is it weird for you?"

Christina's forehead wrinkled as she poured hot water over the tea bags in their cups and set the mugs on the island. "Why would it be weird?"

"Well, you are married to my late husband's brother. I worry that, even if he says he's fine with it, it would bother Holden if I got involved with someone else."

Christina waved a hand through the air as she walked toward her. "Holden really is fine with this, Nic. He wants you to be happy. So dish away."

"There's not much to tell really, except that the other night, after dinner, Daniel and I were talking and we …" *This was a bad idea. It's going to sound like a lot more than it was.*

"You what?"

Nicole shoved the last of the plates onto the pile and reached for a glass. "We had a good time, that's all." She stood on her toes to set the glass on the top shelf. "What are you and Holden doing this week—"

Christina grabbed her arm and turned her around. Her hazel eyes searched Nicole's face. Refusing to meet them, Nicole let her gaze wander around the room, trying her best to keep an innocent look on her face.

Christina sucked in a breath. "He kissed you."

"No."

Her sister-in-law tilted her head.

Nicole held out for a few seconds under the intense scrutiny before sighing in resignation. "He didn't kiss me. I kissed him."

Still clutching her arm, Christina pulled her over to a stool on the other side of the island. Settling beside her, she swiveled it to face Nicole and clasped her hands together on her knee. "Talk."

Nicole wrapped her still-cold hands around the warm mug. "Don't you have a spotlight you'd like to shine in my face?"

Christina lifted her shoulders. "Oh, I'm sorry. Does this feel like an interrogation? It's not, I promise." She leaned forward. "Now confess everything. Immediately."

Nicole choked back a laugh. "We had a great time at dinner. Daniel taught Jordan how to flip burgers on the barbeque and showed him his gun. He was so good with him, the two of them got along like …"

"Father and son?"

"Yeah."

Christina touched the back of Nicole's hand. "It's all right for you to want that for Jord. Of course you do. And Daniel would make a great dad."

Nicole bit her lip. "It's a bit early to think that way, especially since …"

"Since what?"

"Since he didn't exactly respond positively when I kissed him."

Christina's eyebrows rose. "I find that hard to believe. Tell me what happened."

"Jordan fell asleep on the couch after dinner, so Daniel and I went into the kitchen for a hot drink. We had a great conversation and I felt really close to him, so I kissed him."

"And he pulled away?"

"Not at first. He kissed me back and it was amazing, but then, yes, he did pull away. And he looked at me and said that I didn't owe him anything."

Christina winced. "Ouch."

"No kidding. That wasn't why I kissed him, although …" She paused and pressed a finger to her lips. *I'm such an idiot.* "I guess I can see how he might have thought that, since I had just been thanking him for risking his badge for Gage, and for everything else he's done for us."

"What did you do?"

"I went into typical Nicole mode. I stormed out of the room and woke up Jord and told him we had to go."

"You left like that?"

"No. Thankfully he went into typical Daniel mode and stayed calm. He apologized and said it hadn't been fair for him to say that and asked if we could try again next week."

"And?"

"I said I guessed we could give it one more shot." She took a sip of the berry-flavored tea, hoping it would help her relax.

"Glad to see you didn't put any unnecessary pressure on yourself, or him."

Nicole grimaced. "That's exactly what he said."

The corners of Christina's mouth twitched. "So the kiss was great?"

Her cheeks warmed and she set down her mug and pressed the backs of her hands to them. "It was, actually. But maybe he was right, and I was doing it for all the wrong reasons."

"Don't over-analyze this, Nic. You don't have to have a reason to want to kiss Daniel—what woman wouldn't?" Her gaze lifted over Nicole's shoulder, and she raised her voice a notch and added, "A woman who is madly in love with her husband and carrying his baby, that's who."

Holden shook his head as he came through the door and crossed the room to her. "A shameless attempt to use our unborn child to get yourself out of trouble."

"Did it work?"

He grabbed her knees and spun her around to face him so he could lean in and kiss her on the lips. "Sadly, yes."

Christina pressed a hand to her stomach. "Whoa, might want

to watch the spinning for the next few months, cowboy.”

He covered her hand with his. “Don’t try and pawn that off on the little one. I made you light-headed long before you were pregnant, simply by walking into the room.”

“And a little nauseated, that’s true, now that you mention it.”

Holden grinned. “Can I make you something for dinner? I was thinking I could assume that responsibility for the next few months, so you could take it easy.”

Christina punched him lightly in the arm. “Don’t you go blaming the baby for that either. My cooking has always made you nervous.”

“And a little nauseated, that’s true, now that you mention it.”

She made a face at him. “I handed you that one, didn’t I?”

“Like a great big present with a bow on top. Thank you.” He leaned in and kissed her again.

Nicole rested her head on one hand and waited. They’d both clearly forgotten she was in the room which, the way things were headed, could get dangerous fast, but she loved watching them together.

Thankfully, after a few seconds, Holden glanced sideways at her and straightened up. “Hey, Nic.”

“Hey.” Nicole lifted a hand in the air. “Don’t mind me.”

“Oh, okay.” Holden leaned in again, but Christina stopped him with a hand on his chest. He laughed and reached over and squeezed Nicole’s shoulder. “Can you stay and eat with us?”

She swallowed the last of her tea and carried the mug to the sink. “Thanks, but I can’t. I promised the crew I’d help with the dinner rush.”

Christina followed her as she headed for the front door.

“I hate to head outside when I just got warmed up.” Nicole grabbed her coat off the chair and pulled it on.

Christina sighed. “Memories of a great kiss will do that to you.”

Nicole wrinkled her nose. “I’m pretty sure it was the mug I was holding.”

“Are you?”

She ignored that and hugged her sister-in-law. "Thanks for the tea, and for listening."

"Anytime." Chris straightened the collar on Nicole's coat. "So what are you going to do?"

"I'm not sure. A couple of weeks ago I was perfectly content with the way things were. Jordan and I were doing great with only the two of us. Suddenly, even though I've only seen Daniel a couple of times, the condo seems emptier, my life seems emptier ..."

"Your bed seems emptier ..." Christina's hazel eyes gleamed.

Nicole blew out a breath in exasperation. "That seems to be a running theme today. I really was happy on my own, you know."

"I guess it's easy to feel like you're happy on your own until you realize how unhappy you are that you aren't with someone else, isn't it?"

They stared at each other for a few seconds before bursting into laughter. Christina shook her head. "I have no idea what I said either, but I have a sneaking suspicion it was brilliant. The bottom line is, I know you thought you were already happy but judging from the way your eyes light up when you're talking about him, I think you knew as soon as you saw Daniel again that you would be far happier if you were together. Am I right?"

"I don't know. Maybe."

Christina took her hands in hers again. "There's no maybe about it, Nic. It's written all over your face. I know it's scary, starting over after you've lost the person you love, but the idea of never opening your heart to someone again has to be a lot scarier, don't you think?"

Nicole studied her sister-in-law's earnest face for several seconds before nodding slowly. "You're right. It is."

Christina squeezed her hands. "Then go for it. Everything will work out, I'm sure, but on the off chance it doesn't, Holden and I will be here for you whenever you need us."

"I know." Nicole summoned a weak smile. "Thanks."

She hugged Christina and pulled open the door. The cold,

northern breeze cut through her coat as she stepped onto the porch. A shiver swept through her and she shoved her hands into her pockets. It didn't help much. The hair on her neck prickled and she glanced up and down the street. A blue car was parked half a block away, but no one appeared to be in it.

The first few months after Gage died, she'd experienced the eerie sensation, off and on, that someone was watching her. Not protecting her, like Daniel, but with something far more threatening in mind. All part of the lingering trauma of seeing her husband gunned down in the street, according to her therapist. The last couple of weeks the feeling had surfaced again, possibly triggered by the re-entry of Daniel into their lives, stirring up barely dormant memories.

You're fine, Nicole. No one is watching you. Leave the past in the past. The self-talk helped. Sometimes. She gave her head a shake and grimaced as she pulled open the door of her car and settled onto the front seat. Maybe Molly was right. Maybe there was something better than a coat or a temperamental car heater to take her through the long cold nights of winter.

Nicole rubbed her hands together, trying to warm up her fingers. *Who am I kidding?* She'd been married, briefly. She knew there was.

The only question now was whether that better thing was willing to take the chance that she wouldn't break his heart again like she had done once before.

Chapter Twelve

Nicole entered the code on the panel on the door to her condo. She reached for the knob, but before she could grasp it, Jordan had twisted it and tumbled through the opening.

"That jail was so cool!" He nearly tripped over his feet in his excitement.

"Careful there, buddy." Daniel grabbed his arm to steady him.

Jordan didn't miss a beat. "Did you hear how loudly those doors clanged shut when I hit that button? I wish some bad guys had come in while we were there. We would have locked them up good, wouldn't we, Daniel?"

"You bet." Daniel followed him into the apartment and pulled off his leather jacket.

Nicole ruffled her son's dark curls. "Make sure you always stay on the right side of those bars."

Daniel grinned at her as she took his coat, and it occurred to Nicole that the odds of that would go up exponentially if he stayed in their lives. Something in that thought sent a pang through her. *What is that about*? She pressed a hand to her abdomen as the truth hit her. It wasn't apprehension that he *could* become part of their lives, but anxiety over the still very real possibility that he might not. Nicole bit her lip. Since when had she become so eager to give her heart away, to take a chance that it might get trampled and tossed to the curb?

Hurt by parents who had abandoned her as a child, she grew up terrified that everyone else she cared about would leave her and had always avoided men like pylons on a test course. Nicole pursed her lips, remembering how hard she had pushed Gage away when they first met. And how stubbornly he had refused to let her. And how much it had hurt when, as she had feared, her heart had shattered into a million pieces. Her grin faded.

Nicole started when Daniel touched her hand lightly. "You all right?"

Her face warmed when she realized he was watching her intently. "Yes, I …" She what, had been thinking about her dead husband? And how badly she wanted Daniel to take his place? "I zoned out there for a minute, sorry."

"No need to be." His smile was warm, although his eyes still searched hers. Being with a detective could be a definite liability. A vague uneasiness settled in her stomach. Hiding what she was thinking and feeling from him would be a challenge. Unless, of course, she made it a lot easier on him—and herself—by not hiding anymore.

"Mom?" A small hand slid into hers. "Can Daniel tuck me in tonight?"

"Oh, I don't know if he …"

"I'd be happy to." Daniel rested a hand on Jordan's shoulder. "If you're all right with it."

Nicole nodded. "Sure." Crouching down in front of her son, she pulled him into her arms for a hug then brushed the hair off his forehead. "'Night, Jord. Say your prayers."

"I will." The two of them walked down the hallway, Daniel's hand still on her son's shoulder. For a few seconds a paralyzing fear gripped her. She and Daniel needed to figure out whatever was between them, and fast. If it wasn't real, she had to get him out of their lives as soon as possible, before the free-fall she and Jordan were in ended in a very sudden—and painful—crash landing. With a deep sigh, Nicole shook off the fear and forced herself to walk, on slightly weakened legs, into the living room to start a fire.

Jordan finished his rigorous brushing and spit into the sink before dropping his toothbrush into the purple cup on the counter.

"All set?" Daniel had waited in the hallway for him and

stepped aside now as the boy came barreling out the door. He was quickly coming to realize that Nicole's son did pretty much everything at top speed and with great enthusiasm, something Daniel found unexpectedly refreshing and contagious.

He followed the boy to the door of his room. Jordan snatched up the long-sleeved blue shirt lying across the end of his bed and held it out. "Can you give this to my mom? She couldn't decide whether to wear it or her green one before you came to get us tonight, so she asked me which one I liked better."

"Sure. Hold on." Daniel suppressed a grin as he took the shirt and carried it across the hall to hang it on the knob of her bedroom door, resisting the urge to push the door open slightly and look in.

"Here." Jordan pointed to the book lying on his bedside table when he returned to the room. "My mom reads this to me every night. There's a bookmark so you know where we are."

Daniel opened the book and read the short devotional about how God was big and good and in control of all things. Although it was written in kid language, the truth of it flowed through Daniel, the timely reminder relaxing the muscles that had tightened across his shoulders. When he finished and closed the cover, Jordan's eyelids were half-closed, his curls tousled and dark against the pillowcase. His flannel pajamas were covered in basketballs, baseballs, and soccer balls, and the sheet he had crawled under had Batman and the Batmobile all over it. Daniel set the book on the bedside table and pulled the covers up to Jordan's chin.

"I used to have sheets like these when I was your age."

The boy's eyes widened. "Really? They had Batman then?"

"Yes, even in the Stone Age when I was a kid." He tucked the blankets around Jordan securely. "Do you want to say your prayers now?"

"Sure." Jordan closed his eyes. Daniel knew he should close his too, but he couldn't take his gaze from the earnest face in front of him. "Dear God, thank you for this great day, that Mom and I could go with Detective Grey to jail and see all the awesome stuff there. Watch over us tonight while we sleep and tell Dad I said hi. Amen."

Daniel blinked at the words. They made sense, he supposed. Somewhere along the line Nicole must have told Jordan that Gage was in heaven, and since God was there too, of course the boy would figure he could pass along a message to the father he'd never met. Which he very well could, as far as that went.

Jordan opened his eyes. "Good night, Detective Grey. Thanks for taking us to your work tonight. It was awesome. I hope I see you again soon." The words came out thick and a little muffled, as though the boy was already half-asleep.

"'Night, Jord." Daniel rested a hand on the dark curls. "I hope I see you again soon too." He waited another couple of minutes, until the boy's eyes had fully closed, and his breathing had grown deep and even, marveling at how quickly kids could succumb to sleep. It likely had something to do with not carrying the weight of the world around on their shoulders, or maybe not yet realizing how dark and scary that world could be. Of course, depending on how much Nicole had told Jordan about Gage's death, he might have at least an inkling of that. Or maybe he completely trusted that the God he had asked to watch over them actually could and would do so, something most adults— including himself—could take a lesson from. With a sigh, Daniel pushed to his feet and left the room, pulling the door shut behind him.

Daniel slipped into the living room and crept over to the coffee table. Lowering himself quietly, he settled onto it and watched Nicole as she knelt in front of the woodstove, stoking the fire. When flames were leaping high in the stove, she shut the door with a clang and turned around, reaching for the table to push herself to her feet. She stopped, inches from his knees, when she saw him, and sank back on her heels.

"Hi." Her cheeks were pink, although he wasn't sure if that was from suddenly finding herself so close to him, or from the heat of the fire. He really hoped it was the former.

A slow smile crossed his face. "Hi."

"Did Jordan settle all right?"

"Yeah, he's already asleep." He rested his elbows on his knees. "By the way, I'm glad you went with the green shirt."

"What do you mean?"

"I watched you go back and forth between that one and the blue one, and I was hoping you'd pick this one. It really brings out the color of your eyes."

Nicole went completely still.

Daniel managed to keep a straight face for a few seconds before the corners of his mouth quirked. "I'm joking. Jordan told me you couldn't decide which of those shirts to wear, so you asked him his opinion."

Nicole smacked his knees with her palms. "Don't do that. I'm still not good at telling when you're kidding. I've been changing in the dark for a week now."

He grinned. "Really?"

"No, although I have stopped getting dressed in front of the mirror."

Daniel pressed his lips together, then laughed when she smacked his knees again and exclaimed, "What?"

"Nothing. I was going to make a crack about how that does explain some things, but I didn't think that would be nice."

"Like making me believe I'm being watched all the time in my own home is nice?"

His lips twitched again. "You're right, I'm sorry."

"You don't look sorry." She lowered her head.

Daniel slid two fingers under her chin and lifted her face until her eyes met his. "Don't."

"Don't what?"

"Check to see if you're having some kind of wardrobe malfunction. I was giving you a hard time again. For the last time tonight, I promise. You look perfect and beautiful. As always."

Nicole contemplated him. Her eyes sparkled like emeralds in the light of the flickering flames.

He let go of her chin and ran the back of one finger down the side of her cheek. "What is it?"

"I hear you visited my son's school a while back."

"Ah." He dropped his hand. "Something else I kind of hoped you wouldn't discover."

She rested both hands on his knees. "I'm glad Jordan told me. I need to thank you for getting those boys to stop bothering him on the playground."

"No. You don't."

The words came out more forcefully than he'd intended, and Nicole blinked.

With a sigh, Daniel picked up both her hands and brought them to his lips. "You don't have to thank me for any of it. Watching you and Jordan, being a small part of your lives, even from a distance, has brought me more happiness since I've been back in the city than I can tell you. It wasn't a favor, or an obligation, or a way to relieve guilt; it was a joy, pure and simple." He lowered their clasped hands. "While both my timing and my delivery were clearly wildly off the other night, I did mean it when I said you didn't owe me anything."

"Got it." She rose up on her knees, her face inches from his.

Daniel's heart thudded against his ribs as the familiar fragrance of apple blossoms drifted toward him.

"Now that we have firmly established that neither of us has done, or is about to do, anything out of a sense of obligation ..." Nicole leaned in and pressed her soft lips to his.

Daniel let go of her hands and framed her face, for a few seconds drinking in the feel and scent of her. Then the same fear that had risen the last time she had kissed him gripped him, tightening his chest until he couldn't draw in air. He lifted his head and closed his eyes, not wanting to see the confusion or anger on her face.

To his surprise, she laughed. "You have got to be kidding me."

Daniel wrapped his arms around her. "I'm so sorry. Please don't go."

She didn't speak or move, simply rested her head against his chest until his thudding heartrate had slowed to normal.

When she lifted her head, a small smile crossed her lips. "I'm not leaving, this is my place."

"Oh yeah. I knew coming here was a good idea."

Her face grew serious as she studied him. "What is it, Daniel? Am I completely misreading this situation?"

"No." He shook his head. "No, Nic, honestly, that's not it."

"Because the whole watching out for us thing infers a level of commitment to us, to me, that kind of led me to think you might want to see where this could go as much as I do."

"I do, I promise." Daniel loosened his hold on her. "Whatever the problem is, I can assure you it's not that I don't want to kiss you or be close to you." He drove his fingers through his hair. "There's pretty much nothing I want more, in fact."

"Then what is it? Because I hope you know that I don't make a habit of throwing myself at men. A few of them have asked me out over the years, but I always said no."

"Why did you?"

"For the first two or three years it was because of Gage, because it was way too soon. Going out with anyone else was inconceivable; it would have felt like a betrayal."

"And after that?"

Her eyes held his steadily. "I told myself that what Gage and I had was so good, so strong, that I couldn't imagine having it with anyone else. But I never entirely convinced myself that was the real issue. After I ran into you, I realized you were the reason I never went out with anyone else. On some level, I think I always knew you were there, still in my life like you were still in my heart."

For all her wonderful qualities, transparency had never been Nicole's strong suit. Gazing up at him now, though, her face innocent and child-like in the glow of the fire, she was holding nothing from him. Everything she felt came out in her words and was written across her face.

The last bit of his heart, the part he'd only had a tenuous

hold on since the day he'd come out of hiding in the park, slid from his grasp. Everything in him longed to pull her to him again, to cover her mouth with his until she was as breathless as he was.

Instead, he pushed to his feet and walked over to the fireplace. Crossing his arms, he stared into the flickering flames.

Her feet padded across the thick beige carpet. She stopped behind him and rested a hand, warm and comforting, on his back. "What is it? Tell me."

"I don't really understand it myself, so I have no idea how to help you to."

Her hand moved in small circles, drawing out the tension. "Maybe I understand better than you think I do."

He let out a short laugh. "Can you explain it to me then?"

"I can try." She stepped closer, close enough that when she spoke again, he could feel her breath, warm on his neck. "I know I hurt you, Daniel." Her voice caught and she cleared her throat. "Whatever you might feel for me, as much as you might want to be part of our lives, the terrible fear that I'll hurt you again is keeping you from acting on that.

"I understand that because I felt the same way when Gage and I first started getting close. Part of me wanted to grasp what was happening between us and pull it to me, but another part pushed it away with everything I had. After the way my parents basically abandoned me as a kid, I decided I would never let anyone into my life again. It made perfect sense to me that if no one got close to me, no one could leave me. And it worked. I didn't experience any devastating losses. The problem was, I didn't experience any great joys either. I was surviving, not living. I didn't even realize that until Gage came into my life and showed me how much I was missing. Even so, I was terrified, and I tried to push him out the door."

Daniel turned around and uncrossed his arms. His back, where her hand had been resting, felt suddenly cold. "What happened?"

"He wouldn't go. He forced me to admit that I wanted to be with him as much as he wanted to be with me, but that I was scared."

"And what did he say to that?"

"He said that was good, he could work with scared."

Daniel offered her a small grin.

Her eyes locked with his. "Then he told me he wasn't going anywhere. Those few words had the power to draw out my fear and give me the courage to take a chance on us. And even though he did end up making choices that took him away from me, I don't regret giving him my heart that day. As painful as losing him was, the joy he gave me, that I feel every time I see him in his son, somehow manages to ease the heartache I felt the night he died, even though that heartache will always be a part of me."

Nicole reached for both his hands and held them tightly in hers. "I'm not going anywhere either, Daniel. I promise. Okay?"

Something deep inside him—the part that had shriveled up the night she had walked away from him—slowly unfurled, like the bud of a flower to the warmth of the morning sun.

Daniel let go of her hands and pulled her to him. The words Tom had spoken, about the miracle of holding the woman you know you are meant to spend the rest of your life with, echoed through his mind. The fact that he'd been tricked into listening to a lecture didn't lessen the truth of what his friend had said. It was definitely time to step up and be a man, to treat that woman the way she deserved to be treated.

For a long time they stood like that, in each other's arms, her head resting against his shirt as orange tongues of flame flickered off the walls and cast a warm glow over the room.

Then Daniel lifted his hands to cup her face. When she looked up at him, her eyes softly lit, he whispered, "Okay." A smile crossed her face as he leaned in slowly to press his lips to hers. He braced himself, prepared to face the fear down this time like he would a suspect waving a gun, but no deep, choking fear rose in his chest. Instead, something far more powerful flooded through him, a feeling he didn't have the courage to put a name to yet, but that he knew would always be a part of him now.

Chapter Thirteen

Troy yanked at the tab on his cup of black coffee and snapped it into the little slot. He took a sip before reluctantly pushing open the door of the coffee shop and stepping into the frigid night air. A shiver rolled through him, and he clutched the collar of his worn denim jacket to his throat. A bitter gust of wind picked up a pile of dirt and garbage and sent it swirling through the air around him. Troy coughed into his sleeve then tipped back the paper cup, hoping the hot liquid would warm him.

His vision blocked by the drink, Troy didn't see anyone coming until a man clipped him in the shoulder as he passed by. Coffee splashed onto the front of his coat as Troy muttered a curse word and twisted his head to look behind him.

"Sorry." The man stopped and raised a hand.

Any lingering warmth in his body drained out. Hastily lifting the cup in front of his face, Troy nodded. That had been way too close. If the detective had recognized him …

Troy's fist tightened until the cup in his hand crumpled and the rest of the coffee poured out, spilling over his half-frozen fingers. Another swear word exploded from his mouth as he dropped the cup and swiped his hand across the front of his jacket. Rage gripped him and he spun around, barely in time to see the man pull open the door of Joe's Diner and step inside.

Troy shook his head. What was *he* afraid of? He'd served his time—the cop couldn't touch him now. Clutching his stinging hand to his chest, he stepped into the doorway of a closed shop, beyond the reach of the light that spilled from the large front window of the diner. He peered through the glass, his eyes fixed on the detective as he made his way around tables and chairs until he reached *her*. Resting a hand on the small of her back, the cop leaned in close and said something to the woman and they both laughed.

Troy gritted his teeth. No way she should be laughing, not after everything he'd been through. He spat on the sidewalk in disgust. What *was* he worried about? Nobody had anything on him; he'd paid his debt to society. And if he accumulated more debt by doing what he planned to do, well, he'd take care of that too.

He shoved both fists into the pockets of his jean jacket. Although, as far as he was concerned, society owed him a little something now. He'd already paid a lot more than he should have, seeing as how he'd been the victim of everything that had happened. His dark eyes narrowed to slits as he stared at the woman through the large pane of glass.

Maybe now it was time for someone else to start paying.

Chapter Fourteen

The freezing November temperatures had transformed the early morning dew to sparkling white frost smudged across each blade of grass. Nicole rubbed her arms with gloved hands, the chill in the air sweeping away the drowsiness that had clung to her like cobwebs when she'd left the house.

Pressure built in her throat as she made her way across the perfectly manicured lawn. Intent on making sure she stayed close to the backs of the carved headstones so as to not tread on anyone's grave, Nicole's forehead wrinkled when she neared her destination and looked up.

A woman stood in front of Gage's headstone, one hand resting on top of the marble monument. Shimmering black hair was pulled into a sleek ponytail that fell down the back of the green coat cinched tightly around her waist. Nicole contemplated the woman's face, her high cheekbones and porcelain skin, and she bit her bottom lip.

Pain swirled in the startling, charcoal-gray eyes. When her gaze shifted to Nicole, though, the pain disappeared so quickly Nicole wondered if she had imagined it. The woman regarded her somberly for a few seconds before the corners of her full red lips lifted slightly. "Mrs. Kelly."

"Yes." Surprised, Nicole inclined her head. "I'm sorry, have we met?"

"No. But I knew your husband. We were colleagues." The woman's voice was deep and sultry, hinting at a distant, European heritage.

"You're with the Crown Attorney's office?"

"No, I'm employed by an independent agency, but Gage and I collaborated on several cases before he died. I would have liked to have come to the funeral to express my condolences, but unfortunately I was out of the country at the time." She extended a black satin-gloved hand toward Nicole. "I realize this is very belated, but I was so terribly sorry about your husband's passing and have hoped for the opportunity to extend my sympathies to you in person."

She took the woman's hand in hers. "Thank you." A tremor passed through the fingers that pressed against hers before the woman let her go.

Nicole's gaze dropped to the base of the stone. A dozen red roses filled the vase welded to a stand. Several times over the years, roses had graced the foot of the headstone when she had arrived at the cemetery, and she'd often wondered who had left them for her husband.

The woman looked down, her eyes resting on the flowers for several seconds before her gaze met Nicole's. She must have seen the question there, because she nodded in acknowledgment. "I hadn't known your husband for long, and I didn't know him all that well, but he impressed me from the start. There was something … exceptional about him. A genuine courage and goodness that are exceedingly rare. His death affected me deeply, and leaving the roses helps somehow. I hope you don't mind."

Nicole shook her head slightly. "No, of course not. Gage would have appreciated your thoughtfulness, and it would have meant a lot to him to think he'd had such an impact on someone's life."

"Like I said, I didn't know him for long, but even during our short acquaintance I witnessed first-hand many lives being powerfully and positively impacted by your husband. An impact that continues to this day. I hope he knew that, and I pray it helps you in some small way to hear it."

Nicole blinked back tears. "It does, thank you."

"I'm glad." The woman touched the headstone again. "I've been here a few times over the years, but I'm leaving the country soon and it is unlikely I will be back in Canada, so this will be my last visit. And maybe, all this time, I've been hoping to see you, to tell you how very sorry I am." The pain was back in her eyes. "I'm glad I had the chance to finally speak with you."

"So am I, Ms. ...."

The woman hesitated before lifting her chin. "My name is Natalya." She took a step backward and lifted a gloved hand. "It was a pleasure to meet you, Mrs. Kelly."

"Thank you. You too." The woman turned before she could say any more. Nicole watched as she strode across the cemetery, the footprints of her black, high-heeled boots leaving dark outlines on the frosted grass. Nicole kept her eyes on her until she reached a silver sports car parked on the side of the road that wound through the cemetery. Not until the car had disappeared around a curve did Nicole force her gaze back to the grave.

A layer of frost coated the top of the stone, and she wiped it off with the fingers of her white wool glove. When she reached the spot where the woman's hand had rested, she hesitated over the faint outline before brushing it away with the last of the frost. Slightly shaken from the odd and unexpected encounter, she rested both hands on top of the headstone. The woman's stunning beauty might have concerned her if she wasn't so sure that Gage had not only adhered to a strict moral code but had also loved her with all his heart. She sighed. The past was the past, and it was time to let it go.

Gage wasn't here, so while she had come by every few weeks since his death to make sure the area around the site was being taken care of, Nicole hadn't made a regular practice of coming here to talk to her husband. Today, though, she had felt the need to be here, at his final resting place.

Her voice trembled a little when she spoke. "Gage, I'm pretty sure you don't have any idea what is going on down here, but in case you do, I thought maybe we should talk about what is happening in my life. Daniel has come back." She ran a hand over the marble, the cold seeping through her gloves.

"He's a good man, Gage. I don't know if you realized that when you met him. Maybe not, since the circumstances weren't exactly ideal, but he is. He tried to help you, you know, to stop you before you got hurt, and he still feels badly that he wasn't able to." She pressed a gloved finger to the pool of moisture gathering in the corner of her eye.

"It's taken me a long time, but I believe I'm ready to see if he and I can make a life together. I hope you know how much I loved you, and that you will always have a place in my heart. Every time I look at our son, I am reminded of the joy you brought into my life, and that I miss you terribly. But it's time for me to move on. I need to let you go and ..." Her voice broke and she caught her trembling lip between her teeth.

"I want you to know that I'm good. Jordan and I, we're both doing well. Daniel really cares about us, and I think there's a good chance we could become a family. Jordan likes him too, a lot, and I can already tell that the two of them are going to be close. I'll still talk to Jordan about you, make sure he knows what an amazing person his father was, but he needs more than that in his life now. He needs someone who can be there for him, someone he can talk to and who can teach him everything he needs to know about being a man."

Nicole pressed both hands against the stone again, her legs trembling. "I couldn't have done this before now, but I'm finally in a place where I've been able to find the courage to try again. I hope you can be happy for me."

She stepped back and traced the words *Beloved Husband* with her finger. "There was a woman here today, Natalya, who says she knew you and knows for a fact that you had a big impact on a lot of people's lives. I believe that's true because you impacted my life in ways you never knew, that will continue to affect and influence me the rest of my life. I'll never forget you, Gage, but it's time for me to say goodbye." For a long moment she gazed at the tombstone. Finally, a deep ache settling in her chest, she nodded and turned away.

Nicole made her way through the frosty grass back to her little white Corolla. She climbed into the driver's seat and dropped her face into her hands. After a couple of minutes, she pulled a tissue from her pocket to wipe the moisture from her cheeks.

With a heavy sigh, she leaned forward and turned the key in the ignition. Her hand stilled on the gearshift when warm air poured from the vent.

It had to be a coincidence. Gage hadn't reached down from heaven to fix the heater in her car. Still, a smile crossed her face as the warmth flowed around her like an embrace. She basked in the comforting heat as she drove through the tall stone pillars marking the entrance of the cemetery and headed toward home.

Chapter Fifteen

"Tell me a Lala story, Mom." Jordan folded both arms behind his head as she pulled the blankets up over his chest.

Nicole sat down on the edge of his bed. "Old one or new one?"

His green eyes glowed in anticipation. "A new one."

"Hmm." Nicole thought hard. She'd created Lala when Jordan was three years old and decided he didn't want her to read the same old picture books any more. Over the years she'd had a lot of fun coming up with new and interesting scrapes for the adventurous little blond girl to get herself into.

"You remember that Lala has a big orange cat named Pumpkin, right?"

Jordan nodded.

"Well, one day Lala and her best friend LaToya …"

Jordan giggled and Nicole ruffled his dark curls. He was too young to have heard of the Jackson Five, which worked for Nicole since he thought she had come up with his favorite name in the Lala series all on her own.

"Anyway, LaToya and Lala decided it was time for Pumpkin to have a makeover. LaToya held his paws out, one at a time, while Lala used her world-famous artistic abilities to paint his nails a brilliant hot pink color."

Jordan groaned. "Pink? Pumpkin's a boy."

"I know. And he felt the same way you do. It was bad enough that his nails were being painted at all, but when Lala finished and he realized she had painted them pink, he was not impressed. In fact, he went completely insane. He wriggled out of LaToya's arms and raced around the house, leaping up onto the kitchen counters, jumping in and out of the bathtub, and sprinting across every bed and piece of furniture in the house. The problem was, Lala had used way too much polish on those tiny nails, and it hadn't had time to dry. By the time the two girls finally caught that crazy cat and shooed him out the front door, the entire inside of the house was so covered in pink dots it looked like it had caught the chicken pox."

Jordan erupted in giggles. The sound was so infectious that Nicole started laughing too. The more they tried to stop, the harder they laughed, until both of them were holding their stomachs. When the outburst had subsided to an occasional hiccup, Jordan unfolded his arms from across his middle and grabbed her hand. "Was Lala's mom mad?"

"Well, she wasn't very happy when she saw the mess, that's for sure. But she'd realized a long time ago that it didn't do any good to lecture her daughter. Lala didn't go looking for trouble—trouble always seemed to find her somehow. So her mom walked around the house, shaking her head and clucking her tongue in frustration. When Lala wasn't looking, a big smile would break out across her face, but she quickly pressed her hand over her mouth to keep from laughing out loud at the new and creative disaster her daughter had caused. And she tried to look stern and disapproving whenever Lala was brave enough to sneak a peek at her.

"When she finished her investigation of the house, she marched into the kitchen, pulled a pack of sponges out from under the sink and gave one to each of the girls, then handed them a bottle of nail polish remover. 'When I come back, I don't want to see a single pink dot anywhere in this house,' she instructed them. Then she did what all moms do when their house is such a mess they don't even know where to begin to clean it up. She got into her car, drove to Starbucks, and sat there for an hour, sipping on a double chocolate chip Frappuccino and watching all the other moms whose kids were driving them crazy coming in and ordering their own drinks.

"When she was pretty sure the nail polish would be gone, she got in her car and drove home again and, sure enough, the pink had disappeared. In fact, the house was more sparkling clean than it had been in a long time. Lala's mom was so happy she made hot chocolate and her famous oatmeal raisin cookies with extra cinnamon for Lala and LaToya, and they sat around the table and talked about how silly Pumpkin had looked with his nails covered in polish. So it all turned out all right, although Lala did have to promise her mom that she had given Pumpkin his first and last makeover. Like all the other promises Lala has made in her life, she has kept that one until this very day."

Jordan gave a contented sigh as he wriggled farther down under the blankets. His long dark lashes brushed his cheeks.

"All right, Son. Time for sleep."

When she started to get up, his eyes flew open. "Are we going to see Detective Grey soon?"

Nicole settled back onto the bed. "We're supposed to go with him to his partner's house for a barbeque on Friday night. She has two daughters who are a little older than you, nine and eleven, I think. Sound good?"

"Sure." His eyelids drooped.

She rested her hand on his cheek. "We might be seeing Detective Grey quite a bit from now on. Would that be all right with you?"

His eyes closed, he nodded his head. "Yeah. I like when he's with us so we have more boys than girls."

"Hey," Nicole protested. "Why do we have to have more boys?"

"Because when you have more girls than boys, the girls make you do silly stuff. Like when Lala and LaToya painted Pumpkin's nails."

Using my own story against me. Nicole shook her head and tucked the blankets in tight against his ribs. "Well, as long as the two of you don't make me do silly boy stuff like burping and rolling around on the floor trying to get each other to say 'Uncle' which I have never really understood, I guess it's fine."

Jordan giggled again, but the sound was faint as he drifted off to sleep. Nicole studied his peaceful face, overwhelmed as always by the tidal wave of love that flowed through her whenever she looked at Gage's son.

Leaning down, she pressed her lips to his forehead before getting up and crossing the room. Her phone vibrated, and she pulled the door shut behind her and crossed the hall to her own room as she tugged her cell from the pocket of her burgundy hooded sweatshirt. A smile touched her lips when she saw who the text was from.

Nicole propped her pillow against the headboard and sank down on the bed, cross-legged, leaning against the pillow as she pushed the button.

Hey. Thinking about you. Is Jordan asleep?

She typed a reply with both thumbs. *Yes. He nodded off right after his Lala story.*

There was a pause before the phone buzzed again. *I'm sorry. Lala?*

Nicole laughed then tapped in the answer. *A little blond character I created a few years ago. Constantly in trouble but somehow always manages to land on her feet.*

Are you sure you created her? She sounds like a beautiful diner owner I know.

Nicole pursed her lips. *Hmm. Never thought about that, but you may have a point.*

What did the little troublemaker do tonight?

She painted her cat Pumpkin's toenails hot pink.

Another long pause, then: *Tell me Pumpkin is a girl cat.*

No, sorry. But trust me, you couldn't be more disgusted about the whole thing than Pumpkin and Jordan were.

So what happened?

The cat took off running through the whole house, leaving a trail of pink polish everywhere he went. Lala's mother was not impressed.

What did she do?

She went to Starbucks.

What? She didn't seek comfort and understanding at her local, friendly diner? You missed a golden opportunity to stick it to the cold, soulless chain coffee shops.

Wow. Did not even consider using my son's story time as a chance to promote my own personal agenda–what is wrong with me?

Nothing flashed across the screen for thirty seconds. When the words appeared, she could detect, even via electronic transmission, a sudden shift in the tone of the conversation. *Not a thing, as far as I can see.*

This time Nicole paused, her thumbs hovering over the keyboard as a fluttering sensation she hadn't felt in years started up in her stomach. Slowly she lowered her fingers to the keys. *Maybe you're not looking hard enough.*

Well, it is a bit tricky, not to mention incredibly frustrating, trying to see you through the phone.

You'll have to do it on Friday, then.

Friday's a long time away.

Nicole bit her lip. It was only a couple of days, but now that he mentioned it, Friday did feel at least a decade off. Before she could respond, the phone vibrated again.

Could I come over? I won't stay long. I thought I could say good night to you over this darn machine, but somehow, it's not the same thing at all.

It really isn't. But that's probably not a good idea.

No, it's probably not. But that's never stopped us before, as I recall.

You're right. It's also gotten us in trouble before, as I recall.

I have it on good authority that, even when you get in trouble, you always land on your feet.

If she didn't want him to come as badly as he wanted to, maybe she could have stood her ground. She sighed and pressed the keys. *Maybe for a few minutes.*

On my way. No more texting. Very embarrassing to get pulled over by guys from another station. See you soon.

Nicole ran a finger over the words on the screen. The prohibition on texting was probably less about him worrying about a ticket, and more about him being afraid she would change her mind. And she should. She definitely should send him one more text calling the late-night visit off before it was too late. Before she could over-think it, she tossed the phone onto the nightstand, slid off the bed, and headed into the washroom.

Although she told herself it was ridiculous, she reapplied a light version of the makeup she'd removed before changing into her sweats. Then she pulled the hoodie over her head, exchanged the sweat pants for jeans, and tugged on a red T-shirt. After running the brush through her hair, she stepped back from the mirror. *Good enough.* Daniel had seen her at her worst and it clearly hadn't discouraged him from wanting to be with her.

Nicole cast one more look into the glass. She'd seen him at his worst too, when he'd driven himself to exhaustion trying to track down those missing children seven years ago. The ones her husband had abducted.

She gripped the sides of the sink. Forget what she was wearing. If she had any hope that her relationship with Daniel would last, she was going to have to let go of the past and concentrate on what the future might hold for the two of them.

Chapter Sixteen

A strange tapping sound on the door startled Nicole. She dropped the brush into the bathroom drawer and shut it. When she crossed the living room and reached the door, she took a deep, calming breath before turning the knob and pulling it open. The smile she hadn't been able to stop from crossing her face at the thought of seeing Daniel faded slightly when she saw him, one shoulder propped against the door frame, clutching a broken yardstick in his hand. Which explained the tapping sound.

She cocked her head. "Most guys would have gone with flowers or chocolate. You get points for creativity, I guess."

Daniel chuckled as he pushed away from the frame. "Not yours, I take it?"

Nicole stepped back as he came into her condo. "No, why? Was it near my door?"

"Yeah, lying right outside it." He pursed his lips as he tapped the stick on his palm. "Who would have left it there?"

Her neck prickled again, but Nicole resisted the urge to lean past him and check out the hallway. She closed the door and, although she didn't usually, casually flipped the lock. Not casually enough to fool him. His gaze flicked from the lock to her face, but he didn't say anything. Nicole lifted her chin, owning the paranoia. "Probably no one on purpose. There are a lot of kids in the building, and I often hear them running up and down the hallway. Likely they were playing some kind of game with this earlier and dumped it when it broke." If it was kids, though, why were they being so rough? She'd have to make sure Jordan never went out into the hallway alone, or … Nicole straightened her shoulders. *Let it go, Nicole. The building is safe.*

Daniel's shoulders slumped a little. Had he been hoping

there'd be more of a case for him to try and solve? Poor thwarted detective. All those skills and nowhere to use them. Her angst dissolved, and she grinned as she waved a hand toward the box beside the wood stove. "Throw it in there if you want—I'll burn it next time I have a fire."

Daniel carried the stick over and tossed it into the box. When he came back, he stopped inches in front of her.

Nicole swallowed. "Hey."

"Hey, yourself."

He leaned in and kissed her on the cheek. "Thanks for letting me come by."

"I'm glad you did. It's good to see you."

His blue eyes connected with hers. "It's good to see you too."

"How did you get into the building without buzzing up?"

A tiny frown lowered his eyebrows. "Actually, it was a little too easy. A woman was trying to pull the door open with her hands full of shopping bags. I held it for her and followed her in. She didn't seem at all concerned. In fact, she chatted with me all the way up in the elevator."

"Hmm. A young woman?" If so, no wonder she hadn't thought twice about letting Daniel in. *Maybe the building isn't as safe as I thought.* She swallowed as she batted away the thought like a pesky fly.

"I guess. I didn't pay much attention. The point is that I wasn't too impressed with the lack of security. I noticed you locked the door when I came in, but could you do me a favor and always lock it when you and Jordan are here alone? And use the peep hole before opening it to anyone?"

"I suppose."

His frown deepened. "You suppose?"

She sighed. "I've never had any issues here, and I've never heard of anyone else having any either, but if it would make you feel better, I'll keep the door locked and use the peephole."

"It would. Thank you."

"Can I get you a drink?"

"Do you have decaf?" He pulled off his brown leather jacket and tossed it onto the chair by the door.

"Sure." He wore jeans and a long-sleeved, royal blue T-shirt that matched his eyes perfectly. *Uh oh.* When she realized her gaze had settled on his mouth, she spun around and headed for the kitchen. Why had she talked to Molly and Christina about him? Both of them mentioning something about her bed had her thoughts taking off in new and extremely dangerous directions, heedless of her attempts to reel them in. Well, maybe not so new, but definitely dangerous. Nicole pushed through the French doors and went straight to the cupboard above the coffeemaker. She didn't use the decaf very often, and she'd stuck it on the top shelf.

"Here." Daniel rested a hand on her back and reached up to grab the green can. The warmth of his fingers, and the hard leanness of the body pressed against hers, sent her pulse racing.

Daniel handed her the can and stepped back. "So, Lala."

Nicole drew in a shaky breath, grateful for the neutral topic of conversation. "Yeah. Jordan loves those stories. I've been telling them to him for years."

He sat on a stool and propped an elbow on the island. "What other messes has she gotten herself into?"

Nicole scooped grounds into the filter and flipped the switch on the coffee maker. "Let's see … she and LaToya once snuck Pumpkin into school in Lala's backpack. When they went to get him out at recess, he was gone. They couldn't find him anywhere until later that afternoon, when the principal was talking to the entire school as well as all their parents at an assembly. Pumpkin suddenly dropped down from the rafters, landing on his head and pulling off his toupee on the way down. The principal was not amused. Lala and LaToya got detention for a month for that one."

Daniel laughed. "Those stories are hilarious. You should write them down—kids would love them."

"I've thought about that. Maybe I will sometime."

"Where do you come up with the ideas?"

"I'm not sure. The stories started off really simple, things like the two girls eating ice cream cones and one of them losing her ice cream, or swinging in the park and trying to touch the clouds with their toes, that sort of thing. Over the years they've gotten more and more involved, but I really don't know how or why. They come to me somehow."

He studied her until she ran her fingers through her hair. "What?"

"I was thinking how strange it is that I feel as though I know you so well, but there are still so many things I don't know about you. I had no idea you were creative, for example."

"I've never really thought of myself that way."

"Maybe I know you better than you know yourself." He smiled, but the intensity of his gaze tightened her stomach muscles.

"Sometimes I think you do." She scrambled for safer footing. "Which means I have a lot of catching up to do. Does your family live around here?"

A faint shadow crossed his features. "My mom is gone. She died nine years ago, but I still really miss her." His face brightened. "My dad's in a senior's home at the south end of the city and doing great. He's eighty-five, but he's a tough old guy. And I have a little sister, Rebecca, a high school drama teacher who lives outside the city with her husband Austin and their three kids. Olivia is seven, Josh is five, and Ava is almost two."

Nicole's breath caught. *The photo.*

Daniel cocked his head. "What is it?"

She shook her head slightly. "When I came to your office the night Gage took Matthew Gibson, I saw a photo of your family. With everything that happened after that, I'd forgotten about it. But I remember thinking at the time how lovely your family was, especially your sister. I'd like to meet her sometime."

"I'd like that too. I think the two of you would hit it off. She's great."

"Do you see them often?"

"Not nearly as often as I'd like. It's a drive out to their place, and they're so busy. I try to get out there every few weeks though, do the uncle thing."

"I bet you're amazing at it."

He shrugged. "They're amazing kids."

Nicole cleared her throat. "The coffee's ready."

Daniel hopped off the stool. "I'll get your cream."

Nicole grabbed two mugs out of the cupboard and set them on the counter. Her hands shook when she picked up the pot and coffee splashed onto the counter.

"Here." Daniel took the pot and finished pouring before sliding it back into the holder. Nicole grabbed the dishcloth and wiped up the spilled coffee while he added cream to her mug and stirred her coffee. She reached for it, but he pulled it back and caught her chin in his hand. "Everything all right?"

"Yes, fine." Nicole forced a smile and took the coffee. "Want to sit in the living room?"

"Sure." He didn't look convinced, but he dropped his hand and followed her.

She decided against starting a fire—there was enough heat flowing back and forth between them. In fact, finding a way to cool things off a bit would probably be a good idea. Nicole settled into an armchair, pulling her knees up and clutching her mug close. Daniel's eyebrow rose slightly, but he didn't comment as he sat down on the couch and took a sip of his coffee.

"So how are things at work?" Her voice trembled slightly, and she bit her lip, trying to steady herself.

"Always interesting. Sharleen and I are working a case right now that's pretty big. I can't talk about it yet, but when it breaks, I'll tell you about it."

"Jordan's looking forward to going to Sharleen and Tom's Friday night."

"Yeah, that's always a good time. Their girls are adorable." He hesitated before asking, "Have you talked to him about you and me seeing each other?"

"Yes, actually. He's fine with it. He told me he likes having you around so there are more boys than girls. Apparently, he lives in fear of being outnumbered by girls who might make him do silly things like paint his nails hot pink. I may need to rethink some of my Lala stories as they're clearly traumatizing him on some level."

"Well, if it helps him to have me around, I'm more than happy to oblige. Although I have to admit my motives wouldn't be completely altruistic. I know I saw you a couple of days ago, but I've been missing you like crazy."

Nicole shifted in her seat. "I've missed you too. So, is there something I can bring for dinner Friday?"

Daniel regarded her silently for several long seconds. Nicole lowered her gaze to her cup of coffee, studying the thin delicate strands of cream that swirled around the top of it in a desperate attempt to avoid making contact with the blue eyes scrutinizing her.

He leaned forward and set his mug on the table. "Out of curiosity, Nicole, who is it you don't trust, me or yourself?"

Her head jerked. "What do you mean?"

"Every time our conversation has headed anywhere close to intimate tonight, you've acted strange, spilling coffee when I know very well you know how to pour a cup, pulling away from me, changing the subject, and now sitting halfway across the room. I felt closer to you when we were texting over the phone. Do you think I'm going to try something, or pressure you to do anything you're not comfortable with?"

Nicole sighed and set her cup on the table beside her chair. Wrapping both arms around her knees, she hugged them closer to her chest. "No, of course not."

"Then what is it?"

"The thing is … I'm very attracted to you." Heat rushed into her cheeks.

"And that's bad?" His voice was gentle, teasing, and the tight knots in her stomach loosened.

"It kind of is. The thing is, it's been a long time since … well, since I've been close to anyone. And I've been really lonely. And then Molly made this crack about the things that help you get through cold winter nights, and Christina said something about how my bed likely feels emptier since you've come back into my life, and suddenly I'm thinking about things I shouldn't be thinking about. And then you show up tonight looking"—she waved a hand up and down the length of him—"way better than you have any right to, and we're here alone, and Jordan is sleeping... So yeah, keeping a little distance between us seemed like an extremely good idea." She lowered her gaze to her knees.

"Nicole."

There was no amusement in his voice, like she'd feared, only a tenderness that gave her the courage to lift her head. He got up from the couch and came over to drop onto the coffee table in front of her. She bit her lip when his fingers wrapped around her calves, but his touch was firm, secure, not at all provocative.

"I'm *very* attracted to you too. And since we're clearly going for all-out honesty here …"

She offered him a wry grin.

"I'll tell you that nothing would make me happier than to fill that empty bed for you and help you through this cold night. For a few hours. Then I wouldn't feel anything except shame and regret." A shadow flickered across his face and the pressure on her calves increased slightly. "Seven years ago, I crossed a line with you. More than one, actually. I didn't respect you or the relationship you had with another man nearly as much as I should have. And I carry guilt over that to this day. I hope, by God's grace, that I'm a better man now. I know I want to be. So I'm not crossing any lines this time. As much as I want to be with you, I want far more to honor you—and to honor God—by doing all of this the right way this time."

Daniel let go of one leg to brush his fingers over the side of her face. "If you can't trust yourself, Nic, you can trust me. Okay?"

She caught the hand still resting on her cheek and held it tightly in both of hers. "Okay."

"Good. Now will you come and sit beside me on the couch?"

Nicole let out a shaky laugh and let go of him. "Yes."

Daniel stood and held out both hands. When she grasped them, he pulled her to her feet. Lowering his head, he brushed his lips across hers, a kiss so sweet and gentle she would have swayed on her feet if he hadn't been holding her so tightly.

When he let her go, she smiled up at him. "Do you think this is how we're going to spend all our time together, talking each other off the ledge?"

"Maybe." He sank onto the couch and pulled her down beside him. "But I'm good with that. Crisis management is what I do."

"Thank goodness." Nicole rested her cheek against his soft blue shirt as a long-forgotten sensation settled over her like a warm blanket. The feeling had become so alien to her—she hadn't felt it since Daniel first came into her life, bringing with him his suspicions about what Gage might be involved in—that it took a moment for her to be able to name it.

She felt safe.

Chapter Seventeen

"Glad to see you took my advice." Tom tipped his can of cola in the direction of the house. Through the sliding glass door, Daniel could see Nicole in the dining room, helping Sharleen set the table. It was too cold to eat outside, but Tom was the type to barbeque all year round, so the two of them stood out on the deck, freezing while they talked.

Daniel snorted. "Advice? Is that what that was? If so, it was the most underhanded attempt at advice giving I've ever been the victim of. I was halfway home before I even realized you'd guilted me into taking a chance with Nicole."

Tom set down his can and flipped a burger on the barbeque. "That was the idea. Although I'm guessing you didn't really need me to tell you what to do. You're not an idiot; you know second chances don't come along that often in life, especially with a woman as great as Nicole. If anything, I nudged you slightly in the direction you were already headed."

"I guess."

"Then we're good?"

Daniel shook his head. "I still think you broke the guy code, tricking me like that. But since it turned out okay, then yes, we're good." Through the slight opening in the door, he caught the sound of Nicole laughing. Daniel's gaze was captured by the look on her face and the way her blond hair flowed down over her shoulders when she tipped back her head. Warmth rushed through him. Tom was right. As much as he might have hesitated to jump back into something with Nicole, there was no way that, in the end, he could have walked away from her. He wasn't that strong. Or that stupid. Like his friend had said, only an idiot would throw away a second chance like that.

Tom nudged him with his shoulder. "Just okay, huh?"

Daniel tore his gaze from Nicole. "All right, considerably more than okay."

"What about Jordan?"

"What about him?"

"I take it Nicole hasn't really dated since Gage died. How does he feel about all this?"

"Nic said she talked to him the other night, and he seems fine with it."

"Hmm." Tom flipped another burger.

Daniel cocked his head. "What?"

"Jordan's had Nicole to himself his entire life. Seems like you wanting to come in and change all that on him is worth a conversation between the two of you. Man to man."

Daniel contemplated him until he lifted his hands, one still clutching the flipper, into the air.

"What? Too blunt for you? You gave me a hard time earlier about being too subtle, so I thought I'd go the other way this time." He waggled his fingers in an I'm-so-scared gesture. "Wouldn't want to break the *guy code* again or anything."

Daniel gave him a dark look. "Anyone ever tell you that you can be a real smart—"

"Those burgers about ready?" Sharleen slid open the door and stepped onto the deck. Daniel's heartrate picked up when Nicole came out after her and flashed him a smile.

"Almost." Tom flipped the last one. "Why don't you call the kids and I'll bring in the food."

"I'll round everyone up." Sharleen headed back into the house.

Daniel held out his hand and, when Nicole crossed the deck to him, wrapped his arms around her waist as she leaned back against him.

Tom slid the first burger onto the plate and glanced over at him. "You were saying?"

Daniel leveled a warning glare at his friend then attempted an innocent expression when Nicole twisted her head to look up at him. He shook his head. "You really don't care about the code at all, do you?"

Tom let out a short laugh. "No, I really don't."

"What code?" Nicole's eyes fixed on Daniel's. Her close proximity was muddling his thoughts somewhat, and he struggled to come up with a satisfactory response.

"Go ahead, Daniel." Tom finished loading the plate with burgers and shut off the grill. "Tell her all about the code. I'll go help Sharleen get the kids started on dinner."

Daniel gritted his teeth at the smirk that crossed his friend's face when Tom passed him, headed for the dining room.

Nicole turned around in his arms. "So?"

"It's nothing." Daniel kissed the tip of her freckled nose. "A stupid guy thing."

"Ah. Then why—"

Daniel dipped his head. The taste of her strawberry gloss, and the feel of her lips, soft beneath his, emptied every thought from his head. He could only hope his kiss was having the same effect on her, since that had been his original intention.

When he lifted his head, her cheeks were pink, and she looked a little dazed as she shot a glance toward the house. The three kids were settling onto chairs around the table, and no one seemed to be paying any attention to the two of them out on the deck.

"Sorry."

Her smile was mischievous. "Don't be. I'm not. That was a pretty decent reward for pretending not to know what the guy code is."

He stared at her until she laughed. "What? That code is the worst-kept secret in the world—every woman knows about it." Her green eyes danced as she stepped out of his arms and reached for his hand. "Hungry?"

"Uh, yeah … sure." Feeling a little dazed himself, Daniel

followed her across the deck to the sliding doors.

His attempt at distraction had been a waste of time. He let that bother him for about two seconds before he shrugged and tightened his grip on her hand.

If he was going to waste his time, he couldn't think of any better way to do it than that.

Chapter Eighteen

Daniel followed Nicole and Jordan into their condo and pushed the door shut behind them. "Here." He reached for Nicole's coat when she slid it off her shoulders.

"Thanks." As always, her smile warmed something deep inside him, and he winked at her before sliding the coat onto a hanger and sticking it into the front closet.

Jordan tossed his red winter jacket onto a hook behind the door. Nicole ran a hand over his dark curls. "Go brush your teeth, please. It's getting late."

His little face darkened. "I wanted to stay up and watch a movie with Detective Grey."

Nicole crossed her arms over her chest. "When is your bedtime on Friday?"

Jordan kicked at the carpet with a sock foot. "Nine o'clock."

She uncrossed her arms and held one out in front of him. "And what time is it now?"

"Ten o'clock," he muttered.

"Either you get ready for bed now or no TV for a week. Your choice."

Jordan heaved a sigh, as though he bore a burden no six year old should ever be asked to bear. Daniel suppressed a smile as the boy mumbled, "I'll get ready for bed."

"Thank you. I'll come tuck you in shortly."

Her son nodded before trudging across the room, shoulders slumped.

Daniel watched him until he disappeared into the hallway. "You're doing a great job with him."

"Thanks. It hasn't been easy, doing it on my own, but I'm thankful every day that so far he seems to be turning out okay."

"More than okay." Daniel followed her into the living room.

"Of course, as you saw, he does obey a little reluctantly at times."

Daniel lifted his shoulders. "Don't we all?"

She laughed at that as she dropped onto the couch. "I suppose we do."

He settled on the arm and rested his hand on her shoulder. "Trust me, I see the kids who aren't doing okay all the time, even kids as young as Jordan. And a lot of them use the excuse that they don't have a dad, but Jord is living proof that doesn't have to define your life—or destroy it."

He guessed, from her sad smile, that she was thinking Gage's death had nearly destroyed *her* life. Nearly wasn't completely, though, and she'd come a long way back since that dark night—he knew that better than anyone.

"Do you want me to make a fire?"

The sadness cleared from her face. "Sure, if you want to. There's kindling in the box with the wood and a lighter on the mantel. I'll see how Jordan is doing. After the three cupcakes he had at supper, he'll need to do a good job brushing his teeth." She got up and headed down the hall after her son.

While she was gone, Daniel concentrated on getting the fire started, his mind going over and over their evening. He hadn't been too sure how Nicole would feel about being at Sharleen's house. The last time the two of them had crossed paths was the night Nicole had come to the police station looking for him, desperately hoping he could get to her husband in time to stop him from committing another dangerous crime. Two hours later Gage was dead.

Daniel blew on the fire, coaxing the small flames slowly consuming the newspaper and tiny pieces of kindling into life. He wished it had been as easy to coax life back into Nicole. And into himself, as far as that was concerned. It had taken him months to let go of the guilt over not saving Gage, of letting Nicole down. And he probably still hadn't let it go completely. Every once in a while, something would happen, like the sadness on Nicole's face, that brought it all rushing back.

He sighed. In spite of all that, she had been amazing tonight. Whether being around him and his partner had failed to dredge up the memories of that horrible night, or whether she'd refused to let them affect her, Nicole had been funny and outgoing and seemed to enjoy herself all evening. When Sharleen had given her a hug at the door, Nicole had hugged her back as though the two of them had become fast friends over the course of the evening which, under the circumstances, was pretty remarkable.

Daniel sighed again as he shut the woodstove door with a clang and stood. Flames leaped high behind the glass, and he nodded in satisfaction. Something ancient and primal deep inside him always responded powerfully to the sight of fire, especially one he had built with his own hands.

He didn't realize Nicole had come back into the room until her arms slid around his waist from behind and he felt the warm pressure of her head against his back. A smile crossed his face as he folded his arms over hers, reveling in the feel of her soft flesh beneath his hands.

"What's all the sighing about?"

Daniel hesitated, not sure how much of what he had been contemplating to share with her. "I was thinking about tonight and how well it went. You and Sharleen seemed to hit it off."

"We did. She's an incredible woman. I don't know how she does it, working with you, keeping her house looking so good, raising those two adorable girls. I'm a little in awe of her, but I really like her too. She kept me laughing all night."

"She'll do that." Daniel turned around to face her. "She is pretty remarkable, I know, but Tom helps out a lot. You have every bit as much on your plate, with raising Jordan on your own and running the diner. I hope you know how remarkable you are too."

The color on her cheeks heightened and she started to pull away, but Daniel tightened his hold on her and waited until she looked up at him again. "You are, Nic. Tom said as much tonight."

"He did?"

"Yes, he told me that second chances don't come around often in life, especially with a woman as great as you, and I'd be an idiot to throw this one away."

Her eyes met his. "Then don't be an idiot."

"Well, it would set a new precedent, but I'm definitely going to give it my best shot. This is way too important to me." He slid both hands along her jaw line, framing her face. "*You're* way too important to me." His voice grew husky when he realized the look on her face was one of complete trust. That tore into his chest and, deep down in that primal place where he'd felt the effects of the fire, the fierce desire to protect her from any more pain or suffering in her life flared up.

Slowly, he lowered his head until his mouth found hers. His hands slid farther back, into her hair, and he tangled his fingers in the soft silkiness of it, drawing her closer.

"Mom?" From down the hallway, the small voice broke through the haze that had descended over him, and Daniel broke off their kiss. Nicole rested her forehead on his chest, and he cupped the back of her head for a few seconds.

"Sorry." The word was muffled against his black T-shirt.

"It's fine. Duty calls. Go see him."

She nodded and stepped back, and he reluctantly let her go. In spite of the warmth of the flames behind him, he shivered at the sudden cold that moved through him. His eyes followed her until she had crossed the room and gone down the hallway, then he faced the fire, crossing his arms and waiting for the pounding of his heart to subside.

If he was going to keep the promise he had made to her the other night, it would probably be best not to engage in too many kisses like that one. Not everything primal was necessarily good, and in this case, it could be very, very dangerous.

Daniel turned around when he heard her footsteps padding across the carpet again. "Is he asleep?"

"Not yet. He's reading. Still coming down off that sugar high, I'm afraid. I don't know if he's going to be able to—" The cell phone she'd set on the coffee table jangled.

Nicole peered at the screen. "It's Connie. I should probably answer it."

"Go for it." He waved a hand through the air.

She picked it up and hit the button. "Hi, Connie."

Daniel watched her, intrigued by the soft smile that crossed her face when she said the name of the woman who was like a mother to her. The two of them had always been close, but clearly they'd grown even closer in the years since Connie's husband Joe had passed away.

"What is it? What's wrong?" The fear in her voice reined Daniel's wandering thoughts in sharply. The smile had faded from her face, replaced with an alarm that sent trepidation slithering through his gut.

"Do you want me to call an ambulance?" She waited a few seconds. "Lie down and I'll get there as soon as I can." Nicole hit the button and looked up at him, her eyes glazed with fear.

"What is it?"

"Probably nothing, but she's been having some pain and heaviness in her chest and thinks she should go to the hospital and get it checked out." Nothing in her expression indicated that she believed this was probably nothing, but he admired the way she forced calm into her voice, even if her lips were trembling when she finished speaking.

She shot a glance down the hallway. "I can take Jordan with me if you want to head home."

"No." He placed his hand in the small of her back and guided her toward the door. "You go. I'll stay here with Jordan."

"Are you sure? I have no idea how long I'll be and—"

He brushed his lips over hers, cutting her off. "I'm sure. Go. We'll be fine here. And it doesn't matter how long you are. I don't have to work tomorrow, so I don't care when I get home." He lifted her chin, his heart sinking at the wildness in her eyes. "Are you sure you're good to drive though?"

Nicole nodded. "I'll be fine."

Not completely convinced, he dropped his hand, knowing she needed to see Connie as soon as possible. Reaching into the closet, he pulled out the coat he'd hung there a few minutes earlier and held it for her as she slid her arms into the sleeves. "Drive carefully."

"I will."

Daniel slumped against the door frame and watched her until she reached the end of the hall and stepped into the elevator. Before the doors shut, she lifted a hand and he raised his in farewell. When she disappeared from sight, he pushed himself away from the frame and walked back into the condo, his heart heavy with concern for her and for Connie.

Please let her be all right. He sent up the quick prayer—not entirely sure himself which of the women he was referring to—as he crossed the living room and started down the hallway toward Jordan's room.

Chapter Nineteen

Troy straightened up behind the wheel so quickly some of his soda leaked through the star-shaped straw hole and splashed over the edge of the plastic cup. *Where is she going at this time of night?*

He'd expected the cop but hadn't thought even he would be out for a while, since the happy little family hadn't been at *her* place that long. When he'd watched them crossing the parking lot earlier, she had been laughing and talking to the other two as if everything in her little world was perfectly wonderful. Like she'd forgotten she was supposed to pay the price for *his* world being destroyed. His grip on the cup tightened until more liquid splashed out onto his jeans. Cursing, he rolled down the window and dumped the soggy mess onto the pavement of the visitor parking lot.

He would have to remind her. *He* was still paying. Every day. Every second. Why should she be off the hook? What gave her the right to move on with someone else and be happy again, as though the past had never happened? Absolutely nothing, that's what.

He gritted his teeth and leaned forward to start the car. Apparently his first message hadn't made much of an impression. But that would change, and soon. Pressing down on the accelerator, he backed out of his spot and swung the car around toward the exit. A block ahead, her brake lights flashed at a red light and her left turn signal came on. The streets were mostly deserted—he shouldn't have a problem following her.

He could stop her. A simple rear-ender at a red light would bring her out of her car and right into his trap. Without her detective friend around, he could really have some fun with her.

Scare her a little, maybe, enough to remind her that it wasn't over. That it would never be over.

Shaking his head, Troy turned at the lights, checking to make sure she was still up ahead. *Not tonight.* It was too soon, he had to stick to the plan. Everything had to be perfect or it would all be for nothing. For now, he'd follow her, see where she went and what she did, find out her areas of greatest vulnerability. Good things came to those who waited.

And if there was anything he had learned while locked up and staring at the same four walls twenty-four hours a day, seven days a week, it was how to wait.

Both hands on the door frame, Daniel stuck his head into Jordan's room. "How's it going in here?"

Jordan looked up from his book, his face placid, the minor tantrum in the living room clearly forgotten. "Good. I'm not tired though. I was about to call my mom and ask her for a glass of milk."

"She had to go out for a bit, so it's you and me. Is that all right?"

The boy regarded him solemnly. Daniel was struck again by how much he resembled Gage. After a few seconds, he nodded. "Yeah, that's all right."

"I'll go get you some milk. Be right back."

"Thanks."

Daniel grabbed the pitcher out of the fridge and filled a glass, then carried it back to Jordan's room. "Here you go."

Jordan set the book down on the bed and reached for it. "Thanks." He took a sip and looked up at Daniel, traces of the white liquid clinging to his upper lip. Daniel suppressed a grin and pulled a tissue out of the box on the bedside table. "Here you go. You have a moustache."

Jordan wiped it off then leaned over the side of the bed to drop the tissue into the wastebasket. "Where did my mom go?"

Daniel had been hoping he wouldn't ask. He walked to the

desk in the corner and grabbed the black chair, wheeling it over beside the bed and dropping down onto it. He leaned forward and clasped his hands between his knees. "She went to see Connie because she wasn't feeling well. She should be back soon."

He had tried to keep his tone light, but the little guy in front of him didn't miss much. "What's wrong with Grandma Connie?"

He'll know if I'm not telling him everything. "She had some pains in her chest and thought she should go to the hospital. But I'm sure she'll be fine. Your mom can tell you all about it in the morning."

Jordan studied his face for several seconds and then, apparently satisfied Daniel wasn't holding out on him, he nodded and took another sip of milk.

"Actually, Jordan, I'm kind of glad the two of us are alone here, because there's something I wanted to talk to you about, man to man."

"All right." Jordan reached over and set his glass of milk on the bedside table. "One second." He propped his pillow higher against the headboard then leaned back against it and folded his hands in his lap. Apparently, he was going to give Daniel his undivided attention.

Impressive. And slightly intimidating. Daniel worked to keep a straight face as he pulled his chair closer to the edge of the bed. "I know your mom talked to you a couple of nights ago about me coming around more often, but I wanted to ask you myself what you thought of that. I know it's been you and your mom for a long time, so I want to make sure that you're good with me being here, and spending time with the two of you."

Again, the green eyes scrutinized him solemnly. Even at six, the boy seemed to have an innate sense that the question was bigger than the words implied, and he wasn't about to take that lightly. "You really like her, don't you?"

Daniel nodded. "Yes, I do. I've really liked her for a long time now, since before you were born. And I want you to know that I would never do anything to hurt her."

"That's good. I would never want anyone to hurt my mom."

"Neither would I."

Jordan raised his head. In the mirror above the dresser in front of him, Daniel could see what he was staring at—a framed picture of Gage sitting on top of his bookshelf. When his gaze flicked back to him, his forehead was wrinkled. "Are you going to be my dad?"

Daniel sent up a quick prayer for the right words to say to that. "Your dad was a good man, Jordan. And even though he can't be with you, he'll always be your dad. But I would be very happy, and proud, to be like a dad in your life, and do all the things with you that I know your dad would love to have done if he could have."

Jordan's face lit up. "Like playing Crazy Eights and Checkers?"

"Sure."

"And football and baseball and maybe going fishing or camping? Alex's dad takes him camping all the time, but Mom doesn't like it; she says the ground was not made for sleeping on, beds were made for sleeping on."

Daniel laughed. "Well, I don't mind sleeping on the ground. I love it, in fact, and games and fishing and football too. We can do all of that, as long as you're sure that you're good with me being here with you and your mom."

He nodded, his eyes shining. "I'm good with that."

Daniel's chest tightened and he clenched his hands together tighter, a little overwhelmed by the intense emotions sweeping through him.

"Good. But Jordan, I want you to promise me one thing. I know you're used to having your mom all to yourself, and I'm really grateful that you're willing to share her with me. But if you ever feel like you need some time alone with her, you have to tell me. I'll understand that and try to give the two of you some space." Daniel unclasped his fingers and held a hand out toward the boy. "Deal?"

His face suddenly serious, Jordan slid a small hand into his and shook it. "Deal."

Daniel nodded and let him go. "Can you do something else for me?"

"What?"

"Could you call me Daniel? I feel like we're getting to be pretty good friends, and Detective Grey sounds a little formal. What do you think?"

"I want to, but I think I should check with my mom first, because she told me to call you Detective Grey."

"Fair enough. You can let me know what she says next time I see you." Daniel stood up and returned the chair to the corner. "Did you say your prayers?"

Jordan nodded, his eyes starting to look heavy. "I said them with my mom."

Sugar levels must be coming down. Daniel repressed a grin as he rested a hand on the boy's head. "Get some sleep then. I'll be in the living room if you need me, and your mom should be here in the morning when you wake up."

"Okay. Good night."

"Good night." Daniel stood and watched Jordan for a couple of minutes before turning to leave the room. When he reached for the door knob, his gaze fell on the picture sitting on the shelf. He paused and regarded the portrait. *I'll take care of them, Gage, I promise.* He nodded once in the direction of the picture before pulling the door shut behind him.

Daniel made his way to the living room, perused the shelf of books on the wall beside the woodstove, pulled down an Agatha Christie mystery, and settled into the armchair closest to the fire. Balancing the book on the arm of the chair, he stared into the flickering flames, going over the conversation with Jordan.

A grim smile crossed his face as he picked up the book and flipped open the cover. The talk had gone well, better than he'd hoped, and he was extremely glad they'd had a chance to have it.

But man, he really hated it when Tom was right.

Chapter Twenty

Nicole slowly closed the door behind her. Her eyes not leaving Daniel, who had fallen asleep in the armchair in front of the now cold woodstove, she tiptoed across the living room and into the hall.

She paused in the doorway of Jordan's room. In the soft glow of the baseball nightlight, his face was peaceful and calm. As much as she loved his energy and enthusiasm, the sight of his little face, relaxed in sleep, curls tumbling over his forehead like Gage's used to do, always filled her with a deep joy.

Nicole continued down the hall to the washroom where she brushed her teeth and got ready for bed. When she stepped back into the hallway, she pulled open the linen closet door, grabbed a soft, cream-colored knit blanket, and padded quietly back to the living room. She had thought to drape it over Daniel and go to bed, but when she reached him, she couldn't help herself—she sank down on the coffee table and watched him, as relaxed and peaceful in repose as her son.

Warmth flooded through her. She hadn't realized how much she had hurt him until she saw how terrified he was to let her back into his life again. Nicole pressed the heel of her hand against her chest. He was such a good man—he hadn't deserved that. What if she hadn't been able to convince him to give them another chance? As content with her life as she had thought she was before she and Jordan ran into him at the park that day, she wondered now how she had been able to live the last few years without him. She blinked. It had only been a few weeks. Could she really be falling for him this hard already?

Their situation was unusual, to say the least. Yes, they had only been together for a short while, but the seeds of their feelings for each other had been planted a long time ago. Those seeds had clearly taken root and grown over the years, and now that they were together, they were growing into something breathtakingly beautiful.

I wonder how it went with him and Jordan tonight. Daniel was so good with her son, so patient. And he was remarkably skilled, for someone who didn't have children of his own, at not talking down to him, no doubt the reason Jordan was taking to him so quickly. And a big part of the reason she was so willing to give him her heart, even though it had only been a short time. Well, seven years plus a short time. A smile crossed her face and she stood up to lay the blanket gently over him.

Before she could step back, Daniel reached up and grasped her hand. His eyes opened and met hers.

Nicole squeezed his fingers. "I'm sorry. I didn't mean to wake you."

Not letting go of her, he straightened in the chair. "It's fine. I was hoping I'd wake up when you came in. How did it go? How's Connie?"

Nicole sank back down onto the coffee table. "She's all right. They did a bunch of tests and didn't think she'd had a heart attack. The doctor said it was most likely angina and gave her nitro-glycerin spray to use if she needs it. She's supposed to follow up with her family doctor as soon as possible, but she was feeling a lot better by the time we left the hospital. I tried to convince her to come here and stay in the guest bedroom, but she wanted to go home."

His eyes searched hers. "You must have been scared."

"I was. It reminded me of the day I found Joe …" Her voice broke and she pressed her lips together to keep them from trembling.

"Here." Daniel lifted the blanket she'd laid over him and tugged on her hand until she came and sank down beside him on the chair. He adjusted the blanket over them, then wrapped his arm around her and drew her close. Resting her head on his chest, she let the fear and anxiousness of the last few hours slip away.

"Did everything go all right with Jordan?"

"Yeah, great." His breath was warm on the top of her head. "We had a good talk, man to man, about me being around more often."

Nicole tilted up her head to study him. "You did?"

"Yep. He said he's good with it, but I made him promise that if he feels like he needs time with you, he'll let me know and I'll give the two of you space. We shook on it, even, so it's a binding agreement now."

"That's great. I'm glad you talked to him."

"Me too. I also asked him if he would call me Daniel, but he said he had to check with you first."

Nicole smiled. "I'll tell him tomorrow that it's fine." She reached up and traced his strong jaw line, loving the feel of rough dark stubble beneath her fingers.

He caught her hand and pressed her palm to his lips. When he lowered it, his eyes were soft in the glow of the lamp on the table at the end of the couch. "What time is it, anyway?"

Nicole winced. "Three a.m. Did you want to go home?"

He brushed a strand of hair back from her face. His fingertips moving over her skin left a trail of tingling warmth wherever they touched. "Not really, unless you want me to. I'm pretty comfortable here."

"Me too."

"Good. Get some rest." Daniel leaned down and pressed his lips to hers gently. The tenderness of the kiss drained the last of the worry from her, and when he lifted his head, Nicole sighed and settled herself against him more comfortably. The strong, steady rhythm of his heart beat against her cheek, soothing her.

A small smile crossed her face. As unusual as their situation was, she *had* fallen for him. As hard and as completely as she had fallen for Gage. Her throat tightened. Which meant that, if anything happened to him, she would be dragged back to that dark place again where despair overwhelmed her, and she could barely summon the strength to face another day. And this time, so would Jordan.

Chapter Twenty-One

Mikayla set down the paint brush and reached for a rag to wipe her hands. For a long moment, she stared at the canvas in front of her. Darkness had crept into it somehow. It did that sometimes, in moments when she lost herself completely in the work, when her unconscious mind took over. That's when the truth came out, unbidden, through her fingers, obliterating the color and light for which her work was rapidly becoming known.

The flame that always simmered, like a pilot light deep inside, suddenly flared to life, the rush of heat consuming her. Mikayla shot out an arm, sending the canvas hurtling to the gray-tile floor. Leaping to her feet, she stepped over it and strode to the window. Ominous clouds gathered in the distance, and a low rumble of thunder hinted at a storm to come. But the storm within her had blown in already.

Why?

That single word, the only prayer she'd been able to muster for months, echoed through her mind, as it had so often since that black day. *Why, why, why, why, why?* From endless past experience, she knew God wouldn't answer that question. Even understood, on some level, that it wasn't the right question. Still, when the dark shadows slithered through her, that was the question they dragged with them. Mikayla had hoped painting would keep them at bay. Had prayed she'd be able to forget the significance of this day, but clearly her mind would not allow her that luxury.

Today was the anniversary. Exactly one year ago, her parents had been killed in a car crash, struck by a drunk driver who walked away from the scene without a scratch. Far less wounded than Mikayla, who hadn't even been there.

A fact that still haunted her in unguarded moments.

She *should* have been there. Her parents had invited her to join them for lunch at a new restaurant they wanted to try. But Mikayla had declined, her work calling to her. If she'd gone, maybe they would have left the restaurant later, or she'd have driven faster than her father who was more inclined to take his time and enjoy the scenery. Her presence could have altered the timing in any number of ways so that they wouldn't have been in that intersection at that precise moment. Her parents would still be with her. Still dropping by at all hours with dinner, cajoling her away from her easel so they could watch a movie together. Still serving God and others. Still laughing and teasing her out of that deep state she often descended into while painting. That world that claimed her until she lost all sense of the real one surrounding her.

Instead, they were gone. Since she was an only child, she had no family left. She was completely alone in the world. Except for Leigh. When she was finally able to pray again, Mikayla thanked God over and over for her agent. She wasn't sure where she would be if her closest friend didn't check in on her constantly, dragging her back from the edge. An edge she didn't creep as close to these days as she had in the weeks and months following the accident.

Not usually, anyway. Only sometimes, on days like today, did the shadows in her mind lengthen. Wrap around her like a damp fog on an eerie night on the English moors, suffocating her.

Heart pounding, Mikayla flung open the window. The tip of her nose pressed against the metal screen as she drew in mouthfuls of air so unseasonably hot and still, she could practically feel it drifting over her tongue. For several moments she watched the sky, mesmerized by the jagged streaks of lightning as they grew closer and more frequent. Not until a deafening crash of thunder rattled the window did Mikayla close it with a sigh.

The cup of tea she'd made herself earlier was no longer steaming, but she reached for it and carried it into the living room. She sank onto the couch, clutching the mug to her chest with both hands. The peace that came a little more often now, even when she didn't know how to ask for it, seeped into her soul as slowly, but as surely, as the warmth of the mug seeped into her fingers. That peace brought with it the other question she asked now—where do I go from here?

As far back as she could remember, she'd known where her path was taking her. Could see it stretch out endlessly before her with clearly marked road signs and milestones. The crash that had closed the road on the other side of town had effectively shut down the one in her mind in the same instant. Now she couldn't envision an endless path. Couldn't, most days, make out even a foot or two in front of her through the haze. For someone who always wanted to know what step she would take next, and in what direction, the loss of her plan left her feeling as though the power had suddenly been cut and she had to maneuver her way, arms flailing, through unfamiliar terrain in total darkness.

Your word is a lamp to my feet and a light to my path. Mikayla repeated the verse over and over in her mind as she had hundreds, maybe thousands, of times since her parents had been torn from her and she'd lost her way. Although the storm raged around the red-brick house in the old Chicago neighborhood, nuggets of hail clattering against the glass, the one inside her stilled. Her fingers twitched, aching to pick up the brush, and Mikayla clambered to her feet.

When she opened the window in the kitchen this time, the air was fresh and cool, the band of stifling heat that had blanketed the city lifted at last. The hues of the rainbow danced inside her again. Like the cool wind that had swept through the city, they drove away the darkness suffocating her.

Mikayla picked up the brush, and beneath her deft strokes the colors spilled onto the blank, white canvas.

Chapter Twenty-Two

"So, how's it going with the cute cop?" Molly finished drying the coffee pot and slid it back onto the burner.

Nicole didn't look up from counting the receipts she'd spread across the counter in the diner. "Fine."

"Fine?" Molly laid a hand over Nicole's calculator until she looked up. "Umm, I don't think so. Fine is how you describe dinner with your Aunt Matilda, or a meeting with your financial advisor. Fine is not the word you use to describe the start of a relationship with a hot detective."

"Molly!" Warmth crept up Nicole's neck. Her friend cocked her head and stared at her until Nicole sighed. "All right. It's more than fine. Quite a lot more. Is that better?"

Molly sat down on one of the red leather barstools. "Only negligibly. What I'm holding out for here are details. As many as possible. I haven't been seeing anyone lately, and I need a little vicarious excitement in my life."

"I seriously doubt your life is lacking in excitement," Nicole said dryly.

Molly lifted her slim shoulders.

Nicole shook her head as she came through the opening in the counter and sat down on the stool beside her. "Details, huh? All right, here goes. It took us a while, but I think we're both finally at the point where we want to give this a chance and see where it goes."

Molly clapped her hands. "That's fantastic, Nic. So where is it going so far?"

"Nowhere too fast. Neither of us wants to rush into anything—we're spending time together at this point, getting to know each other."

"In the biblical sense?"

"For Pete's sake, Mol! You have a one-track mind, do you know that?"

"Okay, okay." Molly held up both hands. "I know you aren't the type to spend the night with a guy you aren't married to. But …" Her eyes narrowed as she studied Nicole's face.

Nicole pushed herself off the stool. "Well, nice chatting with you. I really need to get back to—"

Molly grabbed her arm and spun her around. "You spent the night with him?"

Nicole shot a look at the swinging kitchen doors before leaning closer and lowering her voice. "No. At least, not the way you're thinking."

Both Molly's eyebrows rose.

Nicole sat back down and folded her arms on the counter. "We were at my place last night when Connie called to say she was having chest pains."

Molly sucked in a quick breath. "Is she all right?"

"She's fine. The doctor thinks it's angina and gave her some medication. Anyway, Daniel offered to stay with Jordan while I took her to the hospital. I didn't get back until about three in the morning and he had fallen asleep in a chair in the living room, so I covered him with a blanket, and he stayed the rest of the night."

Molly huffed her displeasure. "That's it?"

Nicole picked at a small sliver of wood protruding out from under the counter.

Her friend brightened. "What aren't you telling me?"

"Not much, except that he did wake up when I put the blanket on him, and he knew I'd been really scared about Connie so he …"

"He what?"

Nicole pressed the backs of her hands to her warm cheeks. "He pulled me down on the chair with him and held me and we both fell asleep."

"That was it? He held you?"

"That was it. Sorry to disappoint."

Molly pursed her lips and tipped her head from side to side, weighing what Nicole had told her. "No, it's all right. That was pretty sweet, actually. I can live with that. For now."

"It was pretty sweet. And it did make me feel better." A small smile crossed her lips. *Until I went into Nicole mode and panicked again.* Her smile faded.

Molly let out a low whistle. "Does he know?"

"Does he know what?"

"How bad you've got it."

The protest jumped to her lips, but even as she opened her mouth to speak the words, Nicole knew she was wasting her time. No matter what she said, neither of them was going to believe it. "I don't know. Maybe."

"And he's baby-sitting your kid, and spending the night trying to comfort you … I'd say you're not the only one who's got it bad."

Nicole stood up and walked back through the opening in the counter to pick up her calculator. "Like I said, Mol, we're taking it slow, seeing where it goes."

"Well, if I were you I wouldn't take it too slow or …"

Nicole looked up at the sudden silence.

Molly pointed a perfectly manicured fingernail toward the counter. "*What* is that?"

Nicole followed her gaze to the tip jar at the cash register with her name on it. Her nose wrinkled in disgust as she reached for the old, broken black comb sticking out of the jar. "Seriously? I've gotten some bad tips before, but this is ridiculous."

"No kidding. Somebody must have found a hair in their burger or something."

"Maybe, although no one complained about anything." Nicole shuddered and tossed the comb into the lost and found box under the counter as the last customer in the diner walked toward the cash register, bill in hand. When she'd finished ringing him in and accepting payment, she picked up a receipt off a pile and started typing numbers into the calculator. "Why don't you head home? I'm almost done here."

Molly reached behind her back to untie her apron strings. She pulled the apron over her head as she walked past Nicole. "Are you sure? I could wait around until you're done and make sure everything's all cleaned up before …"

Her voice trailed off as she pushed through the swinging doors and disappeared into the kitchen. Nicole chuckled and picked up another receipt. For a few minutes she typed in numbers, trying to get the till to balance. Unfortunately, her mind insisted on drifting to things other than receipts and the daily intake of earnings, and the total kept coming out wrong.

Finally, she tossed the pencil onto the counter. How was she supposed to get anything done when thoughts of Daniel kept pushing themselves into her brain?

Nicole gathered up the receipts and shoved them under the tray, then shut the till with a clang. She could do the math tomorrow; right now she needed to head out so Connie, who'd gone to Nicole's to meet Jordan after school, could get home to bed. Connie had insisted she was perfectly fine after her recent health scare. In fact, she claimed time with Jordan was the best medicine for her. Still, Nicole didn't want Connie to have to care for him more than a few hours at a time. After Connie left, she may or may not check her phone for texts, she'd have to think about that.

Who are you kidding, Nicole? You'll be checking your texts before you leave the building. Like you've been checking them every hour on the hour all day.

Nicole shook her head as she crossed through the kitchen, grabbed her coat, and pushed out the back door into the cold night air. The rest of her employees had gone home before Molly, so she shoved the door shut and locked it. A clattering sound in the alleyway behind the diner froze her in place. *What was that?*

Nicole swiveled slowly to survey the narrow opening between the two brick buildings. "Hello?"

The word came out as a nervous croak and was met by silence. Should she go back inside? A group of people strolled by the opening onto the sidewalk, laughing and talking. Somehow it felt safer out here, where other people were within shouting distance, than inside the empty building.

Her legs trembled, but Nicole forced herself to take a step in the direction of her car. Why had she driven? Most days she walked and would have left by the front door, but they'd been short-handed for the evening shift, and she knew she would get out after dark.

She took another step. Only a few more and she would reach her vehicle. Nicole hit the button on the remote. The click of the locks releasing seemed to echo off the walls like a gunshot. When the sound died away, she strained to hear into the darkness. The blood pounded in her ears so loudly that if anyone was following her, she wouldn't be able to hear his footsteps.

Abandoning caution, she lunged toward the car, threw open the door, and slid behind the wheel. Only when she had locked the doors behind her was she able to draw a ragged breath.

In the glow of her headlight, shadows flickered across the bricks. Nicole shoved the key into the ignition and started the engine. Without waiting to see if the shadows would morph into something real, she squealed out the back of the parking lot and onto a side street.

Chances were it had been a cat. Or maybe a large rat. Nicole shook her head. The alarm bells still ringing in her head told her that whatever—or whoever—it was that had been lurking in her alleyway had something much more sinister in mind than scrounging through dumpsters for food.

Chapter Twenty-Three

Daniel's hands gripped the steering wheel tightly, and Nicole reached across the console and grasped his arm. "Are you nervous?" She hadn't told him what had happened outside the diner a few nights before, because she didn't want him to worry. By the time she'd arrived home, she'd shaken off the fear that had gripped her when she heard the clattering sound. Whoever had been there must have wandered into the alleyway searching for a bit of shelter from the wind for the night, and probably wouldn't be back again.

He looked over at her. "I guess I am, a bit. This *is* a fairly odd situation."

"Why?"

"Why? Because I'm about to go to the home of my girlfriend's brother-in-law. And I have no idea how he's going to feel about his late brother's replacement showing up and sitting at his table casually eating dinner with him."

Nicole made a face. "You are not Gage's replacement."

"What else would you call it?"

"I don't know, but there has to be a better way to look at it than that."

He sighed. "Whatever way you look at it, however you spin it, Nic, that's what I am. Holden has to be struggling with me coming as much as I am—probably more."

She squeezed his arm. "You don't have anything to worry about. Holden is a great guy, and Christina and I are on your side."

His eyes widened. "Side? Are you anticipating that *sides* will be drawn tonight?"

She laughed. "No, I meant that we'll be there for you. And

Holden is fine with you coming. When you first came back into my life, he told me that he was happy for me, and that Gage would want me to move on too."

"Yeah, Daniel," Jordan piped up from the back seat. "Uncle Holden likes you. When Mom and Aunt Christina were talking about you, he said there was something appealing about a man with a gun."

Nicole whipped around, too late to stop the spew of words. "Jord!"

"Ha!" Daniel smacked the steering wheel. "I told you I would find out what Jordan was about to say that night."

She shifted back around. "You said you would use your superior detective skills to ferret it out. I wouldn't exactly say that was what happened here."

"I believe *superior* is your word, not mine. And it doesn't matter how I found out. The point is, I did. And that I was right."

"About what?"

"I knew what I found out would be very interesting. So you and Christina find me appealing, do you?"

Nicole slumped against her seat. "That is not what we said. It was Holden who suggested that a man with a gun was appealing, and he only said it because he was making fun of us for …"

He shot her a sideways glance. "For?"

Heat crept up her neck. "I don't remember," she mumbled, turning to look out the car window.

"Nic."

She traced the leafy patterns of frost on the glass with her fingernail.

"Nicole Louise Kelly."

Pressing her lips together, she faced him. "Yes?"

"Don't make me pull this car over. What did you and Christina do that Holden was making fun of?"

Nicole twisted around to look into the back seat. "Are you going to help me out here, Jord? You're the one who got me into this mess."

"Sorry." He shrugged and went back to reading his comic

book.

"That's helpful, Son, thanks."

Daniel flipped on the right turn signal and touched the brakes.

Nicole gripped the armrest. "All right, all right. Holden somehow got it into his head that whenever your name came up, women would blush. Actually, I believe the word he used was swoon."

Daniel moved his foot back to the accelerator. "Which women?"

Has it always taken this long to get to Holden and Christina's place? "You mean specifically?"

He took his attention off the road for a few seconds to look at her. The amusement in his blue eyes only added to her discomfort. "Yes, specifically."

"Me and Christina. But of course he was mistaken."

"About what?"

"About Christina."

Daniel laughed and reached for her hand. "Thank you for that. If you were trying to make me feel better, it worked." He lifted her hand to his mouth and kissed the back of it, then kept her fingers clasped in his as he maneuvered his way through the side streets of Holden and Christina's neighborhood.

"Out of curiosity, what would you have done if you had pulled over?"

"I have no idea. I was hoping you wouldn't call my bluff. All I knew was that it always worked for my dad when I was a kid. I still get chills when I hear the clicking of a signal."

"So basically, you just scared yourself more than me."

The corners of his mouth twitched. "Basically."

She grinned. "What was your mother like?"

The pause before he answered told her more than words could. Even after all these years, it clearly hurt him to talk about her.

What would it have been like to have parents like that? How different would my life have been?

"She was the best mother ever, a sweet, loving woman who lived to help anyone in need." Daniel's voice thickened. "We didn't even realize how many lives she'd touched until she died. So many people came to the funeral to pay their respects and tell us how much she'd meant to them they had to have overflow seating outside the church. I was blessed and proud to have her for a mom."

They were both silent until he squeezed her hand again. "I'm sorry."

"Don't be." She managed a weak smile. "I'm glad you had such an extraordinary mother. I wish I could have known her."

"Me too."

Nicole studied his strong profile as he pulled up in front of the house and turned off the engine. For the first time since Daniel had come by the condo to pick them up, he looked relaxed and ready to face the evening ahead.

In spite of her attempts to reassure him, she couldn't stop the fleeting thought from going through her head that she hoped Holden was as ready as Daniel was for them to arrive.

Chapter Twenty-Four

Holden met them at the door and stuck out his hand. "Daniel, hi. Welcome to our humble abode."

"Hey, Holden. Thanks." Daniel shook his hand firmly before letting go and following Nicole and Jordan into the house.

"J-man." Holden held out a fist, and Jordan bumped his against it. "Hi, Nic." He kissed her on the cheek and held out his hand for her coat.

Nicole slid it off and gave it to him, then helped Jordan take his off.

"Welcome, everyone." Christina came down the hallway from the kitchen and hugged Nicole. When she let her go, Jordan rushed over and wrapped his arms around her waist.

"Gently, Jord," Nicole reminded him.

"That's right—I hear congratulations are in order." Daniel took Christina's hand in both of his. "Good to see you, Chris."

"Thanks, you too. Glad you could come."

"Me too."

"Dinner's not quite ready. If you guys want to go hang out in the basement for a few minutes, we'll call you when we're all set."

Holden nudged Daniel with his shoulder. "Up for some pool?"

"Always."

"Great. Let's go." He gestured toward the stairs.

Jordan took off with the two men trailing behind. Nicole's eyes followed Daniel until he disappeared down the basement stairs. When she tore her gaze away, Christina was watching her.

"How's he doing?"

"Who, Daniel? He was pretty nervous about coming." Nicole

followed her sister-in-law down the hallway toward the kitchen. "What about Holden? Is he good with Daniel being here?"

Christina picked up a pair of tongs and started tossing the salad. "I asked him about that earlier and he seemed fine with it. I'm sure on some level it's hard for him, watching you move on with someone else, but he really is happy for you, Nic."

Her shoulders relaxed. "That's good. I'm happy for me too."

"So am I, and Daniel looks happier than I've ever seen him, so we're all one big happy bunch."

Nicole tilted back her head and sniffed the air. "So where did dinner come from tonight? It smells incredible."

Christina made a face. "I'll have you know I made this meal all by myself. Well, Holden and I did. He's actually a decent cook, and he's been teaching me a few things. I put a roast in the Crock Pot this morning, which is the easiest meal ever, meaning even I can handle it. I think." She dropped the tongs into the salad bowl and hurried over to the stove. "Holden did the potatoes and the gravy, so all I have to do is make sure the carrots don't burn and cut up the meat." She turned the burner off under a pot that had been steaming vigorously.

"I'm impressed. What can I do to help?"

"You can slice the bread. That did come from the bakery; I'm not quite ready for homemade bread yet, but I'm getting there. Funny thing is, before I found out about this little one …" she rubbed circles on her stomach with one hand, "… I never had any interest in learning to cook. Now I'm not only doing it, I can't seem to learn fast enough. I'm even going on the Internet, looking for new recipes to try."

Nicole picked up the bread knife and pulled the cutting board with the bread closer. "You're nesting. I remember doing that too. For a few months all I wanted to do was cook and clean. Thankfully that passed shortly after Jordan was born."

"Oh no, don't tell Holden. He's thrilled about the new me."

"My lips are sealed."

"Speaking of your lips, how are things going with you and Daniel?"

Nicole choked out a laugh. "Speaking of my lips? What are you talking about?"

Christina picked up the tongs again. "Come on, the two of you are clearly young and in love—you must have some juicy details you can share about what you've been doing."

The knife caught Nicole's baby finger and she dropped the blade onto the counter with a clatter. "Ouch."

"Oh, Nic, what did you do?"

She grabbed a napkin off the counter and wrapped it around her finger. "I'm fine. I barely nicked it."

"Here." Christina reached for a first aid kit on top of the refrigerator and popped it open. She rummaged around in it and pulled out an adhesive bandage. "Sorry, I shouldn't have sprung the l-word on you when you had a sharp knife in your hand."

"You shouldn't have sprung it on me at all. It's way too early for that."

Christina pulled the wrapper off the bandage and handed it to her. "Really?"

"Yes, really." Nicole wrapped her finger and picked up the knife again. "Why do you sound so skeptical?"

"I don't know. Obviously I haven't seen the two of you together very much, but as soon as you walked into the house tonight, I felt it."

"Felt what?" Something prickled across Nicole's skin, like a faint electrical current pulsing through her body.

"Something really deep and powerful between you and Daniel. I know it's only been a short time, but it's also been years. I could be wrong Nic, but I think you feel a lot more for him than you're willing to admit." Christina stuck the tongs into the lettuce and carried the bowl over to the table. When she came back, she handed a basket to Nicole and squeezed her shoulder. "When I was trying to figure out how badly I had fallen for Holden, I asked myself how I would feel if he walked out of my life the next day and I never saw him again. You might want to try …" Her face softened. "Oh honey, I guess that answers my question."

"What does?"

"The look that crossed your face. That thought clearly didn't sit well with you."

Nicole tossed the slices of bread into the basket. Her fingers trembled, but she managed to get them all in and hand the basket to Christina. "No, I guess it didn't."

"There you go then."

Nicole swatted Christina's arm with the back of her good hand. "What did you have to go and do that for?"

"Do what?"

"Put thoughts like that in my head right before we all sit down to dinner together. Daniel's nervous enough about tonight. Me being a basket case on top of everything else is not going to help."

Christina set down the bread and hugged her. "You're not going to be a basket case. This is a good thing, trust me. I know Daniel feels the same way, and the two of you are blessed to have found each other. Relax and enjoy every minute of it."

The current prickling across her skin subsided, replaced by a warm tingling sensation in her stomach. Chris was right—this thing was huge and terrifying and life-changing.

But it was definitely good.

"I think that's it." Christina set the gravy boat on the table and stepped back with her hands on her hips, clearly proud of her efforts.

Nicole arranged the last set of silverware on either side of a plate. "I'll go get the guys."

"Thanks. I'm going to sit down and rest for a minute. I just remembered the other reason I like to order out. All this preparation is exhausting."

"You relax, I'll be right back." Nicole headed for the basement door and padded down the gray carpeted steps. Halfway to the bottom, she caught a glimpse of Daniel, standing beside the pool table leaning on his cue. As though he could feel her looking at him, he turned and their eyes locked. A smile crossed his face and he winked as she reached the bottom step and crossed the room to him.

Across the table, Holden leaned over, setting up a shot. On the far side of the room, Jordan stood in front of a big screen TV, clutching a Wii remote. When she came up to stand beside him, Daniel ran a finger down the side of her hand. His smile faded as his fingers closed over hers and he lifted her hand. "What happened?" He nodded at the bandage.

"A minor tussle with the bread knife, which I lost."

He frowned. "Are you all right?"

"I'm fine. Just a flesh wound. I'm not dead yet."

"Quoting Monty Python—now that's impressive."

The tingling in her stomach intensified as she grinned. "Chris sent me down to tell you supper's ready."

Balls clunked together. Daniel let go of her and surveyed the table. "Nice shot. That's your game."

"You gave me a run for my money, though. You've played a few times before."

"A few times." Daniel walked over and fitted the pool cue into the rack on the wall. "Although it's been a while."

"Oh great, that was rusty? I better practice before you come over again."

Holden's casual acceptance of the fact that Daniel was going to be around from now on sent a thrill of happiness rushing through Nicole. She flashed her brother-in-law a smile as he came around the table. The smile he returned to her was easy, and the last of the tension melted away.

"Come on, Jord. Time to eat."

Thankfully, the easiness remained throughout dinner. When her plate was empty, Nicole took a sip of water and leaned back in her seat. "Chris, I'm really impressed. Everything was delicious, especially the beef and the carrots."

Holden set down his fork. "Hey, I made the potatoes and gravy."

"I know."

Christina chuckled, and Holden elbowed her. "Watch it, or I'll leave those for you to do next time too."

She winced. "I could handle the mashed potatoes, but you're going to have to teach me how to make the gravy."

"I don't think so." Holden tugged the gravy boat closer to his plate. "If I teach you all my secrets, you won't have a reason to keep me around."

"Come on, I keep you around for more than your culinary skills, you know."

"Really? What else?"

"I'm not about to change all those diapers myself. And someone is going to have to get up in the night to bring me the baby. Then there's the late-night runs to the drugstore for fever or teething medication and, eventually, the math homework and the parent-teacher interviews and paying off the student loans ..."

"So essentially I'm good as long as we keep having babies."

"Essentially." Christina smiled at him.

"Plus, you'll keep getting great meals like this." Nicole nodded at the dishes on the table. "Nesting is good for that."

The heads of both men swiveled toward her. Holden raised an eyebrow. "Nesting?"

"Nic." Christina lifted both hands, but Nicole ignored her.

"Yeah, it's the urge women get when they're pregnant to cook and clean the house."

Daniel tapped her arm with a finger. "Did you get that?"

"Yes, but thankfully I got over it. Like the flu."

Holden swept an arm over the table. "So all of this is going to go away?"

"No." Christina frowned. "I really like cooking. And it's not because I'm having a baby." She shot a pointed look at Nicole. "Although ..." she turned back to Holden "...if all of this did go away, would *I* still be here?"

He hesitated long enough for Daniel to start a laugh that he quickly turned into a cough into his fist.

His face serious, Holden reached for his wife's hand and held it in his. "Of *course* you'd still be here, my love. If I was only keeping you around for your culinary skills, you'd have been gone a long time ago."

This time Daniel did laugh. Nicole pressed her lips together when Christina yanked her hand from Holden's and pointed a finger at her. "Don't you dare. You started all this, you do *not* get to enjoy it."

Nicole pushed back her chair. "I'm sorry. As penance, I'll do the dishes."

"I'll help her. You guys relax." Daniel gathered up a pile of plates and followed her over to the sink.

Holden's voice accompanied them. "Wow. I could get used to this treatment. You are definitely invited to come every week with Nicole and Jordan, Daniel."

"Thanks. I think I might. Although next time I plan to give you a harder time at the pool table."

"You can try."

Grateful relief flowed through Nicole. Knowing Holden, she shouldn't have worried about tonight. With everything he and Gage had been through, somehow, with the help of God and their own close relationship, they'd both grown into remarkable men.

It was hard for her sometimes to be around Holden, he reminded her so much of his brother. Like it had to be hard for him to welcome Daniel into the family so freely. But it was something they were both willing to do because that's what they were, a family, the first real family she'd ever had. And families put each other's needs ahead of their own.

Daniel's fingers brushed hers when he took the dishes from her and set them on the counter. She watched him as he turned on the tap and began filling the sink with water, a revelation suddenly flooding through her.

The kind of loving family Daniel had grown up in, and that they'd experienced in this house tonight, was the kind of family she wanted to have with Jordan and Daniel.

If she could only subdue the panic over everything she could lose that occasionally inserted its presence inside her like an unwanted guest at a party, maybe that's exactly what she would find.

Chapter Twenty-Five

"Here you go, Pop." Daniel handed his dad a slice of pizza on a paper plate and sat down on the forest-green-and-tan plaid couch. The mingled smells of melted cheese, tomato sauce, and pepperoni drifted through the apartment and he inhaled deeply.

"Thanks, Son." His dad lifted the slice to his mouth in hands that, while wrinkled now and spotted with brown, still had the ability to clench his in a vice-like grip, as Daniel well knew. "This sure beats the seaweed-tofu-who-knows-what I'd be eating in the dining hall if you hadn't shown up."

"It's great that they serve healthy food here, Pop; you know it's good for you."

"Good for me? How can you say that? The stuff's killing me inch by painful inch."

Daniel scooped up a dangling piece of cheese and shoved it into his mouth. "They do run a tight ship. If they knew I'd smuggled this pizza in for you, I'd be banned from the place forever."

"I'll tell you what, I miss your mother all the time, but never more so than when I sit down to dinner here. All I can think about the whole time I'm trying to choke it down is how great her cooking was. Remember her Sunday roast beef dinners? And her chicken and dumpling stews and her meatloaf? That woman could cook, let me tell you."

The ache that had dulled over the years, but that still flared at the mention of her name, gripped Daniel. Now that his dad mentioned it, he missed his mom's cooking too. She'd shown him the way around the kitchen, although he never could make anything as good as she had made it, even using her recipes.

Realizing his dad was still talking, Daniel forced himself

back to the conversation.

"You find yourself a woman who can do that, and I promise you'll be a happy man."

"Sorry, Pop, I faded out there thinking about the great food Mom used to make. What were you saying I should look for in a woman?"

"Someone who cooks great, laughs often, and loves you and the good Lord. That's all it takes. You come across a woman like that and you grab her and don't let go. That's my advice."

"I don't know about that. It may have been different in your day, but these days women don't tend to take it well when you grab them and refuse to let them go. In fact, that's often when they call me to come and arrest the guy."

The backhand caught him across his leg, and Daniel almost dropped his pizza.

"Not literally, smart-mouth. You know what I mean."

Rubbing his jeans, Daniel grinned. "Actually, I do. In fact, I think I might have found a woman exactly like that."

His dad shifted in his dark brown recliner until he faced him. "Really?"

"Yeah. She's a great cook—in fact, she owns a diner downtown. She has a great sense of humor and loves God, and she's also smart and a great mom and—"

"Whoa." His dad held up one hand. "She's a mother?"

"Yes. She was married, briefly, but her husband died, and she had their son Jordan a few months later. He's a great kid. We get along really well and …" Daniel's eyes narrowed. "What?"

"She's that Kelly kid's wife, isn't she?"

He sighed. "Yes. Nicole."

His dad cocked his head and contemplated him in silence, before a slight smile crossed his face. "So you're hearing the birds singing pretty loudly these days, aren't you?"

Daniel leaned forward and set his plate on the coffee table. "I have no idea what you're talking about." He grabbed a napkin and wiped the grease off his fingers. "You mean like in Bambi where the animals are all twitter-pated and the birds are chirping over their heads?"

His dad let out a choked laugh. "No, although you might be experiencing that too. I hope you are. I was referring to the Bible, Song of Solomon to be exact, where it says, 'The winter is past, the rain is over and gone; the flowers appear on the earth; the time of the singing of birds is come'."

Daniel shook his head. "Still not following."

"The first time you talked to me about this woman, she had married someone else that day, and I pointed out that you were going through a long, dark night of the soul. Remember?"

"Like it was yesterday."

"Well, I've watched you work your way through the cold and dark for years, and now it seems as though the winter may finally be drawing to a close. Which means that it's time for the singing of birds. Am I right?"

"I guess you are. You're definitely right that it's been a long, hard season. I never thought it would happen, but God finally brought Nicole and me together."

His dad clapped his hands. "That's great news, Danny-boy. I'm happy for you. And very glad to see you never lost your faith, even through that dark time."

"I couldn't lose it. Most days it was the only thing that kept me going, and I clung to it like a drowning man."

"And now the morning has come. Which is one of only two things God promises about the darkness—that he'll walk through it with you and that, if you persevere, the light will come again, one way or another. And from the look in your eyes, I'd say it's shining pretty brightly on you right now. Got it bad, don't you?"

"You could say that. I'm thinking about asking her to marry me, but I'm worried it's a little fast."

"Fast? You were already in love with this girl the first time we talked about her, and that was years ago."

"And she was in love with someone else at the time. And then grieving his death. She hasn't exactly been waiting around for me to show up at her door."

"Even so, like I told you before, if she's the one, you gotta grab her and hold on with everything you've got. Trust me, a woman like that doesn't come along every day. You move too slow and lose her, you'll regret it for the rest of your life."

Daniel pursed his lips. "You might be right."

"That's pretty much a given. Although you being smart enough to take my advice might not be. Here." The footrest creaked back down into place as his dad grabbed the cane he'd rested against the side of the chair and struggled to his feet.

Daniel watched him as he crossed the room and disappeared into his bedroom. A minute later, he reappeared in the doorway carrying a small, blue velvet box. "Maybe this'll help." He thumped across the room and handed the box to Daniel before settling back in his chair.

"What's this?"

"Open it up and see." His dad took another bite of his pizza.

Daniel lifted the lid and caught his breath at the sight of the small, heart-shaped cluster of diamonds set in a gold band. It was the ring he'd seen on his mother's hand every day for thirty years. He looked up at his dad. "This was Mom's. I can't take it."

"She wanted you to have it. I've been waiting for the day you'd come here and tell me you had a woman whose finger you wanted to put it on. I'd about given up hope, being honest."

"Me too." Daniel's gaze dropped again to the box in his hand. After a moment, he snapped the lid shut and nodded. "Thanks, Pop."

His dad waved a hand through the air. "Talk is cheap, Son. Give me a couple more grandkids if you really want to thank me."

Daniel shoved the box into the pocket of his jeans and picked up his plate. "Let's not get too far ahead of ourselves here. I haven't even proposed to Nicole yet, and I have no idea if she wants more children. If she does agree to marry me, though, I'll bring your future step-grandson around. You'll get a kick out of him."

"Bring them soon. I want to meet him, of course, but I'd particularly like to meet the woman so special you've been carrying a flame for her for years.”

“I will. I’d really like for you to meet them both.”

His dad’s eyes lit up. “Did you say she owns a diner? Maybe she can smuggle me in a big juicy burger with a side of fries. She’d have *my* heart forever if she did.”

“Pop, we can go out to eat whenever you want to. You don’t have to break the rules just to enjoy a burger once in a while.”

His dad snorted. “Where’s the fun in that?”

Daniel grinned, picturing Nicole trying to get past the front desk with a hamburger hidden under her coat or in her purse.

“Good point. I’ll see what I can do.”

Chapter Twenty-Six

Daniel slid into a corner booth and propped his head on one hand. He was so preoccupied with watching Nicole as she worked, he didn't see the server approaching his table until she spoke.

"Evening, Detective."

Daniel glanced up. "Oh hey, Molly."

"Nicole's almost done with that last group. Anything I can get you while you're waiting?"

"Sure, I'll take a coffee." He nodded at the pot in her hand and slid the white mug to the edge of the table.

Molly poured the cup and nudged it back toward him.

"Thanks."

"My pleasure." Molly shot a look over at Nicole then set down the pot and slid into the booth across from him. "Do you mind if I ask you a personal question?"

"You can ask."

She offered him a grim smile. "What are your intentions toward Nicole?"

He almost laughed, until it occurred to him that Nicole really didn't have anyone else in her life to ask that question of him. He lifted his mug and took a sip of the hot, black coffee, pondering the question for a few seconds. He was surprised at how quickly the answers came to him. "All right, I guess that's a fair question. My intentions are to take care of her and Jordan, do everything in my power to help her understand what an incredible person she is, and to always put her happiness ahead of my own."

"And love her?"

He set the mug back down on the table. "Can I ask you a question?"

"You can ask."

"Why are you so interested?"

"Because I care about Nicole too, a lot. She doesn't have any family around, and I don't either, so she's become like a sister to me. As you know, she's been through a lot, and I really don't want to see her get hurt again."

"Neither do I." He glanced over at Nicole, who was gathering plates and glasses from a family with several kids. The table was covered in French fries, spilled soda, and splotches of ketchup and he sighed, knowing the clean-up would take a while. Nicole didn't seem to mind. She smiled and chatted with the kids and, as he watched, rested a hand on the curly, sandy-haired head of a child in a highchair. His dad's request came back to him. If Nicole was willing, he really would be happy to have a child or two with her. Probably that would be a good discussion to have before they …

"Hello?" Molly waved a hand in front of his face.

"Look, Molly. I appreciate that you care about Nicole and that you're trying to protect her, so I'll make you two promises— one, that I will never intentionally do anything to hurt her, and two, that if she'll let me, I'll spend the rest of my life trying to make her happy. How's that?"

Her shoulders relaxed. "Pretty good. As a bonus, you even answered the question you so deftly avoided earlier."

"Which was?"

"Whether or not you loved her."

Daniel lifted both his hands, palms up.

Molly moved to the end of the bench and stood. He looked up when she gripped his shoulder. "For what it's worth, Detective, you have my blessing."

"Thank you. It's worth a lot, coming from such a good friend of hers."

"Don't forget the sister she never had."

The words struck him like a punch to the gut, but he forced a smile. "That too."

She squeezed his shoulder and went to fill the coffee cups at another table, leaving him alone with his whirling thoughts.

"Ready to go?" Nicole stood at the end of the table, a pile of dirty plates in her hand. She lifted them and gave him a tired smile. "I'll take these to the kitchen and grab my coat."

"I'll meet you at the door. I have to pay Molly for the coffee."

Nicole waved a hand through the air. "Don't worry about it, it's on the house."

"No, I'll pay her. She gave me great service, not to mention a lot to think about."

"Such as?"

"I'll tell you on the way home. It's such a nice night I came through the park, but if you don't feel like walking home, I can call us a cab."

"No, don't. As long as we can take our time, I'd like to walk."

"Sure. I'm not in any hurry."

"No hot date or anything tonight?" Her green eyes gleamed.

"Well, my date is always hot, although she's also looking pretty tired, so the evening will likely be fairly low-key."

"That sounds perfect. Although, if I get some fresh air I might rally." She inclined her head toward the kitchen. "I'll only be a minute."

Daniel nodded and reached for the wallet in his back pocket. Pulling out a ten, he dropped it on the table. It was a little steep for a coffee, but a small price to pay for the blessing of someone close to Nicole.

Someone almost like a sister to her, who—he winced at the thought—unknowingly filled the void left by the one Nicole didn't realize she'd once had.

Daniel stopped outside the market Nicole often shopped at on her way home. "Want to grab a few things in here to make dinner with?"

"Sure."

He held the door open for her then followed her into the brightly lit store. "Feel like anything in particular?"

"Anything but burgers and fries. I saw enough of those today to do me for a while."

"I'll bet. How about chicken? I make a decent stir-fry, or so I've been told."

Nicole lifted an eyebrow.

"By my friends." Daniel grabbed a basket and headed for the produce department. "And my family."

She trailed along after him. "Speaking of which, I'd like to meet your dad sometime."

"Funny you should say that. I was at his place a couple of weeks ago, and he said he wanted to meet you too."

She grabbed his arm and turned him to face her. "You talked to your dad about me?"

"Well, yeah. I was over visiting him. We got talking about what was going on in our lives, and your name came up."

Nicole scrutinized him. "In what context, exactly?"

"I snuck a pizza in for him, because he hates the healthy meals they force him to eat at the seniors' home, and he mentioned how much he misses my mom's cooking. He said if you find a woman who cooks, laughs a lot, and loves God, you should grab her, and I told him I already had."

The corners of her mouth turned up. "What, found her or grabbed her?"

"Just found her so far, although the night is young."

She laughed at that, and Daniel smiled at the sound.

"Anyway, he said to bring you by some time, he'd like to meet you. And Jordan."

"You told him I had a son?"

Daniel's gaze dropped to the empty green plastic basket in his hand. "He already knew that, actually."

He looked up when she didn't answer and sighed. "It's a long story, but he's known about you since the day you and Gage were married. I was hurting that night and went to see him. I can never hide what I'm feeling from him, so he forced me to tell him what was going on. He told me he was the cop who went to the house the night Gage and Holden's parents died."

She let go of his elbow. "Oh yeah, Holden figured that out when we were on our way to find Gage at Matthew Gibson's, but I'd almost forgotten it."

"Well, he's never forgotten Gage. He really impressed my dad that night, the way he fought so fiercely to protect Holden. He was sorry to hear about what happened to him and has asked me about you occasionally over the years, so that's how he knew about Jordan."

"Ah." Her voice was tinged with sadness, but she pushed back her shoulders and smiled. "So he wants to meet me."

"Yes, but he has an ulterior motive. He's hoping you'll smuggle a burger and fries in to him. He says, if you do, you'll have *his* heart forever too."

"Too?"

"Like I said, I can never hide anything I'm feeling from him."

Pink colored her cheeks as she slid her hand through the crook of his arm. "We'll have to go see him soon, then. In the meantime, all this talk about food is making me hungry. Look at those gorgeous peppers. Should we get a couple?"

"Sure." Daniel followed her. The little blue velvet box burned in his coat pocket as he contemplated whether or not the timing was right to offer it to her. She was tired, but if she rallied during their walk like she thought she might it could possibly work.

She felt one pepper after another. Buying food for the diner had obviously instilled a good eye and feel in her for when foods were at their best. When she dropped a huge yellow pepper into the basket and reached for a red one, inspiration struck him.

Keeping one eye on her to make sure she didn't turn around suddenly and catch him, Daniel reached slowly into his coat pocket and drew out the box.

Chapter Twenty-Seven

Nicole slid her hand into Daniel's as they crossed the street. She hesitated slightly at the entrance to the park. The few times she had been held up at work and still ventured into the park in the dark, the sense that she was being watched had done more than raise the hair on the back of her neck. Apprehension had sent prickles of electrified ice skittering down her back and arms, and by the time she had half-jogged along the path and reached the sidewalk across from her building, she had been struggling to draw in air.

The pathway was lit by lampposts planted every thirty feet or so, but beyond their soft glow, darkness pressed in on both sides, conjuring up the image in her mind of the walls of water held back for the Israelites to cross between. *I am not alone. I am not alone.* The God who had held back the seas that day was as powerful today as He had been then and would protect her the way He had His people. Reminding herself of that fact over and over, she'd clench her fists and force herself to keep planting one foot in front of the other, but it would take entire conversations of self-talk to slow the beating in her heart as she crossed the street and made her way to the front entrance.

You're safe tonight with Daniel. Still, her fingers closed around his a little more tightly as they started down the path that wound through the park. She inhaled deeply, forcing her tense muscles to relax. Thankfully, the arctic temperatures they'd experienced over Christmas and New Year's had abated briefly— enough that they could get outside and enjoy fresh air again. She was definitely not a hibernator, although she did appreciate the extra business the bitter weather brought to the diner. Nothing was more appealing on a cold winter night than hot coffee and a warm smile, as Joe always used to say.

"Want to sit?" Daniel's voice pulled her from her musings.

"Sure, if you don't mind waiting a bit longer for dinner."

"I don't mind. We've got all evening, right?"

"Yeah, Alex's mom said she'd bring Jordan home around 8:30, so we're good." She followed him to the bench in the center of the park. In spite of the relatively warm evening, the park appeared deserted, likely a combination of the snow that slushed beneath their feet as they walked, and the fact that darkness had thrown a cloak over the city while they'd been in the store shopping.

Daniel sat down and held out his arm and Nicole settled beside him, resting her head on his shoulder. As always, the solid warmth of him calmed her, and she inched closer on the bench.

They sat in silence for a few minutes, until Daniel shifted to face her and she lifted her head. "Do you remember the day we first spoke?"

"Of course." Nicole's gaze swept along the lit pathway. "After you'd rescued me from that purse-snatcher, you stalked me through the park and accosted me right about here, I believe."

"In my line of work, we'd say that I tailed you and instigated contact, but all right, essentially that's what happened."

"And then my grocery bag ripped, and everything went flying and you happened to be there to rescue me again, like a white knight swooping in to help the damsel in distress."

Daniel shrugged. "It's what I do."

"I seem to remember something else you do. Weren't you impressively adept at juggling vegetables? I have a vague recollection of the show you put on after you walked me back to the condo."

He grimaced. "I'm glad that's how you remember it. Since you do, I won't bring up the fact that I pretty much destroyed your peppers and lettuce that day which, considering I was a complete stranger, you handled with extreme understanding and grace."

Nicole lifted both hands. "It's what I do."

Daniel laughed and squeezed her shoulder. "That's true. Thankfully for me."

"Have your skills improved any over time?"

"I doubt it. Believe it or not, juggling vegetables is not something I attempt on a regular basis."

"Let's see you try." Nicole reached for the bag of groceries, but he pulled it away before she could get to it.

"Definitely not a good idea, Nic, unless you want to make vegetable soup again like you had to do the last time."

"I'll take my chances." She grabbed for the bag and snagged it this time before he could pull it out of her reach. When he let go of it, she slid it onto her lap and pulled out the orange, yellow, and red peppers they'd purchased. "Come on, give it a go."

He exhaled loudly. "All right, but remember, you asked for this." He pushed to his feet and she handed him the brightly colored vegetables.

For a couple of seconds, he tossed them lightly between his hands, and then he attempted to juggle them. He kept them in the air for several seconds before having to grab all three and clutch them to his chest to keep them from falling onto the cleared cement pathway.

"Not bad." Nicole held out her hands. "Let me try."

He angled away from her. "I don't think so."

"What? Why not? I'm pretty sure I can beat your record."

He snorted. "I'm pretty sure you cannot. I've seen you do this before, remember? And I really don't feel like rainbow pepper goulash for dinner."

Nicole stood up and made a grab for the peppers, but he held them over his head. "Come on." She tried to pull his left arm down so she could grab the pepper he clutched in that hand, but with no success. Finally, she stepped back and crossed her arms as she studied him. "I'll *bet* you I can juggle longer than you did."

He slowly lowered the peppers. "What do you bet?"

"If I beat your time, I'll give you a kiss."

"And if you don't?"

"Then I'll do the dishes myself tonight."

"Hmm. Sounds like a win-win for me. Go for it." He held out both hands and she took the peppers from him.

Like he had, she tossed the vegetables lightly in her hands for a few seconds before starting to throw them up in the air.

After about twenty seconds, considerably longer than he had juggled them, he held up both hands in protest. "I think I've been hustled. You've been practicing, haven't you?"

Nicole concentrated on keeping the peppers in the air. "Jordan saw a juggler at a birthday party a few months ago and wanted to learn, so we've been doing it together."

Sliding an arm around her waist, he lifted her off the ground. "Definite breach of the rules, withholding vital information like that."

"Hey!" Giggling, she grabbed for the peppers, but they slipped from her grasp and smashed onto the sidewalk. "Looks like you'll be doing the dishes tonight."

He set her back on her feet. "Oh no, that wasn't the deal. The deal was you'd do the dishes by yourself if you didn't beat my time and kiss me if you did. Nothing in there about me doing the dishes."

"Rats. I didn't think that out very well, did I?"

"I think you did it perfectly. Now pay up, lady."

Nicole stepped closer to him. The teasing look faded from his eyes as he watched her. Slowly, she lifted her hands and framed his face, then slid one hand behind his head to pull him down to her. She pressed her lips to his and gave him a long, lingering kiss.

When she let him go, Daniel brushed a strand of hair from her face. "Wow. You're showing off your skills all over the place today, aren't you?"

"If you've got it, flaunt it, I always say."

"Well, you've definitely got it, and you can flaunt it with me any time you want." Daniel tapped her lightly on the nose before glancing behind her on the sidewalk. "Looks like goulash tonight for sure."

Nicole whirled around. "Oh no. That poor yellow one really took a beating, didn't it?" The biggest of the three peppers had smashed open on impact, spilling its seeds out over the hard sidewalk. She knelt down and started to scoop up the mess, then froze.

Something bright and shiny in the center of the pepper glinted in the light of the lamp post. "What is that?" She reached for it and gasped, pressing one hand over her mouth.

Then Daniel was in front of her, bending down on one knee and reaching for the ring she'd pulled out of the pepper with trembling fingers.

"Nicole." Daniel caught her fingers in his free hand. "I know we haven't officially been together that long, but I lost my heart to you that day in the park, years ago. And even when we had to be apart for so long, my heart stayed with you, so that a big piece of me was missing until you came back into my life again. You are the only woman I have ever loved, and I love your son too. There's nothing in the world I want more than for the three of us to be a family. Will you marry me?"

Nicole's mouth dropped open slightly. A proposal was the last thing she'd expected. Daniel was right—they'd only been together for a few months. But he was also right about the fact that there had been something powerful between them for a lot longer than that.

She couldn't make the same claim he had—she had loved Gage with all her heart. But she knew with a deep certainty that she loved Daniel too. Like Tom had said, second chances didn't come along that often in life, and she would be an idiot to let this one—this man—slip through her fingers.

A smile broke across her face. "Yes, I'll marry you. Of course I will." The words ended in a laugh that was almost a sob as he held up her hand and slid the ring onto her fourth finger. It fit as though it had been made for her. Nicole studied it in wonder for a few seconds before she lifted her gaze to meet his. "It's perfect."

"It was my mother's." Daniel leaned in and touched his

mouth to hers. The kiss was gentle and sweet, full of promise for their future. He rested his forehead against hers. "Thank you, Nicole. For saying yes. You've made me happier than you will ever know."

They stayed like that for a moment, as her heart overflowed with a deep gratitude that God had gifted her with another wonderful man to share her life with.

Then he lifted his head. "It's getting colder. We should probably head back." Daniel pushed to his feet and held out his hands to her.

She hadn't realized she was shivering until she stood up. Daniel scooped up the peppers and tossed them into the paper bag before sliding an arm around her shoulders and turning her toward home.

"How on earth did you get the ring into the pepper?" Nicole glanced sideways at him as they walked.

"When you were sorting through every single one in the bin, I took the opportunity to work it inside."

"How did you know I'd pick that one?"

He grinned. "You didn't. You did throw it in the basket, but then you found one you liked better and tossed this one, ring and all, back onto the pile. I had to keep an eye on it and snag it when you headed for the snow peas."

"Good thing you grabbed the right one."

"No kidding. Someone would have gotten quite a surprise when they were making supper tonight."

"They wouldn't have been any more surprised than I was."

"Good surprise, I hope."

"Great surprise. Possibly the best one ever."

"Do you think Jordan will be good with this?"

She considered the question before nodding. "I think he'll be great with it." She stopped and faced him. "He loves you, Daniel. You're the only father he's ever known." Her voice broke, but she lifted her chin. "He's very blessed to have you in his life. We both are."

Daniel pressed his lips to her forehead. "I'm the one who's

blessed." He reached for her hand again.

They walked in silence until Nicole started to laugh. "That was a pretty elaborate scheme. How did you know I'd try juggling those peppers?"

"I knew if I did, you wouldn't be able to resist trying to show me up. I didn't anticipate you actually bringing up the subject, or betting me a kiss you could do it, but that was a nice bonus."

"For me too. Don't forget *I* knew that I had been practicing." She stopped again and looked up at him. "Did you put as much thought into what comes next?"

"Next?"

"Yeah. Like when you want to get married?"

His face grew serious. "I'd marry you tomorrow. But I know you didn't get a big wedding last time, so if you want to do the whole white gown, hundreds of guests, fancy dinner at a big hotel in June thing, then that's what we'll do."

A shudder moved through her. "That all sounds horrific."

"So what *do* you want?"

"Something small and simple. You and me and a very few friends, and Jordan of course. And June is way too far off."

"Valentine's Day?"

"Too cliché. And besides, I don't want to give you an excuse to hand me one thing with a Happy Anniversary to my Valentine card on it." She tapped a finger on her chin. "How about Groundhog Day? Not one of your overly commercialized holidays, which is good."

His eyes widened. "That's three weeks from today."

"Too long?"

He grinned. "My kind of girl." Sliding his free hand behind her neck and pulling her close, he kissed her until she was weak in the knees and wondering if three weeks actually *was* a little too long for their engagement.

When he let her go, he grabbed her hand and started down the path. "Seriously, stop distracting me. You're freezing and I'm starving. Let's go home."

"That sounds good. And speaking of home, have you

considered where we would live?"

"I haven't, actually. But it makes sense for me to move into your place, right? It's bigger, and it would be less disruptive for Jordan."

"That's true." She squeezed his fingers. They had almost reached the other side of the park before Nicole spoke up again. "Of course, that day with the thief and the park wasn't our first encounter."

Even in the dim glow of the lamps, she could see the flush cross his cheeks. "If you're referring to that time in the diner, I have blocked that out of my conscious memory."

"Really? I remember it as clearly as if it were yesterday. I asked you why you were leaving without eating your breakfast, and you made that crack about your bed being more appealing than anything on the menu and then got really embarrassed. I still think of that sometimes when I need a good laugh."

"Always happy to entertain." Daniel lifted her hand to his mouth and kissed the back of it.

"Oh, you do. And I look forward to a lifetime of laughing."

"With me or at me?"

She shrugged, a mischievous glint in her eyes. "Either. It doesn't matter to me."

Funny, it didn't matter to him either. After all the suffering and loss she had endured, all he cared about was that she *could* laugh again.

And he'd spend the rest of his life making sure that never changed.

Chapter Twenty-Eight

Daniel closed the front closet door, his eyes on Nicole as she crossed the living room and sank onto the couch. She lifted the hand with the ring he'd given her, turning it so it glinted in the light of the lamp on the table beside her.

"You must be exhausted." Daniel walked over to stand in front of her, setting the bag of groceries on the coffee table.

She lowered her hand and offered him a weary smile. "I am, but I'm also incredibly happy."

"Good." He settled at the far end of the couch. "Here." He tapped his knee. "Give me your feet."

Nicole stretched out on the couch and rested her feet on his knees. When he took one in his hands and began massaging it, she closed her eyes and groaned. He worked on her feet for several minutes before his hands stilled. "Why don't you go have a bath while I fix dinner?"

Nicole opened her eyes. "I'd love that, but I should probably wait. Jordan will be home in a few minutes, and I need to talk to Sherry and thank her for having him."

"I could do that." He made the suggestion tentatively, not sure if she was ready for him to assume that role in their lives.

Although he was listening for it, there wasn't a trace of hesitation in her voice when she answered, "Would you?"

"Sure." He squeezed both her feet. "And I'll put Jordan to work in the kitchen, helping me salvage those vegetables you mangled earlier into something edible. By the time you get out, dinner should be ready."

"I'm going to get awfully spoiled if you keep treating me this way."

"With God's help, I plan to. And if I ever feel like slacking off in that department, I'll remind myself how blessed I am to have been given this second chance with you, and that will re-motivate me." A twinge of guilt shot through him at the words.

"What was that?"

He worked his expression back to neutral. "What was what?"

"You winced when you were talking. What's that about?"

Daniel sighed. "I keep talking about how happy I am to have this second chance with you, and it suddenly struck me that it's a really insensitive thing to say."

Wrinkles appeared in her forehead. "Why?"

"I'm keenly aware that the only reason I have another chance to be with you is that the man you were supposed to spend the rest of your life with had his cut short. That must cross your mind every time I say it."

Nicole pulled her feet from his knees and sat up. "Daniel, no. I promise you it doesn't." She reached for his hand. "My time with Gage was a gift, and a beautiful chapter in my life, at least before it all came crashing down. And like all chapters, that one will have an impact on the rest of the story. But I'm not going to keep reading it over and over. I need to turn the page. Part of me will always love and miss him, especially since I see him so strongly in Jordan, but Gage is my past. You are my future. You and I have chapters of our own to write, and I'm looking forward to living out every one of them." She tightened her grip on his hand. "If I truly was supposed to spend the rest of my life with Gage, he would still be here. Which means that you're the one. It's you I'm meant to grow old with, to share my life with."

Daniel ran a finger down the side of her face. "Thank you for that."

"You're welcome. I mean it."

His finger trailed along her jaw line and she swallowed. "Why don't you go have your bath? I need to talk to Jordan anyway."

A smile curved across her lips. "Another man-to-man talk?"

"I believe it's called for." Daniel stood and pulled her to her feet. "I need to ask him for your hand in marriage."

Nicole stood on her tiptoes to kiss him. When she left to go take her bath, he headed for the kitchen to start dinner. A few minutes later, the buzzer sounded from the lobby. Daniel wiped his hands on the towel he'd slung over one shoulder and pushed through the French doors into the living room. When he reached the door, he stabbed the intercom button with one finger. "Hello?"

"It's Jordan."

A thrill shot through him at the sound of the boy's voice. He hadn't seen Jordan for a couple of days, and he'd missed him more than he would have believed possible. "Come on up, buddy."

A minute later, the door to the condo pushed open, and Jordan bounded into the room. Alex and his mother stood in the hallway, and Daniel grasped the knob and pulled the door open wider. He held his hand out toward the woman. "Hi, I'm Daniel."

She shook his hand firmly. "Sherry." She let go of him and wrapped an arm around the shoulders of the boy beside her. "And this is Alex."

Daniel held out his hand to Jordan's friend, and the boy slid his small one into it and shook it. "Good to meet you both. Nicole can't come to the door, but she asked me to thank you for having Jordan, and for bringing him home."

"It was our pleasure. Jordan is a delight, very polite and well-behaved. We're always happy to have him."

It took Daniel a few seconds to realize that the warmth that flooded his chest was pride. "I'm glad to hear that." He looked back over his shoulder. "Come here, Jord."

When Nicole's son walked up to stand beside him, Daniel placed a hand on his shoulder. "Is there something you want to say to Alex and his mom?"

Jordan nodded. "Thank you for having me."

"You're welcome. Any time." Sherry shifted her gaze back to Daniel. "Tell Nicole we said hi."

"I will. Thanks again." He waited until they had gone a ways down the hall before shutting the door softly behind them.

He kept his hand on Jordan's shoulder as he guided him toward the kitchen. "I'm making dinner for your mom and me. Are you hungry?"

Jordan shook his head. "No, we had pizza at Alex's and stopped for ice cream on the way home. I'm full."

"Come and tell me about your day while I work."

Jordan settled himself on one of the barstools at the island as Daniel moved around to the other side and picked up the knife he'd been using to chop the vegetables. "What did you and Alex do?" Lifting the cutting board, he scraped the peppers, onions, and snow peas into the pan on the stove.

"Not much. We hung out, played video games, then took his dog for a walk."

"Sounds like fun."

"It was. What did you and my mom do?"

Daniel came back around the island and sat down on the stool beside him. "Actually, I wanted to talk to you about that. First of all, I want you to know how much I like being around you and your mom."

"We like having you around too."

"Good. I'm glad. The thing is, I was wondering how you would feel if I was around a lot more."

Jordan cocked his head. "How much more?"

"Well, I love your mom very much. And I love you too. So tonight I asked her if she would marry me so the three of us could be a family."

The boy's eyes widened. "What did she say?"

"She said yes, that she also wants us to be a family. But I wanted to make sure that was all right with you, because it's important to me that you want this as much as your mom and I do."

For several seconds Jordan didn't say anything then he nodded once, firmly. "Yep, it's all right."

"Are you sure?"

"Yeah, it's cool. Are you going to live with us?"

Daniel repressed a grin. "I thought I might, after the wedding."

"When's that?"

"In three weeks. Sound good?"

"Yeah, except …" A frown furrowed his forehead.

Daniel's chest tightened. Was Jordan going to ask about his dad again? "Except what?"

"I don't have to wear a suit, do I?"

He bit his lip to keep from laughing. "You'll have to talk to your mom about that, buddy. As far as I'm concerned you don't, but she might have other ideas. And it's always best to go along with the bride when it comes to wedding plans. That's a good lesson to remember for the future—might save you a lot of heartache."

"What's a good lesson to remember?"

Daniel looked up as Nicole, her cheeks flushed from the warm bath and her hair up in a ponytail, blond wisps curling around her neck, walked through the French doors. His stomach flip-flopped. Even dressed in a sweatshirt and jeans, she still took his breath away.

"Always make sure the bride is happy."

"Ooh, that is a good thing to remember." Nicole walked over to Jordan and gave him a quick hug. "Did you have fun with Alex?"

"Yeah. We had pizza."

"Good." Nicole lifted her chin and sniffed. "Although something in here smells way better than pizza." Her arm still around Jordan's shoulders, she gave Daniel an uncertain smile. "So the two of you talked?"

"Yep. I told Jordan I asked you if you would marry me so the three of us could be a family. He said that was cool, as long as he didn't have to wear a suit. That's why I was telling him that it was up to you, that it's always best to follow the bride's wishes when it comes to weddings." Daniel slid off the stool and went to the stove to make sure the vegetables weren't burning.

Nicole took his place. "Tell you what, Jord. This is a really important day for me, for all three of us actually, and I do want you to look nice. But you can go shopping with me and help pick out something for you to wear that we both like, deal?"

"Deal."

Daniel tossed the pieces of chicken he'd cooked earlier into the frying pan with the vegetables, and stirred everything around with the lifter, watching the two of them out of the corner of his eye as Nicole reached over and grasped her son's shoulder.

"Do you have any questions or concerns about Daniel and me getting married? Because we both want you to be honest and tell us how you're feeling."

Jordan yawned and covered his mouth with one hand. "I'm feeling tired right now. But I'm good with it. Since I already ate with Alex, can I go get ready for bed?"

"Sure. Brush your teeth and put your pajamas on, and I'll be right there to tuck you in."

"All right." Jordan hopped off the stool and trotted toward the kitchen doors. "'Night, Daniel. I'm glad you're going to live here. Then we can play games whenever we want."

"You got it, buddy."

Nicole flashed Daniel a smile that did nothing to still the flip-flopping in his stomach. When Jordan had disappeared through the swinging doors, Daniel set down the lifter and came around the island, pressing a hand to the countertop on either side of her.

"How about you, beautiful?" Daniel leaned in and pressed his lips to the curve of her neck. Her freshly scrubbed skin was warm and damp and smelled like roses, and his breathing grew shallow. "Are you glad I'm moving in so we can play games whenever we want?"

Nicole pressed her lips together as though trying not to laugh. "Pretty close to breaching the law here, aren't you, Detective?"

He pushed himself off the island. "You're right, I'm sorry. There's a time and place for everything, and I guess this isn't it."

"Three more weeks and it will be game on."

Daniel kissed her lightly before stepping back. "Bring it, lady."

Chapter Twenty-Nine

"Ready for bed, Jord?" Nicole tapped on the bathroom door then stepped back when it swung open and her son charged through the doorway.

"Yep. See?" He stopped and opened his mouth.

Nicole stifled a laugh, remembering how she had often "shown" her parents that she had brushed her teeth, not sure even now what it was she thought they could see when she did.

"Good job." She placed a hand between his shoulder blades and directed him toward his room. "Hop in." Her hand still on his back, she gave him a gentle shove toward the bed, and he leaped on top of the covers.

When he had snuggled under the Batman sheets, Nicole sat on the side of the bed. She pushed his dark curls back from his forehead. "So you're really fine with Daniel and me getting married and the three of us being a family?"

Jordan nodded, his eyes suddenly serious. "I'm good with it, if you and Daniel are."

Nicole detected a slight hesitation in his voice, and in the glance he darted over her shoulder. "What is it, Jord? This is going to affect your life too, so you have to say if there's anything that concerns you so we can talk about it."

"I was wondering ..." he bit his lip and contemplated her for a few seconds. "Do you think Dad would be all right with it?"

A needle-prick of pain dug into her chest. "All right with what?"

"With me doing things with Daniel like card games and football and camping. Daniel said Dad will always be my father, but he'd be happy to do the things with me that Dad would have done if he was here."

"I think he'd be fine with this, Jord. He would be really happy to know that you had someone in your life to do those things with you, since he can't." She rested a hand on his arm. "I also think that God has doubly blessed you."

"What do you mean?"

"I mean that you had a good father who would have loved to be here with you, watching you grow and doing fun stuff with you. But since he can't be, you have another good man who loves you and wants to spend time with you. Some kids don't have any dads at all, and God gave you two great ones."

Jordan contemplated her words. It always amazed Nicole that her son could be so energetic and full of life and enthusiasm one minute, and deeply introspective the next, a complicated but admirable balance few people she knew had ever achieved.

The soft glow in his green eyes told her he'd worked it out in his head. "You're right, Mom. That is pretty great." He yawned again, and Nicole pulled the sheets up under his chin.

"Okay, Son, time to …" She stopped and sniffed the air. "Jord, what is that smell?"

The eyelids that had been half-closed flew open, and he lifted his nose and inhaled. "I don't know."

Nicole stood up and walked around his bed, sniffing the air. When she reached the little table on the other side of his bed, she leaned down and pulled open the drawer. "Ooh, Jord, gross. What is this?"

Reaching into the drawer, she drew out a lumpy brown mass. She sniffed it and then quickly turned her head away. "Was this a potato in another life?"

Jordan's face cleared. "Oh yeah, I found that a while ago."

"How long ago? And where did you find it?"

"I don't know, a couple of weeks, maybe? I was going with you to get groceries, and you were scraping the back window on the car. I was trying to brush the snow off the hood and I found the potato."

"On the hood of the car?" Nicole's forehead grooved.

"Yeah."

"Why didn't you tell me?"

"Because it was cool and I wanted to keep it. If I told you, I knew you'd make me throw it in the garbage."

"Yeah, I would have, so that what ended up happening—your room getting all stinky—wouldn't have happened. And what was so cool about a wrinkled-up potato, anyway?"

"It had a piece cut out of it, so it kind of looked like an old man with his mouth open."

Nicole shook her head. "Well, cool or not, this old man is going straight into the garbage, and no more food in your room, understood?"

"Understood."

Holding the potato as far from her nose as possible, Nicole bent down and kissed him on the forehead. "Good night, Jord."

"'Night, Mom."

Nicole carried the potato gingerly between two fingers through the living room and into the kitchen.

Daniel was dishing the food out onto the plates, but he looked up when she came into the room. "What is that?"

"A rotten potato. I found it in the drawer of Jordan's bedside table." Nicole opened a cupboard door and pulled out the composter. Lifting the lid, she dropped the offending object into the dark green container and snapped the lid down tight. "There." She shoved the container back into the cupboard and shut the door.

Daniel slid the frying pan onto the burner. "Umm, I realize I'm new to the whole parenting thing, but is it usual for kids to keep things like that in their bedside table drawers?"

Nicole scrubbed her hands with soap and rinsed them under the tap. "No, that's a new one. Although I will say it's not the grossest thing I've found in his room. I used to come across old bottles under his crib with spoiled milk in them, or peanut butter sandwiches that he'd tossed behind the books on his shelf. And don't even get me started on some of the vomit and excrement issues I've dealt with over the years. Lucky for you, you missed that fun stage. A potato will likely be the worst thing we'll find now." She grabbed the towel hanging from the handle of the stove.

Daniel leaned a hip against the counter and reached for her hand to pull her closer. Twining his fingers through hers, he looked down at their clasped hands. "Speaking of which, I've been meaning to ask you if you've ever thought about having more children."

Nicole studied him. "To be honest, I haven't given it a lot of thought. When Gage died, I wasn't thinking about ever getting married again, so I guess I shoved the thought of more kids out of my mind. Why, do you want children?"

"It isn't something I've thought about much either, but I have to say I am loving spending time with Jordan. The more I do, and the closer you and I get, the more I think that having a child with you would be pretty great."

Nicole exhaled. "Definitely something we should discuss before we get married. But to tell you the truth, I'm too tired to even think straight tonight, let alone make a big decision like that. I will consider it, though."

"Fair enough." Daniel let go of her hand and picked up the two plates. "Want to eat in here or in the living room?"

"The living room would be nice. Although I can't guarantee I'll be able to stay awake very long in front of the fire."

"Let's eat out there anyway. If you get really tired you can go to bed and I'll let myself out."

Nicole poured two glasses of water and followed Daniel to the living room. She set the glasses down beside their plates on the coffee table and settled onto the couch with a sigh. "This is it, the moment I've been looking forward to all day."

Daniel put down the plates and sat beside her. Reaching for her hand, he prayed a blessing over their food and over their lives together. Of all the powerful things that had happened since he'd picked her up at the diner, his simple words struck her as the most profound, and she blinked back tears.

When he finished, he squeezed her hand as his eyes met hers. "I was thinking I'd like to come to church with you and Jord tomorrow. I like mine, but of course I want us to go together, as a family. What do you think?"

"I'd love that." Nicole's heart filled again as he handed her a plate and settled back on the couch with the other one. Smiling, she lowered her head and inhaled. "This smells so good." She waved her hand through the air toward her, trying to capture more of the aromas of teriyaki sauce and chicken. "Thankfully, it's driving the lingering odor of rotten potato away."

"Where did the potato come from, anyway?"

"That's the weird part. Jordan said he found it on the hood of our car a couple of weeks ago."

"Really?" Daniel's eyes narrowed as he looked at her. "That's kind of weird. Why would there be a potato in the middle of a city parking lot?"

"I have no idea." Nicole took a bite of snow peas, peppers, and chicken and chewed thoughtfully before swallowing. "If it was someone's idea of a joke, it wasn't particularly funny. Especially since whoever left it had cut a big chunk out of it, which is even stranger. Kind of like ..."

"Like what?"

The furrows in her forehead deepened. "Now that I think about it, people have been dropping other strange items off to me lately."

"What items?"

"A few weeks ago, someone stuck this old black comb into my tip jar at the diner. I told Molly I'd gotten bad tips before, but that had to be the worst."

"What did you do with it?"

He wasn't touching his food. Nicole could actually see him going into cop mode. *I shouldn't have brought this up. Not tonight.* There was no way around it now, though, as his radar was clearly up, and he wouldn't let it go until she'd told him everything. "I don't really remember. I think I might have tossed it in the lost and found box under the counter."

"Hmm." Daniel set his plate on the coffee table without taking a bite. "What else?"

"That broken yardstick you found outside my door a few months back." Nicole set her plate down and got up and walked over to the box beside the stove. She moved a few of the larger pieces of wood out of the way until she spotted the stick and pulled it out. "Remember?" She held it toward Daniel, but he didn't reach for it.

"Could you set it down on the coffee table? The less either of us touches it, the better."

Frowning, Nicole set it down. "You don't really think this could be anything ominous, do you? I mean, it's a broken yardstick."

"Probably not, but it's better to be careful." He leaned forward and examined the stick. "You're right, these are all odd things for someone to have left for you."

"But they're not exactly scary or threatening objects, only a little strange. Do you think the same person left all three things?"

"I'm not sure what to think. On their own none of the items seem that threatening, but putting all three of them together, it feels like a pretty big coincidence. Think about this, Nic, how did you feel when you got each of the objects?"

"A little creeped out, I guess, with the comb and the potato anyway. And if I had found the yardstick outside my door when you weren't here, that would have felt weirder."

"That's your subconscious telling you that something isn't quite right. Promise me you won't ignore that feeling. That you'll tell me immediately if it happens again."

"I promise." Nicole clasped her hands together in her lap. "Is this you being a cop, or overly protective, or could this actually be something potentially dangerous?"

Daniel's gaze dropped to the yardstick on the table, and he didn't speak for a moment. When he did, his tone was grim. "It might be me being a cop, and maybe, if this happened to someone else, I wouldn't be as worried about it." He gripped her knee. "I don't want to scare you, but it does concern me that someone left something for you at your home, your vehicle, and your place of work. And while the objects themselves seem innocuous, it's quite possible there's a pattern among them as well. And when a pattern emerges, seemingly harmless objects can suddenly become very threatening."

Nicole pressed a hand to her stomach. "I guess so."

"I'll take the potato and the yardstick with me tonight. You check at the diner tomorrow, and if you find that comb, drop it in a Ziploc bag and let me know right away. I'll come pick it up and take all three things to the lab. Likely they won't find anything, and this will turn out to be a bizarre coincidence, but I don't want to take any chances with you and Jordan."

She nodded, her stomach tightening into knots. This was not how their wonderful evening was supposed to end.

Daniel must have caught her concerned look, because his face softened. He reached over and brushed the backs of his fingers across her cheek. "Don't worry, I'm sure it's nothing. But if you do see anyone strange or something happens that feels a little off, please text me. Night or day."

"I will."

"Good." He squeezed her knee. "Better eat up before it gets cold. I'll take care of those things after."

In spite of his reassurances, he didn't take more than a few bites of his dinner. She couldn't eat much either and pushed her plate away after a couple of minutes. "I'm sorry. I thought I was hungry, but I'm realizing now that nothing on my plate is as appealing as my bed."

"That's very cute." He offered her a weak grin and pushed to his feet. "I understand, though, it's been a long day. I'll put the food in the fridge for tomorrow then I'll grab that potato and get out of here so you can go to bed."

"I'm sorry I'm not very good company."

"You're always good company, but you happen to be particularly sleepy company tonight. Go, rest. I'll talk to you tomorrow."

"If you insist." She clambered off the couch.

"I do. And Nic? Everything's going to be fine. Although I do want you to be careful, I also want you to enjoy the next couple of weeks, getting ready for the wedding. Please don't let any of this spoil that for you."

"I won't." Going up on her tiptoes, she pressed her mouth to his. "I really am looking forward to you moving in and to starting this new chapter together."

"Me too."

He was clearly trying to keep his voice light, to not let her see how concerned he was about the objects she'd shown him. But she felt his eyes on her as she trudged across the room and headed down the hall. Nicole sighed. No matter how much he tried to reassure her, until they found out who had sent those things, she wouldn't enjoy the wedding preparations nearly as much as she would have liked to.

Chapter Thirty

Troy leaned forward and peered out the front window of the beige Ford Focus, the most inconspicuous vehicle he'd been able to find. His gaze followed the cop as he pushed open the front door of her building with his hip and crossed the parking lot. He clutched something in his hands, but Troy couldn't tell what it was until he passed underneath one of the big lampposts that littered the parking lot.

He squinted to focus on the packages the cop was carrying. A smile of satisfaction crossed his face as he leaned back in the seat. The cop definitely had the yardstick, and no doubt he had one or two of Troy's other little presents tucked somewhere in there as well. The potato had been a calculated risk. The woman was likely to toss that out without seeing the significance of it, but even if she had, they still might be able to figure out what he was trying to tell them.

It would take them a few days though—at least he hoped it would. Even if they did make the connection between the items fairly quickly, they wouldn't be able to trace them to him, not until it was all over. Then everything would be clear, and they would understand what he had done, what he had been compelled to do.

Troy watched the cop as he tossed the stick onto the passenger seat and started his car. He kept his gaze on the black Miata as it left the parking lot. When the taillights disappeared around a corner down the street, he leaned forward and turned the key to start his own engine.

Soon he would have what he'd been longing for—not for his suffering to be over, since that would never happen as long as he drew breath—but for *her* to start suffering along with him.

Misery loved company, and he was about to open the door to his living nightmare and welcome her right in.

Chapter Thirty-One

"So what do you think?" Daniel spun around in his desk chair to face his partner. Nicole had texted him right after she'd arrived at the diner to let him know she'd found the comb, still under the counter where she'd tossed it. He'd driven by on his way to work and picked it up. After making one more obviously futile attempt to assure her everything was fine, he'd come straight to the station. "A little weird, right?"

Sharleen nodded, a small v furrowed between her eyebrows. "A little weird, yeah. Did you hear back from the lab?"

"Not yet."

"Likely it's nothing, but it's good you're checking it out."

"Thanks for saying that. I'm not the most objective person when it comes to Nicole and Jordan, so I was hoping I wasn't over-reacting."

"So what if you are? There's no harm in looking into it, since you do have a lab at your disposal. There has to be one or two perks to this job, right?"

"Other than the stellar coffee, you mean?" Daniel sipped from his paper cup, then grimaced and set it on his desk.

"Right, besides that. So how non-objective are you, anyway?"

He looked up at the abrupt change in topic. "About what?"

"Not what, who. Whenever you're at our place, it looks like things are going really well with the two of you."

"Yeah, I keep meaning to thank you for that, by the way. I wasn't sure if Nicole would be completely comfortable hanging out with you given that, until a few weeks ago, she hadn't seen you since the night Gage died. But she says you always make her feel welcome."

"It's my pleasure. She's really great, Daniel. Tom and I like her a lot. But you didn't answer my question."

He'd been hoping she wouldn't notice. Not that she ever didn't notice something he'd done. Or hadn't done. With a sigh, he leaned back in his chair and crossed his arms. "Fine. I'm about as non-objective as it's possible to be, I guess. I don't have to tell you how I feel about Nicole, and after spending quite a bit of time with the two of them, I've developed a pretty tight relationship with Jordan as well."

"How tight?"

"Very. I've even started thinking I could get into the dad thing, something I've never really considered before."

Sharleen's dark eyes probed his. "You're thinking of marrying her, aren't you?"

Daniel shook his head. "Sometime it would be nice for me to be able to break news about my life to you without you figuring it out before I have a chance."

"So you are? Have you asked her?"

Before he could answer, she clapped her hands together. "You have, haven't you? What did she say?"

"For Pete's sake. I was about to tell …"

Sharleen sank back in her chair, her face wreathed in smiles. "She said yes, of course, or you'd have been mooning around the office all morning. Did you set a date?"

Daniel lifted both hands in the air. "I think I'll let you try and read that on my face too, and if you get it wrong then I guess you'll miss the whole thing."

"I'm not psychic, Grey. I do know how to read what you're feeling. I should, after all this time."

"I can't read you like that."

"You do pretty well, for a guy. But seriously, when are you doing this momentous thing that will change your life forever?"

"First of all, thanks for the added pressure, exactly what I needed. And February 2nd."

Her quick intake of breath gave him immense satisfaction.

"You mean two weeks from this Saturday? That February

2nd?"

"That's the one."

She pursed her lips and studied him before lifting her shoulders. "Why not? You've waited long enough for this woman. Why put it off any longer?"

"My thoughts exactly. Although, for the record, it was Nicole who suggested that date. I started in June and when she said that was too far away I moved back to Valentine's Day, but apparently she's waited long enough for me too."

Sharleen rolled her eyes before pushing to her feet. "Seriously, Grey, it's fabulous news. I'm really happy for both of you. I know it's been a rough journey, and I'm glad it's all turning out so well. You deserve it. And don't let this go to your head or anything, but Nicole's a lucky woman—she's getting one of the last of the good guys."

Daniel's throat tightened. He and Sharleen had been friends for years and had weathered quite a few storms together. They knew pretty much everything about each other and were as close as brother and sister, although they never really talked about their relationship. Daniel stood and pulled her into his arms for a hug. "Thanks, Shar. That means a lot to me."

She stepped back and nodded. "I mean it. Tell Nicole I said congratulations."

"I will."

Sharleen started for the door, but then she stopped and rested an arm on the top of the cubicle. "Did you ever tell her?"

"Tell who, what?"

"Nicole. Did you ever mention that she had a twin sister and that you re-opened the cold case file on her disappearance a few years ago, trying to find out what happened?"

Daniel shifted his weight from one foot to the other. "No."

Sharleen raised one eyebrow.

"I've thought about it, but I haven't been able to bring myself to do it. I still keep an eye on any reports of missing people, and I know Rick in the Missing Persons Unit follows every lead he can think of, but absolutely nothing new has turned up. After all this time, the possibility of her sister being alive is slim to none. What would it serve to bring up the subject? She'd have to grieve the loss of someone else close to her, and she's done enough grieving the past few years to do her for a lifetime."

Sharleen shook her head. "I know you want to protect her from getting hurt again, Daniel, but that's really not your call. She has a right to know about Ella, and you keeping that from her is a bad way to start off your marriage."

Daniel leaned against his desk. "I know. I don't like keeping secrets from her either. I'm not sure what's the right thing to do."

"Aren't you?"

He shoved both hands through his hair. "All right, I do know the right thing to do. I'll try to broach the subject sometime between now and the wedding. Does that satisfy you?"

She hesitated for a couple of seconds, long enough to let him know she didn't entirely approve of his failure to make a stronger commitment than that, before she shrugged. "Sure. Far be it from me to tell you what to do."

He let a derisive snort stand as a response to that.

She carried on as though she hadn't heard. "In the meantime, let me know if anything comes back from the lab on those things you brought in, and I'll keep thinking about a possible connection between them."

"Great, thanks."

Sharleen nodded. "I really am happy for you, Grey. And Nicole. Let me know if there's anything I can do to help."

"Actually, there is one thing."

"What?"

"You could stand up with me."

"Seriously? You want me to be the best man?"

"We don't have to call it that, but yeah. I mean, it has to be someone I'm close to, and you take up so much of my time I don't really have room in my schedule for much of a social life."

Sharleen smirked. "You seem to be finding a way to carve out the time these days. But yes, of course I'll stand up with you."

"Good. Then I think my part of the preparations is done."

"That sounds about right. Except for maybe planning the honeymoon."

"Oh yeah, the honeymoon. I wasn't thinking about that."

"Sure you weren't."

He grinned.

Sharleen smacked her palms together. "All right, enough chit-chat. Time to get to work. Starbucks?"

Daniel hesitated, although he knew the lab wouldn't get back to him with any results for hours, possibly days. And he really did like the way his partner thought. "Let's go." Grabbing his jacket, he followed her out the door.

Chapter Thirty-Two

"Here you go, Mik. What do you think?" Leigh unrolled the poster she'd tucked under her arm and held it up.

Mikayla looked up from her easel and clapped her hands, tiny drops of paint from the brush she still held scattering like confetti across her jeans. "It's gorgeous! Stu did a fabulous job with it."

She set down the brush and reached for the poster, carrying it over to the window as though it were a breakable object. The thin Chicago winter sun peeked through the glass, bathing the announcement of her first-ever art showing in soft light. Mikayla pressed a hand to her chest. "I can't believe it, Leigh. My own show. I've dreamt about this since I was a kid. If only …"

Leigh's heels clicked on the hardwood floor as she strode over to stand beside her. "I know. You wish your parents could have lived to see this." She rested a hand in the middle of Mikayla's back as she leaned in to study the poster. "I'm so sorry they won't be there, Mik, but a lot of people have already RSVP'd to say they're coming. And the article coming out in *The Tribune* next week should capture a lot more attention. That reporter was almost as enamoured with your work as he was with you, so I'm sure the write-up will be glowing. And of course, Terry and I will be there. We're not quite the same as family, I know, but hopefully close."

Mikayla let go of one corner of the poster and slid an arm around the shoulder of her friend. "Definitely the next best thing." She rested her blond head against Leigh's for a few seconds. "Thanks, Leigh. I appreciate your support so much, and your friendship. I don't know how I would have gotten through this past year without it." She lifted her head and offered her friend a weak smile.

A shadow crossed Leigh's face. Leigh had taken the death of Mikayla's parents almost as hard as Mikayla had. Her agent had accompanied her to every court appearance until the drunk driver that had killed them had finally been sentenced to six months in prison and given a two-thousand-dollar fine.

She'd lashed out at the defendant's lawyer as he'd passed them in the courthouse hall after the verdict had come down. "One thousand dollars—that's the value of a life these days, is it?"

He'd kept his eyes straight ahead, refusing to look at either of them as he pushed doggedly past reporters and through the door. No doubt he'd heard it all, and worse, before.

Mikayla had clutched Leigh's hand and begged her not to say any more. The court had made its decision, and nothing could bring her parents back anyway.

For months she had stared at the empty canvas, not even able to lift the brush, let alone paint bright, vivid pictures full of life. Not until spring had come. Spring, her mother, the avid gardener's, favorite season. Slowly, slowly, the chirping of birds and the damp, earthy smell of buds beginning to open to the warmth of the sun began to penetrate the heavy shroud that had draped itself around her the day she'd heard the news.

And once she had started, once the blackness had lifted slightly, Mikayla hadn't been able to stop. She'd worked diligently, almost feverishly, filling canvas after canvas with bright, bold color. After two weeks of this, Leigh had come by. Mikayla would never forget the look on her face when she stepped into her tiny apartment and her gaze had fallen on the pieces of artwork that filled every available space.

Leigh had stood so still, so uncharacteristically silent, that Mikayla, who had anticipated a strong, loud reaction from her, started toward her, half afraid her friend would drop to the floor before she remembered that she needed to draw a breath.

When she did turn to her, Mikayla's own breath had been swept away at the look of pure joy and wonder on her agent's face. She would never forget that look, or the way it had driven away a little more of the darkness still lurking inside her. For that she would never be able to repay Leigh, although she had tried with a portrait that couldn't fully, but did come close to, capturing the look on her face that day.

That picture, while not for sale, would be the centerpiece of the gallery showing Leigh had immediately secured for her. Mikayla had been assured by all those who had seen her work that this show would firmly establish her as a bright new star among American artists. Two more weeks, and one of her dreams, the one first planted in her heart when her parents had given her a paint and brush set for her sixth birthday, would finally come true.

The other dream—that the ones who had nurtured and encouraged her artistic endeavours until they came to fruition would be there to share in the celebration of them—had died along with her parents in the fiery crash that had taken them from her forever.

Chapter Thirty-Three

"Connie." Nicole closed the door of the apartment above Joe's Diner and leaned in to kiss the papery cheek of her friend. She reached for her hands and held them both in hers, standing back to study her. The weariness around Connie's eyes bothered her. Even though she saw her often, each time her friend seemed older, battle-weary somehow, as though she was done with this life and already preparing herself for the next.

In many ways, Nicole understood. In the days and weeks after Gage's death, the only thought that would crystallize in her head was that she knew where he was, and she knew how to get to him. It would be so easy … Many days it had been a struggle to push back that thought, even after she found out about Jordan. Thankfully, time had done much to heal that gaping wound. After all these years, though, Connie still seemed to miss Joe and long to be with him—even more than she had that terrible night a heart attack had stolen him from her. She was living out her remaining years with a sweet spirit and quiet faith, but she appeared ready to go. Although Nicole knew she would never do anything to speed up the process, she didn't seem to be fighting against the inevitable end either. *I'm still not ready to let you go.* She smiled at her friend. "I've got news."

Connie squeezed her hands. "Come in and let me pour you a cup of tea and we'll sit. From the look on your face it's big news, and I don't take that kind of thing standing very well anymore."

Nicole followed her toward the bright yellow kitchen of the small apartment above the diner. A thin sliver of pain pricked her chest, dimming the smile on her face as she passed through the living room. While she'd gotten used to not seeing Joe at the diner, and had, for the most part, stopped expecting to see him standing at the grill when she pushed through the swinging kitchen doors, her eyes still wandered to the beige easy chair in the corner, the one with the worn patches on the back and seat, every time she came here. And she still felt the sting of grief when she didn't see Joe, sitting there in the light of the tall brass floor lamp, reading one of the western novels he loved so much.

Pushing back her shoulders, she walked over to the white wooden table in front of the window and pulled out a chair, settling onto one of the stuffed yellow-and-white-striped cushions with a contented sigh.

"How's my boy doing?" Connie placed the milk pitcher and the honey on the table in front of Nicole.

"He's great. He got a report card from school this week and the teachers had nothing but positive things to say about his attitude and his performance."

"I'm not surprised. He's a good boy, that one. And he's got a good head on his shoulders. He's going to go far one day."

"As long as he doesn't go far away, I'll be happy."

"I'm sure he won't. For someone who hasn't had a daddy around to show him how, he's got a strong desire to take care of you and be there to help you any way he can."

"That's true, he does." Nicole ran her fingers over the cream-colored crocheted place mat in front of her. "Although I think it has affected him, not having a male role model in his life."

Connie carried the tea pot to the table. "Of course it has, sweetie. But you're doing the best you can, and with God's help, he's turning out real well." She braced both hands on the table as she slowly lowered herself on to a chair with a low groan.

"I know God's been watching over us, and I'm well aware that we couldn't have made it this far without Him but, as you know, I've been seeing Daniel Grey for a few months. He really cares about Jordan and Jord loves him too. I think Daniel could be that role model in his life that he needs so much."

Connie leaned back in her chair, her soft blue eyes twinkling. "Does your big news have something to do with this Daniel Grey then, by any chance?"

Nicole picked up the tea pot and poured a cup for Connie, the soft gurgling sound and the scent of cinnamon and apples soothing her. She inhaled the spicy fragrance as she poured herself a cup and set the pot down. "Daniel Grey *is* my news, Connie. He asked me to marry him."

Connie pressed both palms to her cheeks. "Oh, Nicole." Lowering her hands, she covered the fingers Nicole had clasped on the table with her warm, soft ones. "I'm so happy for you, sweetheart. From what I've seen, and in spite of the rough start the two of you had, Daniel is an extremely good man. I've watched him in the diner and his eyes never leave you as you work. It's brought a deep comfort to my soul to see how much he loves you, and to know that he will be there to take care of you if …"

"If what?"

"If anything happens to me."

"Connie."

"Now, now, none of that." Connie lifted one hand and batted it through the air. "I'm not going to live forever, you know. When Gage died, all I could think was that if I went too, you'd be all alone in the world again, blessed girl. But the good Lord's taken care of that. He sent Jordan along to help heal that broken heart of yours, and now he's blessed you with another good man to fill any remaining empty places in your heart and in your life."

Nicole turned her hands over and grasped both of Connie's, running her thumbs over the raised blue veins criss-crossing the backs of them. "Even with Jordan and Daniel in my life, I'm not nearly ready to let you go yet."

"Well, I'm not planning on leaving tomorrow. But when God calls me, I'm not going to lie to you and tell you I'll mind heading on up to see Him and Joe."

"I know you won't, but I will. You've been my closest friend and the nearest thing to a mother I've known in my life."

Connie tugged her hands free and placed them on Nicole's cheeks. "Now look what we've done. You came here to tell me this happy news and we've gone and gotten all weepy. Enough of that, sweet girl."

"But ..."

Connie let go of her and shook her head emphatically. "I mean it now. This is a wonderful day, and we should be celebrating." She lifted her cup of tea. "To you and Daniel. May God bless you both and give you many, many years together. And may they be every bit as happy as the ones I spent with Joe." She raised her cup higher before lifting it to her mouth to drink.

Pushing back her fear, Nicole raised her own cup before taking a sip of the tea. When she set it on the saucer, the tightness in her throat had eased. "I think we will, you know."

"You will what?"

"Be very happy together. He *is* a good man, and he'll be a wonderful father for Jordan. We're blessed that he's come back into our lives."

"I couldn't agree more. Now reach behind you in that cupboard and bring out the package of chocolate cookies I've been saving for a special occasion. If this doesn't qualify, I don't know what will."

Nicole twisted in her seat to grab the cookies. Knowing the gnarled fingers would struggle with the tight packaging, she slid a nail along the top of the roll and pulled back the plastic before handing them to Connie.

"Thank you, darlin'." Connie tugged a cookie from the package before nudging it toward Nicole. For a few seconds Connie munched contentedly then she set the cookie on her saucer. "So tell me, when is the big day?"

"That's the other news. We wanted to keep it more of a simple day than a big one, so we don't have to wait months for the wedding. In fact ..." she brushed a couple of crumbs off the table with her fingers, "... we've decided to get married in two and a half weeks." She braced herself for shock or surprise to cross Connie's face, but her friend's expression remained placid.

"Did I ever tell you how Joe and I met?"

"No. How?"

"He came to the city in 1952 to train as a soldier at the

school on the Canadian Forces base. We met at a hall one Friday night and got to dancing. When the evening ended, he offered to walk me home, and we walked and talked all night. When we finally arrived at the door of the building where two other girls and I shared an apartment, it was nearly dawn. He kissed me, the sweetest, gentlest kiss I'd ever gotten. In those days of celebrating the end of one big war and staring down the barrel of another one brewing in Korea, kisses were handed out shockingly freely, so that's saying something. When he lifted his head, I looked into his face—strong and kind and filled with laughter—and I fell right in love then and there. He must have felt the same way, because before I left him to go upstairs to my apartment, he asked me if I would marry him the very next day."

Nicole's mouth dropped open. "What? Did you say yes?"

"Of course I did, honey. He'd gotten his orders. He was shipping out to the Korean Peninsula on one of those big destroyers three days later, and I had no idea if I'd ever see him again. I wasn't foolish enough to let a good man like that go without having things settled between us, so the next day we took ourselves off to city hall. We had two wonderful days together before he left, and I didn't see him again for a year. Then he came home with a bullet wound in his right leg. I've never been so happy to see anyone hobbling along on crutches as I was the day he hopped down the steps of that train, as handsome as ever in his uniform. We barely spent a day apart after that for nearly sixty years, until God saw fit to take him along home ahead of me."

"You never regretted marrying him so quickly?"

"Never. Sometimes, when it's so right you know it in your very bones, time holds about as much meaning as a sieve holds water." Connie picked up the tea pot and re-filled Nicole's cup.

Nicole sipped absently. "Thank you for telling me that story. I always knew you and Joe had something special. And I believe Daniel and I have a chance at that very same happiness."

"So do I, honey."

Nicole ran a finger over the rose pattern on the side of the cup. "Connie, I don't have any other parents around to share this day with me, so I was wondering, would you consider giving me away?"

The wrinkles around Connie's mouth deepened. "I'd be honored. You know you're every bit as much a daughter to me and Joe as our flesh and blood would have been if God had seen fit to bless us with children of our own. I'd be delighted to be part of your special day. You know I could never give you to just anyone, but I don't have a second's uneasiness about placing you in Daniel's care. I know he loves you and that he'll always be there for you and for my precious boy."

"I believe he will be too." Warmth spread through Nicole's chest, as real and comforting as the warmth tingling through the fingers wrapped around the delicate china cup.

Chapter Thirty-Four

Daniel scanned the report that had come back from the lab a few minutes earlier. He read it over twice more before leaning back in his seat and driving his fingers through his hair. *This is not good.*

The results confirmed his worst fears. While there wasn't much they could get off the potato, it looked like the same person had dropped the yardstick and the comb off to Nicole, and his—or her—intentions did not appear innocent.

Daniel peered at his watch. Nicole would be getting off work soon. Maybe he'd meet her at the diner and let her know what he'd found out. He shoved his arms into his jacket and stuck his head through the doorway of Sharleen's office. "I'm heading out, Shar. I got the results back from the lab and I want to fill Nicole in on what's going on."

She swung her desk chair around. "What *is* going on?"

He leaned against the door frame. "It doesn't look good. The lab didn't find any prints other than Nicole's or mine on either the yardstick or the comb, so it looks as if they came from the same person, and that, whoever he is, he's trying to cover his tracks."

She pursed her lips. "You're right, that doesn't sound good. What are you going to do about it?"

"There isn't a whole lot I *can* do about it at this point, other than ask her to be careful and pay attention to anything that doesn't seem right, which I've already done."

"And of course you'll be devoting extra time to keeping an eye on her and being around, in case she needs you."

"I took an oath to serve and protect, Shar, and I take that very seriously."

"With certain civilians more than others."

He shrugged. "If I'm going to save the world, I have to start somewhere."

"You're a real hero, Grey."

"That's what I keep telling you."

Sharleen waved a hand toward the door. "Go. All joking aside, Nicole really does need to know about this, and hopefully she won't take it lightly."

"I'll make sure she doesn't. See you later."

Daniel jogged toward the bank of elevators and rode down to the parking garage. His mind whirled. What could they mean, the things someone had sent to Nicole? On the surface, there was no obvious connection. However, he'd learned over the years that connections were rarely obvious, but that it usually only took one small breakthrough for all the pieces to start to fall into place. And of course, there could be more pieces coming …

He jumped into his car and started it, anxious to get to the diner and see for himself that she was all right. A few minutes later, Daniel pulled to the curb around the corner from Joe's, dropped a handful of change into the meter, and went inside.

As usual, the place was filled with families at every table and several older men seated at the bar drinking coffee and chatting like old friends. Which they likely were. Joe's was like that, the same customers came back week after week, sometimes day after day, and the regulars all knew each other and spent most of their time in the restaurant poking their noses into each other's lives and business.

Nicole thrived on it.

Daniel slid into his favorite corner booth and waited for her to see him. When she did, his heart squeezed at the way her face lit up and she came straight over to him.

"Hey, you." She grabbed his white ceramic mug and poured him a cup of coffee. "I wasn't expecting you to come by tonight."

"I know." His fingers brushed hers when she handed him the mug.

"Either you couldn't go another minute without seeing me, or …" The smile faded. "You got the results back."

He nodded. "Do you have a minute to talk or should I wait?"

"Actually, I'm due for a break. I'll let Molly know."

She was back before he could take more than a few sips of coffee. Tightening her ponytail, she dropped onto the red leather bench across from him. "I only have a few minutes."

"This won't take long. I'm sorry to bother you at work, but I wanted to let you know what I found out." He leaned in closer so no one would overhear their conversation. "The results showed that the only fingerprints on the yardstick were yours and mine, and only yours were on the comb."

For a few seconds she contemplated him, and then her eyes darkened. "Whoever left them for me wiped his, or hers, off."

"Looks like it."

"Then it was probably the same person."

"That's what we're thinking. And whoever it is doesn't want us to know who he is, not yet anyway, so it's likely these items are more threatening than they first appeared. If we could figure out a link between them, that might help us to know what he's planning to do next."

Nicole bit her lower lip. "Isn't it possible this is someone playing a joke?"

He hesitated. "It's possible, but it's a pretty elaborate joke, and not one that someone who cares about you would play. It's hard to see any humor in any of it either, which makes it a dud of a joke, if that's what it is." Daniel reached across the table and gripped her arm. "I think we have to assume that whoever is doing this has something more ominous in mind than making you laugh."

"Still, if someone really wanted to scare me, wouldn't he use objects that were creepier than these, like a doll missing a head or something?"

"Not necessarily. Like I said, if we discover a link, or a pattern of some kind, seemingly harmless objects can start to look every bit as creepy as a headless doll. Although a pattern can also be useful as it often acts as a decoder to help us decipher the message the person is trying to send. I don't want to scare you, Nic, but I do want you to take this seriously. In my experience, the harder someone works to send you a message, and the more cryptic that message appears at the outset, the more dire it generally turns out to be when we do figure it out."

"What do you want me to do?"

"Like I told you before, the most important thing is staying alert for anything or anyone that seems strange or not quite right, and of course letting me know the second you sense anything at all unusual. Also, I know you like to keep a regular schedule, but changing that up as much as possible is always a good idea. Being predictable makes you an easy target, and that's the last thing we want you to be."

Nicole tugged her arm from his grasp and clasped her hands in her lap. "I don't want this, Daniel. I don't want to live in fear, looking over my shoulder all the time and jumping at every little sound or moving shadow. I do that enough al—" She broke off, as though she hadn't meant to add that last part, and her gaze shifted away from him.

Daniel frowned. "You've been living in fear? Why?" And how had he not known that? Apparently, he wasn't the only one keeping secrets … He pushed back that thought, trying to stay focused.

She lifted her clasped hands to the table and stared at them. "No, I haven't. At least, not all the time. But ever since Gage …" She closed her eyes for a few seconds then opened them and exhaled. "Since the night Gage was shot, I have struggled with being afraid, off and on. My therapist has helped a lot, and when I feel it starting to grip me I pray and tell myself I'm fine, and it usually subsides. In fact, I thought I was pretty much over it. But the last few months, when I'm out walking alone somewhere, I do sometimes get this creepy feeling that someone is watching me." Her head shot up. "You don't think that's because I actually am being watched, do you?" Her voice had taken on a tinge of hysteria, and Daniel covered her hands with his as he shot a look around the diner. The clamor of kids and conversation appeared to have drowned out her words for everyone else, but he lowered his voice as he leaned in, her fingers trembling beneath his.

"That's what I'm trying to figure out. But Nic, I'm so sorry. I had no idea you've been going through that. I'm not sure why you haven't told me, but that's another conversation. For now, let's talk about this feeling you have sometimes, that someone is watching you. When and where do you experience it usually, can you remember?"

Her eyes closed again, and her forehead wrinkled, as though a thick fog had drifted through her brain on the tail of the hysteria and she was mentally pushing her way through it. After a moment, she opened her eyes and he was relieved to see the anxiety had subsided. "In the park at night, walking down the sidewalk around the diner or near my building, outside Christina and Holden's. Other times I can't remember specifically, but always when I'm away from home."

Which makes her theory not that far-fetched. Daniel's stomach tightened. Who would be watching his fiancée and why? He forced calm into his voice as he squeezed her hands. "I know you don't want to live in fear, and I don't want you to either. But I also don't want anything to happen to you. I'll make you a deal. Don't spend a lot of time worrying or being afraid. Make sure you're aware of what's going on around you and, as often as possible, don't go anywhere alone. And most of all, don't keep anything else from me, all right?"

Hypocrite.

Daniel hid a wince. Was that Sharleen's voice or his own conscience speaking? He couldn't tell anymore—the two tended to blend together in his head. Either way, it was true. He *was* being a hypocrite, and the sooner he could tell Nicole about her sister so there were no more secrets between them, the better.

"I won't."

"Good. And for my part, I'll do everything I can to try to figure this out as quickly as possible so you can go back to living your life without this hanging over your head."

"That sounds good."

"And I may, purely in the interest of your safety, have to spend extra time with you between now and the wedding. Would that be a problem?"

For the first time since he'd started talking, her shoulders relaxed. "If it's in the interest of my safety, I guess I can't refuse."

"Good." Daniel let go of her hands and slumped against the back of the bench, drained. What bothered him more, the fact that she'd been struggling with this for so long, or that she hadn't shared her fears with him? He and Nicole needed to have an even bigger discussion than he'd thought. Maybe not tonight, since she was dealing with enough at the moment, but he couldn't wait much longer. "Can I pick something up to bring over and have for dinner with you and Jordan?"

"He did ask me this morning if we could get pizza today."

"A man after my own heart. How soon can you get away?"

Nicole twisted her wrist to check her watch. "Half an hour or so. I only have two tables left, and they're both almost finished."

"Why don't I go down the street to the pizza place and pick one up then come back here to get you?"

"I have my car."

"I know. I'll walk you out and follow you home."

She sighed. "As happy as I am that we'll be seeing more of you, I'm not thrilled at the reason."

"Me neither, but hopefully we can figure out who it is that's doing this soon and all of this will be over."

Nicole unclasped her hands and reached for one of his. "If I start to complain about all these precautions, you have my permission to remind me how much I appreciate you doing everything you can to keep me safe."

"You got it." He squeezed her hand before letting her go and sliding to the end of the booth. "I'll be back soon." When she nodded, he turned and made his way through the crowded restaurant, looking around with new eyes. Was whoever they were looking for here, even now? He had been, at least once, had possibly even spoken to Nicole, or brushed by her. A shudder moved through him at the thought.

Daniel scanned the restaurant as discreetly as possible, but nothing struck him as out of the ordinary. Even so, he clenched his jaw when he pushed through the door and out into the cold night air. He had to find out who was doing this and soon. Or the next time this guy was in such close proximity to Nicole, the encounter might not be one she would survive.

Chapter Thirty-Five

"Here, Nicole. Someone left this at the back of the church for you."

One of the ushers handed Nicole a small box wrapped in gold and silver paper. A tag with the words *Nicole Kelly* typed neatly across it was taped under a small gold bow on the top of it. Clearly an early wedding present. Or maybe not that early, since the wedding was in two weeks. She smiled at the thought.

"Who's it from, Nic?" Connie set down her Styrofoam cup of tea. The smell of fresh-baked pies permeated the old fellowship hall, where most Sundays they all gathered after the service for coffee and refreshments.

Nicole studied the tag. "I'm not sure. There's no signature." She scanned the hall. Daniel stood on the far side of the room, deep in conversation with the pastor. Her gaze lingered on his face, overwhelmed by the fact that in a few short days they would begin their new life together.

Connie nodded at the box. "Aren't you going to open it?"

"I should probably wait for Daniel, since this is our first present."

"Yes, you probably should."

She sent another glance in his direction. "Oh, who am I kidding? He's going to be talking for ages. I can't wait that long."

Connie settled back in her seat to watch.

Nicole ripped at the paper, not bothering to try and salvage it. The layers peeled back, revealing a small, white box. She tore off the last of the paper and let it drop onto the table before pulling off the lid. A gold watch rested on a bed of soft white padding. Her body went suddenly cold.

"Nicole?" Across the table, Connie leaned forward. "What is

it?"

Nicole didn't answer. She lifted her head and sought out Daniel. As though he could feel her eyes on him, he turned his head and his gaze connected with hers.

He'd been laughing, but he sobered immediately when he saw her. He said something to the pastor, who nodded and gripped his hand. As soon as he let go, Daniel made his way toward her. When he reached her, he slid onto the seat beside her.

"What's wrong?"

She wasn't sure how to tell him without alarming Connie. When she didn't answer, Daniel turned to the older woman. "Connie? What is it, did something happen?"

Connie looked bewildered. "I'm not sure. Someone gave her a wedding present, and as soon as she opened it, she got all upset."

Nicole slid the lid back on the box and cleared her throat. "I'm not upset. It isn't a wedding present after all, it's someone's idea of a joke." She forced herself to smile. "I guess we'll have to wait a few more days to get our first gift."

Connie didn't look convinced, but a friend of hers came up behind her and rested a hand on her shoulder as she leaned in to talk, and her attention was diverted from Nicole and Daniel.

He didn't speak, simply held out his hand for the box.

Nicole set it on his palm. "Remember how you wanted me to tell you when something unusual happened?"

"Yes." His voice was grim.

"I'm pretty sure this qualifies."

Daniel lifted the lid and studied the contents for a few seconds before replacing the lid. "I think you're right." He slid the box into his pocket. "Who gave this to you?"

"Devin Brown." She inclined her head toward a young man sitting a few tables over, eating a piece of pie. "He was ushering this morning, and he said someone left it for me at the back of the church."

"I'll go talk to him and then take a look around the building."

Nicole nodded. "I'll stay here with Connie. I think I scared her with my reaction, and I want to make sure she knows everything's all right."

Daniel rested a hand on her knee. "Stay here in the hall and I'll come back to get you as soon as I'm done." He squeezed her knee and pushed back his chair.

Nicole watched him as he crossed the room and pulled out the chair across from Devin Brown. The two of them chatted for a couple of minutes, but she could tell from the look on his face that Devin didn't know anything. Whoever was doing this was working hard to keep his identity a secret, and she hadn't really expected that he'd walked in and handed the present to someone in the church. When Devin lifted his hands as Daniel rose to his feet, her suspicions were confirmed.

"Nicole?"

She looked across the table. Connie's friend had gone, and Connie was watching Nicole intently, lines of worry creasing her forehead.

"What is it? What was in the box?"

"It was a watch." Nicole worked to keep her voice light. "But it was broken. It must have gotten dropped or something before it reached me. Not a big deal."

Her friend's blue eyes searched hers. The problem with trying to keep something from someone who had lived more than eighty years on the planet was that there wasn't much she hadn't seen during her lifetime. And Connie was more perceptive than most, especially when it came to Nicole. Clearly she could read Nicole's concern on her face, in spite of her attempts to brush the incident off as nothing. Fortunately, Connie also seemed to have learned the trick over the years of not pushing herself on others but waiting for them to come to her when they were ready. The lines on her forehead didn't disappear, although she nodded and didn't pursue the subject.

Daniel was gone for ten minutes. When he came back, he gripped the back of her chair. "We should get going. Are you ready?"

Nicole gathered up her coat and purse. "Do you need a ride,

Connie?”

“No, thank you. A couple of the girls asked me to join them for lunch. They offered to drive me and drop me off afterwards, so I’m fine. You two run along now. Let me know if there’s anything you need, Nicole.”

“I will.” The offer sounded like a casual one, but she knew her friend well enough to understand that it wasn’t.

Daniel touched her shoulder. “I’ll get Jordan.”

Nicole nodded and pulled on her coat as he went to the far side of the room where several kids were playing a game of basketball. By the time she was ready to go, Daniel was walking toward her, his arm around Jordan’s shoulders. In spite of her anxiety, warmth spread through Nicole at the sight.

“Can Alex come over, Mom?” Jordan grabbed her hand. “Please?”

Nicole regarded Daniel over her son’s head. He lifted his shoulders. “Might give us more of a chance to talk. We can drop Alex off when we go to my dad’s later.”

A sudden revelation struck Nicole. She’d never had anyone to consult with before when making decisions about her son. Until, with a few words, he’d put a shoulder under her burden and lifted it from her slightly, she hadn’t even realized what a weight that had been. Nicole brushed a dark curl off Jordan’s forehead. “All right, Son. Go ask him if it’s okay with his mom and dad.”

Jordan ducked around Daniel and took off toward the table where Alex sat with his parents. Nicole watched him as he talked to his friend and the two parents conferred quietly.

“What is it?”

“What is what?”

He circled a hand in front of his face. “That look you have, as though you’re somewhere far away.”

“Watching Alex’s parents discussing the plans for the day, making a decision together, it occurred to me that I’ve never had that with Jordan. It’s always just been me.”

His expression softened. “Well, it’s not just you anymore.”

Nicole smiled. "I think I like that."

He let out a short laugh. "I hope so, because you're stuck with me now."

The corner of the white box stuck out of his pocket and she swallowed. "Did you find out anything?"

He shot a look at Jordan and Alex who were running toward them. "Not really. I'll tell you about it when we get home."

Nicole waved at Alex's parents before the four of them started for the door. Daniel caught her fingers in his and she gripped his hand tightly, the strong sense of safety his presence always gave her making whatever dangers may be lurking outside feel as unsubstantial and ethereal as a summer breeze.

Chapter Thirty-Six

Jordan and Alex shoved the last bites of their grilled cheese sandwiches into their mouths and begged to be excused from the table.

"Dishes, Jord," Nicole reminded him as he scrambled down from his seat and started for the door.

With a heavy sigh, he and Alex returned to the table and grabbed their plates and cups, depositing them into the sink with a clatter before bolting through the French doors.

Nicole shook her head. "Three meals a day for six years. You'd think he'd get it by now."

"I seem to recall my mother still reminding me as late as my teens, so I think you'd better settle in for the long haul."

"Great." Nicole groaned and reached for her plate.

Daniel touched her elbow. "Can we talk for a minute?"

Her chest squeezed at the seriousness in his voice, and she let go of the plate.

"I know I've already warned you to be careful, and there really isn't a lot more you can do than that, but I wanted to repeat the warning. After this morning, I'm more concerned than ever."

"Why?"

"I don't like the fact that this guy has left something at the four places you spend the most time. And I really don't like that he wrapped today's gift in wedding paper, so he obviously knows we're getting married. There's no way he could know all of that unless …"

"He's been watching me recently."

Daniel nodded. "The presentation was also much more formal this time, as though he was making sure no one could mistake this gift for something someone might have simply dropped by mistake. The most disturbing thing to me is that it had your name on it. That means he's not targeting some random stranger, he knows exactly who you are, and he wants you to know that he knows. All of that indicates an escalation in his activity. We are going to have to be especially vigilant now, Nic. I'll spend as much time with you as I can, but you have to promise me you won't walk anywhere alone, and that you'll vary your schedule as much as you possibly can."

Cold shivered over her skin, but she managed to nod.

Daniel rubbed his hands up and down her arms. "It won't help to panic. In fact, it's absolutely critical that you stay calm and alert."

"I'm trying. But I don't have your training for these types of situations."

"I know. That's why I'm going to be around as much as possible. And the good thing about today's gift is that he's given us more to go by now. I have a sense that we're right on the verge of cracking his code and figuring out what he's trying to say. Usually, as soon as that happens, things come together very quickly, and we can bring this to a close."

"Good. I wouldn't want to have to go on like this for long."

"Me neither." His hands stilled on her arms. "Nic, you're shivering. Come here." He pulled her into his arms and rubbed his hands over her back. "We're going to figure this out, I promise. Please don't worry."

She relaxed into his embrace for a moment before she sat up. "I'll try. I definitely don't want to give this guy the satisfaction of thinking he's got me hiding in my house and living in fear."

"Good for you. Cowards like that get off on destroying people's lives through terror. If he sees he can't do that with you, he might lose interest and go find easier prey."

The word *prey* sent fresh chills coursing through her, but Nicole straightened her shoulders. "I wish he would come out of hiding. I'd rather face him than know he's out there somewhere, watching and waiting."

"I'd much rather it be me that faces him than you. Which is why I'll be devoting every spare minute to shadowing you and to figuring out what this guy wants and what his next move is going to be. I'll do everything in my power to keep you and Jordan safe—you know that."

Some of the tension left her muscles. "Yes, I do."

"Good. So tell me what's happening with the wedding plans." Daniel scooped up both their plates and carried them to the sink. "Do you have a dress yet?"

Nicole knew he was trying to take her mind off their conversation, and she appreciated it, but nothing was going to distract her from thinking about the guy who was stalking her, least of all a discussion of dresses and vows and cakes. Not when she knew he might be out there, watching her and possibly plotting to hurt or even kill her for some unfathomable reason.

Her fists clenched as anger knifed through her. Who was this guy, and how dare he terrorize her and her family like this? She'd never done anything to hurt anyone. When she found out …

"Nic?"

She blinked rapidly. "I'm sorry, what?"

"Wow, you were miles away. What was that about?"

"Sorry. Too much on my mind right now. Let's see, a dress. I did find a couple I like, but I haven't bought one yet because I want to get Christina's opinion. She's off on Wednesday, so we're going then."

"Sounds like you have it under control. The big question is, have you given any thought to our honeymoon?"

"You know, I haven't even thought of that. Have you?"

He let out a short laugh. "You do realize guys only put up with the wedding stuff so they can get to the honeymoon part, right?"

Warmth flooded her cheeks as he set down the dishcloth and walked toward her. Nicole swallowed at the look he was giving her, so intense she could almost feel it brushing over her skin. Maybe *something* could distract her.

Capturing her face in his hands, Daniel lowered his head and pressed his lips to her mouth. And for the next few minutes at least, the last thing on her mind was some stranger who may or may not be watching her from the bushes outside.

Chapter Thirty-Seven

Nicole clutched Daniel's hand tightly as they strolled down the hallway to his father's room. Jordan traipsed along beside her, greeting the man and two women who shuffled by pushing walkers. All three smiled and returned his greeting, and one of the women stopped, patted him on the head, and called him a handsome young man.

Nicole grinned and relaxed her grip on Daniel's fingers. Since Gage hadn't had any family but Holden, and she'd never allowed any other relationship with a man to reach this point, today was the first time anyone had ever brought her home to meet his family. What if his dad didn't like her? Daniel was extremely close to his family. Without his father's blessing, would he reconsider marrying her? She swallowed hard. *You're being ridiculous.* Even if she failed to impress the man, Jordan was sure to win him over, the way he did most of the adults he met. Everything would be fine.

Still, when Daniel let go of her so he could rap on the door with his knuckles and push it open, she clutched her bag to her abdomen. The slight warmth and mild aroma of grease wafting from it comforted her as she followed him into the small apartment. "Pop?"

"Come on in." A large man with thick white hair hobbled toward them, leaning heavily on a cane as he crossed the room.

Nicole had seen a picture of him in Daniel's office, years ago, so she already knew that, even in his eighties, Daniel's father was a handsome man. What she hadn't expected was his commanding presence, how thoroughly he took over the tiny space as he came toward them, his free hand outstretched. No wonder he had been such a decorated police officer—criminals must have cowered before him when he stormed onto a scene or strode into an interrogation room.

He stopped in front of them and leaned his cane against the arm of the couch. Nicole let go of her son's hand so Daniel's father could shake the smaller one firmly. "Master Jordan, I presume?"

Jordan's eyes widened slightly, and Nicole bit back a laugh. Her son had likely never heard that salutation before. Clearly Daniel's father was a proponent of old-school manners, which explained why Daniel was such a gentleman.

"It's nice to meet you," Jordan said, solemnly.

Daniel's father nodded. "You too." His face was as serious as Jordan's, although Nicole detected a glint of amusement in his warm blue eyes when he let go of her son. "And this must be the lovely Nicole."

"Yes." Daniel slid an arm around Nicole's waist. "Nicole, this is my father, Philip Grey."

"It's a pleasure, Mr. Grey."

"The pleasure is mine." He reached for his cane. "I've heard so much about—" He stopped and sniffed the air. "Wait. Is that what I think it is?"

Nicole laughed and slid the bag off her shoulder. She set it on the coffee table and reached inside to extract a brown paper bag. "Burgers from my diner, Joe's."

"And fries?" The older man looked so hopeful Nicole couldn't help laughing. "Yes, and fries. Neither as amazing as Joe used to make, but still pretty good."

Daniel's father shifted his gaze to his son. "This one's a keeper, Son."

"Way ahead of you, Pop." Daniel lifted Nicole's left hand. The ring he had given her sparkled in the light of the chandelier hanging in the center of the room. "Remarkably, she said yes."

"Well, well." Mr. Grey hung his cane over his arm and clapped his hands. "This calls for a celebratory dinner. Why don't you take Jordan into the kitchen and set the table? Maybe mix up a salad to go with the burgers in case the health police drop in while we're eating."

Nicole raised an eyebrow. "Health police?"

Daniel grinned. "They're pretty strict about what the residents eat here. I'm surprised no one stopped us on the way in to confiscate those burgers." He clapped a hand on Jordan's shoulder. "Looks like we're on kitchen duty, buddy."

Nicole watched as Daniel guided her son into the next room, her heart squeezing a little, like it always did when she saw the two of them together.

"Looks like my boy has lost his heart."

A smile touched Nicole's lips at Philip Grey's words. "He's amazing with Jordan."

His face softened. "I can see that, but I wasn't talking about Jordan."

"Oh." The tips of her ears warmed. A framed picture on a bookshelf caught her eye, and she wandered over. A couple stood, entwined in each other's arms, in the middle of a dance floor. A large crowd surrounded them, but clearly the man and woman had eyes only for each other.

The shuffling, thudding sound of feet and cane grew louder as Daniel's father came up to stand beside her. "That's my wife Cara and I on our fortieth anniversary." He ran a finger across the top of the frame, as though brushing away invisible specks of dust. "She's been gone nine years. Still miss her every day."

Nicole's throat tightened. "Of course you do. Judging from this picture, you'd lost your heart too."

"On day one." His arm dropped to his side. "Of course, it wasn't always easy. Although Cara was a woman of incredible faith, it bothered her a little every time I headed out for a shift."

"I'll bet it was tough, being married to a cop." Nicole studied the woman's face. Years of worrying hadn't left a mark on her smooth skin. "But you made it through okay, right?"

He tapped his left knee with the cane. "Took one here that forced me into retirement, but otherwise, yeah, the good Lord watched over me."

Nicole pressed a hand to her heart. It thudded hard against

her palm. "You were shot?"

"Yep." He sounded vaguely proud of that fact.

"What happened?"

"Drug bust. We thought we'd cleared the house, and I was about to holster my weapon when this kid bursts out of a closet firing. My partner and I dove behind the bed. He was fine. I was about two seconds too slow." Mr. Grey reached for the photo and lifted it closer to his face. "Cara didn't love what I did, but she loved me, and she loved God. If she hadn't, and I mean with everything she had in her, she might not have stuck it out. Lots of spouses don't."

He's warning me. "I—"

"Lunch is ready." Her son's enthusiastic announcement cut her off.

Daniel's dad held out his arm. "Shall we?"

She slid her hand through the crook of his elbow. "We'd better. As good as our food is hot, it's not very appealing when it cools off."

His eyes twinkled. "Let's get to it then."

Daniel turned the key to start the car. The visit with his dad had gone well, but he was interested to hear what Nicole thought of him.

"Your dad is great." Nicole fastened her seatbelt.

Daniel glanced over his shoulder to make sure Jordan was buckled in before he put the car into reverse and backed out of the parking spot. "I'm glad you think so. From the smile on his face the whole time we were there, I'd say he was taken with the two of you as well."

"I'm pretty sure that was about the burgers."

Daniel chuckled. "That could be true. If you were trying to win him over, I'd say the bag of greasy food did it." He steered up the ramp and merged onto the highway. Traffic was heavy, and they were both quiet for a few minutes as he maneuvered around a slow-moving truck and then changed lanes to get out of the way of a red Corvette, its driver clearly not concerned by anything as pesky as the speed limit. Daniel frowned, but there wasn't much he could do about it.

"I'm sorry your sister and brother-in-law weren't able to make it."

"Me too. They're dying to meet you and Jordan, but Becca thought showing up with three kids covered in chicken pox—or chicken pops, as their son Josh calls them—might not make the best first impression."

"I hope they'll be able to come to the wedding."

"Ava's had them for a week, and she's the last one to get them, so they should be fine by then."

"Good." Nicole scratched at a small spot on her jeans. "Your mother was a beautiful woman."

Daniel shot her a sideways glance as he exited the highway. "Where did that come from?"

"When you and Jordan went to get supper ready, I saw the photo of your parents dancing at their fortieth anniversary party."

"Ah." A wistful sadness drifted like mist through his chest.

"You still miss her."

"Yes, I do."

"Your dad told me he does too, every day. He also mentioned that it was hard for her sometimes, him being a cop."

Daniel winced. "I wish he hadn't."

"He was trying to prepare me, I think. For how difficult it might be."

He let go of the steering wheel with one hand and squeezed her knee. "They never let it get in the way of their happiness."

Nicole checked the back seat. In the rear-view mirror, Daniel could see Jordan, his little chin bobbing against his chest every time Daniel hit a bump in the road. She leaned closer and lowered her voice. "Not even when he was shot?"

So he'd told her that too. What was his dad trying to do, scare her away? The burger and fries churned a little in Daniel's gut. "You two had quite the conversation. I didn't realize it had taken us that long to make the salad."

She didn't answer. After a few seconds, Daniel blew out a

breath. "I should have told you about it. I'm sorry."

"Why didn't you?"

"I didn't want to freak you out, I guess." He signaled before turning into Nicole's parking lot. Neither of them spoke until he pulled into her space and killed the engine. Then she shifted in her seat to face him.

"The one thing I can't take is you keeping something from me. Even if you think you might freak me out or hurt me or scare me, I need to know that you will always be honest with me, okay?"

Tell her. Only thirteen more days until their wedding. Lately he'd become acutely aware of every minute that passed, as though a giant pendulum swung in his mind. Daniel reached for her hand. "Nic, I do need—"

"Mom?" Jordan stirred in his booster seat and yawned. "Are we home?"

"We are, but give us a minute, okay? Daniel and I were discussing something."

He couldn't bring it up in front of Jordan. Daniel shook his head. "It's fine. We can talk tomorrow."

"All right. Dinner at my place? Jordan is having a sleepover at Connie's."

"Sounds good. Want help getting him inside?"

"No, you go. You're on the early shift in the morning and need sleep." She kissed him lightly. "Sleep well."

"You too." Somehow he doubted it, though, with their pending conversation on his mind.

Nicole helped Jordan out of his seat. Daniel watched until they had crossed the parking lot and disappeared through the double front doors of their building. Tomorrow night. Twenty-four hours from now she would know he had kept a secret from her for seven long years. How would she react? Given what she'd just told him, she was not going to be happy. He had no choice, though. He had to tell her and then pray that she would understand why it had taken him so long.

The pendulum swung in his mind. Tick tock. Tick tock.

Chapter Thirty-Eight

Daniel slid behind the wheel of the car and settled the bottle into the holder between the front seats. After four cups of coffee, his usual Monday morning jump start, he'd gotten a little jittery and decided it might be good to switch over to water. The radio crackled to life and Sharleen, who'd been fastening her seatbelt, paused as they both turned toward it.

"All units. Robbery in progress, Dundas and Yonge. Suspect fleeing on foot."

Daniel leaned forward to peer out at the street sign on the corner ahead of them. "Dundas and Yonge? That's—"

"There!" Sharleen pointed with her left hand as she yanked open her car door.

A guy in baggy jeans and a black wool hat raced down the sidewalk across the street from them, knocking people out of his way as he ran.

Daniel leapt from the car and into the street, holding up his badge to stop the traffic coming in both directions. He and Sharleen splashed through the slush lining the curb to leap onto the far sidewalk and sprint after the suspect. When the guy crashed into a grocery cart being pushed by an old lady in a man's long brown coat and fell onto the sidewalk, Daniel closed the space between them, Sharleen right on his heels. They kicked their way through the plastic bottles and cans, ignoring the indignant protests and arm-waving of the old woman as the suspect scrambled to his feet and took off again.

"Stop. Police!" Daniel shouted out a warning, but the guy in the black hat whipped around a corner and headed into an alley. Everything in Daniel screamed at him to follow, but he'd made that mistake before and paid for it. He and Sharleen stopped at the edge of the last building before the alleyway. He held up a hand and peered cautiously around the corner to his left. A ten-foot-tall chain-link fence cordoned off the end of the alley. Dumpsters lined the brick walls on either side. The suspect was nowhere in sight.

Daniel pulled back. "I don't see him. He must have ducked behind a dumpster. There's a fence at the back and I want to make sure he doesn't climb it. Did you see if he had a weapon?"

She shook her head. "No."

"Call for back-up. I'll keep an eye on him."

Daniel leaned around the corner again, a little farther this time, straining to hear any sounds. Behind him, Sharleen called for assistance. Suddenly the sound of gunshots peppered the air. He ducked back around the corner and pressed against the brick wall as he reached inside his jacket and grabbed the Glock strapped to his chest. "I guess that answers that question."

When the sounds stopped, he carefully peered around again. The suspect was sprinting for the fence.

"He's making a break. I'm going in."

"Careful, Grey."

He nodded and lunged into the opening of the alley. Adrenaline pumped through his system as he sprinted for the nearest dumpster. When he peered around it, the suspect had reached the bottom of the fence and grasped the metal with both hands. Judging by the speed he'd hit it at, it would only take him a few seconds to make it up and over. Daniel started running. The man had shoved his gun into the pocket of his black hoodie. Daniel could see the butt of it hanging out, so he didn't bother with cover as he charged toward him.

"Police. Freeze!" He yelled the warning again. The man kept climbing. Daniel stopped, planted his feet, and lowered his weapon, taking careful aim. The suspect was almost at the top of the fence. If he missed, the guy would be off and running and the chances of him being picked up would be drastically reduced. He squeezed the trigger. The bullet caught the man in the calf. He yelped and fell back onto the cement.

"Stay down!" His weapon straight out in front of him, Daniel advanced toward him slowly.

The suspect clutched his leg but didn't reach for the gun in his pocket.

"Hands where I can see them."

Sprawling onto his back, the guy lifted both hands, covered in blood, over his head. Now that he was closer, Daniel could see that he was a kid, maybe sixteen or seventeen. The eyes that met his were almost all whites. Daniel's senses went on high alert. A terrified suspect could go one of two ways—into a state of over-compliance where he couldn't do what he was asked to fast enough, or he could lose it completely and figure that if he was going down, he was taking as many people with him as possible.

Thankfully, this one went compliant. He didn't move as Daniel closed in and yanked the gun from his pocket.

Daniel kept his Glock trained on him as Sharleen strode around behind the kid, reached into his other pocket, and grabbed a wad of cash that she stuck into her own coat pocket.

"Sit up."

The kid rolled onto his side and struggled to a sitting position. She read him his rights and pulled the handcuffs from her belt, snapping them on his wrists before moving around to check out his leg.

Daniel lowered his weapon as she pulled the blue scarf from around her neck.

"He shot me." The suspect's voice shook.

"Yeah, I gathered that." Sharleen wrapped the scarf around his calf. The kid let out a string of curse words that she ignored as she pulled it tight. "You'll be fine."

"What did you have to shoot me for?"

He was going from terrified to belligerent fast. Daniel tightened the grip on his gun. "You didn't stop when I told you to. Bad things happen when you do stupid stuff like that."

"Yeah, didn't your mama ever teach you to do what you're told?"

Daniel watched the kid's face, interested in his reaction. Sharleen often made a point of asking a question like that, and it almost always elicited a strong response from the perpetrator. Either his features would twist in hatred or bitterness, which shed a lot of light on what was happening, or they'd soften with a gut-wrenching remorse that saddened Daniel, knowing that, if the mother of whoever it was in his custody was still alive, she was about to get a phone call that would break her heart.

The kid's face softened for a few seconds before his jaw tightened and he swung back toward Daniel, his eyes flashing fire. Whatever he'd been about to say died on his lips, though, as the color drained from his face.

Sharleen must have taken in his reaction, because she spun around on her heels to examine Daniel. A grim look crossed her face. "Dang it, Grey. You've been hit too. Now I'll be stuck doing paperwork for the rest of the day." The slight tremor in her voice belied the impatient-sounding words.

Daniel glanced down. Crimson seeped through the shoulder of his jacket. The last bit of adrenaline left his body as the pain slammed into him like a fist.

Sharleen pointed a finger at the kid on the ground. "Stay put." She strode over to Daniel. "Let me see."

He winced as she slid the jacket off his left shoulder. "I'm good." He waved his right hand through the air, his gaze still locked on the suspect. "Let's get this guy taken care of." Daniel took a step backwards, his legs feeling suddenly weak.

"Oh yeah, you're perfectly fine." Sharleen moved to his side and took his arm. "Here, sit down for a minute." She directed him back a couple of steps to a beige plastic garbage can.

Daniel wanted to protest, to insist they stay with the kid, but his head was starting to feel fuzzy and he couldn't seem to form the words. He glanced down again. *Man, that's a lot of blood. Nicole is not going to be happy about this.* He felt the garbage can against the back of his legs and sank down on it.

Sharleen shot a look at the suspect and then back down the

alley. "Where are those guys?"

"I think we should suggest that, in the future, every ES person in the city should maybe not take their lunch break at the same time. What do you think?"

Her smile was tight. "It does seem like that."

Daniel rubbed his eyes with the thumb and forefinger of his good hand before attempting to focus on the kid. If he was going to try anything, this would be a good time. Fortunately, that threat appeared low. All the fight seemed to have left him when he realized he'd shot a cop, and he sat, slumped against a dumpster, his head hanging down.

Daniel pursed his lips as a new thought occurred to him. A few bad choices into the future and the kid on the ground could be Jordan. He'd have to make sure he spent a lot of time with Nicole's son, doing all the things Jordan had asked him to do with him. Mothers were great, and most single mothers bordered on saints, shouldering the load they had to all alone. But, as he well knew, the prisons were packed full of men with great mothers and no positive male role model in their lives.

He'd rested his head against the brick wall behind him, but he lifted it when he heard the sound of sirens in the distance.

"Finally," Sharleen muttered.

Daniel looked down and realized she had folded up his shirt to cover the wound in his shoulder and had pressed her hand against it in an attempt to staunch the flow of blood. An ambulance screeched to a halt halfway into the alley, and two EMTs jumped out of the vehicle, unloaded a stretcher, and came toward them at a jog. They headed for Daniel first, but he waved them off. "Take care of the kid."

"Stay with me, Grey."

He hadn't realized he'd started to drift off until her words yanked him back. While they worked on the suspect, peeling off Sharleen's scarf and bandaging up his calf before lifting him onto the stretcher, Daniel attempted to focus on the dark eyes that searched his face. "Don't tell Nicole."

Sharleen snorted a laugh. "I can not tell her all you want, but I think she might guess when she sees the hole in your shoulder, or you lying in a hospital bed, or the headlines on TV tonight." She inclined her head back toward the opening of the alley. A news truck had pulled in, and as he watched, a cameraman jumped out the side door.

Daniel grimaced. "All right, call her, but downplay it for me, would you? She's already had one man in her life gunned down in the street—this is really going to freak her out."

"I'll do what I can."

Another ambulance pulled in behind the news truck. Sharleen stepped back as two more paramedics hopped out and hurried toward them. A police car squealed up to the scene and she jerked her head toward it. "I'll go talk to them, fill them in on what happened."

Daniel grabbed her hand. It was slippery with blood, his blood. His stomach lurched. "Thanks, Shar."

"You're welcome." She squeezed his fingers before letting go and striding over to meet the two cops walking toward them.

The three of them appeared to be moving through a swirling mist. Daniel squinted as he attempted a glance at the sky. Could it be getting dark already?

"Can you walk to the stretcher?" One of the paramedics, a tall muscular guy with short, blond hair, gripped his left elbow.

Daniel forced himself to his feet and nodded, then wished he hadn't as the world suddenly tilted beneath him.

He didn't like that he needed it, but he couldn't help appreciating the strong hand under his elbow as he stumbled toward the stretcher. When he reached it, he sat down and gingerly swung his legs over the edge, pain stabbing through his shoulder as the paramedic lowered him down with both hands under his back.

They raised the stretcher carefully. Daniel braced himself, but they were clearly used to working in the city and managed to maneuver around the boxes and wind-blown garbage lying on the ground without jostling him too much, for which he was extremely grateful. After sliding him into the back of the ambulance, one of the attendants hopped in with him. Seconds before the other one slammed the doors after them, Daniel caught a glimpse of Sharleen's face, looking uncharacteristically anxious. Then they were moving, and he closed his eyes and with everything he had, he fought the darkness that threatened to overtake him.

Chapter Thirty-Nine

"Did you call her?"

Sharleen hesitated. "Yes. She's on her way." She pulled an extra pillow off the shelf near the bed and stuck it behind him. "Here you go."

Daniel winced as he leaned forward slightly, the arm the doctor had secured in a tight sling aching. His sister Becca, who had been substitute teaching at a school downtown and flew into his hospital room minutes after Sharleen called her, adjusted the pillows on the other side of him. Daniel settled back against them, his eyes searching out his partner's. The fact that she was working hard to avoid meeting his was not a good sign. "What aren't you telling me?"

"Nothing."

"Shar."

She sighed and sank down on the chair beside his bed. "You were right."

"About Nicole?"

"Yes."

He contemplated her. "She freaked out."

"Not exactly, which is what was so disturbing about it."

"It's been a long day, Shar, not really in the mood to pull teeth."

"Sorry. The thing is, she sounded really calm, but something crept into her voice, like tightly reined in hysteria. I had to admire her composure, but at the same time, the juxtaposition between that and the terror reminded me of when they use sweet, innocent kids in horror movies and make their heads spin. It kind of freaked *me* out, to be honest."

Daniel blew out his breath. "Did you tell her there was no

major damage and I'm fine?"

"I tried to. Not sure how much of that she heard. And her definition of major damage may be a little different than yours."

"Well, thanks for trying. Hopefully when she gets here and sees for herself that it's not a big deal, she'll calm down."

"I'm sure she will." Her tone of voice did nothing to reassure him as she sat down on the chair beside his bed.

Becca slid to the edge of a green leather chair she'd pulled up to the other side of the bed. "When are they springing you?"

"I tried to talk them into letting me go home since the bullet went in and out cleanly, but they said I lost a lot of blood, so they want to keep me overnight. I should be out of here first thing in the morning."

"That's good."

Her voice shook a little, and Daniel reached over and grasped her arm. "I'm fine, Bec."

She drew in a shuddering breath. "I know. But when you have a dad and then a brother who's a cop and a husband who is a firefighter, the sound of a phone ringing is a bit of a trigger. Today reminded me why."

"I'm sorry."

She managed a wan smile. "Don't be. I'm proud of you all."

Daniel pulled back his arm. "Speaking of Austin, is he with the kids?"

Becca shook her head, her long, dark ponytail swishing against her back. "No, they're at the baby-sitter's." She glanced at her watch. "I'll call him, see if he can leave work early and pick them up."

"No, don't." Daniel started to sit up but changed his mind quickly and sagged against the pillows. "You go. There's nothing you can do here. Nicole is on her way and I'm going to sleep soon anyway."

His sister shot a look at the door. "I think I'll stay a few more minutes. I can't believe that, other than brushing by her in the stairwell outside your apartment that one time, I haven't met this amazing woman who finally convinced you to settle down."

Daniel grinned. "For the record, I convinced her. It required absolutely no convincing on my part."

"Even so, I've been dying to have you two over, but six straight weeks of one child or another down with chicken pox kind of wiped out those plans. And me."

"I'll bet. Everyone's good now though?"

"Yes, finally. We'll all be at the wedding, but it would be nice to meet my future sister-in-law before then."

Sharleen slid on her coat. "Well, I've met her, so I think I'll head home, see how Tom and the kids are doing."

"Give my girls a hug for me." Daniel pointed at his shoulder with his good hand. "Might be a while before I can do it myself."

"I will." Sharleen reached for the door knob. "You get some rest. I need my partner back ASAP."

A soft knock sounded at the door.

A look of sympathy crossed Sharleen's face. "That's probably Nicole. Good luck."

Daniel grimaced. "Thanks."

She pulled the door open. "Nicole, hi." Sharleen stepped back to allow Nicole into the room. His partner touched Nicole's arm. "He's fine. They're letting him go home in the morning."

Nicole's smile was barely discernible and didn't get anywhere close to her eyes. "Good. Thanks."

Sharleen looked over at him. "I'll talk to you tomorrow."

Daniel nodded, his eyes not leaving Nicole's face. She waited until the door had shut behind Sharleen before lifting her chin. "Are you really all right? And please don't lie to me."

Oh boy. Sharleen was right. Anger and fear and concern twisted through her voice like three strands of rope. *Not easily broken.* He repressed a sigh. The concern he could live with— even appreciate—but the other two had to go.

"She's telling you the truth Nic, I'm fine. It's a clean wound. It'll leave a scar, but otherwise ..."

It was no use. He could read it on her face. She knew he wasn't going to die. Beyond that, apparently all that would register was that he could have.

"Nicole?" Becca stood up.

Nicole's gaze shifted to her and she blinked as though only now realizing there was someone else in the room. "Rebecca?"

His sister came around the end of the bed and threw her arms around Nicole. After a brief hesitation, Nicole returned the hug. Over Becca's shoulder, her eyes met Daniel's. The sight of her face, pale and drawn, gouged his chest like fingernails. His sister stepped back and held her at arm's length. "I'm sorry about the circumstances, but I'm so happy to see you, Nicole."

Nicole ran the side of a shaking hand across her forehead. "I'm sorry too. Definitely not how I wanted us to meet."

Becca smiled and let go of her. "We'll have lots of time to get to know each other better. For now, I'm going to leave the two of you alone."

"You don't have to go."

"I do, actually. I need to pick the kids up from the sitter." Becca walked back to Daniel's side and rested a hand on his good shoulder. "Do what the doctor tells you, please. I want to see you strong and healthy at the wedding."

"I will. Say hi to Austin and the kids for me."

"All right." She squeezed his shoulder and turned back to Nicole. "Take good care of him."

Nicole nodded but didn't speak. Becca touched her elbow as she passed her and then disappeared out the door, closing it behind her. When Nicole didn't move, Daniel gestured toward the chair beside his bed with his good arm. "Would you sit down, please?"

She walked woodenly over and perched on the edge of the chair, her fingers clasped in her lap. "What happened?"

"Sharleen and I chased a suspect into an alley. We followed protocol and waited at the opening, but I did check around the corner every few seconds. When he made a break for it, he got off a few wild shots, likely trying to provide cover for himself. We ducked back and waited until the firing stopped, then I ran a few steps into the alley. He was headed for the fence and I yelled at him to stop, but he kept going, so I shot him in the leg. At no point did I really feel we were in danger. I didn't even realize one of his wild shots had caught me in the shoulder until Sharleen calmly pointed it out. Scared the suspect more than it scared me, to be honest. He went white as a sheet when he saw the ... that I'd been hit. He was only a kid and suddenly realized he was looking at a whole lot more time than he'd thought. I actually felt sorry for him."

"I thought ..." Her voice broke and she dropped her gaze to her hands. "I thought the risk would be lower for you since you're a detective and not in uniform anymore."

He measured his words carefully. "It likely is. I'm definitely not in the direct line of fire as often. Today was an exception since Sharleen and I were the only cops in the vicinity when the call came through."

Daniel reached over and tugged her hands loose, pulling one of them into his grasp. He forced himself to not let the pain that shot through him at the movement show on his face. Her hand was ice cold, and he ran his thumb in circles over the back of it. "Normally, I'm probably not in much more danger than any civilian who walks down the street at night. Anyone can get shot, even sitting in their homes sometimes. Thankfully it doesn't happen all that often in Canada, but it does happen. There are no guarantees, for any of us."

"I suppose not."

"But Nic ..." He lifted their hands, pressing his palm to hers and linking their fingers. "If the worst did happen, I'm ready to go. You know that."

"But I'm not ready to let you." The words were soft but woven through with steel and a hint of bitterness that tightened his muscles.

Daniel rubbed his thumb over the diamond ring on her finger, silently pleading with her to remember how she'd felt when he gave it to her. "You said yourself that mentally unstable people come into the diner sometimes; something could easily happen to you too, especially since ..."

"Someone might be threatening me."

"Yeah." A cold shudder he couldn't repress moved through him.

"It's not a pleasant thought, is it?"

"No, it's definitely not, so I do understand how you feel. The thing is, we can't let fear and uncertainty rob our lives of joy. We have to be wise, of course, and careful, but after that we have to put each other in God's hands and let go. He's the one who brought us together—we have to trust that He is watching over us."

The tightness around her lips eased, releasing some of the corresponding tightness in his chest. "I guess you're right."

"I am. Trust me on this, okay?"

"I'll try."

With the relief came a renewed awareness of the throbbing pain in his shoulder. Daniel let go of her hand and patted the bed. "Come sit with me?"

She glanced toward the door. "I don't know if I should. What if someone comes in to check on you?"

"What if they do? We're not doing anything wrong." Daniel did his best to look pathetic. "Come on, Nic. I've been through a terrifying ordeal. I stared death in the face today. My entire life passed before my eyes. Can you really be heartless enough to deny me a little comfort?"

She started to laugh but bit her lip to hold it back as she rolled her eyes. "What happened to 'at no point did I feel I was in danger and I didn't even realize I'd been shot?'"

"That *was* the truth, but as soon as I finished giving you that version, I realized it might not get me a whole lot of sympathy or TLC, so I thought I'd attempt to put a different spin on what happened."

"First of all, I always prefer to get the true, completely unspun version. And second of all, seeing as how, of the two of us, I seem to be the only one at all worried about what happened to you, I believe *I* should be the one getting comfort and TLC."

He held out his right arm. "Me comforting you, you comforting me, I don't care what you call it. Either way, all I want is to hold you in my arms. Or arm, anyway."

Nicole sent another look toward the door then, shaking her head, rose to her feet. She took off her coat and draped it over the chair then straightened her blue shirt. Kicking off her winter boots, she climbed up on the bed beside him.

Daniel watched her, suddenly as aware as she was that he might never have seen her again. The pain that thought carried struck him harder than the pain in his shoulder had earlier. "I was wrong about that shirt."

She tilted her head and her soft blond hair spilled over one shoulder. "What do you mean?"

"That you look every bit as beautiful in it as the green one."

She pressed her lips together as though she was trying not to smile. "Don't say things like that. I'm still mad at you."

"Anything I can do to help with that?"

"Yes. Promise me you'll be careful. I can't ..." Her voice broke.

He nodded, relieved that she had asked him something he *could* promise her. "I know. And I will." He wrapped his arm around her and pulled her down until her head rested against his chest. "Where's Jordan?"

"I dropped him off at Connie's to spend the night shortly before Sharleen called me." She moved closer, getting comfortable, and he sucked in a quick breath.

"I'm sorry." Nicole lifted her head. "Didn't they give you something for the pain?"

"They offered it, but I didn't want to take anything before I saw you."

"Why don't you call someone now and ask for it?"

He shook his head, wanting to be awake and alert enough to enjoy the warmth of her against him, the assurance that, while she'd been deeply rocked by what had happened to him, and part of her continued to hold back from him a little, she was still there. And so was he, alive—thanks to a few inches and the grace of God—and holding the woman he loved. "I'm fine."

Nicole studied his face, the look in her eyes telling him he wasn't fooling her. "How about this? While I'm sure a big strong man like you can handle the pain of having a bullet tear through your shoulder, *I* would feel better if you'd take something. So, given what you put me through in the last hour, would you do it for me, as a personal favor?"

"I suppose, if it means that much to you, I could take a little something."

The corners of her lips twitched as she reached for the call button on the side of the bed. "I appreciate it." She hit the button and started to get up, but he tightened his grip on her.

"You're fine where you are."

"But …"

"Nic." He pressed his lips to the top of her head. "Any nurse worth her salt will know that you are the best possible medicine for me. It'll be fine." He ran his hand up and down her arm until she relaxed against him again.

The door swung open and a young nurse with a long brown ponytail and pale peach uniform bounced into the room, clutching an IV bag as if she had been waiting for his call. "Ready for your pain medication?"

"Yes, thanks."

The nurse hung the bag on the hook on the IV pole beside his bed, slid the needle expertly into the back of his hand, and taped it down. "There you go." She rested a hand on the elbow secured in the sling. "You'll feel better in a few minutes. You should get some sleep though."

The words were pointed, and although the woman had barely glanced at Nicole, she clearly didn't approve of the fact that she was there. He ignored the inference.

"Given what you're dumping into me at the moment, I doubt I have a choice. But thank you."

The nurse nodded. "Thank *you*. And feel free to call me if there's anything at all that you need." She pointed to her name tag. "It's Stephanie, and I'll be here until eleven o'clock tonight."

"I will, thanks." When the door closed behind her, Daniel looked down at Nicole. She was studying him, both eyebrows raised. "What?"

"You're actually enjoying this, aren't you?"

"No, of course not."

She waved her hand in a circle in front of him. "This whole thing is some kind of badge of honor for you guys, isn't it?"

There was no good answer to that, so Daniel kept his mouth shut.

"That's what I thought. You have the same look on your face your dad did when he told me about getting shot in the knee. You're both proud of yourselves and this elite club you belong to now. Unbelievable. And don't give me that pathetic puppy dog face. You've clearly already been getting plenty of TLC today."

Daniel laughed. "I have no idea what you're talking about. There's only one woman in the world I want to get TLC from, even when she's being ridiculous." He shifted slightly so he could see her better. "Believe it or not, some people consider a cop taking a bullet while bringing down a dangerous criminal heroic. She was merely expressing her appreciation for my efforts."

"Sure she was."

He lifted his hand to stroke her hair. "Will you stay with me?"

"I think I better. Won't they kick me out at some point though?"

"Oh no, we heroes tend to get special treatment, so I think we're good."

"Not entirely convinced it's your heroism she's attracted to. She couldn't take her eyes off you. I'm not sure I've ever felt so completely invisible in my life."

"Well, *I* see you." His face grew serious. "Can that be enough for you for tonight?"

The smirk faded from her face as her eyes locked with his. "It can be enough for me for the rest of my life."

Fog drifted through his mind in pastel-colored, cotton-candy wisps. Nicole's words came to him in slow motion, as though she was talking under water, as the pain in his shoulder slowly receded. The words he wanted to say in response floated off like a balloon tugged from the chubby fingers of a toddler by a sudden gust of wind. Daniel gave up trying to speak and allowed the effects of the medication to carry him away too.

Chapter Forty

Nicole pushed open the door of the dressing room and stepped out. Christina pressed the fingers of both hands to her mouth. "Nic, you look gorgeous! That is definitely the one."

Nicole faced the floor-length mirror and smoothed down the front of the blue gown, so pale it was almost white. *Who is that woman?* "I think so too."

"Daniel isn't going to know what hit him when he sees you come down the aisle in that."

Her cheeks warmed. She hadn't walked down the aisle to Gage, as they had gotten married in a small room behind the sanctuary. The thought of that moment, Daniel standing at the front of the church watching her as she passed by the small gathering of friends and family in the pews, sent a ripple of anticipation through her.

Nicole tucked a strand of hair behind her ear. "Do you think I should wear a veil of any kind? I feel a little silly since this isn't my first marriage, but maybe it's—"

Her sister-in-law gasped softly behind her and Nicole whirled around. Christina's face had gone pale and her hand cupped her rounded belly. "Chris? What is it? Is something wrong?"

Christina blew out a few short breaths. "I don't think so. But I do need to sit down."

"Here." Nicole grasped her elbow and guided her to a plush armchair in the corner of the bridal shop. Her hand on her friend's shoulder, she looked up and caught the eye of a saleswoman across the room. "Could we get a glass of water, please?"

The woman shot a look at Christina then nodded and

scurried through a curtained opening at the back of the shop. Nicole crouched down and rested her hands on her friend's knees. "What is it, Chris?"

"I don't think it's anything serious, but I've been getting these weird pains lately." She rubbed her stomach. "I think it's the little one shifting around or something. Catches me off-guard sometimes."

Nicole frowned. "So it happens often?"

"Not often. Every once in a while."

"Should I take you to the hospital?"

Christina shook her head. "No, I'm fine now. I have a doctor's appointment tomorrow and I'll mention it to her."

The saleswoman arrived with a glass of water, and Christina accepted it from her and took a sip. "Thank you."

Nicole studied her. The lines around her sister-in-law's mouth were still tight, but color was slowly seeping back into her cheeks.

"Here." The saleswoman dragged another chair over and maneuvered it into place beside Christina's.

Nicole straightened and sank down on it. "Thanks so much." She offered the woman a grateful smile.

"Do you want me to call an ambulance?"

"No, thanks. She says she's fine. Baby's being a little rambunctious today."

"All right." The woman didn't sound too sure. Nicole wasn't too sure herself, but she couldn't force Christina to do anything. "Please let me know if there is anything you need."

"We will."

The woman nodded before strolling over to another woman in a business suit rifling through a rack of dresses. Nicole laid her hand on Christina's leg. "Feeling better?"

"Yes, thanks." She ran her finger around the rim of the glass. "I never told you this, Nic, but I've been pregnant before."

Nicole's eyes widened. "You have?"

"Yes, twice in the last five years. I lost the baby before twelve weeks both times."

"Why didn't you tell me?"

Christina sighed. "I'm not sure. I think it hurt too much to talk about it, made it all too real. And you were going through enough, losing your husband and raising Jordan on your own. I wanted to be there for you—I didn't want you to feel as though you had to take on what I was going through as an additional burden."

Nicole felt sick. Had she been so wrapped up in her own life, her own struggles, that she was completely unaware of what the people closest to her were going through? "You're my best friend, Chris, and my family. No matter what is going on in my life, I always want to know what you are going through so I can help. That's not a burden, that's a privilege. Got it?"

Christina smiled weakly. "Got it."

Nicole adjusted the strap on her gown. "I'm going to change and then I'll take you home. Holden will not be happy with me if I wear you out."

"He won't be happy with me either. He's been a mother hen lately, hovering over me and not letting me lift a finger at home."

"Good. That's exactly how it should be." Nicole stood and smoothed the gown with the palms of both hands. "I'll only be a minute."

Christina rested her head against the wall. "Take your time. I'm fine here."

In spite of her friend's words, Nicole changed as quickly as she could while being careful not to harm the gown in any way. She slipped it onto a hanger and carried it to the cash register. The woman who had helped them earlier hurried over, rang up her purchase, and zipped the gown into a plastic garment bag. She flashed a radiant smile at Nicole as she held it out. "This is absolutely lovely on you. You're going to make a beautiful bride."

"Thank you." Thoughts of her wedding did slightly lift the heaviness that had pressed on her chest since she'd realized Christina was in distress. Still, she'd feel better when she had delivered her friend home and into Holden's care. *Father, watch over that little one, please. Keep him healthy and strong. He's so loved already.*

Silent prayers still echoing in her mind, Nicole draped the garment bag over one arm and headed for her friend. The excitement had quickly gone out of dress shopping. Like the thrill of her engagement had been overshadowed by the discovery of the potato. Her brow furrowed. Why was that? Were the two of them not destined to be together?

Nicole shook her head as she reached Christina, who had set the water glass down on a small table and clambered to her feet. What was she thinking? She didn't believe in destiny. God had brought her and Daniel together, and He was the one who would protect them and unite them in marriage.

As long as nothing else happens between now and then. Nicole linked her free arm through Christina's, and the two of them wended past rows of gowns, hats, and veils to the exit and outside. As they picked their way carefully along the slick sidewalk, cold shivers whispered across Nicole's skin. Shivers she suspected had nothing to do with the frigid air that froze their breaths into icy clouds as they made their way home.

Chapter Forty-One

Daniel inhaled the aroma of ground beef, tomatoes, and spices as Nicole lifted the lid on the casserole. "Almost done." She shut the oven door. He watched her from the far side of the island as she tossed the oven mitt onto the counter. Sharleen's words, about not starting their marriage with a lie, came back to him. The wedding was in three days. Somehow, he'd let more than a week go by since he'd taken Nicole and Jordan to meet his dad. Of course, he'd been shot in the meantime, which he'd used as an excuse to delay the inevitable. Now, though ... *I'm running out of time.* He had to talk to Nicole about her sister, and he wasn't sure he'd have another opportunity before the wedding. It had to be tonight. After Jordan went to bed, he'd try to find a way to break the news to her gently and hope she'd understand why it had taken him this long to talk to her about it.

He still had one arm in a sling, but she sat down across from him and reached over to cover his other hand with hers.

"I've been thinking about our honeymoon."

His eyebrows rose. "Oh yeah? Me too."

She slapped his hand lightly. "I mean about the *arrangements.*"

"Oh."

"So have you thought about where the three of us could go?"

Daniel stared at her blankly. "Umm, the three of us?"

"Of course. I'm a single mom. I can't run off and leave my child, you know."

"Well, no. But I ... I guess I wasn't thinking ..."

Nicole stared at him for a few seconds, then the corners of her mouth quirked, and she burst out laughing. "Rats. I really wanted to string you along longer than that. But you should see your face."

Daniel pulled his hand out from under hers. "Seriously?"

Nicole pressed a hand to her stomach. "You are such a good guy. It was hilarious watching the struggle between you wanting it to only be us going, but not wanting to say Jordan couldn't come along." She wiped a tear from the corner of her eye. "I'm sorry."

"I don't think you are sorry. But you will be. I'm not sure when or how, but I will get you for that. You'd better watch your back."

Still grinning, she stood and came around the island. He spun around to face her as she walked up to stand between his knees, lowering her voice as she pressed her hands to the island and leaned in close.

"Or, if we don't take Jordan, then *you* could wash my back."

"I said *watch* your back, not wash your back." Daniel struggled to keep a straight face himself.

She pressed her lips behind his ear. "I know." She trailed kisses along his jaw line.

"Nicole."

"Yes?" Her mouth brushed his.

"Stop. You're not getting off the hook that easily."

"Whatever you say." Moving closer, she took his face in her hands and kissed him again, more demanding this time.

For a few seconds, he didn't respond then he groaned and wrapped his good arm around her waist, pulling her to him. "You don't play fair, lady."

"I told you I was competitive. I'll do whatever it takes to win." She crushed her mouth to his, and he tightened his hold, drawing her closer.

When she finally stepped back, his heart was pounding. "If that's losing, I have no problem with you winning every time."

"Then we'll get along fine." Nicole backed up a step to sink down on the stool beside him. Daniel reached out to brush her hair back from her face.

Her eyes grazed the sling and her smile faltered. "How was

work today?"

His antenna went up at the sudden shift in her tone. "Fine. I was mostly in the office. We're still working that big case I mentioned to you before, but we've gotten a few new strong leads to follow, so I'm pretty sure we'll be wrapping it up soon."

"Good. So you weren't out doing field work?"

Daniel studied her, not liking the look in her eyes, in spite of her obvious attempt to keep her voice light. "Nic."

She pulled the pile of plates she'd set on the island earlier toward her and starting to distribute them over the countertop.

"Nicole." He waited until her hands stilled and she looked back at him. "You have to let it go."

Her shoulders slumped. "I know. I'm trying, I really am. But …" she lifted both her hands, "I don't know what I'd do if anything happened to you."

"All I can do is promise to be careful and not take any extra chances at work. The rest of the time you'll have to stay close to me, keep an eye on me yourself. And I'll keep an eye on you. We can wash each other's backs."

She laughed and relief flowed through him. "We could do that."

"I'm looking forward to it."

She rested her hands on his knees. "What I really wanted to tell you was that I talked to Holden and Christina, and they said Jordan is welcome to stay there for a few days. And Molly and Johnny said they're fine running the diner without me, so if you can get some time off, it might actually work for us to get away."

He ran his fingers slowly down the side of her face. "It's good timing because I'm on light duty anyway. And Sharleen can follow up on those leads herself. Shouldn't be a problem to take some time off."

"Good, because I—"

A sharp knock on the door interrupted her.

"Ignore it. They'll go away." Daniel's fingers trailed down her neck. "You were saying?"

"Grey? I know you're in there." A man's voice carried into

the kitchen, underscored by more knocking on the door.

Nicole caught his hand in hers and gently pulled it away. "It's all good. I'll tell you what I was about to say when you come back. In the meantime, I'll take the casserole out of the oven and when you're done, we can eat."

Daniel didn't move until the knocking on the door became pounding. Then, with a deep sigh, he let go of her hand and got up. He shoved through the French doors, leaving them swinging wildly behind him. *This better be good.* Anything short of a national emergency at this point and he was going straight for someone's throat. He crossed the living room and yanked open the door to see his colleague, Detective Rick Thomas, standing in the hallway, clutching a large manila envelope in his hand.

"Rick? What's up? Everything all right?"

"Yeah, it's fine. But I had to see you right away to let you know that … whoa!" Rick craned his neck to peer over Daniel's shoulder.

Daniel looked back as Nicole came out of the kitchen and walked over to them. He turned back to his colleague, one eyebrow lifted.

"Sorry, but she looks exactly like—"

"Hi. I'm Nicole." Daniel moved back as Nicole walked up beside him and held out her hand.

Rick shoved the envelope under one arm and grabbed her hand. "Rick Thomas. Wow. You must be the twin. Actually, it's great that you're here. I can give you the good news too."

Nicole's forehead wrinkled. "I think you might have me mixed up with someone else."

A sudden sick feeling struck Daniel. "Rick, listen," he held out one hand. "We're kind of in the middle of something here. Why don't I take that and call you later?"

Rick ignored the outstretched hand as he pulled the envelope out from under his arm. "You've gotta be her twin. The two of you look identical." Opening the envelope, he slid a large photo out.

"I don't understand." She glanced over at Daniel. "I look

identical to whom?"

"Nic, I …" Daniel had no idea how to finish that sentence. How to justify keeping this from her for so long.

"Ella Hunter. Your sister. The one that disappeared when she was a kid." Rick flipped the picture around. "Look, her hair is shorter, but otherwise the two of you are identical."

Nicole gasped and pressed a hand to her mouth. Daniel closed his eyes for a couple of seconds. This was bad. When he opened them again, Nicole was staring up at him. Taking in the mix of incomprehension and rising fury on her face, he revised that assessment. This was very, very bad.

"Good news is …" Rick continued, the smile on his face showing that the intense silent communication happening between the two people in front of him wasn't registering at all. Daniel cursed the man in his head, wishing he'd put his detective skills to some use. "We found her. She's alive."

Neither Daniel nor Nicole spoke. The smile on Rick's face faded as he shifted his attention to Daniel. "Did you hear me? We found her alive. In Chicago. Although she goes by Mikayla Grant now." His eyebrows drew together. "After seven years of hunting for her, I would have thought you'd be a little more excited to hear that."

Beside him, Nicole jolted, as if the cop in front of her had reached out and pushed her.

The sick feeling in Daniel's stomach intensified. "Nic, I'm sorry. I was going to tell you, but I haven't had a chance."

"In seven years?" Her voice was tight, controlled, but laced with anger and confusion. "You haven't had a single chance in *seven years* to tell me I have a *sister*?"

"Umm." From the corner of his eye Daniel could see Rick glancing back and forth between the two of them, comprehension beginning to dawn. Finally. "Look, Grey. I made a copy of the report for you." He held out the envelope. Daniel stared down at it. "Why don't I leave it here and we can go over it later?"

Numbly, Daniel reached out and took the envelope. "Sure. Thanks Rick." His voice rasped, and he cleared his throat.

Nicole spun around abruptly and strode away from the two of them.

Rick winced. "Sorry, man. I had no idea she didn't know."

Daniel shook his head. "No, this is my fault. I didn't want to get her hopes up until we knew something." He lifted the envelope. "Seriously, this is good news. Fantastic, actually. Once she has a chance to absorb it, she'll realize that."

Rick nodded. "Bring her down to the station tomorrow and we can go over everything we've found." He punched Daniel lightly in the shoulder. "Good luck."

"Thanks." Daniel started to close the door, then pulled it open again as a thought occurred to him. "How did you know where I was, anyway?"

Rick looked sheepish.

Daniel shook his head. "You GPS'd my phone, didn't you?"

"I tried texting, but you didn't answer, and I thought you'd want to get this news right away. Sorry for any trouble I've caused." Rick lifted a hand before striding down the hall.

Daniel waited until Rick stepped into the elevator before slowly closing the door and turning around. Nicole stalked toward him. When she reached Daniel, she strode past him to the closet. He tossed the envelope on the table beside the door. "Nicole, please. We need to talk about this."

"We have nothing to talk about." She yanked on his leather jacket so hard the hanger spun around and clattered to the floor.

His stomach clenched. He'd seen her angry before, plenty of times. The night she stormed out of Gage's apartment after they'd had a fight was the worst, but even that was tame compared to the storm that raged in her green eyes now. The flecks of gold sparked like stone on flint. "Nothing to talk about? How can you say that? Don't you want to hear about your sister?"

Her head jerked as though the word hissed through her like an electric shock. "Of course I want to hear about her. But not from you." Nicole shoved his coat against his chest. "I'll go to the station myself and talk to Detective Thomas."

"But ..."

The words he wanted to say, all the arguments he could use to persuade her, fled when she lifted her eyes to meet his. The fire was extinguished, and the green had gone ice cold. "I don't want you on this case, Daniel. In fact, I don't want you to have anything to do with me, or anyone in my family, ever again."

Jordan. The thought flashed through his mind like a streak of lightning. She wouldn't cut him off from Jordan, would she? He leaned forward slightly at the sudden pain in his gut. "Not have anything to do with you? We're getting married in three days."

She stiffened. "It's not too late to change that, thankfully." Grasping the ring he'd slid onto her finger, she tugged it off and held it out to him.

The room spun around him. Call off the wedding? When he finally had everything he'd ever wanted in his grasp? "Nicole, don't do this." Daniel reached out a hand toward her, but she grabbed it and smacked the ring down on his palm before moving out of his reach.

Reluctantly, he closed his fingers around it and stuck it into the pocket of his jeans.

"*I* didn't do this, Daniel, *you* did this. How could you—?"

"Mom?"

They both turned at the sound of Jordan's voice. Nicole's son stood a few feet from them, a puzzled look on his face. "Why are you and Daniel fighting?"

Nicole pushed back her shoulders. "I'm sorry, Jord. We're not fighting anymore. Come and say goodbye to Daniel. He has to go now."

Daniel searched her face wildly, desperate for any sign that she might relent. Nothing he saw there gave him any hope.

Her jaw tightened. "Jordan, go to your room please."

"Wait." Daniel choked out the word, his throat so constricted he could barely speak. He tore his gaze from Nicole's and squatted down in front of Jordan.

"Goodbye, buddy. I might not see you for a while, but I'll be thinking about you, and I'll miss you."

"Why won't you see me?" When Daniel didn't answer, he twisted his head to look at Nicole. "Mom? We'll see Daniel, right? I thought he was going to live with us. And we're supposed to go to the hockey game tomorrow."

Daniel looked up at her. Nicole's chin lifted. "I'm sorry, Jord. Daniel won't be able to take you this time. Say goodbye now." She reached out and pulled open the door.

Jordan's green eyes—so much like Nicole's that Daniel's stomach twisted again—welled with tears. Unable to say another word, Daniel pulled the boy to him in a tight embrace. When he released him, Nicole grabbed Jordan's hand and pulled him close to her.

Daniel pushed to his feet and grabbed her arm. "Nic. I was only trying to protect you, you have to know that."

Her eyes blazed again. "All I know is that I will never be with a man again who tries to *protect* me by keeping secrets from me. Never."

His hand dropped. There was nothing he could say to that. Panic gripped him as she pulled the door open wider. She really could be kicking him out of their lives for good. Worst part was, he couldn't even blame her. He had betrayed her and trampled all over the trust it was so hard for her to put in another person. Even if his intentions had been good, he wouldn't blame her if she never forgave him, or saw him again.

Summoning every ounce of willpower he had, Daniel stepped out into the hallway. Nicole shoved the door shut behind him. For a long moment he stood, one hand pressed to the wood, before he forced himself to turn and walk away.

Chapter Forty-Two

"Mom, why did Daniel have to go? He didn't even have dinner. And why can't he take me to the hockey game? I thought …"

"Jordan." Nicole sat on the edge of his bed and rubbed her forehead hard with the side of her hand. How could she possibly explain to him that they could no longer be with the man he'd thought was going to be a dad to him? This whole thing was like another death, for both of them.

"I know this is going to be hard for you to understand, but I want you to try, for me. Can you do that?"

He nodded, his dark curls rubbing against his Spiderman pillow.

"Daniel and I aren't … we aren't going to get married now."

His little forehead wrinkled. "We're not going to be a family?"

"No. I'm sorry. I know you care about Daniel, but it isn't going to work out between the two of us."

"Why not?"

"I found out something tonight, Jord, something really great actually. I found out I have a sister, a twin sister, that I never knew I had. Isn't that amazing?"

His eyes widened. "How could you not know you had a sister?"

"Something happened to her when she was really little. She got lost and no one knew where she was. My parents were so upset that she disappeared that they never told me about her. But Daniel found out about her a few years ago and decided not to tell me. When I discovered that tonight, I knew I couldn't marry him because he had kept a secret from me. Not telling someone the truth is the same as lying, so now I can't trust him anymore."

"But Daniel told me he would never do anything to hurt you."

Nicole swallowed hard. "He didn't mean to hurt me. In fact, he was trying to protect me by not telling me but keeping a secret from me did end up hurting me. That's why we can't be a family now. Do you understand?"

His little fingers clutched the blue blanket tightly. "Can I still see him sometimes?"

"I don't think that's a good idea, Jord. I know it's hard right now, but I think it will be easier if he isn't in our lives anymore. If we see him, it will keep being sad and hard because we won't be able to forget him."

He shook his head against the pillow, the dark curls swinging wildly. "I'll never forget him."

Neither will I. "Still, it will be easier if he stays away. You'll understand that when you're older."

"Why can't you forgive him?"

"Even if I do forgive him, Jord, and I'm going to try hard to do that, I still won't be able to trust that he won't hurt me again." Nicole rested a hand on his head. "You know how when we're laughing sometimes, and you want to know what's so funny, and I tell you it's adult humor?"

"Yes."

"Well, this is like that. Some things in life are really complicated, even for adults, but kids really can't understand. Then you have to trust that I know what's best for you."

"I'll try. But I don't think it's best for me to not be with Daniel. He was going to take me camping and play Crazy Eights with me and everything."

"I know, Jord. And I'm sorry. But I can play Crazy Eights with you any time."

"Will you take me camping?"

She hesitated. "Maybe. Or we could ask Uncle Holden. I'm sure he'd take you."

"Uncle Holden is going to have his own kid. I was going to be Daniel's kid."

"But that's even better. You and Uncle Holden can go and take your cousin with you when he or she is a bit older. You'll be able to teach him or her everything you know about fishing and camping. That will be fun, won't it?"

"I guess so. But I'll still miss Daniel."

A tear slid down his cheek and Nicole rubbed it off with her thumb, her chest aching. "So will I. But this is best, for all of us. And you know what's really exciting?"

"What?"

"If I have a sister, that means you have another aunt. And maybe someday soon she'll come for a visit so we can meet her."

He brightened slightly. "That's pretty cool. What's her name?"

"It was Ella, when she was little. But now it's Mikayla. Aunt Mikayla." Nicole tried the name out loud for the first time.

"Aunt Mikayla." Jordan looked thoughtful. "That's a pretty name."

"Yes, it is."

"What do you think she looks like?"

"Actually, I saw a picture of her. You won't believe it, but she looks exactly like me, except she has short hair."

"Really?"

"Yeah." She pulled the blanket up to his chin and tucked it around him securely. "Hopefully you'll get to see her for yourself sometime soon. For now, it's time for prayers."

Jordan pulled his arms out from under the blankets and clasped both hands together in front of him. "Dear God, thank you for helping us find Aunt Mikayla, and please help us to meet her soon. I'm sad that Daniel and Mom and I aren't going to be a family, but maybe we can be a family with Aunt Mikayla. Help her to like camping so we can go together while Mom stays home and sleeps in her bed. Thank you for everything. Amen."

Nicole didn't know whether to laugh or cry at the simple prayer. She settled for leaning down and kissing her son on the forehead. "'Night, Jord."

"'Night, Mom."

She stood up and crossed the room. Stepping out into the hallway, she pulled the door shut and rested her forehead against the cool wood for a few seconds. As painful as that conversation had been, the next few days and weeks of adjusting to the reality that Daniel was out of their lives was going to be even more difficult.

She turned and sagged against the back of the door, crossing her arms and pressing them against her abdomen at the pain of that thought. *I want Daniel.*

Nicole pressed her eyes shut tight as the cruel irony of it struck her. The only one in the world she wanted to turn to for comfort was the one who had torn her world apart, and the one she could never turn to again.

Chapter Forty-Three

"Here you go." Daniel plunked the Starbucks cup down in front of his partner.

Sharleen stared at it. "What do you want?"

"Can't a guy buy a coffee for his partner for no …" The words trailed off as her eyebrows rose. He pulled the black plastic chair in the corner closer to her desk and sat down. "All right, I do want to ask you a favor."

"That's what I thought." Sharleen picked up the cup and pulled back the tab, snapping it down on the lid. If Daniel's stomach hadn't been a roiling mess, the aroma drifting from the cup would have been incredibly appealing. She dropped her gaze to his empty hand. "You're not having one?"

"No, I don't feel like it."

Sharleen set her cup down with a thud. "All right, out with it, Grey. What's going on with you?"

"I'm heading out of town for a couple of days."

"Yeah, I figured you and Nicole would take off for …" She tilted her head. "What's wrong?"

"Nicole isn't coming with me."

"I don't understand. You're leaving her right before you get married?"

"Actually, the wedding's been put on hold."

"On hold?"

He dropped his gaze to the hands clasped between his knees. "More like called off, I guess."

Sharleen waited for him to look up. "I take it she didn't react well when you told her you've been keeping the fact that she had a sister from her."

"Unfortunately, I didn't get a chance to tell her."

"What? I thought you planned to talk to her last night."

"I did, only Rick beat me to it. I was about to sit down with her to tell her everything when he came to the door with the news that, under other circumstances, would have been fantastic, that he'd tracked down Ella Hunter, alive and well and living in Chicago."

Sharleen clapped a hand over her mouth. "You've got to be kidding me."

He grimaced. "Not in the mood to kid, believe me."

"So Nicole was upset?"

Daniel let out a humorless laugh. "Upset would have been great. She was beyond furious. She told me she doesn't want me to have anything to do with her sister's case. In fact, she doesn't want me to have anything to do with her or Jordan ever again. Then she kicked me out."

The memory struck him as forcefully as the bullet had, and he swallowed hard. "You were right, Shar. I should have told her about this years ago. I was trying to spare her feelings, but now I might have lost her for good. And I may never see Jordan again either, and he'd already become like …"

"A son?"

He exhaled loudly. "Yeah." Daniel shook his head. "I really blew it this time."

Sharleen reached out a hand and gripped his. "Maybe you should have told her a long time ago, but you were trying to keep her from getting her hopes up. Give her time to cool off, and I'm sure Nicole will realize that."

"I tried to explain that to her, but she told me she could never again be with a man who tries to protect her by keeping things from her. I can't even blame her for that. The last time a man protected her that way he ended up dead, and she was left to raise their son alone."

"I'm really sorry, Daniel." Sharleen squeezed his hand. "What was the favor you wanted from me?"

"I may not be with her anymore, but I'm still worried about Nicole and what this guy that's been sending her stuff is planning to do. Could you keep an eye on her while I'm out of town?"

"Yeah, sure. Give me her schedule, and I'll try to be there when she's coming out of her condo building or work, make sure she gets to her car safely."

"Thanks. I'd appreciate it. And please text me if anything strikes you as odd."

"I will. Where are you going?"

"Chicago. I haven't taken a vacation day in months, so I booked off today and tomorrow. I fly out in a couple of hours."

"What on earth are you going to do in Chicago?"

Daniel pushed to his feet and zipped up his leather jacket. "I'm going to attend an art gallery showing."

Chapter Forty-Four

It was shocking, seeing Mikayla Grant in person. Daniel wandered around the gallery, intrigued, in spite of his state of mind, by the work he was looking at. He'd never considered himself much of an art person, but he could actually see filling his apartment walls with the brightly colored paintings he was sure would infuse any space with life.

Every few minutes his gaze would stray to the artist as she worked the room, stopping to chat and laugh with everyone she passed by, like Nicole walking through the diner. In a long-sleeved silver blouse and black dress pants, she looked nothing like the eccentric, bohemian, artist type he'd been expecting. Other than the short blond hair tucked behind her ears, the resemblance to Nicole was, not surprisingly, enough to drive the breath from his lungs every time he glanced over.

One painting in particular caught his attention, a small café on a busy city corner. It reminded him of Joe's, although he wasn't entirely sure if it bore any real resemblance to the diner or if his tortured mind was playing tricks on him. He leaned in closer and studied the picture. It really did make him think of Joe's. Even the streetlight on the corner was placed in the same location, surrounded by the same circle of light falling onto the snow that he'd stood in to watch her the night Nicole had re-opened the diner a few months after Gage died.

Daniel tucked his fist under his chin, the tightness in his throat almost unbearable.

"I'm curious. What do you see?"

He whirled around. Mikayla stood behind him, the uncertain smile that always tugged at his heart when he saw it on Nicole playing around her mouth.

She inclined her head. "I'm sorry, I didn't mean to interrupt. You had this look on your face, as though you saw something in the painting that I may not even realize someone could. I'm always interested in that, in someone's interpretation of my work."

He half-turned until he could see the painting and still give her his attention. "It reminds me of a place, a little diner, back in my hometown."

"Which is?"

"Toronto."

Her green eyes widened, revealing tiny gold flecks against the jade background. Daniel bit his lip.

"That's a long way to come for a small showing by a completely unknown artist."

"You may be unknown at this point, but I suspect that won't be the case for long. I'm no art connoisseur, but even I can tell you have a lot of talent." He held out his hand. "Daniel Grey."

She slipped a slender hand into his. "Mikayla Grant."

He couldn't let go of her. It definitely was uncanny, seeing all the features he loved on another woman.

Her smile faltered. "You're looking at me as if you know me, Mr. Grey. Have we met before?"

Daniel released her hand. "No, sorry. But you remind me very much of someone I know."

She angled her head. "Someone you care about, obviously, which is good."

"Why is that good?"

"Because it would be disconcerting if I reminded you of your worst enemy. I might have to call security, and I wouldn't want to have to throw out the one person who seems to appreciate my work."

Daniel scanned the gallery behind her. "I hate to break it to you, but I'm not even close to the only one. There isn't a person in the room who doesn't appear to be impressed by your talent." He inclined his head toward the far corner of the room. "Even that guy, scribbling furiously in his notebook and likely a journalist or critic of some kind, looks like a fan. I'm guessing it won't be long before people are flying from a lot farther away than Toronto to see the work of the famous Mikayla Grant."

Pink tinted her cheeks. "Where is she tonight?"

"Who?"

"The one I remind you of. Why isn't she here with you?"

The pressure in his throat increased to the point of pain.

Her smile faded. "I apologize. It isn't any of my business."

"That's not entirely true."

She blinked. "I'm sorry?"

Daniel shoved his hand into the pocket of his tan dress pants. "I have a confession to make, Ms. Grant."

"Mikayla, please."

"Mikayla. I didn't fly all the way down here to see your work, although you're right, I'm already an admirer. You don't know the woman you've asked me about, at least, you wouldn't remember her, but there is a connection between the two of you that I'd like to discuss with you. Would you by any chance be available to have a cup of coffee with me later, when the showing is over?"

Her eyes searched his.

"If it helps, this sling isn't for show—I'm actually disabled at the moment."

"What happened?"

He hesitated. "I was shot."

She blinked. "Not sure that helps."

His lips twitched. "Not gang related or anything. I'm a detective with Toronto Police Services. I was injured in the line of duty." Daniel reached inside his jacket for his badge and opened it up to show her.

Mikayla glanced down at it. "Is this woman in some kind of trouble?"

"No."

"Am I?" Amusement flickered in her eyes when they rose to meet his.

"No, not at all."

"Well, I have to admit I'm intrigued, Detective." She rested her elbow in one hand and tapped a finger against her lips. "A complete stranger shows up at my first-ever art showing, claiming I remind him of the woman he loves ..."

"Did I say that I loved her?"

"You didn't have to." The gold in her eyes glowed like embers. "Somehow I am connected, or you believe I am, to what I'm starting to think is some kind of tragic tale. And not only that, but I'm gathering from what you said that I actually did know this woman at some point, but so long ago that I would no longer remember her. Do I have that about right?"

"Remarkably close."

She surveyed the room behind her. "It may be a little while before everyone is gone and I'm free to leave."

"I don't mind. I'll wait as long as it takes."

"It's that important to you?"

"I flew to Chicago. In January."

"Good point."

He waited patiently while she scrutinized him. Finally, she nodded. "All right, Detective, I probably shouldn't, but you've been so kind about my work, I'm feeling magnanimous. If you don't mind waiting, I'll come with you as soon as I can get away."

"Don't rush. I know this is a big night for you."

"Yes, it is, although I have a feeling it's about to get a lot bigger."

She waited, as if looking for an affirmation or denial, but Daniel only lifted his shoulders.

"All right"—she waved a hand up and down in front of his chest—"keep that mysterious Canadian thing going; it's working for you. And if you're looking for something to do while you're waiting, you could stroll casually over to that journalist and make loud comments to everyone around him about how extraordinary my work is and how you've never seen anything like it."

"I wouldn't be lying."

A mischievous grin crossed her face. "I think I like you,

Detective Daniel Grey."

Daniel watched her as she made her way slowly through the crowd to the other side of the gallery. *I think I like you too, Mikayla Grant.* Whatever had happened to her as a child didn't seem to have affected her negatively in any discernible way. Somehow or other, she must have ended up in the home of a set of decent parents, or she likely wouldn't have become a remarkable and talented woman with such a great sense of humor. Although somehow Nicole had done it as well.

His chest squeezed. He had to get the two of them together. Once she dealt with the shock of the whole situation, Nicole would undoubtedly see Mikayla as a beautiful and unexpected gift in her life. For his part, he would have really liked to have had her for a sister-in-law.

The thought sent a pang through him, but he pushed it back. It would have to be enough that he had done this one last thing for Nicole.

Yes, he definitely liked artist Mikayla Grant. So much so that he really, really wished he wasn't about to send her world crashing down around her.

Chapter Forty-Five

Nicole shut the door of Holden and Christina's house behind her in a useless attempt to block out the cold that was freezing her from the inside out. She pulled off her black leather boots and dropped her blue coat on the chair inside the door before padding in her sock feet down the marble tiled hallway to the kitchen. Her brother and sister-in-law sat at the table. His hand covered hers as he leaned in and said something to her softly. The scene was intimate, and Nicole thought wildly about backing out of the room and leaving, but before she could move, Christina looked up.

"Nic, hi."

Holden pulled his hand back and lifted it in greeting as he raised his mug to his lips.

"I'm sorry. I knocked, but I guess you didn't hear me."

Christina waved her into the room. "Don't be sorry. Come on in. We're finishing dessert. Do you want some?"

Nicole shook her head. "No thanks. I'm not hungry."

"Sit down anyway and tell us how the plans are coming along. Were you able to get the flowers you wanted?"

Holden pushed back his chair and stood. "If you two will excuse me, I have paperwork I need to finish."

Christina tipped her head back to look at him, her hazel eyes gleaming. "What, you don't want to discuss wedding plans with us?"

"If Daniel doesn't have to sit through this, I don't see why I should." He picked up his dishes. "Where is he anyway? I'm still waiting for that rematch at the pool table."

Nicole swallowed hard as she took the seat across the table from Christina. "I don't know where he is, actually."

His eyes narrowed. "You don't know?"

"No, I …"

Holden set his plate on the table and sat back down. "What's going on, Nic?"

She rolled her shoulders, hoping to relieve some of the tightness in her muscles. "I don't know where Daniel is, because it really isn't my business anymore. We've called off the wedding."

"What?" Christina flung out her hand, accidentally catching her water glass and tipping it over. A dark wet patch spread slowly across the tablecloth. No one paid any attention to it. "What happened?"

Holden's hands clenched into fists on the table. "Did he do something to hurt you?"

"He wasn't trying to hurt me, but yes, he did. At least, he kept something from me that he should have told me a long time ago. When I found out about it last night from someone else, I told him I couldn't marry him, that I would never be with a man again who lied to me, even if he was only doing it to try and protect me." Her gaze darted to her brother-in-law. "I'm sorry, Holden."

"No, I understand. Gage did lie to you, to all of us, and it cost him his life. I don't blame you for not wanting to go through anything like that again."

Christina took her hand. "Honey, what did Daniel keep from you?"

Nicole shook her head slowly, still trying to comprehend what Rick had told them. "Something I'm having a hard time wrapping my mind around. We were about to have dinner last night when someone Daniel works with showed up at the door. He had a picture of my … of someone who looked exactly like me, and he said she was my twin sister."

Christina's mouth opened slightly. "Seriously? Did you believe him?"

"I didn't have a choice. This woman, Mikayla Grant is her name, looks identical to me. It's kind of hard to deny we're related. Apparently, she disappeared from a park shortly before we turned three, and when the police weren't able to find a trace of her, they eventually closed the investigation, and everyone assumed she was dead. I guess that's why my parents pretty much left me to be brought up by a nanny—I would have been an extremely painful reminder to them every time they looked at me of what they had lost."

Christina and Holden both looked shell-shocked. Nicole might have laughed if she hadn't been feeling so shell-shocked herself.

"If the police have a picture of her now, are you saying that she's alive and they've tracked her down?" Holden picked up his fork and tapped it against the table.

"Apparently."

"And Daniel knew about her all along?"

"For the last seven years. He didn't know she was alive until yesterday, but he knew she had existed."

"Then where is she? Was she adopted? Will you have a chance to meet her?" Christina let go of her and pressed both palms to her temples. "Ahh, I have so many questions to ask, my head is spinning."

Nicole smiled faintly. "Mine too. But I don't have any answers for you, except that she's living in Chicago, and she's some kind of artist. That's how they found her. The police had sent my picture around to several cities in the States, and when a cop saw a poster for her upcoming art show, he recognized her and let the police here know."

Holden tented his fingers in front of his face and tapped them on his chin. "Wow."

"My sentiments exactly. I can't begin to figure out how to feel. One minute I'm so angry with Daniel for keeping this from me I can hardly see straight, the next minute I'm thinking about this woman and getting kind of excited at the thought that I might actually have a sister out there I could soon meet. I can go from laughing to crying in an instant, sometimes both at the same time." Nicole propped her elbows on the table and dropped her face into her hands. "There's a distinct possibility I could be losing my mind. That's why I came over here tonight. Jordan's at Alex's for a sleepover, and I was scared to be alone in case I lost it completely." *Or in case some psycho broke into the place and attacked me.* Her stomach churned. *God, it's too much. I don't know if I can take any more.*

Christina picked up her water glass and grabbed a napkin to dab at the wet spot. "I'm glad you came. We'll watch girl movies and eat chocolate and ice cream all night. That's the best cure for a broken heart that I know."

Nicole offered her a sad smile. "I think it might take a little more than chocolate and ice cream to heal my heart this time."

"I guess you're right. Never mind."

Nicole reached for another napkin to help her mop up the water. "No, no, I didn't say I didn't want to do it. Chocolate and ice cream and something with Colin Firth in it may not cure what ails me, but it may send me into enough of a stupor that I can forget about everything that's going on, for a few hours anyway, and that's pretty appealing right now."

"How does the five-hour version of *Pride and Prejudice* sound?"

"Perfect."

"We may have to send Holden out for supplies, but we'll make it through this night, Nic, together."

Holden stared at them. "Seriously? That's how you deal with a major crisis in your life?"

Christina nodded. "Of course. Why, what would you do?"

"Go to the gym, take out my frustrations on a punching bag for a couple of hours, then come home and blow through three or four bags of chips while watching the hockey game. I promise you, after that I'd have a completely new outlook on life."

"Ooh, the punching bag thing sounds good too." Nicole clenched both fists and jabbed them in the air. "I think I could get into that tonight."

"We could do that, or we could stick with the ice cream and Colin Firth, your choice."

Nicole dropped her fists. "That's easy. Whenever there's a choice between Colin Firth and anything, Colin is going to win."

"It's true." Christina nodded solemnly.

Holden shook his head and rose to his feet again. "I'll take care of the dishes, you two get started on your Jane Austen fest. Let me know what you want, and I'll make a run to the store when I'm done." He came around the table and reached for Nicole's hands, pulling her to her feet and into his arms. "I'm sorry about all of this, Nic. And I'm sorry Daniel hurt you. Do you want me to go beat him up?"

The corners of her mouth twitched. "I don't think so, but thanks for the offer."

The look of relief that crossed his face when he stepped back made her laugh, confirming her suspicions that there was no other place she could be tonight.

Holden grasped her arms. "I hope the two of you can work things out. He's a great guy, and I know he messed up here, but I also know he really loves you and that he's probably completely devastated at the moment. I wouldn't be surprised if *he* was in a gym somewhere, working it out on a punching bag right about now."

Nicole's eyes watered, but she blinked back the tears. She'd cried enough of them into her pillow the night before to do her for a while. "I don't know if we can, Holden. It's too much to think about right now."

He leaned in and kissed her on the forehead. "Then don't think, just be here doing whatever it is you need to do to get through this. Let us know what we can do to help. And I don't only mean tonight."

"I know, and I will, thanks."

The days and weeks to come stretched out ahead of her in one endless blur, but Nicole pushed back her shoulders, determined not to let thoughts of the future overwhelm her. One day at a time, that was all she could handle. Or maybe an hour at a time. At least the next five or so were covered.

"Shall we?" Christina slid an arm around her and flipped her long auburn hair over her shoulder as she guided her toward the living room. "It really is remarkable news, Nic."

Nicole dropped down on the sofa and bit her thumbnail. "It is, isn't it? It's horrible and tragic and wonderful all at the same time."

Christina stuck the disc into the Blue-ray player and pressed a hand to her rounded abdomen as she sank down beside her. "Are you going to call your parents?"

A cold chill passed over Nicole's skin. "I guess I will. Of course, we'll have to let them know. Maybe they'll be able to carve out time in their busy schedule for the daughter they never thought they'd see again, at least." She pulled her knees up and smacked her hands on the top of them. "Sorry, I shouldn't talk like that. I'm going to have to pray pretty hard before they come that I can get over this bitterness I feel toward them. At least now I have a reason for why they left, and that's helping."

"Good." Christina squeezed her arm. "Let me know when you're going to call them, so I can be praying too."

"I will, thanks. How are you feeling anyway?"

"Better. When I saw the doctor, she didn't think there was anything to worry about. And I haven't had any weird pains today. In fact, the little guy's been pretty quiet the last twenty-four hours. I'm hoping he's settled down and we can cruise through the last twelve weeks to the finish line."

"I'm sure you will, but please promise me you'll take it easy. Get lots of rest."

"Don't worry. Holden doesn't give me much of a choice there." Christina picked up the remote. "Ready?"

"For Colin? Always." Nicole grabbed a cushion and wrapped both arms around it as she pulled it to her. A pillow, chocolate, Christina's company, and a classic movie—none of it would eliminate the problems she faced in her life, but all offered at least a degree of comfort in their own way.

And tonight, she'd gladly take every bit of comfort she could get.

Chapter Forty-Six

Daniel leaned against his rental car. Mikayla stood inside the glass door of the gallery, deeply involved in an animated conversation with a short, red-headed woman with big gold hoop earrings. Whoever she was, she did look more like the bohemian artist type he'd expected to encounter, with a loose, long-sleeved white blouse over royal blue pants and a bright, multi-colored scarf looped several times around her neck.

The frown on her face made it clear she was not happy about Mikayla going out alone with a total stranger. He didn't blame her for that. In fact, he was glad Nicole's sister had someone looking out for her. Even so, he hoped Mikayla was strong enough to stand up to her friend and go with her gut instinct about him so this wouldn't be a completely wasted trip.

Apparently, she was. With a last sharp look in his direction, the red-headed woman shook her head, the hoops dangling wildly, then stalked back into the interior of the gallery.

Mikayla opened the door then stepped out into the frigid night air. She wrapped a long silver scarf around the collar of her coat as she walked toward him, a rueful grin on her face. "That was my agent, Leigh Connors. She can be a little over-protective. I'm sorry."

"Don't be. I understand her concern. Did you tell her I was a cop?"

"Yes. But that's not a rock-solid guarantee you can be trusted—in her opinion, anyway."

He winced. "Unfortunately, that may be true. Did you mention the woman I told you about?"

"And spoil all her fun? As much as she felt the need to lodge an official protest, I know for a fact that she was secretly delighted I was finally going out with a man. According to her, I am all but married to my paintbrush and palette."

"It *is* a beautiful relationship."

She had a devastating smile. "Thank you. For tonight at least, and for possibly the first time in my life, I'm inclined to believe that." A gust of wind swooping down the street caught her scarf and whipped the end of it over her shoulder, leaving it flapping in the breeze. Laughing, Mikayla grabbed for it, pulled it back around, and tucked it more securely into the front of her long, red coat. "Welcome to the windy city."

Daniel pulled open the door of his rental car with his good hand. "Let's go find somewhere warm and quiet to talk."

The smile wavered slightly as she slid into the front seat. "I know a place a few blocks away. Good coffee and lots of comfy armchairs. There's even a couple in front of a fireplace if we're lucky enough to find them available."

"Sounds perfect." He shut the passenger door behind her and walked around the front of the car. Although he'd spent the time while waiting for her trying to rehearse in his head what he was going to say once they were alone, he still had no idea how to broach the subject. He'd have to see how things went.

They *were* lucky, as it turned out. An older, gray-haired couple had finished their drinks at the coffee shop and gotten to their feet, leaving the plush armchairs facing each other in front of the fireplace empty as Daniel and Mikayla walked over with their cups in hand. A good start. *And a good sign, hopefully.*

Neither of them spoke as he sipped his black coffee and she twirled a spoon through her cinnamon spice latte. He gave her a moment to get her bearings before he set his drink on the little round wooden table between them.

"So, how did you feel about tonight?"

Mikayla met his gaze over the top of her paper cup. "Better than in my dreams, which is pretty remarkable."

"You've dreamt about having a gallery showing?"

"Since I was six years old and my parents gave me my first paint set."

That was a decent segue. He'd take it, regardless. "Tell me about your parents. What are they like?"

Pain flickered in her eyes and she leaned forward and set her cup down beside his before clasping her hands in her lap. "They were wonderful."

"Were?"

She nodded. "They died a year ago, killed by a drunk driver."

Shock buzzed through him. "I'm sorry, Mikayla."

"Thank you." She tucked her hair back behind one ear. "My father was a university professor. He taught English Literature and lived and breathed books. He passed that love along to me, although unfortunately I didn't inherit his quiet, gentle nature. My mother loved to laugh, and she was a real free spirit. I'm definitely more like her than him." She contemplated her hands. "Since I don't have any brothers or sisters, the three of us were very close and I miss them terribly." She lifted her chin. "But you didn't come all this way to discuss my family."

"Actually, I did."

A tiny v appeared between her eyebrows. "I don't understand."

"I know you don't. It's all pretty … complicated, but I'm going to try and explain it as clearly as I can. Tell me, what would you say is your earliest memory?"

Her eyelids flickered in confusion, but she went along with him. "I'm not sure. I guess it would be when I was three or four and my mother took me to a pond near our house and let me throw bread to the ducks. That's certainly the most vivid memory I have. Before that it's all kind of hazy."

Daniel leaned forward and rested his elbows on his knees. Here's where it started to get a little dicey. "These questions might seem a bit odd, but I need to ask you to bear with me. I do have a reason for them, and I'll get to it as quickly as possible."

She nodded, tiny lines appearing around her mouth as her lips tightened.

"Did your parents ever suggest to you that you might have

been adopted?"

Mikayla jerked back as though he had slapped her. "No. Never."

"And you're sure you have no memories before that day at the pond? Nothing that might involve another little girl your age?"

She studied him in silence. Daniel tried to read on her face what was going through her mind. Either she was attempting to remember, or she was wondering how far to let him push her. Or maybe she was considering getting up and bolting from the coffee shop.

Thankfully, she didn't bolt. Instead, as he watched, something fluttered in her eyes, like the stirring of a long-dormant memory. When she spoke, the words came slowly, hesitantly, as though she had woken up disoriented and wondering what day it was. "A little girl?"

"Yes, a blond girl. Her name is Nicole."

Mikayla reached for her latte and brought it to her lips. Her fingers trembled and some of the hot liquid spilled over the edge and onto her black pants.

"Here." Daniel jumped to his feet and strode to the condiments counter. He grabbed several napkins and handed them to her. She dabbed absently at her leg before setting her cup down again.

"Why are you asking me about her?"

"Because she wants to meet you."

"Why?"

"She's your sister."

Her face went so pale, the freckles sprinkled across her nose stood out in stark contrast. "What are you talking about?" she whispered. "I don't have a sister."

Daniel half stood to reach into his back pocket and pull out his wallet. He flipped it open and silently handed it to her.

She took it but kept her eyes on his face as he lowered himself to the chair.

He leaned forward and touched her hand. "I know you don't

know me, Mikayla, and that all of this sounds completely crazy. But I hope you can trust me when I tell you that everything is going to be okay."

For a few more seconds her eyes stayed locked on his, then some of the tension seemed to leave her face and she slowly lowered her head to look at the photo. Her trembling hand drifted up to cover her mouth. For a long moment she stared at the picture. When she raised her head, her eyes glistened. "This is her, isn't it?"

"Your sister?"

"The woman you love."

He exhaled slowly. "Yes."

"How …?"

"You and Nicole were born in Toronto, the only children of Roy and Marion Hunter. Your name was Ella Hunter. Shortly before your third birthday, you were taken from a park. When the police couldn't find a trace of you, your parents assumed the worst. They never told Nicole about you, but my guess is they were so devastated by your loss, and it was so painful for them to be around her when she looked so much like you, that they left her in the care of nannies and rarely saw her over the years. Seven years ago, I found out you existed when I was investigating Nicole's fiancé as a possible suspect in a crime."

"She's married?"

"She was. He was killed a couple of days after their wedding. I made the decision then, right or wrong, not to tell her about you. She'd already lost so many people in her life—I couldn't stand the idea of getting her hopes up and seeing her crushed again if we were never able to find you. I did, however, re-open your case and have been looking for you ever since. I figured I would wait to tell her she had a sister until I knew for sure whether you were alive or dead."

"How did you find me?"

"A colleague of mine sent Nicole's picture to all the major cities across North America a few months ago, re-listing you as a missing person. Someone at a station in Chicago saw the poster advertising your art gallery showing, put the two together, and notified us that you were here.”

Mikayla handed him his wallet. “I can’t believe it. If you didn’t have her picture, and she wasn’t clearly my sister, I wouldn’t have stuck around long enough to hear you out.”

She intertwined shaking fingers and pressed her fisted hands to her mouth. “My parents were good people. They would never have adopted me if they thought I had been stolen.”

“They might not have known. Although they almost certainly didn’t get you through official channels, they could have been given any one of a number of stories about how you came to be available. Usually people are told that the mother is young and desperate, can’t take care of the child and wants to find a good home for her, and that she’s going this route because she needs the money to survive. That eases the conscience of the prospective parents, who are usually fairly desperate themselves.”

Mikayla nodded. “I asked my mother once why they never had any more children, and she told me that I was so special to them, they wanted to give all their love to me. But I could tell the question made her sad, as though she would have had more if she could have.”

Daniel picked up his coffee and took a sip, giving her a moment to take it all in.

“Ella.” She said the name as though she’d put something in her mouth and was tasting it for the first time. “Do I have any other family?”

“Nicole has a son, Jordan.” The name sent fresh pain coursing through him, but he worked to keep his features even. “He’s six, almost seven, and he’s a really great kid. You’ll love him. And your parents are both still alive, although Nicole hasn’t spoken to them in years. If you agree to come to Toronto, you and Nicole can discuss the best way to let them know you’ve been found.”

“And you?”

“And me what?”

"Won't Nicole want your advice about how to handle this?"

"No." The ache was back in his throat. "Nicole won't want anything from me. Although there are other detectives you can consult with on this. In fact, you'll have to talk to them at some point so they can close this case."

She didn't follow the trail he'd tried to lead her down. "Why won't she want anything from you?"

He sighed. "Nicole and I were engaged, and we were supposed to get married the day after tomorrow. Last night I decided I couldn't marry her without telling her the truth about you, so I went over to her place. I was preparing to share everything with her when the colleague I mentioned to you, the one who's been helping me track you down, showed up at the door with the news that he had found you. Nicole was furious when she realized I'd known about you for years and hadn't told her. She said she didn't want me to have anything more to do with her or her son."

"But you came here on her behalf anyway."

"Yes."

"You must really love her."

"I do. And Jordan. But given what happened with her first husband, which is a long and complicated story I'm sure she'll tell you if you ask her, I also understand why she feels she can't forgive me for lying to her or trust me again. And I have to respect that."

"But you don't have to be happy about it."

"No." A wry grin crossed his lips. "I don't."

"So what now?"

"That's up to you. If you want, you're welcome to fly back with me tomorrow, although it's fine if you need more time to think all this through." He pulled a business card from his shirt pocket and handed it to her. "Here's my number. If I don't see you tomorrow, then if and when you decide to come, give me a call. I'll get the detective who found you, Rick Thomas, to set up a meeting between you and Nicole, and the two of you can take it from there. That's assuming you agree to meet with her at all. It's your choice, of course, although we will have to notify your parents either way."

She clutched the card in both hands, bending and straightening it. "This is a lot to take in."

"I know. You don't have to decide this minute. My flight is at two tomorrow afternoon. I'll be at O'Hare by noon. If you decide to come with me, you can meet me there. If you don't show up, I'll completely understand. Call me whenever you are ready, and we'll go from there."

"All right."

Daniel grabbed the wallet he'd set on his knee and slid it into his back pocket. "Can I drive you home?"

"No, thank you. It's been a monumental day. I need to sit here for a bit, try to wrap my mind around all this. I'll call Uber when I'm ready to go."

"If you're sure." Daniel hesitated then rested a hand on her forearm. "If I don't see you again, I'm truly glad I got the chance to meet you."

Although her arm trembled beneath his fingers, she managed a wan smile. "Me too. I appreciate you coming all the way here to tell me this. It helped to hear it from someone who knows Nicole, someone who cares about her."

"I hope so." He pushed to his feet. "Good night, Mikayla." When she nodded, he turned and walked out of the coffee shop and into the cold Chicago wind.

Daniel scanned the ticket on his phone at the kiosk at the airport and checked the time on the device before slipping it back into his pocket. 1:15. He couldn't wait any longer, or by the time he got through customs he'd miss his plane. He wasn't surprised Mikayla hadn't come. Of course, she hadn't. It made perfect sense that she would need time to come to terms with everything he had told her—with the fact that nothing in her life was as she had thought it had been—before she decided to meet with her sister. On top of everything, she was still dealing with the terrible loss of her parents. Did she have anyone in her life she could turn to, someone who would support her through yet another huge shift in the foundation of her life? Her agent, maybe. Leigh had seemed pretty concerned about her last night. Hopefully Mikayla was with her and not alone. He turned away from the kiosk and stopped short.

Mikayla stood a few feet in front of him, clutching a floral carry-on bag in front of her with both hands. Even though he'd spent time with her the night before, the sight of her, so much like Nicole, slammed into him as strongly as it had the first time he had seen her.

"You came."

She grinned wryly. "I can't believe it either. I canceled my Uber three times before finally going through with it on the fourth attempt. That's why I'm so late. I'm sorry."

"Don't be. I'm happy you're here now."

She inclined her head toward the customs area. "We better hurry or we'll miss our flight. I managed to get a ticket on the same one as you."

"Good. Let's get to the gate and then we can talk."

He held out an arm for her to lead the way through customs. His gaze sought her out as he took off his shoes and dropped them into the bucket along with his wallet and phone and as he walked through the metal detector and grabbed his belongings on the other side. She smiled at him while balancing on one foot and tugging a sneaker onto the other. He didn't perform the task as gracefully as she had, since he had to maneuver both shoes on with only one working hand.

He'd have to call Rick before they boarded and arrange for him to meet Mikayla at the airport. As happy as he was that she had somehow found the strength to fly to another country to meet the sister she didn't know twenty-four hours ago existed, he couldn't take being around her much longer. It hurt too much.

A sliver of sympathy for Nicole's parents worked its way through the hostility he felt for them, but he shook his head.

Nicole had ordered him away. If he'd had any say in the matter, nothing could have persuaded him to abandon her. Love didn't do that. It was that love that had driven him to find Mikayla in the first place, even knowing how painful it would be to see her. And it was what would get him through until he could see her safely to Toronto and hand her over to the care of his colleague. After that Mikayla and Nicole would be on their own and he would never see either of them again.

It hurt to take a breath when that thought passed through his mind.

Daniel grabbed his bag and fell into step beside Mikayla as they headed for the gate. Boarding hadn't started yet, so they found two seats beside each other and settled in to wait. Daniel wrapped his good arm around his bag, needing something solid to ground him. "What made you finally go through with the decision to come?"

Mikayla set her carry-on luggage on the floor and crossed one leg over the other. "I couldn't sleep last night. Everything you told me kept whirling around and around in my head like leaves in the wind—it was nearly impossible to make sense of any of it. By my third cup of coffee this morning, though, two things had become clear. The first was that I had caused you a lot of trouble, if unknowingly, and maybe I could help sort that all out somehow. The other was that I needed to see my sister and find out if, after all this time, and after not even knowing that each other existed, we could find a way to be a family. A lot of other thoughts kept muddling those two up, causing me to second and third and fourth-guess my decision, but in the end, I realized that if you could muster the courage to come and see me, I could muster the courage to go see Nicole."

A staticky voice over the intercom informed them that their flight was about to board, and they both grabbed their bags and stood. "That's a good decision. Nicole has been alone all her life. As angry as she was with me when she found out I'd kept you from her, there was also a growing excitement in her eyes about the possibility that she might actually have someone in the world, other than Jordan, who belongs to her."

"Then she and I both owe it to ourselves to see where this goes. And no pressure, Detective, but I'm doing this because of you. I'm trusting in your promise that, as crazy as all of this is, everything is somehow going to be okay."

Chapter Forty-Seven

Nicole wandered around her kitchen, no idea what to do with herself. When Detective Thomas had called the night before to tell her that Mikayla was in Toronto and wanted to meet her, she had felt as if she had been punched in the stomach and might actually pass out before she could draw in air again.

Conflicting emotions rolled through her. Part of her was so excited at the thought that she had a sister that she wanted to climb onto the roof of her condo building and shout the news to the stars and anyone listening on the street below. Another part of her though, the part that fiercely protected her heart and kept her from giving it to anyone too freely, shriveled up at the thought like a leaf tossed onto a fire.

Nicole peered at the sunflower clock in the kitchen. The bright, cheerful yellow flower seemed oddly in juxtaposition to the relentless gold hands marching over the face of it. Detective Thomas would be there in ten minutes, bringing with him a woman who was likely to have such a tremendous impact on her life it would never be the same again. *I wonder how she's feeling right now.* Nicole admired her already. It had taken unbelievable courage to hop a plane on her own and come to a strange city to meet her.

She sank onto the bar stool in the kitchen and lowered her forehead to rest on the palms of her hands. If she thought her world had been rocked, what about poor Mikayla's? At least the parents she'd always known were actually her parents. The police must have told Mikayla that the people who had raised her had gotten her through some kind of illegal means, and if she didn't even know she'd been adopted, everything she had believed to be real and true in her life had been stripped away.

What must that have been like? Answering a knock on the door to find uniformed officers there, waiting to tell her the news. Nicole moaned. Hopefully they'd broken it to her with at least a modicum of sensitivity. Presumably she hadn't been completely devastated, or she wouldn't have come so quickly. Which was part of what Nicole was struggling to deal with.

As glad as she was that her sister wanted to meet her, things were happening awfully fast. Between what had happened with Daniel, and now Mikayla suddenly appearing in her life, it was all more than a person could be expected to process in a lifetime, let alone a few days.

A knock on the door brought her head up sharply. Whether or not she'd been able to process it, whether or not she was ready, time had run out.

Nicole slid off the stool and made her way on trembling legs into the living room. Before she could change her mind, she grasped the knob of the front door and pulled it open.

Detective Thomas stood in the hallway, Mikayla behind him. He nodded at Nicole. "Ms. Kelly, good to see you again."

"Thank you, Detective. You too."

He stepped to the side and held out his hand. "I'd like you to meet Mikayla Grant."

Nicole swung her gaze from the detective's face to her sister's. Her eyes connected with Mikayla's green ones, and some of the tension left her at the mingled apprehension and excitement she detected there. She held out her hand. "Mikayla."

Her sister slid warm fingers into hers. "Nicole. I hate to sound cliché, but it really is like looking into a mirror, isn't it?"

Detective Thomas chuckled. "Do you want me to pick you up when you're done?"

Mikayla let go of Nicole's hand. "That's all right, Detective. I'll take a cab back to the hotel. Thanks so much for bringing me over."

He tipped his head to her, the high color on his cheeks indicating that he hadn't minded in the least providing chauffeur services for the visiting artist.

"Do you need me to come into the station again or did we finish earlier?"

He hesitated, as though he was trying to come up with a reason for her to come back in, then he dipped his head. "I guess we finished. If you think of anything else that might help though, or if you have any other questions, don't hesitate to give me a call."

"I won't, thank you." Mikayla stepped over the threshold and into the condo.

Although the detective hadn't made a move to leave, Nicole nodded at him and gently closed the door. "I think you've made your first Canadian conquest."

Mikayla's eyes danced. "Everyone has been so friendly. I've never been to Canada before, but I'm very impressed so far." She wrinkled her nose. "I guess that's not entirely true, is it? Apparently, I was here as a child, but not that I remember."

Nicole mustered a faint smile. "Would you like a cup of tea?"

"I'd love one." Mikayla gazed around the apartment. "What a beautiful home. I love the fireplace, and you've decorated so beautifully."

"Thank you." Nicole hadn't realized she was trembling until she lifted her arm. "The kitchen's through here."

Mikayla followed her as she pushed through the French doors.

"Please, sit. I'll get the tea."

Her sister settled on a stool as Nicole took the kettle over to the tap to fill it. Some of the water splashed over the edge as she carried it back to the outlet and plugged it in. Glad to have something for her shaking hands to do, she grabbed the cloth and wiped up the spill.

"This room is beautiful, as well. My kitchen at home is pale green and I loved it when I painted it a couple of years ago, but now I'm tired of it. I've been thinking about what color to try next but couldn't seem to decide. Now that I see this shade of yellow, I think that would look really good there, like sunshine streaming into the room. I'm not a morning person, at all, so it might help me when I stumble into the kitchen to make coffee if the place was a little brighter."

Nicole tried to follow the steady stream of words as she worked, retrieving two tea bags from the canister on the shelf above the stove and grabbing two mugs out of the cupboard. Her sister's voice sounded like hers, except with a slight Chicago accent. It reminded her of *The Parent Trap* remake, where twin sisters who didn't know the other one existed ran into each other at camp. They were completely identical, except one had been raised in California and one in London, so their accents were their one distinguishing—

A warm hand covered the one that was reaching for the spoons in the drawer and she stilled.

"Nicole."

She turned slowly and leaned back against the counter. Mikayla moved to stand in front of her, taking both hands in hers. Her smile was tentative but warm, and the tautness in Nicole's stomach muscles eased.

"I think we need to give ourselves a break here."

"What do you mean?"

"I mean, this is obviously an extremely surreal situation. There's no manual anywhere on how to cope with meeting the twin sister you never knew you had for the first time—that either of us remembers, anyway. Look at you ..." she squeezed Nicole's hands, "... you're shaking. And you haven't stopped moving and doing things since I walked into the apartment. As for me, I'm not a big talker, and I've been chatting incessantly since the moment I laid eyes on you. Let's both stop and take a breath here, all right?"

"All right." Nicole's shoulders relaxed as she drew in a deep breath and slowly exhaled.

"Better?"

"Yes."

"Good. Here." The kettle whistled, and Mikayla picked it up and poured the bubbling water into the teapot. "Why don't you take the mugs over to the island and I'll bring the pot. Then we'll sit down, relax, and try this again. How does that sound?"

"Perfect, actually." Nicole hooked both mugs with a finger and carried them over to the island where she set them down with a clunk. "What do you take in your tea?"

"Milk and a little honey, if you have it."

Nicole's eyes widened. "That's exactly how I take it."

"Really?" Mikayla studied her as she set the pot down on the island. "Interesting."

Nicole placed the jug of milk and jar of honey beside the pot then sat on a stool.

Mikayla took the one beside her. For several seconds she contemplated Nicole then she lifted both her hands into the air. "I have a thousand questions buzzing around in my head, and I can't seem to latch onto any one of them. Is there something you want to ask me?"

"I guess what I want to know about the most is your parents, what they're like, if they told you that you were adopted, things like that. I really want to know what happened to you after you disappeared, if you had a good life."

"Wow, that's a lot of questions. And now I have a thousand answers buzzing around in my head. Let's see. Like I told the detective when he flew down to see me, my parents were wonderful. They never told me I was adopted, and I never suspected for a moment that I could be. My father was a university professor and my mother a stay-at-home mom. And yes, I had a good life. A very good life. The three of us were extremely close. Unfortunately, they were killed by a drunk driver last year."

Nicole gasped. "I'm so sorry."

"Thank you." Her sister tucked her blond hair behind her ear. A tiny diamond stud sparkled in the light hanging above the island as she reached for the teapot. "It was terrible, of course. For a long time, I couldn't paint. I wasn't even sure I wanted to live. Thankfully, I had my faith, and good friends who were there for me. While I still struggle a lot some days, it has gotten better.

A day did come, a few months ago, when it struck me that I could see light and color for the first time in months. That's when I picked up my brush and started to paint again, and I haven't been able to stop since." She tipped the pot and poured the steaming tea into both their cups.

"I'd love to see your work sometime."

"I'd love to show it to you. If you come visit me in Chicago, I could take you to the gallery where several of my pieces are being shown."

A thrill rippled through Nicole at the thought. "I've never been to Chicago. Maybe I could bring Jordan and come down in the spring." She added milk to her tea and shifted the handle toward her sister.

"Oh, please do. I'll give you a tour of the city, and we'll take Jordan out for the best pizza in the world."

Nicole stirred honey into her mug thoughtfully before she straightened on the stool. "Did you say Detective Thomas flew down to tell you about all this personally? That was nice of him. I assumed they'd send someone from the Chicago P.D. to talk to you."

Mikayla had lifted her cup to her mouth, but she lowered it without taking a sip. "It wasn't Detective Thomas, Nicole, it was your detective. Detective Grey."

Nicole set her mug on the island so hard some of the tea splashed onto her fingers. "Ouch." She slid off the stool and stumbled over to the sink to run her hand under the cold water. When she turned around, Mikayla was watching her intently.

"Sorry, I guess I should have broken that to you a little more gently."

"No, it's fine." Nicole dried her fingers on a towel hanging from the handle of the stove and pressed her hand to her stomach as she walked back to the stool. "I didn't realize Dan ... Detective Grey had gone down himself to see you. Although he isn't my detective anymore. Did he tell you that he was, or had been? So of course he wouldn't have told me he was going—it isn't any of my business what he does. I'm glad to hear that he went, though, that was good of him. I ..."

Mikayla touched her arm. "Now *you're* babbling. Something else we have in common, I guess."

Nicole propped her elbows on the counter and dropped her face into her hands. "I'm sorry. Today was supposed to be …"

"Your wedding day. I know. He told me. And for the record, he's not coping very well either."

She lifted her head. "How do you know that?"

"Daniel came into the gallery two nights ago. It was the opening night of my first show, and I came up to him while he was looking at one of my pieces. Actually, it was a picture of a small café that he said reminded him of a diner in Toronto. Do you happen to know which one he was referring to?"

"I own a diner downtown, Joe's. I suppose he could have been thinking of that."

"I'm sure he was. When I introduced myself and he took my hand, he had the strangest look on his face, as if he knew me but didn't really, if you can picture what I mean. I questioned him about it, and he said I reminded him of someone he knew. When he asked me if we could go for coffee after the show, I told him I would, because I was intrigued that I reminded him of the woman he loved. He didn't deny it."

Nicole lifted her mug in trembling hands and took a sip, hoping the hot liquid would calm her.

Mikayla wrapped her fingers around her cup and stared down at her tea. "I gathered, from what he told me, that the trouble between the two of you has to do with me, which I was very sorry to hear. I felt partly responsible for coming between you, even though it was done inadvertently. One of the reasons I wanted to come up here was to see if there was anything I could do to help straighten things out."

Nicole sighed. "I don't think there's anything anyone can do. It wasn't you, it was the fact that he kept something so big from me. After what happened with …"

"Your husband?"

Her head jerked. "That must have been quite the conversation the two of you had."

"It was about you, mostly. Daniel only said that it was a

complicated story that maybe you would tell me sometime. He said that because of whatever happened with your husband, he didn't blame you for not being able to forgive him for keeping something from you, or for not being able to trust him anymore."

When Nicole didn't answer, Mikayla squeezed her arm and pulled back her hand to wrap it around her mug again. "Okay, look. Obviously, it's a bit early in our relationship for sisterly advice, so I'll drop it. Except to say that he seems to be a really good man, Nicole. You're right, he could have had officers from the Chicago force come talk to me, and that's probably what he was supposed to do. But having someone who cares about you come all that way to break the news to me made it all so much easier than if a couple of guys in uniform had shown up at my door, all cold and formal, and informed me that nothing in my life was what I had believed it to be. I'm not sure, if that had happened, when I would have been able to work up the nerve to come here to meet you, if ever."

Nicole swallowed the lump that had risen in her throat. "He is a good man."

"And he obviously loves you very much and is completely miserable right now, because in trying to keep you from getting hurt, he ended up hurting you terribly."

Nicole dropped her gaze down to the fluffy pink slippers she had propped up on the rungs of Mikayla's stool. "So this is how it's going to be, is it?"

"How?"

She looked up, a small smile playing around her mouth. "You telling me you're not going to interfere or offer advice and then going ahead and throwing all kinds of it at me."

Mikayla's eyes crinkled at the corners when she smiled, as if it was something she did a lot. The thought sent a rush of warmth through Nicole, thankful that her sister had known happiness with the parents who had raised her, even if that happiness had been cut tragically short.

Mikayla lifted both hands, palms up, her eyes sparkling. "What are sisters for?"

Chapter Forty-Eight

Daniel sent the yardstick clattering across the table in the conference room. "I don't get it. I can't see any connection between these things. I'm sure it's right there in front of us, but somehow I'm missing it."

Sharleen paced the length of the table. "Maybe we're over-thinking this. Let's go back to basics. What have we got?" She picked up the comb and examined it. "A comb missing a few teeth, a watch without a hand, a rotten potato, and a broken yardstick. What's the common denom—"

"Wait." Daniel's head jerked up. "Body parts."

"What?"

He strode over to the table. "Say that again."

Sharleen squinted down at the items. "A comb missing teeth, a watch without a hand, a rotten potato with, okay, I see it, an eye cut out, but the yardstick?"

Daniel grabbed it and held it up in the air. After a few seconds he lowered it, triumph coursing through him. "A foot. It's missing a foot."

"Teeth, hand, foot, eye … how do those four things combine to create a message?"

Daniel tossed the yardstick back onto the table. "I don't know. Unless he's going through every body part, I'm not seeing an immediate connection to these specific ones."

"Let's see. Hands and feet are extremities, but the other two aren't. Could they be connected to senses? Teeth for taste, hand and foot for touch, eye for seeing?"

"Possibly, although it's not perfect, since there are two things for the one sense and teeth aren't really for tasting. This guy seems to think he's pretty clever, so I think he'd be going for perfect.”

“Hmm.” Sharleen tapped a fist against her mouth as she studied the objects on the table. “Something from literature, do you think? Eye, tooth, hand, foot … Sounds a bit like a Dr. Seuss book but not exactly, and you’re right, this guy is likely attempting to be as exact as possible.”

Daniel closed his eyes. “Let’s work through this one part at a time. Teeth: sink your teeth in, long in the tooth, false teeth … nothing there. Eyes on the prize, I have my eye on you, *When Irish Eyes are Smiling*, an eye for an eye …” He dropped his hands. “Could that be it—from the Bible? An eye for an eye, a tooth for a tooth?” He clenched his fists and tapped them against his temples. “How does the rest of it go?” He started for the door. “I’ll go get my Bible.”

“Here.” Sharleen leaned over and typed on her laptop keyboard. “I have the app on my computer.” She sent him a sideways glance, lifting her shoulders when his eyebrows rose. “What? I read it sometimes, mostly to try and figure out what you are always yammering on about.”

Daniel stifled a grin and leaned over her shoulder.

Sharleen clicked a button and words filled the screen. After scanning them for a few seconds, she pointed, “Here it is, Exodus 21:24: eye for eye, tooth for tooth, hand for hand, foot for foot.” She looked at him. “That has to be it. That’s way too much of a coincidence.”

He nodded and read on. “Then burns and wounds.” He repressed a shudder. What did that mean? Would whoever was threatening Nicole try to burn her? Attack her somehow? “So what do you think will come next?” A cold fist gripped his gut as the possibilities flowed through his mind.

Sharleen reached out and gripped his arm. “Here.” Her voice was grim as she pointed to the screen. “Maybe the verse before that one is your answer.”

Daniel leaned in again and the fist tightened. “A life for a life.”

Daniel grabbed his jacket from the back of the chair, shoved his right arm into the sleeve, and gingerly pulled the other sleeve up over his left shoulder. "I need to go see her."

Sharleen grabbed his arm. "Grey."

He stopped and met her gaze steadily. "Shar, I have to make sure she's all right."

She pursed her lips, studying him, then she dropped her hand and nodded. "Fine. I'll go talk to Sergeant Lector, tell him what's going on. With such a nebulous threat, I doubt he'll be willing to commit manpower to twenty-four-hour protection, but you never know. If not, I'll rally the troops, see who might be willing to donate some of their down time to help keep an eye on her."

"Thanks, Shar. I owe you one."

"One? You owe me a lot more than that, my friend."

"I know I do. One of these days I'll pay up."

"Yes, you will." She waved a hand toward the door. "Go. I'll be in touch and let you know what's happening."

Daniel nodded and headed out into the hallway. With or without his boss's support—even with or without Nicole's support, which he suspected he might not get either—he *was* going to protect her and Jordan.

This coward, whoever he was, would have to be a lot cleverer than he thought he was to get past Daniel and hurt the two people he cared about the most in the world. He'd give up his own life in a second to protect the two of them, and he'd gladly take whoever was threatening them with him. As innocent as the objects he'd sent Nicole appeared on the surface, Daniel knew in his gut that the threat was real and likely imminent. Now he had to convince Nicole how serious it was.

Right after he convinced her to let him in the door.

Chapter Forty-Nine

Daniel rapped on the door. He'd pulled out his badge for the building manager so he could get at least this far. Hopefully it would be easier to convince Nicole to listen to him in person than over an intercom system.

Daniel's phone vibrated and he yanked it out and glanced at the screen. A grim smile crossed his face as he shoved it back into his pocket.

He heard movement on the other side and then nothing, and mentally kicked himself for insisting she always look out the peep hole before opening the door. *Please talk to me. Please talk to me.* If she refused to let him in, he'd still keep an eye on her, but it would be considerably less comfortable and much colder sitting out in the parking lot watching the building through the front windshield of his car.

Nicole yanked the door open. Daniel almost winced. Given the look she leveled at him, it might not be any more comfortable—or less cold—in here with her.

"What are you doing here?"

"We need to talk."

"I have nothing more to say to you." She shoved the door toward him. He'd left his sling in the car and, without thinking, he shot out his left arm to stop it with his palm, gritting his teeth against the pain that jolted through his shoulder.

"This isn't about us, Nicole. It's official police business. I could show you my badge if that would help."

She regarded him coolly. "That won't be necessary. You've flashed it in my face often enough in the past. I know what it looks like."

Ouch. Daniel waited in silence until her shoulders slumped and she stepped back. "Make it quick. I need to get ready for work."

He knew for a fact that she didn't leave for the diner until five, but he let it pass. "Thank you."

When he came through the door, her gaze immediately fell on the gym bag he'd kept out of her sight in the hallway.

"Why do you have a bag?"

"That's one of the things we have to talk about."

Her lips narrowed to a thin line, but she didn't answer, simply walked toward the living room. Daniel toed off his shoes and tossed his jacket and the gym bag on the chair by the door before following her. When she faced him, both arms crossed, he held out an arm toward the couch. "Can we sit down?"

She exhaled loudly. "In the kitchen." Not waiting for a response, she spun around and crossed the room to push through the French doors.

Daniel repressed a sigh and followed her. The kitchen was safer, he got that. And he'd take what he could get at this point. Nicole had settled herself on the bar stool on the far side of the island by the time he'd walked into the room. Daniel took the one closest to her. Nicole's arms remained firmly folded against her body, like a shield.

"Is this about those items someone's been giving me?"

"Yes."

"Where's Sharleen?"

"She's working this at the other end, following up on leads at the office."

"So, not following protocol again."

"Another special case."

Nicole started. "Case?"

"Yes. Sharleen is talking to the detective sergeant about launching an official investigation and possibly getting protection for you. He likely won't agree to that at this point, since the threat is fairly vague, and it's not usual to provide twenty-four-hour a day protection for civilians, but we thought it wouldn't hurt to ask. In the meantime, I'd like to be here so I can keep an eye on you and watch for anything that might happen."

"Why you?"

"Because, until the sarge approves protection, I can't really ask anyone else to watch my … to watch you and Jordan voluntarily."

"We're not your responsibility anymore, Daniel."

"I know that. But I still care about you, and Jordan, and I need to know you're both safe before …"

"Before what?"

"Before I'm out of your life for good."

Something flashed across her face that, for the first time since she'd kicked him out of her apartment, offered him the slightest bit of hope.

Then she straightened her shoulders. "I still think you're over-reacting. These things are a bit weird, but none seem terribly threatening."

"I didn't think so either, at first, but now something about this feels really wrong, and I don't believe it's possible for us to be too careful."

"Why, what did you find out that's making you so cautious?"

"Sharleen and I were studying all the objects, and it occurred to me that they could all represent body parts. The yardstick was missing a foot, the watch a hand, the potato an eye, and the comb teeth."

Her face paled. "What do you think that means?"

"We think it might be connected to the verses in Exodus that talk about exacting revenge—an eye for an eye, a tooth for a tooth, a hand for a hand, and a foot for a foot."

"Are those the only things mentioned in that passage, or should I be expecting more gifts at my door?"

He hesitated. "There is one more."

"What?"

"A life for a life."

She stared at him. "So you think someone is threatening my life?"

"I don't know for sure, but it seems like a possibility."

Nicole tapped her fingers on her arm. "Why would someone come after me?"

"That's what I need you to tell me. Really try to think about anyone who might be angry or upset with you for any reason. Maybe someone you ticked off at the diner? You mentioned that a few guys have asked you out over the years and you turned them down. Did anyone seem particularly worked up about that, or persistent in pursuing you even after you told them no?"

Nicole shook her head. "Not that I can think of."

"Well, keep trying, and if anything at all occurs to you, let me know."

"I will. But we live in a secure building—don't you think we're safe here?"

"Nic, you know how easy it is to slip in behind someone going into the building. I did it the night I found the yardstick, and he must have too, since he left it at your door. Or possibly he lives in this building, which is something else to think about. Whether or not anyone here has anything against you for any reason. Either way, it's only a small step from being outside your door to getting inside. Locks help but they're not foolproof. I won't rest easy if you and Jordan are here alone."

"I don't know ..."

Time for the big guns. She'd told him she didn't want to live in fear, but sometimes a little fear could be a good thing. "Think about those items, Nic. All of them were treated violently. The foot was snapped off the yardstick, the eye was gouged out of the potato, the teeth were broken off the comb, and the hand was twisted off the watch and the face smashed, which in itself might be a warning. When you really look at those things, the message someone is trying to send you becomes far more ominous."

Nicole pressed her lips together. She was wavering, about to tip one way or the other, and when she did, Daniel knew there would be no persuading her to change her mind. He leaned forward on his good arm. "Please let me do this for you, Nic."

Her shoulders sagged. "Fine. But only until we figure out who's doing this."

Relief flooded through him. "Understood."

"And if you do get approval for official protection, it would be better if someone else could be here with us. Jordan is going to have a hard time understanding all of this, so the easier we can make it on him, the better."

"Of course. You know I want that too."

She uncrossed her arms and rested her hands on the cold marble island, which Daniel took as a good sign. "How's your shoulder?"

"It's healing quickly. Still aches sometimes, but not bad."

"That looked like more than an ache when you grabbed the door."

He lifted his right shoulder. "When I don't have the sling on, I forget sometimes I can't do things like that. It helps when I think before I move."

"I'm sorry I didn't give you time for that. I really am trying to be a grown-up about all this, believe it or not."

"I know." Daniel brushed a crumb off the counter. "I hear you met your sister."

Her expression softened. "I did. She's incredible. But you already know that, don't you? She told me you went all the way to Chicago to talk her into coming here."

"I thought it would be easier for her to hear such life-changing news that way."

"It was. She told me she might not have come, or it would have taken her a lot longer to work up the courage, if uniformed officers showed up at the door being all insensitive and official about it." Her green eyes met his and an unbearable ache settled in his chest. "So thank you."

"You're welcome."

Neither of them moved for a few seconds, until Nicole looked away and checked the clock. "Jordan will be home soon. Why don't you put your things in the guest room? And when he gets here, will you give us a few minutes to talk, so I can somehow try to explain this to him in a way that won't scare him to death?"

"Of course. What's he doing while you're at work tonight?"

"Mikayla's coming over to spend time with him. She only has a few more days before she flies back to Chicago, and she wants to get to know him better."

"Of course. But if you ever don't have someone to stay with him, it's fine to leave him with me, since I'll be here anyway."

Daniel's initial plan had been to accompany Nicole to the diner, and part of him still wanted to go, to be wherever she was so he could keep an eye on her himself. The text Sharleen had sent him when he was waiting for Nicole to open the door though, had been to let him know that seven of his fellow officers had volunteered to take turns watching the diner when Nicole was there, and the parking lot outside her building as much as possible. The first watch would already be in place by the time she arrived at work, so her condo was probably the best place for him to be in case this guy showed up at her door again. Which, now that he was here, Daniel almost wished he would.

She bit her bottom lip. "We'll see."

He left it alone, not wanting to push her too far. "Do you want me to make dinner for Mikayla and Jordan and me? I didn't have a chance to buy groceries yet, but I will. I don't expect you to feed me while I'm here."

"No, it's fine. If you want to make something, that would be great. Use whatever you can find. I should go get changed for work."

"I'll walk you out when you're ready."

She climbed down off the stool. "All right."

"Nic?"

"Yes?" She stopped, one palm on the French doors.

"Thank you for letting me stay."

She nodded. "I won't be long."

Daniel propped his elbow on the counter and rested his head on his hand, as drained as he had ever felt. He hadn't even realized how tightly his muscles were knotted, worried that she might kick him out of her condo again, until she had agreed, if reluctantly, to let him stay.

Of course, now that he had crossed that hurdle, he had another, bigger one to overcome. He needed to focus on his job and make sure she and Jordan were safe, when all he wanted to do was take her in his arms and refuse to let her go.

Chapter Fifty

Daniel accompanied Nicole to her car and pulled open the driver's side door. When she went to get in, he touched her shoulder to stop her then quickly dropped his hand. "Like I mentioned before, if you could change your routine a bit, that would be good. Maybe park at the front instead of the back and try to get out a little earlier than usual, that sort of thing. The main thing is to not walk to your car by yourself. Promise me you won't do that."

"I won't."

"I mean it, Nic. If you do, I'll know about it." He offered her a small smile. "Molly's my spy down there at the diner."

She didn't return the smile.

"What?"

She shook her head slightly. "Nothing."

He waited a beat, hoping she'd look up at him, but she kept her eyes firmly fixed on her gloved hand gripping the top of the door.

"I'm not interested in Molly, Nic."

Nicole swallowed. "I can't care about what you do anymore, Daniel. Or who you do it with." She slid into the front seat, her eyes still not meeting his as she clutched the steering wheel with both hands. "I'll see you later."

Heaviness pressed in on his chest so strongly he had to work to get out the words. "Be careful."

He stood in the parking lot and watched as she pulled onto the street. When the little white car disappeared around the corner, he crossed his arms and pursed his lips. That was interesting wording. That she *couldn't* care what he did or who with, not that she *didn't* care.

Daniel ran a hand over his head and then spun around to head back into the building. He really had to stop doing that, analyzing every little thing she said and how she said it, or he was going to drive himself crazy. And if he was going to stay alert and keep her safe, it would be really helpful if he was in his right mind.

He took the stairs to the condo, needing to burn off a little of the excess emotion smoldering inside him. When he pushed through the French doors and into the kitchen, Mikayla was setting plates, filled with the spaghetti he'd made, on the table. She looked up when he came into the room. "Perfect timing."

"Smells delicious."

She laughed. "If you do say so yourself."

"Daniel!" Jordan had been sitting at the table, but he hopped off his chair and charged across the room, barreling into Daniel's stomach.

He ignored the pain that shot through his shoulder at the jolt and pressed a hand to Jordan's small back. "Hey, buddy."

Jordan stepped away. "I'm glad you're here."

"Me too." Daniel pulled out a chair for Mikayla before taking the one on the other side of the table. Jordan folded his hands and bowed his head. Daniel closed his eyes, the words Jordan was saying lost in the flood of silent pleas he couldn't form into coherent sentences. When he heard the word *amen*, he opened his eyes and stared down at the plate of food in front of him, the aroma failing to stir his appetite.

Jordan clearly did not share his frame of mind. He dug into the spaghetti as though he hadn't eaten in a week.

"Everything all right?"

He lifted his head to see Mikayla watching him.

"Yeah, not as hungry as I thought, though." He picked up his fork and twirled some of the pasta around the tines before shoving it into his mouth. Anxious thoughts about Nicole's safety insisted on pushing themselves into his head, but he tried to keep them at bay and listen to Jordan talking about everything that had happened at school that day. Daniel didn't know how many more meals like this he'd be able to share with this amazing kid, and he really didn't want to spend this one mentally checked out. He would definitely feel better once Nicole was safely back in the condo though.

"Can I have ice cream?"

"Sure, Jord." Mikayla had taken over, which was right and good, even though it sent a pang of loss through Daniel.

"I'll get it." He pushed back his chair and scooped chocolate ice cream out of the tub and into a bowl. When he set it down in front of Jordan, he looked over at Mikayla. "Ice cream? They have chocolate and pralines and cream."

"Sure, pralines and cream please, my favorite."

"That's Nicole's favorite too."

"Really?" She picked up her spoon. "I can't believe how much we have in common even after being raised hundreds of miles apart."

"It's fascinating, isn't it? The twin thing, I mean." Daniel filled a bowl for her and carried it over.

"Yeah, it is. I've always thought so, but now that I realize I am one, I'm starting to see how real that connection everyone talks about actually is. As soon as I met Nicole—once we got over the initial awkwardness, anyway—I felt as though I had known her forever. She likes all the same things and has the same mannerisms. I can almost anticipate what she is going to say before she says it. It's definitely bizarre, but in a really, really cool way."

"This is cool too." Jordan barely looked up from his bowl as he jumped into the conversation.

Daniel shifted his attention to the boy. "What is, Jord?"

"That you and Aunt Mikayla are both here. Because *you* were going to be my family and now you're not, but then she came and now *she's* my family." Jordan scooped another spoonful of ice cream into his mouth, oblivious to the impact his words were having on the adults at the table.

Mikayla's gaze, soft with sympathy, met Daniel's and he forced a smile.

"The Lord gives and the Lord takes away." Jordan glanced up, the triumphant look on his face undermined by the streak of chocolate smeared across one cheek.

In spite of himself, Daniel laughed as he pushed back his chair and walked over to the sink. He grabbed the dishcloth hanging over the tap and brought it to the table to wipe off Jordan's face. "Where did you hear that?"

"Last week, in Sunday School, we talked about Job, and that's what he said when he lost his family and his servants and everything. And it's right, isn't it?"

"Yeah." Daniel rested a hand on the dark curls. "It's right." That's certainly what had happened to him. "Do you remember what Job said after that?"

Jordan screwed up his face, trying to remember.

"Starts with 'Blessed …"

"… be the name of the Lord!'"

"Good listening. And it's important we say the same thing when God gives us things or takes them away. He's in charge and can do what He wants, and He always does what's best for us, even when it doesn't feel like it at the time. Right?" A good lesson he'd have to try to remember in the weeks and months ahead.

"Right." Jordan dropped his spoon into his bowl with a clatter, clearly done with the conversation. "Did you bring Laurel and Hardy?"

"There are a couple of DVDs on the dresser in my room." Daniel sat back down at the table. Mikayla raised an eyebrow and he shrugged. "I showed him a couple of episodes at my place and now he's hooked, I'm afraid."

"Laurel and Hardy will do that to you. I'm a big fan too. Why don't you go pick one of the DVDs out and get it started Jord, and I'll do the dishes then come watch with you, okay?"

"Okay." He slid from his chair and started for the door.

"Dishes, Jord." He and Mikayla spoke at the same time. Daniel shot her a sheepish look. "Sorry. I keep forgetting I shouldn't be telling him what to do anymore."

"Why not?" She reached for his plate, settling it on top of hers as Jordan dropped his cup and plate into the sink and disappeared through the swinging doors. "The two of you are still close, and he obviously respects you. It won't hurt him to get some male guidance while ..."

"While I'm still here?"

"Yes." She sighed and rested a hand on his forearm. "God gives and takes away. Even when it doesn't feel like what's happening could possibly be for our good. We still need to trust, right?"

He met her gaze steadily. "Do you believe that?"

"I do. My parents always took me to church growing up. I decided early on I couldn't live my life without God, so yes ..." her fingers touched her throat, "... grateful follower of Jesus Christ here."

Daniel smiled. "Nicole came to it a bit later, after she happened into Joe's looking for work and Connie and Joe, who were the owners at the time, hired her. They'd never had any kids of their own, and they basically adopted Nic as their daughter. Joe died a few years ago and left her the diner, but they're the ones who first showed her the love of God."

Mikayla looked thoughtful. "It's interesting, isn't it? I was the one taken away from my family, not her, but I grew up in a loving home while she was pretty much left on her own."

"It is interesting. And sad."

"What you said to Jordan, that was really beautiful. I needed to be reminded of it."

"So did I."

"Although it's happening the other way around in my life right now. God took my parents, but he's given me a new family. And you're right, Jordan is incredible. He stole my heart the moment I met him."

"I feel the same way." Daniel stared at the door Nicole's son had disappeared through. "I'm going to miss him almost as much as I'm going to miss her."

"I'm sorry about all of this, Daniel. The two of you

obviously care about each other so much—it's breaking my heart that you can't be together." She stood up to carry the plates over to the sink.

He exhaled loudly. "Mine too. But I'm going to have to find a way to deal with it. And I really am glad you and Nicole have found each other. It means so much to her to have you in her life." Daniel grabbed the salad bowl and dressing off the table.

"It means a lot to me, as well." Mikayla turned on the faucet.

"Have you talked about getting in touch with your parents?"

"Yeah, Nicole is going to call them as soon as she can come up with a way to tell them. There's so much going on with her right now, she's trying to process what's already happened. She'll probably attempt to get hold of them in a couple of days." She reached for the glasses he'd carried over from the table. "You made dinner, so I'll do the dishes. Do you want to watch that DVD with Jordan?"

Daniel shook his head. "I brought a book with me. I think I'll go read in my room for a while. I don't want to interfere with your time with him, and I really don't want to confuse that poor kid any more than he already is."

Mikayla nodded. "I guess that makes sense."

"Knock on my door when he's asleep though and you're ready to go. I'll walk you out to your cab." Daniel shut the refrigerator door and planted his palms on the island counter. "I don't know how much Nicole told you about what's going on, but if someone is after her, you should take precautions too, since you look so much like her."

"I will, although I'd almost welcome the chance to face this guy. It's crazy how protective I feel toward Nicole already. I guess that's why God gives us families, so we can take care of each other." She ran a plate under the running water and set it in the dish rack.

Gives them and takes them away. Daniel repressed a sigh. *Blessed be His name.* "I guess. I'll see you later." He pushed through the kitchen doors and out into the living room.

Jordan was sprawled on the couch, his arms folded behind

his head. "Can you watch with me, Daniel?"

His heart squeezing, Daniel walked over and squatted down in front of him. "I'd like to Jord, but I think I'm going to go read for a while. Your Aunt Mikayla will be coming out soon, and she's going to watch with you. Only one episode though, and then it will be bedtime. You have school tomorrow."

"Okay. Good night, Daniel." Jordan held out both arms to him.

Even knowing it was the worst idea in the world, at least where his heart—and Jordan's—was concerned, Daniel reached out and pulled the boy to him. The little arms went around his neck, and Daniel buried his face in the soft curls. *God, help me. I can't do this. I can't let them go. Not on my own.* A peace he hadn't felt in days flowed through him, and when Jordan's arms slid from his neck, Daniel leaned back on his heels. "Can I tell you something, Jord?"

"Sure." The emerald eyes fixed on his.

"Even when I can't be here with you anymore, and we can't see each other, you will always be here." Daniel tapped his chest with his fist. "Do you understand?"

Jordan nodded solemnly.

"Good. I'll never forget you, I promise."

"I'll never forget you, either." Jordan clenched his fist and pressed it over his heart.

Daniel reached out and ruffled his hair, attempting a smile he was pretty sure didn't fool the perceptive little boy in front of him. "Good night, buddy." He forced himself to stand and stumble from the room.

His chest aching, he rooted through his bag until he found his book then sank down on the armchair in the corner of the room. Shadows lengthened across the floor as he sat there staring, unseeing, out the window.

When a soft knock sounded on his door, he blinked, only realizing in that moment that, except for the faint glimmer of a tiny sliver of a moon in the night sky, he was sitting in complete darkness, the unopened book still clutched in his hand.

Chapter Fifty-One

"It's been four days, Daniel. Have you heard anything from your detective sergeant about getting approval for protection?" Nicole slammed the kitchen drawer shut and faced him, leaning against the counter.

His eyes narrowed. He'd walked in the door after work two minutes ago and was trying to get a bead on her mood. She crossed her arms and tapped a foot on the floor. *Barely contained frustration, then.* Something he could completely relate to.

"Actually, yes. I was coming in to let you know he called me into his office today to tell me he's not ready to go for that yet."

"What is he waiting for, shots to be fired?"

Daniel sighed. "I did tell you it wasn't likely he would approve the expense."

"So we keep going on like this?"

"Do you have any other suggestions? Because I'm open to them."

"My *suggestion* would be for you to go back to living your life at your apartment, and we'll go back to living ours here. I can be careful about walking around alone, and text you if I see anything that concerns me."

"I don't think that's a good idea. Sharleen and a couple of other detectives are taking turns doing surveillance outside this building and at the diner. Sooner or later—and my guess is sooner—this guy is going to make a move, and hopefully they'll spot him before he can try anything. If not, I'm the second, and the last, line of defense here in the condo."

Her jaw tightened. "I didn't know they were doing surveillance. I don't like the idea of being watched all the time."

"Judging from what whoever gave you those items knows about you, my guess is you're already being watched. At least these are the good guys."

"Even so, please let me know about things like that in the future. I don't appreciate being left out of the loop of my own life."

Daniel walked around the far side of the island to stand in front of her. "You're right. I'm sorry. I should have told you everything that was going on. I will from now on."

Nicole closed her eyes and pressed her fingertips to her temples. "No, I'm sorry. I know you've put your life on hold for us, and I don't mean to sound ungrateful. There's too much going on right now between you, and this person watching me, and Mikayla. I feel as though I'm going crazy."

Daniel stepped closer and grasped hold of her upper arms lightly. She dropped her hands and opened her eyes but didn't pull away.

"It's all right. I get it. This is all more than anyone should have to deal with. But you don't have to handle it alone, Nic. I'm here if there's anything you need."

Beneath his fingers, a tremor passed through her. "I can't turn to you, not anymore."

"Why not? After everything we've been through together, can't we at least be friends?" His thumbs slid up and down her soft skin.

She shook her head, but the look of uncertainty on her face gave him courage.

"Please, Nic." One hand lifted from her arm to cup her face.

"Daniel."

Was that a refusal or an invitation? He couldn't tell by the pleading in her voice, and the conflicting emotions splashing across her face weren't helping. Neither was the soft blond hair drifting over the back of his hand. All he had to go by was that she hadn't pulled away. Yet. His gaze fell to her mouth. Daniel slowly closed the space between them.

"Mom?"

Behind him, the French doors creaked on their hinges. Nicole jerked away, and Daniel dropped his hands as she slipped around him. "Yes, Jord?"

"Can I have a snack?"

"Sure." Daniel caught the trembling in her voice, but when he turned around, Jordan was hopping up on the stool, blissfully unaware of what was going on between the adults in the room. *It's great to be a kid.* Daniel envied that resilience, that God-given ability to unreservedly trust the grown-ups in his life to take care of any problems that might come up. He could use a little more of that trust right now, if not in other grown-ups, at least in the God who had promised to take his cares and worries from him if he could only cast them away.

Too bad He never made any such promises about pain. Daniel's face twisted. Now that was something he'd gladly give up.

"Grandma Connie will be here soon." Nicole's voice brought him back from his musing. She squeezed Jordan's shoulder. "Be good and do what she tells you. Got it?"

Jordan dug his spoon into a bowl of cereal. "Got it."

"Mikayla's not coming?"

Nicole tugged open the refrigerator door and set the jug of milk on a shelf, not looking over at him. "She has a headache so she's going to bed early."

"Connie doesn't have to come out in the cold."

She shut the door firmly. "Yes. She does."

Because you need to stay away from my kid. The message was loud and clear. Daniel pushed himself away from the counter. "Let me know when you're ready to head out."

She nodded, still not looking at him.

Daniel strode into the living room and over to the big front window overlooking the parking lot. For several minutes he stood, scanning the cars and the grassy area beyond, straining to see between the small strands of trees that dotted the endless stretch of snow. *Where are you?* His fists clenched. *Come out of hiding, you coward. Face me like a man.*

He was ready to fight, but until whoever it was made a move, all he was doing was swinging his fists through empty air.

Chapter Fifty-Two

Daniel didn't like the lines of weariness etched deep in Connie's face. He waited until Jordan left the table though, before he brought it up. "Are you all right, Connie?"

The lines deepened when she smiled and reached over to pat his hand. "I'm fine, Daniel. Approaching the finish line after a long race, is all."

Which didn't ease his apprehension. He hated to think about how hard it was going to be for Nicole to let this woman go. From the looks of things, she was going to have to do so before much longer.

"Do you know you're one of my favorite people?"

He looked into the soft blue eyes gazing at him. "I am?"

"Yes. In life and also in the Bible."

"Ah." Daniel had always been one of his favorite characters in the Bible too, his strong faith and courage a continuous source of inspiration for him.

"That story of Daniel and the lions is truly one of the most powerful ones of all. People always talk about David when they're referring to someone facing overwhelming odds, but I'd take a giant any day over a den full of hungry lions. Sure did look like as hopeless a situation as it could possibly be, didn't it?"

He had a feeling he knew where she was going with this, but he nodded. "Yes, it did."

"Of course, it wasn't courage that enabled Daniel to walk into that den, it was trust. Trust that the One he risked his life to worship would hold him in the palm of His hand and bring him through what had to be one of the longest, darkest nights in history."

Daniel started. His dad's words, about facing a long, dark

night of the soul, drifted back. He sure couldn't hear any birds singing at the moment, any more than the Daniel in the story would have been able to down in that hole in the ground. But Connie was right, the Hebrew Daniel would have had absolute trust that God could bring him through, and that he would once again see sunlight and breathe fresh air if he could only hold on through the darkness.

The thin hand, paper light on his, squeezed his fingers before she let him go.

The suffocating heaviness that had pressed down on Daniel for days lifted slightly. "Would you like Jordan and me to take you home?"

"No, don't take my sweet boy out into this cold. I can call a cab. I think I will get going though. What I need right now is a cup of tea, my book, and my own warm bed."

Daniel pushed back his chair. "I'll tell you what. My partner is in the neighborhood and she'd be happy to drive you. I'd feel better about that than you taking a cab home by yourself."

He texted Sharleen, who was pulling the evening shift out in the parking lot. He and Jordan went downstairs with Connie, and he helped her into Sharleen's Jeep. They stood and watched until the vehicle disappeared down the street before heading upstairs. Daniel sat in the black desk chair he'd pulled up to Jordan's bed and waited as Jordan brushed his teeth. A minute later the boy came bounding into the bedroom and jumped onto his mattress, landing on his hands and knees hard enough that the headboard knocked against the wall.

"Oops." Jordan sent Daniel an abashed look. "Mom doesn't like me to do that. I always forget, though, until I hear the bang and then it's too late."

Daniel repressed a grin. "Try to remember for next time. That can actually damage the wall."

"I will."

Daniel held the sheet up for him. A thoughtful look crossed the boy's face as he crawled under the covers and pulled his arms out to rest on top of the Batman blanket.

"Daniel?"

"Yeah, buddy?"

"Why did my dad have to die?"

His heart skipped a beat. For a few seconds he contemplated giving Jordan a pat answer and telling him to go to sleep, but instead he took a deep breath. "Have you asked your mom about that?"

"Yeah. She doesn't want to talk about it. She tells me lots of stories about him, and he sounds really great, but she never wants to talk about how he died or why. She tried once and she got really sad, so I didn't ask her again."

"You're right, Jord, your dad was great."

"Then why did he get killed?"

Daniel sent up a desperate prayer for help, for the words to say to ease Jordan's confusion and pain. "Sometimes when an adult, or even a kid, sees something happening that they know is wrong, they're willing to do anything to try and stop it. That's what happened with your dad. Even though what he did was dangerous, he believed so strongly that what he was doing was right, he was willing to risk everything, including his life, to do it."

"Did you help him?"

Daniel hesitated. "I wanted to. I tried to. Even though I didn't completely agree with what he was doing, I admired him for standing up for what he believed to be right." He brushed a wayward curl back from Jordan's eyes. "The most important thing you need to know is that your dad really loved your mom. He didn't know about you then or he might have stopped what he was doing because he would have wanted to be there for you and be your dad. He would have been really proud of you, like I am. He was a very good man, Jordan. Don't ever let anyone tell you he wasn't."

"I won't. You love my mom, don't you?"

Pain pricked his chest. "Yes, I do. Very much."

Jordan snuggled down under the blankets, a look of contentment on his face. "Good. Then everything is going to be okay."

Daniel studied him for a minute, wishing he had the simple, powerful faith of a child and could believe the same thing. He gripped a pajama-clad shoulder and leaned closer to Jordan to whisper, "Sweet dreams, buddy."

He got up and tiptoed to the door. When he pressed the light switch, a soft glow from the baseball-shaped nightlight stuck into an outlet in the wall filled the room. Daniel stepped out into the hall, pulling the door shut behind him.

Nicole pushed away from the wall and he blinked, startled.

"Nic. I didn't know you were home."

"It was quiet at the diner tonight, so I closed early. I was hoping to tuck Jordan in, but it sounds like you've done a pretty good job."

Daniel lifted his shoulders. "I don't know how much of that you heard, but I'm sorry if I overstepped."

"No." Nicole shook her head. "I heard everything you said. It was … perfect. Thank you." Her voice caught. "He's asked about Gage over the years, and I tell him what he was like, who he was, the best I can, but I've always had a hard time trying to explain how he died and why. I think … I think it might have been better coming from you anyway. He admires you so much, and for you to tell him that you thought Gage was a good man, well, I think that will really help him."

"I hope so."

She tucked a strand of hair that had come loose from her ponytail behind one ear. "Where's Connie?"

"She was tired. Sharleen drove her home a couple of hours ago."

Nicole's forehead wrinkled. "I've noticed that a lot lately. I think she's feeling very worn out these days, and really missing Joe. It's almost like …" A tear rolled down her cheek and Daniel clenched his fists to keep from reaching out and wiping it away. Nicole swiped at it with the back of her hand. "It's like she's ready to go, that all she wants is to be with the one she loves."

Daniel nodded slowly. "Yeah, I get that."

Neither of them moved until Nicole cleared her throat. "I should go to bed. It's been a long day."

"Yeah, me too."

"I'll see you in the morning."

Daniel watched as she whirled around and headed into the washroom. When the door shut behind her, he closed his eyes and pressed the heel of his hand to his chest. While Connie's point was well taken, he'd push it a step further. A towering giant and a den of hungry lions were daunting foes, for sure, but at least they were enemies that were real, that could be seen and grappled with and taken down by force.

A far more difficult foe to overcome, in his opinion, was a heart that didn't know how to let go.

Chapter Fifty-Three

Daniel was deep into a discussion with Jordan about how the Leafs' season was going when Nicole strode into the kitchen and started pulling plates out of the dishwasher, setting them down hard on the counter. Daniel watched her for a moment, stomach tightening. Then he punched Jordan lightly in the shoulder. "Time for school, buddy."

Jordan slid off the bar stool and carried his dishes to the sink. "'Bye, Mom."

Nicole pulled him to her for a hug, then kissed the top of his head. "'Bye, Jord. Have a good day. Maybe the two of us can do a movie night tonight. What do you think?"

"Can't Daniel watch with us?"

Nicole didn't glance over at him. "I'm sure Daniel has work he needs to do. And you should get going or you'll be late." She slid an arm around his shoulders and walked with him toward the kitchen door. When they reached him, Daniel stood and held out Jordan's backpack. Jordan slipped out from under his mother's arm and threw his arms around Daniel's waist. Daniel's eyes met Nicole's over her son. Her mouth tightened, but she didn't speak.

Jordan let go of him and grabbed his backpack before racing for the door. Nicole started after him, but Daniel pressed a palm to the kitchen door. "I'll walk him to the bus stop and make sure he gets on all right."

She hesitated then turned back to the dishes without a word.

Daniel repressed a sigh and followed Jordan out the door. He'd gotten in the habit, the last few days, of walking Jordan to his bus stop to make sure he got there safely. Today, going with Jordan was also partly an attempt to avoid getting into anything with Nicole which, given the way she was tossing the dishes into the cupboard, seemed almost inevitable. She was approaching her breaking point. While he didn't blame her, he felt the need for a little fresh air and exercise to fortify himself for the coming confrontation.

The bus was already coming down the street by the time they exited the building, so Jordan threw him a wave and took off toward it. Daniel didn't take his eyes from the boy until he had climbed the three big steps and disappeared inside. With a sigh, Daniel strode toward the condo building. He grasped the front door handle and then let it go. *Not ready to go in yet.*

Stuffing both hands into his coat pockets, he headed down the street. Four blocks away, he came to a little coffee shop and stepped inside to warm up and grab a cup of the life-infusing liquid. He should be getting to work, but somehow, as much as he could use a little time to get himself together and ready to talk to her, Daniel felt the need to stay near Nicole today. He was as close to the breaking point as she was, and he wasn't sure which of them was going to go over the edge first. *Or what it's going to look like when it happens.*

He sat at a table in the corner, his back to the wall as he watched people come and go. A couple at a nearby table caught his attention, and he cast several glances their way. The obvious closeness between them as they talked, their hands intertwined on the table, dug like a thorn into his chest. Daniel thought again about lions and giants and the need to trust in a power greater than himself as he drained the last of his coffee and stood. *Might as well get this over with.* He crumpled the cup before tossing it into the garbage.

On the walk to her condo, he prayed for wisdom and courage as the ice-tinged February air cleared the cobwebs from his head. He'd only taken a few steps up the walkway to her building when his phone vibrated. Daniel grabbed it from his shirt pocket and scanned the screen. He grimaced. A new lead was breaking in the other case he and Sharleen were working on, and she wanted him in the office immediately.

He tapped a finger against the side of the phone. Maybe

going into work for a couple of hours wasn't the worst idea in the world. It might give him a fresh perspective, and Nicole a chance to cool off. When he returned, they could hopefully have a civilized conversation and find a way to be in the same apartment without dragging each other onto an emotional roller-coaster ride every day.

He sent a quick text to Nicole to let her know he'd be back at lunchtime so they could talk, before he jogged toward his black car, trying not to feel guilty about his relief over the delay in dealing with whatever waited for him upstairs.

Chapter Fifty-Four

The old man shuffled his way carefully down the sidewalk, the pick on the bottom of his cane digging into the ice. The process left a frosty, three-legged trail stretching out behind him. The sound of children laughing and calling to each other filled the air as he approached the schoolyard.

When he reached the group of boys kicking a soccer ball around the snow, he stopped to watch them. The ball smacked up against the chain link fence a few feet from where he was standing, and his eyes followed a young boy in a red ski jacket as he bounded over to retrieve it. The man lifted a hand in greeting and the boy raised a navy mitt in response, flashing him a toothy grin.

As the boy reached the ball, the old man continued his trek down the sidewalk. His black rubber boot slid across a patch of ice, and the cane lifted as his feet came out from under him. He went down with a thud onto the hard cement sidewalk.

"Are you all right, mister?" The boy stood at the fence, the ball tucked under his arm as he grasped the metal with both mitts. The grin was gone now from his cold-reddened cheeks, replaced by a look of concern.

"I … I'm not sure. At my age it takes the body a bit of extra time to get the message to the brain that it's hurting." The man rested both gloved hands on his knees. "I think I can get up, but I'll need my cane." The walking stick had landed a few feet away from him in a snow drift.

"Come on, Jordan." Another boy, clumps of carrot-colored hair sticking out beneath a yellow wool hat, called out, clearly oblivious to the old man's dilemma as he stamped from one foot to the other.

"Here." The boy at the fence, Jordan, tossed the ball toward the group of waiting kids. "I'll be back in a minute."

The old man waited as he jogged to an opening and out onto the sidewalk. When Jordan reached him, the boy pulled the cane out of the snow. He tapped it against the ice until the snow fell off of it before handing it to the man. "Do you need help getting up?"

"If you wouldn't mind." The man extended his hand. Jordan whipped off his mittens and slipped them into the pocket of his jacket, then reached out his little hand and clasped the man's. He grabbed hold of the fence with his other hand and used it to brace himself as he tugged on the man's fingers.

With a loud groan, the man regained his feet, firmly planting the cane into the ice as he recovered his balance.

He touched the rim of his brown plaid cap. "Much obliged, young man."

The boy's forehead wrinkled.

"It means thank you."

"Oh, then you're welcome." The shrill sound of the school bell ringing brought Jordan's head up sharply. "I better go."

"Wait." The old man placed a hand on his shoulder and leaned down to peer at him. "Aren't you Jordan Kelly?"

"Yes, I am. How did you know that?"

The man straightened. "Well, well, Jordan Kelly. I knew your father, Gage."

The emerald eyes widened. "You did?"

"Yes. He was a good man. We were close friends. In fact"—the man leaned closer and lowered his voice to a conspiratorial level—"I was with him the night he died."

For a few seconds the boy stared at him, his mouth open slightly. When he spoke, his voice was hushed. "You were with him? You know what happened?"

"Of course. I saw it with my own eyes. He was a very brave man, your father, and it's quite a tale, but I suppose you'd best be getting back to class now." He inclined his head toward the school building.

Jordan didn't look over. "I can be a few minutes late. Can you tell me about my dad? I ask my mom sometimes how he died, but she doesn't ever want to talk about it."

The old man hesitated. "I wouldn't want to get you into any trouble, but I am a little nervous about the ice now. My car is parked around the corner. If you could walk me there, make sure I don't fall again, I'd sure appreciate it. And I can tell you about your father on the way."

Jordan chewed his bottom lip. "I'm not supposed to go anywhere with strangers, but if you know my name, and you knew my dad, maybe that means you aren't one."

The man held out his hand again. "My name's Robert Green." Jordan took it and shook it solemnly. "There now, we certainly aren't strangers anymore, are we?"

A tentative smile crossed his face. "I guess not." He craned his head to look over his shoulder. "Your car's not far?"

"Right around that corner." The man indicated the direction with a wave of his gloved hand through the air. "It won't take but a minute or two to get there, so you won't be too late getting back inside if we go now."

Jordan twisted his head back to contemplate him for a few more seconds then he nodded his head once, decisively. "I'll help you. If you tell me about the night my dad died."

"Certainly." The man took a cautious step forward, feeling his way along the slippery surface.

"Here." Jordan shifted until he was at the man's side. "I've got you." He took hold of his elbow, and they made their way down the sidewalk toward the corner.

"Thank you, Son." The man reached across and patted his hand. "All right, about your dad. Let me see … It was a warm night in July. I had gotten out of bed because, you know, when you're old like me, it's pretty hard to make it all the way through the night without waking up to use the washroom."

Jordan giggled. "I have to do that too sometimes. So it was the middle of the night?"

"Yes, about twenty minutes after midnight, to be exact. I

know that because I looked at my clock radio when I woke up, like I always do so I know how much sleep I've gotten and how much longer it is until morning." The old man shuffled a few more steps. "Here we are at the corner already. And that's my car." He lifted his cane and pointed to a large brown Impala parked at the curb about twenty yards away.

"Good." Jordan threw a nervous glance over his shoulder. "I should be getting back. Will you be …?"

The old man's boot skidded across another patch of ice and the cane came off the ground, thudding against a red wooden bench beneath a bus stop sign.

Jordan let go of his elbow and wrapped an arm around his waist. "I've got you."

"Thank you, Jordan." The man steadied himself with a hand on his shoulder and the boy let go of his waist. "If you need to go, I'll be all right. Maybe I can tell you the rest of the story another time."

"No, no, I'll help you. We're almost there." Jordan took his arm again.

Suppressing a smile, the old man shuffled along beside him. "Very well. Now where was I?"

"You had gotten up to go to the washroom."

"Ah yes. I was on my way back to my bed when something moving outside the window caught my attention."

Jordan swiveled his head to look up at him, a dark curl escaping his red hat and falling down over one eye. "What was it?"

"It was a man, out on the sidewalk."

"My dad?" Jordan whispered.

"Yes." The old man nodded. "Ah, here we are." They reached the brown sedan and he rested a hand on the hood to catch his breath.

"What was he doing?"

"That's exactly what I wondered, of course. In fact, I was so curious I grabbed my camera off the dresser and zoomed in and took a few pictures."

"You have pictures of him?"

The man reached out to pat the boy on his head. "I do. As a matter of fact," his hand stilled on Jordan's head as though something had occurred to him, "I think I might have them with me, in a bag in my back seat. I came across them recently and wondered about giving them to the police, or your mother." He pursed his lips as he studied the boy. "Would you like to see them?"

Jordan nodded his head vigorously.

"All right then." The man fumbled in his pocket for his car keys. He pulled them out and hit a button on the remote control. The locks disengaged with a loud click. The man tapped on the back window with one gloved finger. "See that brown bag there?"

"Yes."

"If you want to grab it for me, I'll show you what's inside."

Jordan yanked open the back door. He reached for the bag. It was on the floor on the far side and he couldn't quite get it from the sidewalk, so he knelt on the back seat and stretched out his hand.

The old man peered up and down the empty street then slid onto the seat behind him. He shoved the boy out of his way and slammed the door, hitting the remote button to engage the locks again.

Jordan spun around. "What are you doing?"

"I'm showing you what's in that brown bag, like I said." He'd dropped the old man voice, and the look of confusion—tinged with fear this time—crossed the boy's face again. "Give it to me Jordan, now." The man held out his hand.

The boy stared at it for a few seconds then reached for the bag. When the old man grabbed it from him, Jordan turned quickly and pulled on the door handle, but nothing happened.

"Child-proof locks." The man held up his hand. The remote dangled from one finger. "A great invention. Almost as good as this one." He reached into the bag and pulled out a roll of silver duct tape.

"Help!" Jordan pounded on the window with two small fists.

The man calmly pulled a length of tape from the roll, ripped it with his teeth then reached over Jordan's head to slap it over his mouth. Jordan whirled around, the eyes peering out from under the unruly curls so huge the color was almost lost in a sea of white.

"Hold out your hands."

Jordan shook his head and the man pulled off his glove and slapped the boy across the face, snapping his head to the side. "I don't want to hurt you Jordan, but you need to do what I tell you. Do you understand?"

Tears welled in his eyes, but he nodded.

"Then let's try this again. Hold out your hands."

Jordan slowly lifted shaking arms and held them out toward him.

"That's better." Troy ripped off another length of tape with his teeth and wrapped it around the slim wrists. "Now, I could do your feet too, but I'm going to give you a chance to show me you can listen to me and do what I say so I don't have to. Can you do that?"

The boy nodded again.

"Good." He slid his hands under Jordan's arms and pulled him over until he was sitting in the middle of the backseat. He fastened the seatbelt around the boy's waist. "We want you to be safe now, don't we?" A mocking smile twisted across his face. "You and I are going to go for a little drive together. Sit still back here and don't move, and we'll be there before you know it."

He slid to the door, hit the unlock button with the remote, and shoved it open. Turning back to Jordan, he held out a finger to the boy, who hadn't moved. "Stay where you are and everything will be fine."

Troy slammed the door behind him, shoved his hand back into his glove and picked up the cane he'd dropped into the snow outside the car. For the benefit of anyone who might drive by, he hobbled around the front of the car and slid behind the wheel.

He adjusted the rear-view mirror until he could see the boy's terrified face. Troy leaned forward and jammed the key into the ignition, put the car into gear, and glided out into the street.

That had gone well. Far better than expected. He'd studied the boy for weeks now, and it hadn't taken long to determine his weakness—what some people might consider compassion, but he regarded as an over-inflated hero complex. Troy knew he wouldn't be able to resist helping him if he fell. Just like his bleeding-heart father. Troy's hands gripped the steering wheel until his knuckles ached inside his brown leather gloves. Gage Kelly had appointed himself judge and jury over the parents he deemed *unsuitable* to raise their own children and taken it upon himself to *save* every one of those children he could.

Well, that compassion had cost him his life, and now that same weakness would cost his son. A grim smile crossed his face at the irony. He hadn't lied to the boy about that, anyway, he *had* been there the night his father died.

Because Troy was the one who'd aimed his shotgun and pulled the trigger.

Chapter Fifty-Five

When Daniel came back into the kitchen, Nicole was sitting on a stool at the island, an untouched sandwich in front of her. She grabbed her plate when she saw him and stood up. After carrying it over to the refrigerator, she set it on a shelf inside and slammed the door.

Daniel's stomach tightened. *So much for cooling off.*

"What are you doing here, Daniel?"

His eyes narrowed. "I'm *trying* to do my job. Keep you and Jordan safe and find out who's threatening you. Why? What do you think I'm trying to do?"

"I won't let you use my son to try and get to me, or to get back into our lives."

Heat surged through him, but he forced his voice to remain steady. "I would never do that. Don't you know how much I care about that kid?"

"All I know is that you being here is confusing him. I told him you weren't going to be around anymore, now suddenly you have moved right in with us. I don't want you here, Daniel."

"Yeah, I got that, Nicole. Loud and clear. Although maybe Jordan isn't the only one around here who's confused."

"What is that supposed to mean?"

"It means that last night you seemed quite happy that I had talked to him, even grateful. Today you're furious with me for doing the same thing. I know *I'm* confused, and I'm getting the impression you don't have any idea what you want either."

"What I want is to be able to trust the people closest to me."

Daniel blew out a long breath in exasperation. "I'm not sure you do want that."

Nicole lifted both hands in the air. "How can you say that?"

"Look, I messed up. I know that. But I did it because there is nothing I wouldn't do to keep you from being hurt. Because I love you, Nicole. And I believe you love me. But you left me even before you found out I'd kept a secret from you."

Her head jerked at that, but he pressed on before she could speak. "You promised me you weren't going anywhere, Nic, but you broke that promise. I knew it the day you came to the hospital. I could see in your eyes that you had realized you could lose someone else to a violent death, and you weren't willing to accept that. And I know you didn't physically leave right away—you waited for me to open the door for you before you bolted—but on every other level you were gone from that point on. So even though I think you know, deep down, that you can trust me, that I would die for you, it's a lot easier to use what I did as an excuse to push me away so you can go back to living in your nice safe world again."

Her eyes flashed fire. "How dare you say that? And how dare you be angry with me? All I've ever done is trust you."

"Not enough to believe that I might have had a good reason for what I did. You never even gave me a chance to explain, just ripped the two people I care about the most in the world out of my life."

"How can you possibly explain lying to me? You had no right to do that."

Daniel shoved his fingers through his hair, stopping short of grabbing a handful and yanking. "I know that. I'm not saying it was right. I wrestled for years with telling you the truth, but in the end, I couldn't do it."

"Why not?"

"Because it almost destroyed me to watch what you went through when Gage was killed. I couldn't get your hopes up, only to see you suffer through another loss. Not until I knew for sure whether your sister was dead or alive." He came around the island and stopped in front of her.

"It was wrong not to tell you. And I'm sorrier than I can say that I hurt you. But I can't undo the past. All I can do is promise to never lie to you again. If that's not good enough for you, if you cannot forgive me, then you have to let me know that now. Because I can't go on this way, clinging to hope if there isn't any hope left to cling to. It's killing me. I need to know one way or the other. So say the word, Nicole. Tell me to stay and I'll do my best to never hurt you again, or tell me to go, and as soon as all of this is over, I will be out of your life, and Jordan's, forever. Decide."

She sagged against the counter. "Daniel, I—" Her phone rang, cutting off whatever she was about to say. Daniel clenched his teeth in frustration as she glanced down at the screen. "It's the school."

He nodded and she picked up the receiver. "Hello? ... Yes." She listened for a few seconds. "What?" The color drained from her face as her eyes met Daniel's. "I'll be right there." She disconnected the call and dropped the phone onto the counter. She swayed as though she might faint and pressed a hand to the top of the island.

Alarmed, Daniel grasped her elbow. "What is it?"

She looked up at him, eyes wide with terror. "It's Jordan. He didn't come back into the school after lunch." She shook free of him and started for the kitchen door. "I have to go."

Daniel strode after her. "No, Nic, wait."

When she turned, he took hold of both her arms. "Listen to me. I'll go. I'm sure he wandered off with some of his friends and lost track of time. But on the off chance someone did take him, you need to be here in case the guy calls."

A battle raged across her face until her shoulders slumped. When she spoke, her voice was raw with fear. "Please let me know as soon as you know anything."

"I will. I promise." He waited until she met his gaze again and he knew she'd heard him. Leaving her standing there, Daniel strode across the living room and grabbed his leather jacket. He winced as he slung his left arm into the sleeve, but he ignored the pain and yanked open the condo door.

He covered the distance from her door to the elevator almost at a run. As much as he had tried to reassure Nicole that it was probably nothing, Daniel had a deep, terrifying feeling that the man he had attempted to will out of hiding had finally come out.

And now Jordan might have to pay the price.

Chapter Fifty-Six

Gripping the steering wheel with one hand, Daniel fumbled in his shirt pocket, attempting to retrieve his cell phone. When he finally pulled it out, he hit a number and pressed the phone to his ear. His partner answered, but he waited until he had wheeled around a corner before speaking. "Shar? Jordan's missing."

"What? You mean he's lost, or someone took him?"

"That's what I need to find out. I think maybe he's been the target all along, not Nicole. I'm driving to his school right now, but you have to do something for me."

"Name it."

"Get the word out. I need a couple of officers to go to Nicole's condo to set up a trace on the phone and keep an eye on her, and as much ground force as possible to cover the area around the school and do some door-to-door. Can you tell the detective sergeant what's going on? I'll send you one of the pictures of Jordan I have on the phone if you can get approval to implement an amber alert."

"I'm on it."

"Thanks."

"Do you want me to come out?"

"Actually, I'd prefer to have you there, investigating any lead you can think of. We're missing a small piece of the puzzle, and if I figure it out, I'd like to be able to call you for information."

"All right. Let me know if you think of anything. And Grey?"

He took another turn almost on two wheels. The school loomed a couple of blocks down the street. "Yeah?"

"How's Nicole doing? She must be freaking out."

"She's freaking out without freaking out again, which, given the circumstances, shows remarkable control. Frankly, I can't even imagine what is going on in her head right now. Jordan's all she has in the world."

"He's not all she has."

The quiet words slammed into him, and he closed his eyes for a couple of seconds. "Well, at the moment he's all she can see. We have to find him."

"We will. Keep in touch."

"You too."

Daniel shoved the phone back into his pocket and screeched up to the curb in front of the schoolyard.

Leaping out of his vehicle, he strode up the walkway and into the front foyer of the school. Staff members stood around in groups of two or three, speaking in hushed tones. Like a funeral. Daniel pushed that thought away as everyone turned their heads toward him, and he held up his badge. "Detective Daniel Grey. Someone reported a missing child?"

A tall woman with short, stylish white hair disengaged herself from a group of people and came over to him. "Of course, Detective. Come into my office; we can talk there."

He followed her into a small room off the main office. She held the door for him then shut it after he walked inside.

"I'm Eileen Watkins, the principal here." She walked around her desk and lowered herself onto the chair, her face etched with worry. "And yes, one of our first-grade students, Jordan Kelly, failed to return to class after lunch. At first we assumed he'd gone a little too far off the property and didn't hear the bell, but now it's been ..." she twisted her head toward the standard school clock, silver rimmed with a white background and big black numbers, hanging on the wall, "... over an hour, and we are starting to get very concerned."

"I'm concerned too. Jordan's mother has received a few threats recently, and we're worried his disappearance might be connected to those somehow. Do you know exactly when Jordan went missing?"

"I spoke to one of his friends who said he had been playing soccer with them on the field, so he was here for at least part of the lunch recess. Why don't I call that boy down and see if he can give you any more details?"

"I'd appreciate it, thank you."

The principal pressed a button on her phone and spoke to a classroom teacher. Daniel clenched his hands in his lap, his eyes drawn to the clock. The ticking seemed suddenly deafening in the quiet room, each incessant click representing a turn of the wheels carrying Jordan farther and farther from his reach.

It seemed to take forever, but the door finally opened and a small, red-headed boy around Jordan's age stepped into the room. The principal rose to her feet. "Come in, Trevor. This is Detective Grey. He's a policeman who's going to help us find Jordan."

Daniel stood too and held out his hand. The boy, his eyes wide with awe, shook his hand silently.

Mrs. Watkins pointed to the chair beside Daniel's. "Why don't you sit down? Detective Grey has a few questions he'd like to ask you."

Daniel tamped down his impatience to get going and sat, forcing a relaxed expression onto his face that belied the turmoil raging inside. "Thanks for coming down, Trevor."

The boy nodded.

"Mrs. Watkins said you were playing soccer at recess?"

He nodded again.

The principal shifted on her chair. "Answer the detective out loud please, Trevor."

The boy scratched his freckled arm. "Yes."

"Was Jordan playing with you?"

"He was for a while."

"Then what happened?"

"An old man was walking past the school, and he slipped and fell on the ice. Some of us thought it was kind of funny ..." he shot a guilty look at the principal, "... but Jordan was all worried. He went over to the fence to talk to the man then he went out the gate to go and help him up. Last time I saw him he was walking down the sidewalk holding the man's arm like he was helping him so he wouldn't fall again."

Daniel pushed back a rising panic. "Can you describe the old man to me, Trevor? Do you remember what he looked like, or what he was wearing, anything like that?"

"He had on a long coat and gloves, and he wore a hat like my grandfather always wears. And he had a cane and white hair. That's all I remember."

"That's really good. Did it look like he was making Jordan go with him, like maybe Jordan didn't want to go?"

"No. They were talking and then Jordan nodded and went around to his side and took his arm. He looked like he wanted to go with him."

"Did you see where they went?"

"Not really. I know they walked toward the factory, but then we started playing soccer again and I wasn't watching anymore."

Daniel glanced over at Mrs. Watkins. "The factory's to the east," she told him, the worry on her face deepening to fear.

He shifted his attention to Trevor. "Thanks so much for answering my questions. If it's all right with Mrs. Watkins, you can go back to class now."

"That's fine. Thank you, Trevor."

"You're welcome." The chair legs scraped on the floor as Trevor hopped off and left the office.

Daniel waited until the door closed behind him before facing the principal. "What is it?"

"Although the factory is still operational, the area around it is pretty deserted. If this person, this old man, had a vehicle parked on that street, it's quite possible he could have forced Jordan into it and driven off without anyone seeing anything."

Daniel nodded and stood. "If you don't mind, I'm going to take a quick look around the school yard then I'll head over that way and see if I find anything."

"Of course. We're going to keep the children in during their afternoon recess, at least until we hear anything further. Please let me know if there's anything else I can do. Jordan …" her voice broke and she cleared her throat, "… of course we would be devastated if anything happened to any of the children, but Jordan is a special little boy. It doesn't surprise me that he would go over to this man and try to help him. The idea that someone could take advantage of his sweet nature like that infuriates me."

"Me too." Daniel's voice was grim as he edged toward the office door. "Thank you again. I'll let you know if we find out anything."

"I'd appreciate it."

He dipped his head in her direction before exiting through the office and going out into the yard. The cold hit him like a slap to the face. Wherever he was, he hoped Jordan was warm. Although, if he'd been taken inside, the chances of them finding him dropped substantially, unless the cop's best friend, a nosy neighbor, phoned the police to tell them he or she had seen something suspicious. The best scenario would be if he was in a car and Daniel was able to find someone along the street who might have noticed an old man and a young boy climbing into one and taken down the license plate number.

Daniel pushed back a wave of nausea, knowing neither of those options was all that likely. He scanned the area in front of him. Someone somewhere knew something, and he was going to find them and get it out of them if it took tramping around in the snow and ice all day and all night.

Nothing unusual stood out to him in the yard. Recalling what Trevor had told him, he made his way through the snow to the fence and gazed up and down the sidewalk before heading for the gate. As he stepped through it, a Toronto Police Services vehicle pulled up behind him.

Daniel explained what was going on to the two uniformed officers as quickly as he could. "If you could go door to door on this street, find out if anyone saw anything at all, that would be great. Apparently, they headed in that direction," he pointed east, "so you could do the houses on both sides from here to the corner." He pulled up a picture of Jordan on his phone and texted it to the cell numbers they gave him.

Another police car pulled up to the curb. One of the officers he'd been talking to clapped Daniel on the arm. "We'll fill them in and get them doing one side of the street while we do the other. You go do what you have to do."

"Thanks." Daniel nodded, lifted a hand in the direction of the two female officers walking toward them, then headed down the sidewalk.

The footprints in the snow caught his attention. He could make out round cane marks with a smaller, deeper hole in the middle of them, clearly a pick of some kind. Halfway across the yard, a smooth patch suggested that might be the spot where the old man had fallen. Daniel searched around, but nothing appeared to have dropped to the ground either when he fell, or when Jordan helped him to his feet. Daniel continued down the sidewalk. Every once in a while, a patch of snow blown across the ice showed the cane marks alongside two sets of footprints, one larger and the other a small set that tightened his throat whenever he saw it.

He crouched and took several pictures of each of the marks, making his way painstakingly to the corner. When he reached it, he scanned the area in front of him and then to his left. The cross-street dead-ended at the back of an old, crumbling brick factory building. The principal had been right. The street was so quiet it appeared deserted. No houses lined the road in this industrial district. Any windows on the back of the building at the end of the block were either thick with dust and grime, or boarded up, so the likelihood that anyone passing by one might have happened to glance out and see anything was slim. He'd still send a couple of the uniforms in to check out the possibility though, since even a slim likelihood was better than none at this point.

His thoughts churning, Daniel took a step forward and cracked his shin against something hard. A red bench covered in a layer of snow. Something lay on the ground beneath it, and his heartrate accelerated when he realized it was a small navy mitten. He picked it up in his gloved hand and looked inside the opening at the top. The words *J. Kelly* written on the tag inside in black marker hit him in the chest. Why had Jordan taken off a mitt? And what had caused him to drop it? Daniel stood in one spot and slowly turned, scanning the area around the place he had found the mitten. He picked up what looked like a spot where the adult-sized boot had slid on the ice. Had the old man slipped again? If he had knocked against Jordan, or if Jordan had grabbed for him, he could have dropped a mitt he'd stuck in his pocket earlier, maybe when he was playing soccer, or when he reached out to help the man get to his feet outside the school.

Daniel gritted his teeth. All speculation, and precious little to go on, but it did make sense and was starting to paint at least a vague picture of what had happened to this point. He glimpsed the footprints he'd been following farther down the sidewalk leading to the factory. At least he knew they'd turned here and not gone straight ahead, narrowing the investigation area somewhat.

Daniel followed the footprints for another eight or ten yards before they ended. He went back to the spot where he'd seen the last ones and looked carefully around. The snow that had been cleared off the sidewalk was piled up at the curb. Daniel found the footprints again, sunk deep into the snow and leading to the edge of the street. His heart sank when he saw tire marks beyond them. They must have gotten into a vehicle here. He looked carefully, but there didn't appear to be any sign of a struggle, or any indication that Jordan had been pushed or dragged into the car. For some reason, he must have gotten in willingly. Most likely the man had enticed him in somehow, and Jordan wouldn't have realized anything was wrong until he wasn't allowed to get back out again.

Daniel pushed back the rage that roared through him. He had to keep his emotions in check and stay focused if he was going to be any use to Jordan. Yanking out his phone, he snapped several pictures of whatever tire marks he could find and sent all the photos to Sharleen to pass along to the lab. He also texted her a request to send someone from forensics to check out everything he'd found.

He was putting his phone away when the first pair of officers showed up at the corner. Daniel hurried toward them. Even before he reached them, he knew they hadn't discovered anything.

One of them shook his head as he approached. "No answer at most of the houses. The two people that did come to the door hadn't seen or heard anything unusual."

Daniel nodded. He'd expected that, but the disappointment still stung. "I followed their footprints down this street"—he waved an arm toward the factory—"about ten yards before it appears they got into a vehicle. If you could go into the factory down there and nose around a bit, see if anyone happened to see anything through one of those back windows, or while out in the alley having a smoke, anything like that, I'd appreciate it." He tugged off a glove and reached for one of his cards. "Let me know if you find out anything at all. I took a bunch of pictures, but otherwise I don't think there's much more we can do here until forensics arrives."

The man stuffed the card into his coat pocket and nodded. "We'll keep in touch."

"Thanks." Daniel made his way back to his car, his eyes glued to the ground for any small clue he might have missed. When he got to his vehicle, he shook his head in frustration. Boot prints, a mitten, and tire marks. Not a lot to go on, although slightly better than nothing.

An unmarked car pulled up to the curb. Daniel recognized the officer getting out as Tim Hopkins from the lab. They shook hands when Tim reached him, and Daniel went back over everything he'd seen and knew so far about what might have happened.

When they arrived at Daniel's car, Tim gripped his shoulder. "I hear this case is personal for you."

What exactly had Sharleen told him? "It is."

Tim nodded. "I'll do everything I can to find out something for you then, and let you know if I have any luck."

"I appreciate it."

Daniel watched him as he turned to go to work. Luck wouldn't help Jordan any. *Only you can do that, Lord. Please watch over that boy now and show me how to find him.* He left the forensic investigation in Tim's hands and climbed into his car.

Knowing there was nothing more he could do at the scene, he decided to drive back to Nicole's and grab something of Jordan's they could use if they needed to bring in a dog. *She must be frantic.* He'd feel a little less sick about returning to her condo if he had more to offer her than what he'd been able to find out so far.

Chapter Fifty-Seven

The kid stumbled and nearly fell on the last step before the second floor. Troy yanked him up by the elbow and dragged him down the hallway and into a bedroom with a mattress shoved into the corner. "Here. Sit." He pushed Jordan onto the makeshift bed.

The boy dug his heels into the mattress and scrambled away from Troy until his back was pressed against the wall.

Troy studied him. The green eyes above the duct tape regarded him intently. The terror he'd seen in them in the car had diminished. *Not happy about that.* When Matthew was here—the hot flush of anger that always poured through him at the necessity of speaking of his son in the past tense filled him now—things had always gone smoother when his little blue eyes were wide with fear. When a child overcame fear, defiance quickly moved in and gained a foothold. If there was anything his father had taught him growing up, it was that defiance could never, ever be allowed a foothold inside a boy's heart and mind. It needed to be viciously attacked and dug out by the roots, like an ugly weed.

Troy took a step toward him and Jordan pressed farther into the corner. *Good.* He hadn't completely lost control of him yet. He knelt down on the mattress and reached for the boy. Jordan shrank from him, but Troy grabbed hold of one end of the duct tape and ripped it from his face.

Jordan let out a cry of pain and shock.

A cold smile crossed Troy's face. "Go ahead, cry all you want. This room is one hundred percent soundproof. You can yell and scream until you turn blue, but no one will hear you. Do you understand? I made it that way when I had a little boy and he used to holler and holler when I left him here."

Jordan nodded. His eyes had filled again when Troy had ripped the tape off, and one tear slid down his cheek now, but he quickly swiped his face across the shoulder of his coat. "I was trying to help you."

"What?"

"When you fell on the ice, I was trying to help you. Why did you bring me here?"

Troy sat down on the edge of the mattress. "Remember when I said I knew your dad?"

"Yes."

He leaned in closer to the boy, wanting to make sure he heard every word. "Well, I wasn't lying about that. I *was* lying when I said we were friends, and that he was a brave man. The truth is, your dad was a big yellow coward."

Jordan brought his hands, still bound together with duct tape, up so quickly Troy didn't have time to react before they connected with his jaw and his head snapped back.

He whipped around and raised his hand to strike. The boy lifted his chin, eyes fastened on Troy. For a long moment Troy stared at him then he slowly lowered his hand. "All right, you're sticking up for your dad. Family is everything, so I'll let you get away with that. This time. Raise a hand to me again though, and I'll teach you a lesson you won't soon forget. Do you hear me?"

Jordan swallowed and nodded.

"Good." Troy rubbed his jaw with the back of his hand. "Do you read the Bible, Jordan?"

"Yes. My mom reads it to me. And we read it at church."

"That's good. There's some helpful things in that book, if you know what to look for. Like the verse, 'the sins of the fathers shall be visited upon their sons.' Did you ever read that one?"

"No. We usually read stories about Jesus and David and Goliath and Jonah and the whale. I don't know that one."

"That's too bad, because it's the reason I brought you here."

"I don't know what you mean."

Troy grunted as he pushed himself up off the mattress. "I have to go downstairs for a little while. You think about it while

I'm gone and see if you can figure it out."

"I want to go home."

"I'm sure you do. But I'm afraid that's not possible, Jordan. I've been planning for your visit here for a very long time, and now that you've finally arrived, I think I'm going to keep you here for a while. At least until it's time."

"Time for what?"

"Time for your surprise. The one that has something to do with the verse I told you." Troy tromped across the worn hardwood floor in his black rubber boots.

"Daniel will come and get me."

He whirled back around. "Who's Daniel?"

"He's our friend, my mom's and mine, and he has a gun."

Ah yes, the cop. "You better get one thing straight in your head, little man. No one in the whole world knows you're here, except me. No one's coming for you. Not tonight, not ever. You got that?"

The little chin lifted higher. "Daniel will."

Troy snorted. "Believe what you want. In a little while it won't much matter anyway." He stepped into the hallway then pulled the bedroom door closed and locked it. Gripping the handrail, he made his way down the stairs to the kitchen. He rummaged through the cupboards and pulled a can of soup off the shelf. Might as well have something to eat. It wasn't time yet, and he didn't want to rush the surprise. He wanted Jordan to wonder where he was and why he was there and when he'd be allowed to go home.

Like Matthew must have wondered all those things. *Maybe he's still wondering.* Troy slammed the can opener down on the counter under his open hand with a loud clang. His son must have been so scared that night, wondering what was going on. And he didn't deserve that. He'd already been through enough sorrow in his life, watching his mama die like she had.

Troy's fingers tightened around the can opener. "Rosie." He whispered the word, the name still sending debilitating pain through him. She'd suffered too. And like the night his son was taken, there was nothing he could do to help her. He swallowed around the thickness in his throat. Too much suffering. Him. Rosa. Matthew. Jordan. Was there never going to be an end to it? Maybe he should let the boy go. That might finally finish …

His head lifted. No. Gage Kelly hadn't let Troy's son go. He died making sure Matthew was taken so far away from him he would never be able to find him. He hadn't been able to muster up an ounce of sympathy or mercy, not even while staring down the barrel of a shotgun. And if he wouldn't show Troy's son any mercy, Troy sure wasn't about to show his son any. The sins of the father would be visited upon the son, like the Bible said.

Troy dumped the contents of the can into a pot, splashed in some milk, and stirred it around. He'd take his time eating and then gather up everything he would need to get the job done. Let the boy sit for a few hours, alone, scared and confused about what was going on. It all had to happen at twenty past midnight, same as it had with Matthew. There was no need to hurry. As he'd told Jordan, no one in the world knew they were there. No one would be able to figure out what had happened to Jordan in time to stop Troy from doing what he had to do. What the Good Book told him he should.

Take a life for a life.

Chapter Fifty-Eight

Nicole stood at the large window in the living room, staring out the glass. Somewhere out there, her little boy was lost and frightened, probably wondering where she was and why she wasn't coming to rescue him. She pressed a fist to her mouth to stifle a sob.

She spun around at the sound of the intercom buzzer and hurried across the room to stab at the button with her thumb. "Daniel?"

"No. It's Mikayla."

Disappointment slashed through Nicole, but she shoved it away. "Come on up." She pushed the other button and braced herself with a hand pressed to the wall. Maybe it was a good thing that Mikayla had come by. She was going crazy here all alone, except for the two police officers in the kitchen who had arrived to hook a tracer to her phone in case the kidnapper called. *Kidnapper. What a horrible word.* Nicole bit her lip. The irony that technically that's what her husband had been struck her. She wasn't a believer in karma, but it did seem to be beyond all rational explanation that her son would suffer the same fate as other children had at the hands of his father.

Except Gage was rescuing children and would never have hurt them. She wished she could believe the same about her son's abductor. Nicole moaned and pressed her knuckles to her mouth. Besides that day in the park when Daniel found him, she'd lost Jordan a couple of times when he was younger. Once in a department store when he'd thought it was funny to hide inside a round rack of clothes, and another time at a fair crowded with people. Both times she had stood frozen, the world slowing to a crawl around her, as one clear thought—*I have no idea where my child is*—pushed its way through the panic.

At the time she could remember thinking there was no worse feeling in the world than that. But then, both times, she'd found her son, giggling and oblivious to her fear, in less than five minutes.

She knew now that the thought that followed that one in a situation like this—*and chances are I may never see him again*—was far, far worse.

Nicole jumped at the sound of a knock. Pushing herself away from the wall, she pulled open the door.

Mikayla stared at her. "What is it? What's wrong?" She stepped into the condo and closed the door before taking hold of Nicole's arms. "Has something happened?"

Nicole looked at her, unable to frame a response to that question.

Mikayla let go of her long enough to slip off her coat and drop it onto the chair behind her, then she slid an arm around Nicole's shoulders and guided her toward the couch in the living room. "Never mind, I know something's wrong. I've been feeling it all afternoon, in here." She rubbed a hand over her chest. "That's why I came over. I had to see you and find out if you were all right. Here, sit down and tell me about it."

Nicole sank onto the couch. Mikayla lowered herself onto the coffee table in front of her and reached for her hands. "Nic, you're freezing. What is it, has something happened to Jordan?"

She nodded. "Yes, he …" She pressed her eyes shut for a few seconds. Mikayla waited for her to find the words. Nicole opened her eyes and fixed her gaze on her sister's worried face. "Jordan's missing."

Mikayla's eyes widened. "Missing? You mean someone's taken him?" She drew in a quick, horrified breath. "Do they think it's the man who's been threatening you? Is this what that was all about?"

"I don't know. Daniel's gone to the school to try and figure out what happened. They called to say he didn't come in after lunch, and that's the last thing I've heard." She slumped against the back of the couch. "I've been going out of my mind sitting here waiting and not being able to do anything, but Daniel said I needed to be here in case the kid—in case whoever has him tries to call."

"Oh, sweetie." Mikayla tightened her grip on her hands. "It's going to be okay. Daniel loves your son like his own. He won't rest until he tracks down whoever did this and brings Jordan home to you."

"I keep telling myself the same thing. I know he'll do everything he possibly can, but what if it's too late? What if Jordan's gone and they're never able to …"

Mikayla shook her head. "Don't think like that. You can't lose hope, Nic. If he was taken from school, there would have been lots of kids who saw what happened and can tell the police. They're acting quickly—I'm sure they'll be able to figure out who did this and find Jordan before they get very far. Trust God, Nic, and trust Daniel, that together they will bring your son home."

Trust Daniel. A wave of remorse crashed through her when she remembered the accusation he'd leveled at her that afternoon, that she hadn't trusted him enough. "You're right. I have to trust. Jordan's out of my hands now." She squeezed her sister's fingers. "Thank you for coming over. I don't know what I would have done if you hadn't shown up."

"I'm glad I was here. In fact …" Mikayla dropped her gaze to their clasped hands.

"What?"

"This probably isn't the time to talk about it, but I've been thinking I might possibly move up here to Toronto."

Nicole's mouth dropped open. "Really?"

Mikayla let go and crossed her legs. "I'm thinking about it. I can paint anywhere, and of course there are lots of galleries in this city. I have a few friends in Chicago, but I don't have any family or really strong ties there anymore except my agent Leigh. But she's busy with her own family. You're my family now, and I can't stand the thought of leaving for good and being hundreds of miles away from you. I feel as though you and I have lost so much time together already, I don't want to lose another minute. I want us to have time to really get to know each other, to do all kinds of family stuff together—like celebrate birthdays and holidays and have girl's movie nights and go out for dinner. I haven't even been to your diner yet or toured around Toronto. I know it's kind of a crazy idea, but the minute it occurred to me it felt right. What do you think?"

"Are you kidding? I love the idea. I haven't even been able to think about you leaving, it's been such a depressing thought. And Jordan ..." Nicole stopped and pressed her fingers to her lips. "When Jordan comes back home, he'll be thrilled at having endless amounts of time to spend with his aunt."

"I look forward to that too." Mikayla stood up. "I'll put the kettle on and make us tea. Have you eaten anything today?"

She thought back to the events of that morning. "I had a few bites of a sandwich at lunch. But I don't feel like anything. Maybe in a little while. I think I'll hang out in Jordan's room for a bit."

Mikayla nodded. "I'll bring your tea in there when it's ready."

"Thank you." Nicole stood and grabbed the portable phone off the table at the end of the couch. *Just in case.* Her legs trembled, but she made her way across the living room, feeling her sister's gaze on her as she went. As disappointed as she'd been when she realized who was at the door, she was deeply grateful Mikayla had shown up when she had.

Pressing one hand to the hallway wall as she walked, she reached her son's bedroom and stepped inside. The sight of all the objects he loved—posters of hockey players and his beloved books on the shelf and the super-hero sheets and blankets on the bed—sent sadness rippling through her even as it comforted her.

Nicole climbed onto his bed. She grabbed the pillow she'd slipped his favorite Spiderman pillowcase onto the day before and clutched it to her chest as she leaned against the headboard.

Holden. She should let him know what was going on.

Wanting to leave the land line free, Nicole pulled the cell phone out of her pocket. An image of Christina, her face pale and her hand pressed to her abdomen that day in the dress shop, flashed through her mind. She couldn't worry her, not until they knew for sure what was happening. But Holden had to know. She tapped in her brother-in-law's cell number and gripped the device tightly as it rang. Maybe Holden could find a way to break it to Christina that wouldn't stress her out too much. Nicole really needed the two of them to be praying. She'd love to ask Connie to pray too but couldn't bring herself to frighten her.

"Hey, Nic."

Nicole's throat tightened at the sound of her friend's cheerful greeting. "Chris? I was trying to reach Holden."

"He's at work. He forgot his phone at home today."

"Why are you home?"

"I've been a little tired the last few days, and this morning I couldn't bring myself to get up and go, so I'm working from here. At least, I was. At the moment I'm lying on the bed reading. Do you want me to give him a message?"

Nicole hesitated.

"What is it?" The compassion in Christina's voice nearly undid her, and Nicole pressed her trembling lips together. "Did something happen with Daniel?"

"No." *I can't do this to her.* "Everything's fine, but could you ask Holden to call me when he gets home? I want to talk to him about something."

For a few seconds, nothing but silence filled the air between them. Then Nicole caught the sound of a mattress creaking. "Don't get up, Chris. Please. Everything's—"

"Don't say it. Everything is clearly not fine. So either you tell me what is going on, or I'm coming over there."

Nicole exhaled. "All right. I wanted to let Holden know that Jordan didn't go back into the school after lunch today. But Daniel's looking for him and—"

"Wait. Are you saying Jordan is *missing*?"

Nicole winced. That was exactly what she'd been trying *not* to say, the word was so horrifying. "Daniel thinks he likely wandered off the property with friends, but he's gone to the school to check it out."

"That doesn't sound like something—" A door slammed in the background. "Hang on, I think Holden's home. He'll want to talk to you." Christina said something else, but muffled, as though she'd put her hand over the phone.

Seconds later, Holden's voice came over the line. "Nic? What's going on?"

Her head felt suddenly too heavy for her neck. Nicole rested it against the headboard and closed her eyes. How many times would she have to tell this story? "The school called an hour ago to say Jordan hadn't come in after his lunch recess. Daniel went to look for him. I'm sure it's nothing, but I wanted you to know what was happening."

"I'm coming over."

"No, Holden, don't. Please. There's nothing you can do here."

"Are you alone?"

"No. Mikayla's with me. Please stay with Christina. I'm worried about her."

He blew out a breath. "So am I." He didn't speak for a few seconds. When he did, his voice sounded strained, as though he was being pulled in two directions. Which of course he was. "All right, I won't come on two conditions. One, you call if there is anything you need, and two, you let us know the second you hear anything."

"I will, I promise. But all I need right now is for you to pray."

"You know we will. And I'm glad Daniel is on this—you know you can trust him to move heaven and earth to find Jordan."

Her chest tightened. "Yes, I do. Thanks for praying." Nicole disconnected the call and set the cell phone on the bedside table next to the bobble head figurine of some athlete she didn't even know. *Trust.* She sagged against the headboard. There was that word again. And that was all she could do now. Trust God. And trust Daniel. Mikayla and Holden were right—he loved Jordan and would do everything in his power to save him. A sad smile crossed her face as she recalled their conversation in the park the day he had come out of the shadows, and his joking reference to being a super-hero trying to rid the world of evil. What she wouldn't give for that to be true now. He'd told her once that he'd decided to become a cop when he was three because he still believed then that such a thing was possible. But today, the truth that evil was not only still very much present in the world but had thrust itself into the middle of their lives, threatening to destroy any little bit of hope and joy they had, undermined that belief once again.

Nicole pulled up her knees and rested her forehead on the pillow, inhaling the faint scent of the baby shampoo she'd used on her son's hair the night before.

Please God. Please God. Please God. She couldn't dredge up any other words through the tempest of emotions swirling through her. Peace tried to claw its way through the fear. She caught the faint scent of it, like smoke carried on a breeze from a fire miles away, but it drifted off again before she could fully inhale it. Before it could settle in her soul.

Peace would not come until she knew what had happened to her son and whether or not she would ever see him again.

Chapter Fifty-Nine

Daniel pushed open the door to Jordan's room. "Nic?"

His heart broke at the hopeful look on her face when she raised her head. He lifted a hand. "Nothing yet."

She closed her eyes as he crossed the room and sat on the edge of the bed. Her face dropped to the Spiderman pillow she had clutched to her chest, her knees drawn up tight. The cordless phone lay on the blanket beside her.

"Nic." Daniel touched her knee. "There are all kinds of cops on this, and they've already issued an amber alert. It's only a matter of time before ..."

She lifted her head again. The curtains were drawn, and her face was so pale it almost glowed in the soft glimmer of the nightlight. "Why won't God let me keep anybody?"

The pain and confusion in her voice nearly killed him. All he wanted to do was gather her in his arms and hold her until everything was all right again. His fists clenched at his sides. There was nothing he could do to help her. Except for one thing. "I'll find him. I promise."

She leaned forward and grabbed his hand. "Please, Daniel. Please bring him home to me. Don't let them hurt him. He's so little, he won't understand." She let go of him and covered her face with both hands.

"Nicole." Daniel slid closer and gripped both her arms. The pain that shot through his shoulder at the movement blinded him for a few seconds and he blinked, trying to focus on her face. "Look at me."

Slowly she lowered her hands.

"You have to stay strong, for Jordan. Thinking about everything that could happen is not helping him, and it's definitely not helping you." He increased the pressure slightly on her arms until her eyes locked on his. *Good, stay with me.* "You are not alone. I know you've lost people you cared about, but there are still people in your life who love you, and we're all here to help you. You know that, right?" He waited until she nodded. "I have to go now. I only came to get a shirt or something of Jordan's. But I need you to do something for me. Pray, Nic. Pray like you have never prayed before. God knows exactly where Jordan is, and we need His help to find him."

The confusion cleared from her eyes. "I will."

"Good." He squeezed her arms and let her go. "Where can I find a shirt of Jordan's, preferably one that hasn't been washed?"

She pointed across the room. Daniel rose and went to the clothes hamper in the corner. His stomach lurched when he lifted the lid and pulled out the long-sleeved, navy blue shirt Jordan had worn a couple of nights ago at his hockey practice. He turned to her. "I'll be back as soon as I can."

She nodded and clutched the pillow to her chest.

Daniel stumbled into the hallway and headed for the door of the condo. The knots in his stomach were so tight he could barely walk upright. And his shoulder throbbed every time he moved. But none of that mattered. He *was* going to find Jordan and bring him back to Nicole.

An image of her pale face, twisted in fear and pain, flashed through his mind. Daniel's grip on the little shirt in his hand tightened. When he found out who was doing this to her, whoever it was had better pray that Jordan was all right. If Daniel had to come home and tell her she would never see her son again, he wouldn't do it until he had ripped the man who had taken Jordan from her limb from limb.

Chapter Sixty

Daniel slammed a fist against the steering wheel. Who would want to hurt Jordan? He was an innocent little kid.

A life for a life. A life for a life. What did that mean? Jordan had never hurt anyone or taken a life.

Taken a life. Daniel's head shot up. Jordan hadn't taken a life, no, but his father *had* taken three children away from their parents before he had been stopped. Could one of them be coming after his son now out of some twisted sense of justice?

He grabbed the phone out of his pocket and stabbed his partner's number. "Shar." He didn't wait for her to respond. "Maybe all of this is connected to Gage abducting those kids. A life for a life could be one of those parents feeling like Gage should lose his son like they lost theirs. What do you think?"

"Makes sense. But why would they wait so long?"

"That's what I need you for. I haven't had a chance to check the release list the last few weeks. Can you look at the ones starting from a couple of months ago, see if any names jump out at you? Especially look for anyone who might be connected to those missing kids in any way."

"I'm on it." The sound of clicking keys brought him a small measure of comfort. Something was being done, anyway. "I'll call you as soon as I find anything."

The line went dead, and he shoved the phone back inside his jacket. Not having any idea which direction to drive, Daniel pulled over to the side of the road and ran through a mental list of the kids Gage had targeted. He tapped his fingers against the steering wheel as the name Matthew Gibson ran through his mind. He was the last child Gage had taken, and the one whose father had ended Gage's life. Daniel figured he was down on the list of suspects. He'd already taken a life for the life of his son, so it made sense that the one still seeking revenge hadn't had the opportunity to exact any retribution yet.

Made sense to him, anyway. The problem was, the criminal mind, particularly if mental instability was thrown into the mix, didn't always perceive situations the way the rest of the population might, meaning Daniel's logic might be faulty. Unfortunately, until Sharleen let him know if any of the parents had been recently released from prison, logic was all he had to go by.

Daniel drummed his palms on the steering wheel, desperate to be back on the road and heading somewhere, anywhere. He glanced at his watch. Five minutes after midnight. Twelve hours since Jordan had been taken from the schoolyard. And every minute that passed decreased the chances they would find him. Daniel gritted his teeth so hard they ached. Toronto was a huge city, and Jordan could be anywhere. Maybe he wasn't even in the city anymore. They hadn't been able to find any witnesses who'd seen the car the abductor had driven Jordan away in. He could be sailing down the 401 right now, hours from Toronto, heading east to Quebec or west to the prairies, and no one would know to stop him. Daniel groaned. *I have to do something. I can't sit here another minute.* He reached for the key but pulled back when his cell phone vibrated.

He stabbed the button and pressed the unit to his ear. "Grey."

"It's Troy Gibson." The tightness in Sharleen's voice filled him with apprehension.

"Are you sure?" He was already reaching for the key. So much for logic.

"He was released ten weeks ago after serving six years at The East for manslaughter."

Daniel pulled a U-turn and squealed down the street. Troy Gibson's place was a good twenty minutes away, going the speed limit. He slapped the flashing light onto the dashboard and pressed on the accelerator. "Manslaughter? He killed someone else besides Gage Kelly?"

"Yeah. I talked to his parole officer. Apparently, he lost it after Matthew disappeared. He was already largely out of control, but losing his son a year after losing his wife pushed him over the edge. He started spending every spare minute in bars and ended up shooting a guy during an altercation one night. He was charged with second degree murder but pleaded down to manslaughter and got seven years."

"And he had to serve six of them, meaning his behavior in prison mustn't have been exactly exemplary either."

"That was my take as well."

"I'm on my way."

"I'll meet you at his place. I'm leaving the building now."

"Can you request back-up and ask Williams to bring the dog?"

"Already done."

"Thanks, Shar. See you there."

Daniel swerved around a car pulling out of a driveway and pushed down harder on the gas pedal. He didn't like anything he'd heard from his partner. Troy Gibson, a clearly unstable repeat offender with a fixation on vengeance, had gotten hold of Jordan. Until now he'd been afraid the boy's life was in danger, now he knew for sure it was.

He gripped the steering wheel and concentrated on avoiding anything that might slow him down. At this point, every second counted.

All he could do now was get there as quickly as possible. And pray he wasn't too late.

Chapter Sixty-One

Troy woke up with a start. He'd pulled the heavy dark curtains over the living room window before he stretched out on the couch, and he blinked now in the dim light, trying to get his bearings. *What time is it?* He held his watch up to the thin beam of moonlight drifting into the room through the crack in the curtains. 12:10 am. *Why am I on the couch?* He pressed the tips of his fingers to both temples, trying to think. Then his head jerked. Jordan Kelly was in Matthew's bedroom. And it was time.

He swung his legs over the side of the couch and rubbed his face with both hands, trying to push away the sleep haze. The next few minutes were momentous, the culmination of all his thinking and planning while incarcerated. He wanted to make sure he was awake and alert enough to carry out the clear directive and then to get rid of every bit of evidence. The last thing he wanted was to be behind bars again. A shudder moved through him as he pushed to his feet.

Troy had already gathered up the supplies he would need, for after, and shoved them into a garbage bag. Now he dragged the bag over to the bottom of the stairs and went to retrieve his chosen instrument of justice. Troy carried the long, thin box to the table and set it down. For a moment he rested his hands on the smooth wooden surface, praying for the strength and courage to do what had to be done, then he lifted the lid.

The light hanging above the kitchen table glinted off the shiny metal. Troy lifted the knife reverently out of the box. He inspected one side of it and then the other before nodding, satisfied. He'd sharpened it the day before so it would be ready when his plan came together.

Grasping the handle tightly in one hand, Troy walked over to the refrigerator. The front of it was completely bare, except for a small, two-by-three-inch school picture of Matthew, taken a month before he disappeared. Troy ran trembling fingers over the worn surface of the photo. "This is for you, my son. His life for yours. Like I promised."

Troy turned away from the picture, tightened his grip on the knife, and headed for the stairs. He grabbed the black garbage bag and started up, the bag bumping against each step as he ascended. At the top, Troy set the bag down outside Matthew's bedroom door.

After sliding the key into the lock and turning it soundlessly, he pushed the door a crack and stopped, the sound of the boy's voice catching his attention. *Who is he talking to?* A cold chill passed over his skin. Had someone sneaked into the house and past him somehow while he was asleep on the couch? He leaned closer to the crack in the door, trying to catch the words. After a few seconds, his shoulders relaxed. The boy was talking to himself. He listened, his eyes narrowing.

"LaToya held Pumpkin tightly around the middle while Lala painted his nails a bright pink. Since Pumpkin was a boy, he was not happy that his nails were pink. He wriggled out of LaToya's arms and ran all around the house, over the counters and the beds and the furniture, leaving little pink dots everywhere he went. When Lala's mother came home, she was not—"

Troy flung open the bedroom door, and Jordan's head came up sharply.

"Who's Lala?"

The boy didn't answer. His eyes were riveted on the blade in Troy's hand. Except for a faint splotch of pink where Troy had slapped him in the car, his face went completely white.

Troy smiled.

Chapter Sixty-Two

Daniel snatched the light from the front window and forced himself to let off on the accelerator as he pulled up to the house, not wanting to give Troy Gibson any warning of his approach. Memories of the last time he'd arrived here in time to see Gage gunned down in the street slammed into him. He had to get Jordan out of this guy's clutches before it was too late.

If it isn't already.

He had to stay positive and focused. If Jordan was in the house with Troy Gibson, this was a hostage situation, and those could turn ugly fast if not handled properly.

Two blue, white, and red Toronto Police Service vehicles sped up the street toward him, and he motioned them to the curb, thankful they hadn't come in with lights and sirens blaring. Four uniformed cops, one leading a German shepherd on a leash, climbed out of the vehicles and congregated on the far side of one of the cars, waiting for him as he approached. Another vehicle tore down the street, and Daniel exhaled as Sharleen pulled over to the curb and jumped out. Having her there calmed him. He could count on her to know the best way to back him up, whatever happened.

"What's the situation?" One of the uniformed officers stepped forward as Daniel joined them.

"One male suspect, probably armed, definitely dangerous, holding a six-year-old boy hostage. If they're in the house, as far as we know they're the only ones."

"And the plan?"

"We'll give him thirty seconds to open the door and then we're going in. Here." Daniel handed Jordan's shirt to the cop with the dog. "Keep him from barking if you can."

Williams nodded tersely and held the shirt to the dog's nose as Daniel continued.

"We believe his intent is not to hold the kid for ransom, but to kill him, so time is critical. Not entirely sure what we'll find when we get in, so follow my lead. Everyone ready?"

After receiving nods from all the officers in the circle, Daniel spun around and headed up the walkway toward the house. He climbed the wooden stairs of the porch and reached out to press the doorbell. Thirty seconds was about twenty-five too long, he decided. After fifteen, with no movement or noise from inside the house, he tried the door handle then aimed a kick near the knob that splintered the wood. One more kick and the door flew open.

Daniel waved Williams and the dog in ahead of everyone. The animal raced into the room, stopping to sniff at a pile of clothing tossed onto a chair. Daniel nudged through the pile with the tip of his finger. A long brown coat was draped over the chair, a pair of black gloves, a tan plaid cap, and a white wig piled on top of it. Remnants of the old man who had lured Jordan away from the schoolyard. Now they knew for sure that it was Troy Gibson who had taken Jordan, and that they were in the house. Or had been at some point, anyway.

The dog left the pile and lowered his nose to the ground. Daniel followed him as he loped toward the stairs. The dog didn't hesitate, but led Williams straight up to the second floor, Daniel right behind them. The dog stopped outside a bedroom door and the trainer nodded curtly at Daniel. Sharleen came up behind him. Daniel met her gaze. "Ready?"

She nodded.

Williams and the dog stepped out of the way as Daniel moved to the door, straining to hear any sound or movement coming through the tiny crack in the opening. Jordan's voice, tight with fear, slashed through the thick silence.

"Why do you have a knife?"

"I told you, kid. The sins of the father will be visited upon the son. It's time for your surprise."

With confirmation that the man who had Jordan was armed,

Daniel reached under his jacket and yanked his Glock from the holster. He jerked his head and Sharleen fell in behind him as he kicked open the door and stormed into the room.

On a mattress on the floor, Troy Gibson spun around on his knees, grabbing Jordan across the chest to pull him close as he pressed the knife to the boy's throat. "Stay back!"

Sharleen came up beside him, but the other officers remained out of sight in the hallway.

"Drop your weapons," Troy commanded. When neither of them moved, he dug the tip of the knife into Jordan's neck and the boy cried out.

"Okay, okay." Daniel reached out slowly and tossed his gun onto the floor. Sharleen did the same.

"Kick them over here."

Gritting his teeth, Daniel took a step forward.

"Not you, her." Troy jerked his head toward Sharleen. She stepped up and kicked both guns toward him.

Daniel tensed, prepared to leap for the man if he reached for the weapons, but he didn't make a move as he focused his gaze on Daniel.

"I have every right to do this, take a life for a life. His daddy took my boy, and now I am going to take his daddy's son away."

Daniel's heart pounded at the sight of the blade against Jordan's throat. One quick move by the man wielding it and there wouldn't be anything they could do to save him. He forced himself to take a deep breath to keep the panic at bay. "Jordan didn't have anything to do with that. He wasn't even born yet. It was his dad who took Matthew, not him. And you already took Gage's life. So a life has been taken for a life."

A jolt, like an electric shock, moved through Troy Gibson at the mention of his son's name.

Definite area of vulnerability.

"But I want him to pay like I am, missing his son every single day, not knowing where he is and if he's afraid or sick or sad and wondering why I'm not coming for him."

"Gage is dead, Troy. He won't know that you took Jordan."

"But his mama will know."

"She doesn't deserve this. She had nothing to do with the abductions, either. And you've already punished her by taking away her husband."

A flicker of uncertainty crossed the man's face.

Daniel moved quickly to press his advantage. "If you hurt Jordan, you'll go to jail for the rest of your life. You don't want to go back there, do you?"

The color drained from Troy's face, but he didn't answer.

"And Matthew's case has never been closed. We're still following up on leads and trying to find him. What if we do and we want to bring him home to you, but you've gone to prison? You will have lost any chance you have of ever being with your son again."

Troy blinked several times. "You might still find Matthew?"

"Yes. Every once in a while, a new lead pops up. We don't believe the children were hurt, only given to new families, so we're hopeful we'll be able to track them all down eventually and reunite them with the parents who lost them."

The knife slid a couple of inches from Jordan's throat. Daniel nudged Sharleen in the foot, and she nodded almost imperceptibly.

"My boy might come home?"

"Yes. And you don't want to be locked up in a prison cell somewhere when he does, do you?"

The knife slipped farther. "No." Troy rasped out the word.

Sharleen darted in. Before Troy could move, she'd yanked Jordan from his grasp and pulled him into her arms.

Troy lunged toward them, still kneeling, the knife slashing through the air, but Daniel stepped in front of them, avoided the strike, and grabbed the man's wrist, twisting his arm until the weapon clattered onto the wooden floor. He hauled Troy Gibson to his feet, dragged him over to the wall, and shoved him up against it, face first. Daniel grabbed the handcuffs from his belt and yanked both of the man's arms behind his back to snap them around his wrists.

From the corner of his eye he caught a movement. Other officers poured into the room. Daniel raised a hand to stop them, then spun Troy around and pressed his forearm to the throat of Jordan's abductor. Troy's eyes bulged as Daniel increased the pressure. No one moved for a few seconds.

"Grey." Sharleen's voice was low and warning.

Not letting up on the pressure, Daniel leaned in close. "Stay away from my family." He spat the words out before dragging Troy away from the wall by one arm and shoving him toward the uniformed officers to deal with, since Daniel couldn't stomach acknowledging that the man had any rights whatsoever.

"Daniel."

He spun around as the boy squirmed out of Sharleen's arms and ran to him. Daniel scooped him up.

Jordan flung his bound hands over Daniel's head and hugged his neck. "I knew you'd come. I told that bad man you would." He buried his face in Daniel's shoulder.

Ignoring the screaming pain from the gunshot wound, Daniel wrapped both arms around him and crushed him to his chest. He met Sharleen's eyes over Jordan's head. She was watching the two of them, a faint smile on her face.

He pulled back so he could search Jordan's face. "Are you all right, Jord?"

The boy nodded.

"Are you sure? That man didn't hurt you?"

"He slapped me here." Jordan touched the red spot on his cheek with one finger. "That's all."

Daniel's jaw clenched.

"And then he came in with the knife ..." The little voice quivered.

"Here." Daniel reached behind him to lift Jordan's arms from around his neck so he could set him on the ground. After picking up the knife Troy Gibson had dropped, he lifted it slowly and showed it to Jordan. "I'm going to cut the tape, okay?"

Jordan nodded and Daniel sliced carefully through the duct tape until he could pull it away from the small wrists.

As soon as he was free, Jordan wrapped his arms around Daniel's neck again. "Can I go home now?"

Daniel stood up, holding the small, trembling body close with his good arm. "You bet, buddy. Your mom has been worried sick about you." He looked over at Sharleen. "You all right to finish up here?"

She waved a hand through the air. "Absolutely. Take him to Nicole."

Daniel bent down and picked up his gun, shoving it into the holster as he started for the stairs. "Okay, Jord. Let's go home."

Chapter Sixty-Three

Daniel punched a number into his cell phone. It rang twice and he pictured one of the police officers in the apartment holding up a finger, telling Nicole to wait before she answered it.

On the third ring, she picked up, her voice strained. "Hello?"

"Nicole? I have someone here who wants to talk to you."

Daniel passed the phone over to Jordan, sitting beside him on the front seat. Jordan grabbed it and pressed it to his ear. "Mom?"

"Jordan!"

Even though he wasn't holding the phone, Daniel caught her cry of joy and relief, and an exhausted smile crossed his face.

He could only catch snatches of the conversation from her end after that, but he could pretty much guess what she was saying from the answers Jordan was giving her. "Yes … Daniel found me … I'm okay … Yes, I'm sure … I know, Daniel told me you were worried … No, he didn't … yes, we're coming home … I don't know …" The little boy looked at Daniel.

Daniel held up the fingers of one hand. "Five minutes."

"Daniel says five minutes … yes, see you soon."

Jordan pressed the off button and handed the phone to Daniel. He slid it into his pocket as he stole another glance at the boy in the front seat, something he hadn't been able to stop doing since they'd gotten into the car. He really shouldn't be sitting there, but when Jordan had asked, he hadn't been able to refuse. He understood why Jordan didn't want to ride alone in the back seat, although he also knew Nicole would have to encourage him to do that soon or his fear would quickly turn debilitating. He wished he could be there to help him through it, but …

Daniel shifted in his seat. He couldn't think about that. Couldn't dwell on the fact that these were the last few minutes he'd ever spend with Jordan, or he might wheel around and start driving in the opposite direction.

Jordan and Nicole were safe. That would have to be enough to get him through the next few weeks and months and years without them, until the desperate ache in his chest finally began to ease. If it ever did.

Daniel flicked on the signal to turn into Nicole's parking lot. As he pulled into one of the visitor parking spots, he saw her, her coat flapping and her long blond hair streaming out behind her as she ran for the car. His gaze fastened on her as she came toward them, the sight of her so painful it hurt to breathe. Still, he couldn't look away, like he hadn't been able to take his eyes from Jordan. These last, stolen glimpses of them were so precious they were worth every bit of what they cost him.

Nicole reached the passenger side door and flung it open. Daniel pressed the button on Jordan's seat belt, releasing him a second before she dropped to her knees and tugged him from the car and into her arms. "Jordan."

His throat ached as he watched them.

Nicole held her son tightly, kissing his cheeks and head and burying her face in his dark hair. After a few seconds she stopped and grasped his arms, holding him far enough away from her that she could get a good look at him. "Are you hurt?"

"No. I'm fine."

Nicole's gaze swung over to him. "Daniel?"

"He really is fine, Nic. He said the man slapped him across the face, but otherwise he's just a little shaken up." At some point he'd have to tell her about the knife, or another officer would fill her in on the details, but now, in front of Jordan, didn't seem like the right time.

She pulled her son to her again. "Let's go in, Jord. Aunt Mikayla is here and she wants to see you, and I want you to be home."

"Me too."

Nicole lifted him up in her arms then peered around him to look at Daniel. "Will you come in?"

There was nothing he would rather do. But he wasn't sure, if he prolonged the inevitable much longer, that he'd be able to turn and walk away when she told him it was time for him to go. "I don't know if I should, Nic. I don't want to interfere in your family time."

"You won't be. I really need you to tell me everything that happened today."

He hesitated, as torn as he had ever been about anything. "Someone else can come by tonight, or tomorrow, and fill you in on all the details."

"Daniel." Her jade eyes met his, pleading with him. "I don't want to hear about what happened to my son from anyone else. I need to hear it from you, from someone who was there, someone who cares about him. Please."

Any hope of resisting crumbled, and he nodded. "All right."

Daniel opened his door and climbed out of the car then followed the two of them into the building. She didn't look at him in the elevator but kept Jordan pressed tightly to her with one hand, her other hand stroking his curls as though she couldn't bear not to touch him. He got that. And not only with Jordan.

Daniel contemplated the situation he was going into. He was a professional. That's what he needed to do, treat this like any other job so he could compartmentalize his emotions and stay focused. He would talk to Nicole, fill her in on everything that had happened, then say goodbye to her and Jordan and go. In a couple of hours, he would be back in his apartment, preparing to start his life without her. Again.

When the elevator doors opened, Mikayla was waiting on the other side.

"Aunt Mikayla!"

She opened her arms and Nicole finally let go of Jordan so he could run to his aunt.

"Jordan. I'm so happy you're home." As he and Nicole had done, she held him out at arms' length, needing to see for herself that he was all right. "Let's get you inside."

Daniel walked down the hallway beside Nicole and stood

back to let her go in after Mikayla and Jordan. When he had shut the door, she turned to him. "Can you stay for a bit? I want to give Jordan a bath and get him tucked into bed. But I really want to talk to you as soon as he's settled."

Daniel nodded. "Sure. I should file my report for today anyway. Do you mind if I use your laptop?"

"No, go ahead. You know where it is."

"I told the principal at Jordan's school I'd let her know if I had any news. Is there anyone else you'd like me to call?"

"I only told Holden and Christina, but they'll be frantic. If you wouldn't mind calling them I'd appreciate it. Their number is beside the phone in the kitchen."

Mikayla crouched in front of her nephew. "Jordan, I'm going to go now and let you and your mom spend some time together. But I'll come back tomorrow, and we'll have lots of time together after that."

Nicole brushed a dark curl off her son's forehead. "Yeah, Jord, Aunt Mikayla is thinking about moving to Toronto. What do you think about that?"

Jordan gazed at his aunt, his eyes shining. "Really? That would be awesome."

Mikayla pulled him close for another hug. "I think so too."

She stood and wrapped her arms around Nicole. "I'm so happy for you, Nic. I knew you could trust them."

Daniel's eyes narrowed. *Trust them?* That was a little cryptic. Who was Mikayla referring to? He would have loved to probe, but his decision to keep his time here professional prevented him from asking that personal question.

Nicole's cheeks were pink when she stepped back from her sister's embrace, but since she didn't glance over at him, he couldn't read what she was thinking.

Mikayla squeezed her arms. "I'll see you tomorrow."

Nicole gripped Jordan's shoulders and tugged him back against her as she nodded.

"I'll walk Mikayla out while you take care of Jordan," Daniel offered. He squatted down in front of the boy, his chest tightening in spite of his attempts to keep his emotions in check. "Goodnight, Jord."

Jordan stepped out from under his mother's hands and threw himself into Daniel's arms again. So much for professionalism. Grief billowed through him so strongly that for a second Daniel couldn't speak. He settled for pulling Jordan close and feeling the boy's arms tighten around him for the last time.

"Goodnight, Daniel. I love you."

"I love you too, buddy."

Jordan moved out of his arms. Daniel pushed to his feet and watched him and Nicole as they walked hand in hand across the living room and into the hallway. When he turned around, Mikayla was gazing at him intently. He held a hand toward the door. "Shall we?"

For a moment she didn't move, simply studied him as though there was something she wanted to say, but then she inclined her head. "All right."

He held her long red coat for her as she slipped her arms into the sleeves. As he followed her into the hallway, Mikayla reached into her purse and pulled out her cell phone. "I'll call a cab."

They rode down in the elevator and he waited with her at the door of the building.

After a couple minutes of silence, she turned to him. "Can you really do it?"

"Do what?"

"Walk away from them?"

Daniel had no idea how to answer that, even though he'd been contemplating the same question for days now. "I've let her go before. Twice."

"Have you?"

Her gentle question plowed into him like a truck. How could she be so perceptive when she'd known him for such a short time? He had never let Nicole go. Not even when she was married to someone else and he had no right to cling to hope. Daniel bit his lip to hold back a groan. "Maybe not. But I don't have a choice, not this time. She's made up her mind and there's nothing I can do about it."

"Isn't there?"

"Mikayla ..."

"I'm sorry. It isn't any of my business, except that I care about you and my sister, and it's killing me to see both of you in so much pain. She loves you, Daniel. I know I don't have any right, but I'm going to tell you what I think you should do anyway. Fight for her. Don't let her go so easily. If she tells you that you can't be part of their lives, you won't be any worse off than you are now. But if she doesn't ..."

A yellow cab stopped outside the door of the building. She offered him one last sad smile and grasped both his forearms as she stood on tiptoes to kiss his cheek. "I hope I see you again, but if I don't, please know that I will always be grateful to the man who brought me to my sister, and who brought my nephew home to both of us." She let go of him and pushed through the door before he could respond.

Daniel contemplated her as she climbed into the back of the cab. When the vehicle pulled forward, he caught a last glimpse of her watching him through the window and lifted his hand. She pressed her fingertips to the glass in response, and then she was gone from his sight.

Chapter Sixty-Four

Nicole rubbed circles on her son's back as he drank his milk, determined to never again take for granted the feel of his soft flannel pajamas and warm skin beneath her fingers.

"Jord, we don't have to talk about it tonight if you don't want to, but tomorrow I want you to tell me what happened to you. I know it must have been really scary, but it will help to talk about it and not keep everything locked up inside you. Is there anything you want to tell me now?"

Jordan set his empty glass on the bedside table and stretched out on his side, propping his head up on one elbow. "When I was … with that bad man, I was really scared."

A new flood of rage and helplessness flowed through her. Jordan covered her hand with his. "Don't be upset, Mom. Daniel came and got me before the man could hurt me." He looked up at her, his eyes earnest. "I knew he'd come. I knew Daniel would find me and bring me home. But while I was waiting for him, I told myself all the Lala stories I could remember. They made me think of you, and they made me feel like you were there with me and then I felt better." A big grin crossed his face.

Nicole marveled at the resiliency of kids and sent up a quick prayer that her son's healing would be quick and complete.

"So will you tell me one now?"

"Sure. Do you want an old one or a new one?"

He didn't hesitate. "An old one. The one with the swings and the ice cream."

The first one she'd ever told him, and the one he'd heard the most. Nicole understood that, wanting the comfort of the familiar tonight, of the way things used to be …

She lifted her chin. "One day Lala and LaToya were

swinging at the park, higher and higher, sure that if they could only get high enough they would actually be able to touch the fluffy white clouds with the toes of their worn sneakers. Lala's mom had bought them an ice cream cone from the truck that drove around town, playing loud music so all the children would come out of their homes and run after it, and they licked those as they stretched for the sky.

"They had almost gotten close enough to touch the nearest fluffy cloud with their toes when LaToya's ice cream fell off her cone and splattered onto the gravel below. She was so sad, great big tears started to run down her face. Because they were so high up in the sky, where it is very cold, the tears froze on her cheeks like sparkling diamonds. They both slowed down their swings, and when they stopped, Lala used her fingers to take one of the scoops of rainbow ice cream off of her cone and put it on LaToya's cone, and LaToya was happy again. This time they waited until they were both finished their ice cream and then they started swinging, higher and higher, and this time they did it. They reached the clouds! They swirled those clouds around and around with their toes until the whole sky looked like the pot when Lala's mother was stirring melting marshmallows around to make Rice Krispie squares."

Jordan's eyes had closed. Nicole ran her fingers lightly over his face, her throat tightening at the thought that she might never have seen him again, never had a chance to tell him another Lala story. She was glad he'd chosen that one. For some reason, that story seemed so real to her when she told it, almost as if ... Nicole drew in a quick breath. "Ella."

"Mom?" Jordan's eyes flew open, and Nicole grabbed his hand and squeezed it.

"Sorry, I didn't mean to startle you. But I always thought I was making up my Lala stories, that she was an imaginary friend who only existed in my mind. Suddenly I realized she was actually your Aunt Mikayla." She squeezed his hand. Her heart pounded in her chest. "Those old stories were real, Jord, partly anyway. They were memories of me and my sister. I remember now. I couldn't say Ella back then so I called her Lala." Nicole laughed at the wonder of it. She'd thought she had always been alone, but she hadn't. She'd had a sister, a wonderful sister who had played and dreamed with her and given up her ice cream so Nicole wouldn't be sad anymore.

"That's so cool, Mom. Lala's real." Before she could stop him, he leaned forward and yelled, "Daniel!"

Her breath tangled in her throat. "Jord, no. Don't bother Daniel. He's working. He doesn't have time to hear about our bedtime stories."

"Mom," Jordan said, slowly and patiently, as though he couldn't believe she didn't know this already, "Daniel always has time for us. We're his family."

"We're not his family, not anymore."

He shook his head. "I know you think that, but it's not true. We *are* Daniel's family. He even told that bad man today that we were."

"He did?"

"Yes. He pushed him up against the wall and said, 'stay away from my family,' and he meant us, you and me."

Daniel's footsteps echoed in the hall and she pressed her fingers to her throat. *Breathe.*

"What's up, buddy?" Daniel stuck his head in the doorway, both hands pressed against the frame. Nicole glanced away quickly. "Everything all right?"

"Yeah, it's great. Mom suddenly realized that Lala is really Aunt Mikayla, and those stories she told weren't all made up, they were memories in her head of stuff she and her sister did together when they were little."

"Really?" Daniel walked over to stand at the foot of the bed, searching out her eyes. Nicole met his gaze. Neither of them moved for a few seconds, until he looked back at Jordan. "That's pretty cool. So you already sort of knew your aunt before you even met her."

"Yeah, I guess I did. I never thought of that. And you heard them, so you knew her a little before too, which is great because she is kind of your sister, right?"

Nicole cupped her son's chin in her hand and turned him to look at her. "Jord, we talked about this."

"I know, Mom, but I've been thinking about it, and I know why Daniel didn't tell you about Aunt Mikayla."

"Jordan," Nicole warned, but her son forged ahead.

"It's because he loves you so much, he didn't want you to be sad if he couldn't find her. Like when Aunt Mikayla gave you her ice cream. She probably didn't want to give it up, but when you love someone, you do anything you can so they won't be sad, right, Daniel?"

Daniel cleared his throat as he grabbed the chair from Jordan's desk and pushed it to the side of the bed. Jordan rolled over to face him as Daniel sat down and leaned forward, resting his elbows on his knees and clasping both his hands in front of him. "That's true, buddy. When you love someone, you do want to do anything you can to keep them from being sad. But what I did still wasn't right. You don't keep secrets from people, even if you think the truth might hurt them. That's the same as lying. And when they discover you lied to them, they're even more hurt than if you had told them the truth in the first place. Do you understand that?"

Jordan nodded. "But you said you were sorry, right?"

Daniel didn't answer for a few seconds. When he did, his voice was thick with emotion. "Yes, I did. And I hope someday your mom can forgive me. But that doesn't mean things can go back to being the way they were. Sometimes, if you hurt someone too much, they can't trust you anymore, and then you can't be as close to them as you used to be. That's why it's always best to tell the truth, especially to the people you care about the most. Okay?"

"I guess." Jordan flopped back on his pillow and stared at the ceiling.

Daniel stood and pushed the chair over to the desk. He squeezed Jordan's foot as he walked by the end of the bed. "'Night, Jordan."

"Goodnight, Daniel."

Nicole tucked the blankets more securely around her son as Daniel left, closing the door behind him. As much as she wanted to talk to him, needed to hear what had happened that day, she couldn't bring herself to leave her son's bedroom until he had fallen asleep and she had witnessed for herself the little chest rising and falling for several minutes.

The sound of his deep, even breathing soothed her as she ran her hand over his head and shoulders, reassuring herself that he really was there, before she forced herself to get up and leave the room.

Chapter Sixty-Five

Daniel stood in front of the window, staring into the darkness. He turned when Nicole walked into the room and crossed the thick beige carpet to lean against the wall a few feet from him. He offered her a wry grin. "I didn't ask him to say any of that."

"Oh, I know. Jordan doesn't need encouragement to say anything. It's getting him to stop that's the trick." Nicole's grin was shaky. "Although, after today, I don't think I'll try, ever again. I can't get enough of hearing his voice, and seeing his smile, and feeling his little fingers in mine."

Daniel didn't answer. He felt the same way, but was painfully aware that he didn't have the luxury of time with Jordan to enjoy those things that she did.

Nicole pushed away from the wall, as though she'd realized how her words might affect him. "Could we sit down? I really need to hear about everything that happened today."

"Sure." He trailed across the living room after her. She sat on the armchair and he took a spot on the couch nearby. "By the way, I called Holden. He and Christina were extremely relieved, of course. They're coming over tomorrow to see Jordan."

Nicole nodded. Like the last time they'd sat that way, she pulled her knees up, a barrier between them. "Who was it?"

He blinked at the abruptness of the question then sighed. There was no way to break it to her gently. "It was Troy Gibson."

The name clearly hit her like a fist in the chest. "Troy Gibson?" The words came out in a ragged whisper. "But why? Hasn't he taken enough from me already?"

He searched for the words to rationally explain an irrational act. "Somehow, in his twisted mind, he didn't feel like things would be even until Gage's son was taken away like his son was."

"But Jordan knows better than to go anywhere with strangers. How did he get him away from the school?"

Daniel told her about the old man slipping on the ice outside the schoolyard. "I'm pretty sure that was by design, that he knew Jordan would come over to see if he was all right. I didn't ask Jordan exactly what he said to get him to go with him, but my guess would be that it was something about Gage."

Her fists clenched on her knees. "So he used Jordan's desire to know more about his father to entice him to go with him so he could what, hold him for a while? Make sure he disappeared like Matthew did? Or what was he planning?"

He hesitated.

"Daniel. Tell me. I need to know."

"I think he planned to kill him. When Sharleen and I went into Matthew's old bedroom, where Troy was keeping Jordan, Troy grabbed him and held a knife to his throat. He said something about the sins of the father being visited on the son."

Nicole closed her eyes and pressed a hand over her mouth. Daniel gave her a moment to process what he'd told her, although he knew it would take a lot longer than that.

Finally, she lowered her hand and opened her eyes. "How did you get him away?"

"I told him Matthew's case had never been closed and there was still a chance we would find him and bring him home. I pointed out that if he hurt Jordan he'd go to jail for the rest of his life and then, if we did find his son, he wouldn't be able to be with him. That seemed to get to him and he lowered the knife. As soon as he did, Sharleen moved in and grabbed Jordan and I cuffed the guy and handed him over to the other officers who had come in with us."

Nicole bit her lip, her eyes glistening. "I'll never be able to thank you for that. You kept your promise and brought Jordan back to me, and I will never forget it."

Neither of them moved. The air was so thick with emotion, it seemed to shimmer between them, like heat rising from a sidewalk on a summer day. Then Nicole looked down at her hands and the moment was broken.

Daniel drew in a painful breath. "Troy Gibson will be going away again, for a few years at least. You and Jordan will be safe now, so …" He pushed to his feet. "I'll go grab my things and get out of your way."

A faint smile played across her lips. "You were never in our way."

Daniel nodded and walked down the hall, touching Jordan's door lightly as he walked by. After thrusting the few belongings he'd brought into his bag, he zipped it closed and left the room, leaving the Laurel and Hardy DVDs on top of the dresser.

Nicole stood at the end of the couch, waiting for him. Daniel stopped in front of her. For a moment he studied her, committing her face to memory, then he reached out and brushed his knuckles across her cheek. "Take care of yourself, Nic. And Jordan." There was so much more he wanted to say, but when she simply nodded, he dropped his hand and turned away.

Really, there *was* nothing more to say.

He was almost at the door when something clicked in his brain, like the last turn of the knob of a safe. *Maybe there is.* Daniel dropped his bag and spun on his heel, striding back to stop in front of her again. A startled look crossed her face, but she didn't speak.

He folded his arms over his chest. "You know what? No. I'm not going to leave."

"You're not going to leave." Something he couldn't quite identify flickered in her eyes. Apprehension? Relief? Both, maybe. Hope flickered again.

He shook his head. "No. I want you to hear me out. I think I deserve that much, at least. And when I'm done, if you still want to kick me out of your life for good, well, there's nothing I can do about that. But I'm not walking out of here on my own, because I love you, and I love Jordan. You're my family, and you don't walk out on your family." Blood pounded in his ears so loudly he could hardly hear himself speak, but still it felt good to finally get off his chest what he'd been feeling for days.

"You're right." Nicole met his eyes, whatever he'd seen flickering there growing stronger, less apprehensive.

Daniel cocked his head. He'd braced himself for her anger. What was he supposed to do with her acquiescence? "About what?"

She laughed softly. "About everything, so far. You do deserve to be heard, and we are your family—Jordan reminded me of that tonight—and you don't walk out on family." Her face grew serious. "And you were right earlier today too, when you accused me of being the one to walk away. I didn't realize I was doing it, but I did break my promise to you. "Can you"—her voice cracked, and she stopped and swallowed—"forgive me for that?"

"I already have."

"Thank you." She exhaled the words, as though she'd been afraid to ask. "There's one thing you *were* wrong about."

"What's that?"

"You said that when you keep a secret from someone, they can never trust you again and things can never be the same between you. The truth is, sometimes things *can* be the same. But sometimes, if you're able to find your way back to each other, I believe they can be better, stronger." She rested a hand on his chest.

His heart thudded as hope flared into flame. "Are you saying you forgive me?"

"Yes. And I'm sorry it took so long. I should have trusted in you, in your character and your heart." A sad smile crossed her face when her gaze dropped to the hand pressed against him. "Such a good heart." Nicole looked up at him, her eyes probing his. "Do you think you could ever trust me enough to give it back to me?"

Daniel searched her face before he shook his head. "No."

Her face fell and she started to pull her hand away, but he caught it and held it against his chest.

"I can't give you my heart *back*, Nic, because you've always had it. Ever since that first day in the diner where I earned myself that nickname which we are never going to mention again."

Her eyes glowed when they met his. "I was hoping and praying you wouldn't leave tonight."

"Why didn't you try and stop me?"

"I wanted to. But I was afraid you'd think I was only asking you to stay because I was grateful for what you did today. I *am* grateful, but that's not why I want you to stay."

"Then why?"

"Because I love you. With all my heart. And nothing is right when you're not here. It's like there's a gaping hole in our lives now that only you can fill. I need you, and Jordan needs you." She turned over the hand he'd covered with his and grasped his fingers. "And I'll make you another promise, one that I will keep this time. Now that you're back here with us, I'm going to do everything I can *not* to worry about the future. It—and you and Jordan—are in God's hands, not mine. I thought I had learned that lesson with Gage, but apparently I still had a ways to go."

Daniel slid his free hand into the pocket of his jeans. When he felt the cold, round object he slipped into his pocket every morning, he tugged it out and held it up.

Nicole blinked. "You've been carrying it around with you?"

"I've been hoping and praying too." He tightened his grip on her left hand. "Can we try this again?"

Her eyes glistened, but she managed a smile as she nodded. "Yes. Please."

Daniel lifted her hand and brought the ring close to the tip of her finger. "Before we do this, there's something you need to know."

"What?"

"I've lost you twice and both times it almost killed me. I can't do it again. If I put this ring on your finger, that's it, you will be stuck with me for the rest of our lives."

A wide smile broke across her face. "I certainly hope so."

Daniel took his first deep breath since Rick had shown up at the door with the news that they'd found Mikayla.

He slid the ring onto her finger, praying, as he did, that the shape of the diamonds would be a reminder to her that she carried his heart with her and always would. "For the record, I don't want to plan a long engagement like we did the last time."

Nicole laughed. "Those three weeks were excruciating, you're right. Maybe we *should* go for Valentine's Day, that's only a week—"

"Tomorrow." He leaned down and pressed his lips to the curve of her neck.

"What? We can't get married tomorrow. We need time to tell people, to make arrangements."

"I still have the marriage license, and Mikayla is in town. I'm pretty sure the rest of our friends and family will be willing to shift a few things around in their schedules to be there. And if not, I don't care, as long as you and Jordan and I are there. So …" Daniel's hands slid along her face and into her hair as his mouth moved up to her jawline. "Tomorrow."

"But …"

His lips claimed hers, cutting off any further protests. Nicole tipped back her head as he pulled her closer. Like she'd said about Jordan, he didn't think he'd ever be able to get enough of the feel of her mouth against his, the faint smell of apple blossoms drifting from her hair, her warm skin beneath his fingers.

When the room started to spin around him, he lifted his head.

Nicole's eyes met his, the gold flecks sparkling as she nodded. "Tomorrow."

He pulled back and looked at her. "What are you grinning about?"

"Since I've never been happier in my life than I am at this moment, it could be any number of things. But I was thinking about the story Connie told me recently about her and Joe. She said they met at an army dance on a Friday night, and before he left her at the door that night, he made her promise to marry him the next day. I was wondering if he used the same method you just did to persuade her."

"I only saw the two of them together a couple of times at the diner, but I do remember the way they looked at each other, even after all those years, so I'd say it's entirely likely."

"And it worked out pretty well for them, so I have high hopes for us."

Daniel reached for her, but a sharp pain shooting through him reminded him he'd pushed his shoulder way past endurance today. He worked to hide the wince, but she didn't miss it.

"Daniel, your shoulder. It must be killing you."

"I'm all right. A little TLC and I'll be good as new. Maybe I should check myself back into the hospital for the night."

"Oh no." Nicole moved closer to him and wrapped both arms around his waist. "If you need TLC from now on, you'll be getting it from me, here at home, where you belong."

Here. Home. Belong. He liked the sound of all those words. Daniel made a mental note to thank Mikayla for her good advice the next time he saw her. Yeah, he was going to enjoy having her for a sister-in-law. A flood of joy and relief poured through him at the thought that he would now, and that he'd have another opportunity to face Holden at the pool table, and to bring Jordan and Nicole to Tom and Sharleen's for Friday night barbeques. He could take Jordan camping and be there for him when he went on his first date and teach him how to drive a car. And maybe they'd give him a brother or sister too, possibly both. His heart filled at the thought.

Whatever the future held, he'd be there for every big and small moment in their lives that, ten minutes ago, he hadn't thought he'd be able to share with them ever again.

Nicole tapped his chest. "What are *you* grinning about?"

"I'm listening to the sound of the birds."

"The birds?" Her forehead wrinkled.

Daniel laughed for the first time in days. "Something my dad said. I'll tell you about it soon, but right now there's something

I'd much rather be doing than talking."

Her eyes danced. "What's that?"

"This." He took her face in his hands and lowered his head. As his lips touched hers, he closed his eyes and breathed a prayer of thanks for this third chance that he'd somehow, miraculously, been given.

Author Note

Dear Readers,

Guarded is a story close to my heart, a book more than a decade in the making. I typically become deeply connected to all my characters when I write, but Daniel holds a special place in my affections. In the first book of this series, *Vigilant*, Gage does the wrong thing for the right reasons. In *Guarded*, Daniel does the same thing. He keeps a huge secret from the woman he loves in an attempt to protect her from more hurt and pain in her life.

Is he right to do so? Was Gage right? Do the ends justify the means? There are no easy answers to those questions, but my hope and prayer is that you will think about them, discuss them with others, and contemplate what you would do if you found yourself in a similar situation one day. It might be considered passé to wear a "What would Jesus do" bracelet these days, but the sentiment still holds true. What *would* Jesus do? As He is our ultimate example, it bears asking ourselves that question—in cases such as Gage and Daniel faced and in all others.

Like Daniel and Gage, I have done the wrong thing for the right reasons. More often, I have done the right thing for the wrong reasons. Taken a meal to someone going through a hard time in order to avoid having to do something harder such as deeply invest my time and emotions by walking alongside them on their journey. I've taken on duties at church out of obligation. Served others for the thanks or for the sake of appearances or to feel good about myself. My natural human tendency is to enjoy the praise and adulation of others, rather than to serve quietly, in secret, for nothing but the glory of God and out of gratitude for who He is and all He has done.

Like King David, I need to repeatedly ask God to search me and know my heart, see if there is any unclean way in me. Only when He reveals that uncleanness, those wrong motives—and even then, only with the help and guidance of the Holy Spirit—can I ever hope to do the right thing for the right reason. Only then can I truly do what Jesus would do.

Sara

If you enjoyed *Guarded*, would you consider leaving a review on social media? That and telling others about them is the best way to help authors spread the word about their books.

I would love to connect with you further. You can find me at the following places:
Blog (where you can sign up for my monthly newsletter):
www.saradavison.org
Twitter: @sarajdavison
Facebook: @authorsaradavison
Instagram: www.instagram.com/davisonsara/

Discussion Questions

1. Do you ever find yourself worrying about the evil in the world and being over-protective of the people you love as a result, like Nicole was with Jordan? How do you deal with that? Are there any Scriptures that help you to let go of that fear?

2. Have you ever been deeply hurt by someone you cared about, the way Daniel was hurt by Nicole? Did you find it difficult to trust that person, or to let anyone else get close to you after that happened? If so, how were you able to get over feeling that way?

3. While in prison, Troy's single-minded focus is on revenge. Do you believe he was justified in his desire to seek justice for the loss of his son? Have you ever wanted revenge when someone hurt you? What did you do in that situation? How did it turn out?

4. Stepfamilies come with unique challenges. Do you think Daniel handles his discussions well with Jordan about what role Daniel will play in his life? Are you part of a step-family or close to one? What are the challenges and how did you or the people you know deal with them?

5. Daniel's father tells him, "And now the morning has come. Which is one of only two things God promises about the darkness—that He'll walk through it with you and that, if you persevere, the light will come again, one way or another." What do you think about this statement? Have you been in a situation where you found it to be true?

6. Daniel struggles with keeping a secret from Nicole but feels it is justified because he is protecting her. Is there ever a time when it is okay to lie and/or keep something from someone? Was her

reaction fair? Have you ever felt betrayed by someone who kept something from you? How did you deal with those feelings?

7. Several characters in the book struggle with grief—Daniel lost his mother, Nicole and Connie lost husbands, and Mikayla lost her parents. Have you ever experienced deep grief that threatened to overwhelm you? What helped you during that time? What would you advise people who want to help others who are grieving to say or do? What would you advise them not to say or do?

8. Nicole struggles to forgive Daniel for keeping a secret from her. Is there something deeper going on that contributes to the depth of her feelings? Have you ever struggled to forgive someone? How did you feel before you did? If you were able to forgive, how did you feel after?

9. Jordan tells Nicole that the two of them are Daniel's family. What does family mean to you? What constitutes a family?

10. "The Lord gives and the Lord takes away. Blessed be the name of the Lord." Have you ever experienced great loss? Were you able to say those words? What do you think they mean at their very heart?

Chapter One

Holden bolted upright at the sound of a loud groan. "Chris?"

His wife was curled up on her side, facing him. Her eyes were screwed tightly shut and both her hands were pressed to her royal blue T-shirt, over the place where her belly rounded just above the tops of her flannel pajama bottoms.

"What is it? Are you having contractions?"

Without opening her eyes, she nodded, slightly. "Really bad." The words came out in a breathless whisper.

It's too early. Holden threw back the covers. "I'll take you to the hospital."

She shot out a hand and grasped his arm. "No. I can't move. Call 911."

Holden snatched up the cell phone on his bedside table. With a trembling finger, he punched in the three numbers. "Come on, come on, come on." It seemed minutes before a calm, cool voice came over the phone. "911. What is the nature of your emergency?"

He described Christina's condition quickly and gave the woman their address and the front door code before disconnecting the call. After tossing the phone back onto the table, he searched his wife's face. His chest clenched. Her eyes were open now, but in the dim, early morning light, they were wild, unfocused. Her white-knuckled grip on his hand nearly sent him to his knees beside the bed. Although he was ready to drop to them anyway and beg God to spare his wife and child.

"It's too soon." She gasped out the words.

"I know, love." Holden stroked her wrist with his thumb, fighting to keep the panic out of his voice. As she was just thirty weeks along, his wife's intense contractions were the last thing he thought he'd be dealing with today. For once, he'd have been happy if all he'd had to face was some kind of domestic dispute or even the never-ending pile of paperwork stacked up on his desk at Child Services Headquarters in downtown Toronto. "It's going to be okay."

The words he hadn't meant to say sent remorse coursing through him. He shouldn't make a promise he had no idea if he could keep. *God forgive me.* Still, the wildness in her eyes eased and the fingers clutching his loosened their grip enough that blood began to flow again, so he couldn't bring himself to feel too repentant. *Please make everything be okay so that I didn't lie to my wife.*

For the eighteenth time in the last ten minutes, he shot a glance toward the hallway. Where was the ambulance? They only lived a few minutes from the hospital; how long could it take the EMTs to get there? He pressed his lips together to keep the angry questions from spewing from his mouth and attempted to offer his wife a reassuring smile. From the look on her face, the attempt fell short. Vastly short. "Please, Chris, let me take you to the hospital." Holden tried to gently extricate his fingers from hers so he could get up, but she tightened her grip again. He hid a wince.

"It's too late. I won't make it. Where—?"

The question she'd been about to ask—the same one he'd been silently screaming in his head for several minutes—was cut off by the shrill wail of a siren cutting through the early-morning silence of their neighborhood. The grip on his fingers tightened again. "Holden. I can't lose him. Please ..." Pain contorted her face as another contraction gripped her.

He had no idea what to do. *God, show me how to help her.* More words of reassurance rose in his throat. *He'll be fine. You'll be fine. We won't lose him.* He bit them back as he brushed the long auburn hair, damp with sweat, back from her forehead. "Chris, listen to me." The doorbell rang. Seconds later the door creaked open. Holden glanced at the doorway and called out, "We're upstairs." He turned back to his wife as boots thudded up the wooden stairway. He cupped her flushed cheek with his free hand. "I'll be with you every second. We'll do this together. Okay?"

She nodded and let go of his hand as two EMTs, a man and a woman, burst into the room. They carried a stretcher that they set down beside the bed and lifted up onto its wheels. The woman rounded it and stopped at the side of the bed. "Ma'am, we're going to get you to the hospital."

Christina shook her head against the pillow. "No time." She pushed the words out through clenched teeth.

Holden's heart pounded hard against his ribs. Another contraction? What had it been, thirty seconds? A minute? At Lamaze class they'd told them to go to the hospital when they were five minutes apart. How had this come on so fast?

The female EMT rested a hand on her shoulder. "Don't worry. I'll ride in the back with you, and if anything happens, we can take care of it on the way." She squeezed Christina's shoulder and nodded at her partner.

The tension in Holden's back eased slightly at the confidence in the woman's voice. Maybe everything *was* going to be okay. At least the professionals were here now.

The paramedics moved his wife from the bed to the stretcher in one quick movement. Holden followed them as they wheeled the bed to the top of the stairs, pressed the button to release the legs and swing them back up into place, and carried it down. He passed them at the bottom and whipped open the door, holding it until they had walked through. He grabbed Christina's coat from the hook behind the door and shoved his feet into his tennis shoes before slamming the door behind him and hurrying down the front walk. A brisk February wind swept past him, sending a light dusting of snow swirling around his calves. Holden tossed

Christina's coat over her, trying to protect her from the chill in the air. From the corner of his eye, he caught a glimpse of the faces of a couple of neighbors peering out red-flashing-light-splashed windows.

Holden didn't ask, just climbed into the back of the ambulance after they'd slid the stretcher in and the woman had climbed in after it.

The male EMT didn't comment or try to stop him. Which was wise. Enough adrenaline coursed through Holden that if the man had tried to keep him from his wife and child, Holden might have put *him* in the back of an ambulance.

Holden's entire body shook as he settled on the bench across from the woman and reached for Christina's hand. Her fingers were as cold as a … He slammed up a wall in his brain before it could allow the word *corpse* to fully form. He wouldn't associate that image with his wife, not even for a second.

Sirens wailed again as the driver squealed out of the driveway in reverse, then shot forward down the street in the direction of the hospital. Through the back window, Holden caught a glimpse of Mrs. Barrows, self-appointed keeper of the neighborhood's affairs, as she stepped out onto her porch, clutching a lavender-colored robe to her throat. He tried to smile at her, to staunch the flow of grim speculation on their situation that she'd spread around the street before they could return, but his mouth refused to cooperate. It wasn't likely she could see in through the glass anyway.

Let them talk. He tore his gaze from the back window to study Christina. Her eyes were screwed tightly shut and her lips had gone thin and white. Holden glanced over at the EMT, hoping for more reassurance, but with Christina's eyes closed, the woman had lowered her guard. Concern was etched across her face. After attaching a clothespin type of monitor to one of his wife's fingers, the EMT grabbed a starched white sheet from a cubby bolted to the wall of the vehicle and shook it open. Holden snatched Christina's coat so the EMT could spread the sheet over her before moving to the foot of the stretcher. She fired questions at Holden as she examined his wife. How many weeks along was she? When had the contractions started? How far apart were they? He had no idea what he said in response, if his answers were accurate or even intelligible. He kept his eyes fastened on the woman's face. Whatever she was seeing only deepened the concern that lined her forehead. She lowered the sheet and turned her head to speak into the mic on her shoulder. "Hurry, Darryl."

Through static, Holden caught the words, "Almost there."

Christina moaned. The sound ripped the air from Holden's lungs, but he forced himself to draw in a ragged breath. It wouldn't help his wife any if he passed out. The grip on his hand had weakened. Had the pain lessened, or was she losing strength? Holden swallowed hard and cupped her face again. She shifted her head slightly on the rounded mound at the head of the stretcher, until she faced him. Her eyelids fluttered for a few seconds before opening. The terror in her hazel eyes sent fresh panic coursing through him. *God help her. Please.*

"Something's wrong."

Everything's wrong. He didn't voice the thought. "We're almost to the hospital."

He could see in her eyes that those weren't the words she'd been looking for, but she nodded slightly.

The ambulance careened into the hospital parking lot and screeched to a stop under the awning in front of the emergency room. The EMT leapt to the doors and flung them open. Her partner appeared in the opening and the two of them slid the stretcher out. Holden jumped from the vehicle after them and jogged beside the stretcher as the automatic doors slid open and they wheeled Christina through.

In seconds, they were swarmed by men and women in gowns and masks. His wife disappeared through swinging doors. Holden pushed through after her and followed the horde into a room. A gloved hand appeared before his face and he stepped back. The door swung shut in front of him and he moved forward to peer through the small, round window, clutching Christina's coat to his chest. The faint aroma of the floral scent she wore drifted on the air and he took his first deep breath in what felt like hours.

Holden watched, a pulse pounding in his neck, as people worked frantically on his wife, calling for instruments, reaching for towels. A crimson stain spread across the crisp white sheet at Christina's feet and the hallway spun around Holden. Blindly, he groped beside him for the wall and pressed splayed fingers across the smooth, cool surface of it, attempting to stay on his feet.

God. God. God. It was the only word that would emerge from the fog swirling around in his mind.

The woman working at the end of the stretcher, facing him, straightened, clutching a tiny, red-smeared body in both hands.

My son. He held his breath, shoving the door open a couple of inches with his shoe so he could hear the tiny wail when it came, but there was only a sudden, deafening silence in the room.

The woman's eyes met Holden's through the glass.

And he knew, with an absolute certainty that gripped his gut like a vise, that he was not going to be able to keep the promise he had made to his wife.